THE UTTER-MOST PARTS OF THE EARTH

THE UTTER- MOST PARTS OF THE EARTH

FREDERIC HUNTER

THE PERMANENT PRESS
Sag Harbor, NY 11963

For information, address:
  The Permanent Press
  4170 Noyac Road
  Sag Harbor, NY 11963
  www.thepermanentpress.com

Library of Congress Cataloging-in-Publication Data

  Hunter, Frederic, author.
    The uttermost parts of the earth / Frederic Hunter.
    Sag Harbor, NY: The Permanent Press, [2018]
    ISBN: 978-1-57962-516-0
        1. Suspense fiction. 2. Romantic suspense fiction.

PS3558.U477 U88 2018
813'.54—dc23   2017047516

Printed in the United States of America

In Memoriam Paul and Helen Hunter

ONE

When Kwame Johnson stepped off the plane at Ndjili Airport outside Kinshasa, pickpockets, hustlers, and pirate cab drivers studied him from the observation deck. Not one of them mistook him for an African. Not even in the dark of night, shortly after midnight. No, not an African, for what African would return from Europe in less than a business suit and tie? What Zairean would let his relatives think he had failed abroad? This man wore a Ghanaian tie-dye shirt with embroidery at the neck and jeans stiff with newness; he went barefoot in Mexican huaraches. Undoubtedly an American. In one hand he carried a duffel with a Patagonia fleece stuck under his arm. The other held a small padded suitcase. The men on the observation deck inspected that suitcase. Obviously a laptop computer. That would be something to snatch.

The man had an American way of striding across the tarmac. Tired from the long flight from Belgium, he was still erect, eyes alert, shoulders squared back, seeming taller than his six feet. He carried a passport in his hand, confident of who he was, of his citizenship, and his comparative wealth in this place of poverty. Even so, he glanced about apprehensively. He had heard of the gauntlet of thieves and hustlers that waited to prey on new arrivals as they emerged from customs inspection.

Those hustlers raced down to customs to snatch him as he entered the noise and confusion of the preying ground.

The person who actually snatched him was the embassy greeter. Under the watchful eyes of the giant portrait of Mobutu Sese Seko, Zaire's president/dictator, behind a hubbub of contending bodies, the greeter held up a sign that read: K. Johnson. Kwame smiled with relief and strode toward him. "Mr. Johnson?" The small man in the safari suit, Lebanese from the looks of him, exuded a presence larger than himself. "I'm from the embassy," he said. "Follow me." The man took Kwame's wrist and pulled him through the mass of touts screaming at him: "Taxi, *M'sieur*? Hotel? Taxi?" When an arm reached out to grab the laptop, Kwame became aware of men, tall and well-muscled, walking close to him on either side. The reaching arms withdrew.

Outside, the night air was cooler. Vehicle exhaust fumes replaced the odor of bodies. The greeter led Kwame to a Ford Explorer. The escorts put Kwame's luggage into the rear of the SUV, accepted their tips, and vanished. The greeter sped Kwame into the city. A cloud layer of what seemed like hot, wet cotton hung so close to the earth that Kwame felt he could touch it. Sprawling shantytowns of cast-off metal and palm-frond shacks stood beside the highway, illuminated by occasional naked light bulbs. Men in shorts, tee shirts, and sandals laughed together. The sharp smell of vegetable decay and cook-fires lingered in the air.

The greeter deposited Kwame at the InterContinental Hotel, its lobby decorated with ersatz Bakuba masks. As he registered, Kinshasa rock 'n' roll pulsated out of the hotel bar where couples danced. Silk-suited men wearing gold rings and sunglasses stood outside the bar conducting business by phone. Sunglasses at midnight, Kwame thought. Welcome to Central Africa.

A young Zairean woman in a tight leather dress revealing her thighs approached Kwame, following nodded instructions from a silk suit. She sidled beside him, her push-up bra displaying abundant cleavage, and grazed him with her voluminous headcloth. She whispered in an African language. He examined her: well-modeled face, good cheekbones, and well-turned lips, but with eyes as empty as a vacant house. When he did not answer, she repeated her solicitation, studied him more carefully. She realized that he was a white man, switched to bad French, and asked if she could be of service to him.

Kwame said, *"Merci. But not tonight."*

He followed a bellhop into the elevator. A young white woman entered beside him. She had blonded hair, a starveling's figure, and wore a dress so tight she could hardly walk. "Sidanie did not appeal to you?" she asked. "A good thing." Smiling, she conveyed that she recognized Kwame for what he was: black, but not African. "Her tribe is the BaSida."

Kwame leaned tiredly against the back of the elevator. He observed the young woman. She had a Gallic face like that of a fox—pinched mouth, pointed nose and chin—spoke working-class French out of a mouthful of bad teeth and had cash registers in her eyes. Kwame wondered how many men she had crawled across already tonight, how many fingers and toes and other things she had sucked. She smiled knowingly, dissing the competition. "Be careful of the BaSida," she warned. "They give and they take away." SIDA was French for what Americans called AIDS. "Me, I am very careful," the woman said. "I do not intend to die in this place." She reached a hand toward Kwame's groin. He covered it with his laptop. He wondered if the woman and the bellhop had an arrangement. She asked, "May I be of service to you?"

"I am very careful myself," Kwame told her in French.

"Here is my card," the woman said. "I live quite near the hotel." She stuffed the card into his shirt pocket and let her hand slide against his laptop. As he left the elevator, she sent him a pucker, both sexy and satiric. Kwame followed the bell-hop to his room. As soon as the man departed, he tore up the card. Good god, he thought, why am I here? Thieves are every-where. The women are diseased. What would Joseph Conrad think of this place hardly a century later? He showered, fell into bed, and dreamed of Livie.

SHORTLY AFTER dawn Kwame left the First World ambience of the hotel, with its perfumed opulence, its quietude and order, its muted colors specified by pale-eyed, pale-faced designers several continents away. He entered the Third World, the yak-king and clatter and honking of its waking all about him, its city stench, the odor of things decaying in the heat, freshened by the comparative coolness of the night, his eye delighting in the bright orange-red of its flame trees, the blues and yellows of the mammy cloths passing women wore. The humid hustle of Kinshasa, chaotic even at this hour, replaced the climate-control and soft musical soothings of the hotel. He walked about, feel-ing the city's famous combination of dynamism and lethargy, the one produced by the vigor that had market women setting up stalls at dawn, the other by the pauperization inflicted on the populace by the kleptomania of Mobutu Sese Seko.

Recently America's establishment press had filled long col-umns reporting that the Mobutu era was drawing to a close. What lay ahead for the country Mobutu himself had renamed Zaire none of the punditry could surmise. The dictator's health was rumored to be failing. He lived in seclusion in palaces set away from the shacks of his people, sometimes on a yacht lying off the capital in the middle of the Congo River, which river he called the Zaire, also sometimes in a magnificent and isolated compound in the grasslands of the north near the village where he was born. His army, effective only at plundering and terrorizing citizens, was losing battles in the east of the country. There it had become enmeshed in the Rwandan crisis, the massacres by *génocidaires* of Rwanda's Tutsis and moderate Hutus. Kwame wondered how Kinshasa would react to Mobutu's end, be it death, assassination, or flight. Music would reverberate across the city, he supposed. Dancing feet would pound the floors of bars and brothels, the earth of marketplaces and dusty roads. And then what?

Kwame walked out the Boulevard de 30 Juin away from the city center. When he crossed streets, vehicles honked at him. Cyclists and pedestrians whizzed past, heading toward town. Feeling the contagion of the early morning bustle, Kwame bought bread and coffee from women cooking at a tree-shaded road stand. The patrons sat at crude tables made from packing crates. As Kwame joined them, they stared at him. They perceived immediately that he was not Zairean, not African. Nor working-class like them. He offered, *"Jour. Comment va?"* Their frowns showed that his American-accented French—perhaps any French—was incomprehensible to them.

I am here, he thought, but I am still out of place.

Even so, he was glad he had come to Zaire. Kinshasa seemed real and African to him in a way that Cape Town never had. He wondered if he would see it become unreal in the rejoicing at Mobutu's passing.

At the *Centre Culturel Américain*, his colleagues, the American officers, had not yet arrived for work. He found a computer, logged on, and e-mailed Livie to let her know that he had arrived. He reported that Kinshasa was an electric power plant that might—bang! explode! or whimper!—collapse from exhaustion. That he missed her. That he could not wait till he saw her in Paris at Christmas.

THE VIEW from the twelfth-story balcony in the heart of the city caused the Zairean lunch guests to exclaim with amazement, *"Ooo! C'est Brazza là-bas?"* Kwame's host, the embassy's public affairs officer, who was also his boss, assured them that the city visible across Pool Malebo was, indeed, Brazzaville, capital of the old French Congo, known as Congo-Brazzaville. The Zairean guests giggled with delight. They included an official of the Education Ministry, a vice-chancellor of the university, and a professor of Francophone African literature. All three men wore suits to indicate their position as professionals and glasses to prove their status as intellectuals. The Education Ministry official and the vice-chancellor were both burdened by diamond-studded rings and gold wristwatches. Each man had perfumed his cheeks with French aftershave to show himself an *homme du monde.* Each managed to receive prearranged telephone calls while the guests had drinks.

Warren Judkins, the host, wore neither suit nor glasses, but smiled his lined face beneath an unfortunate African haircut. He introduced Kwame as a newly arrived officer, a specialist in comparative literature, formerly a professor of African literature in the American intellectual capital, Boston. He was, *enfin,* an intellectual like the Zaireans themselves. Kwame offered proof in the flesh, Judkins said, that Americans esteemed African writing. He was also a resource, an accomplished lecturer on works by both African and African American writers. Judkins hoped that his guests would take advantage of Kwame's expertise and arrange lectures for him.

Kwame quickly hit it off with the professor of Francophone African literature. Drinking infusions after the meal they chatted about African cinema, about Idrissa Ouedraogo, Djibril Diop Mambéty, and Ousmane Sembène and compared notes on Sembène's *Les Bouts de Bois de Dieu,* about which the professor had done some writing. The man offered to take Kwame to see the university that very afternoon. But Judkins shook his head. He whispered: "We need to talk—if we can ever get these fellas to leave."

The guests gone, Judkins said, "These fellas mean well and, believe me, surviving in Mobutu's chicken coop requires better political instincts than either of us has got." He slipped out of his seersucker coat, pulled off his tie, and indicated that Kwame should do the same. He added, "You'll have plenty of chance to see the university."

Kwame sensed that Judkins was about to spring something on him. He shed his coat, but remained in his tie. Moments like this called for protective coloration—PC, as he thought of it—his strategy for coping with the white world. It and its namesake, political correctness, had much in common. The rules were these: Appear to share the attitudes of those with whom you associate. Agree with thine adversary whilst he is in thy way. Blend with thine environment so that others can assume thou art "on the team." Kwame blandly smiled. He told Judkins, "It isn't as if I haven't seen an African university."

Judkins locked the door and continued to watch his guest. Kwame continued to smile. "What made you agree to come here?" Judkins asked, stretching out on a government-issue sofa and gesturing Kwame to a chair. The question's directness surprised Kwame. He took a slow look around for a place to set his coat. "I trust it wasn't to further American policy," Judkins said. "Which is a little confused."

"To be truthful, I've asked myself why I'm here," Kwame admitted. "It wasn't easy to explain to my girlfriend or my family."

"Explain it to me," Judkins suggested. When Kwame shrugged, he smiled and suggested, "Perhaps it was personal. You looking for—"

"Myself? I don't think so."

"You never know," Judkins said. "Nothing like an overseas post to reveal you to yourself. Sometimes you're pleased. Sometimes not."

"I guess I wanted to see more of Africa." A fumbling start. He shrugged. "Maybe I thought I could help these people." Judkins studied Kwame in the afternoon silence. Kwame felt as he had in graduate school oral exams when he'd fielded an unexpected question.

"Help them to do what?" Judkins asked.

Protective coloration, Kwame realized, would advise him to acknowledge that Foreign Service officers were charged with furthering American interests. But he was a scholar, presently an FSO of the US Information Service, charged with a cultural mission. Traditional embassy concerns—consular affairs, politics, regional security, commercial arrangements—did not involve him. "Help them become educated," he replied. "Modern, but still African. To get a sense of the bigger world beyond the village, the town, or even this city. To realize that other Africans are wondering the same things they are, raising the same questions. That's what literature can do."

"Literature did that when you were teaching in Boston?"

Judkins was certainly appraising him, Kwame thought. Because he was black? Maybe, but maybe not. "In Boston I was cajoling undergraduates to read books that bored them," he said. "Hardly noble work."

"You expect to do noble work for us here, do you?" Kwame shrugged again, snagged by the words "for us." The point he had just made was that he hoped to do it "for them." He felt caught looking naive. Judkins smiled. "I used to teach myself," he confided. "Perhaps education really is wasted on the young."

"Even here?" Kwame asked. "There's been so little of it here."

Judkins shrugged. He looked supportive. Kwame decided to relax about the color of his skin. They became, more or less, just two Americans in a strange country who had once shared the same profession. "You've gotten a taste of the place," Judkins observed. "Willing to spend two years here?"

"I think so," Kwame said.

Judkins nodded, pleased.

THE TWO men moved out onto a balcony overlooking Pool Malebo. Under the canvas awning the air was hot and motionless. Kwame stood in the sun by the railing where a slight breeze stirred. He gazed at Brazzaville obscured by haze on the opposite bank of the great river. Below the balcony, idle wharves and shanties clustered; they looked like the leavings of a garbage truck. The stench of the shanties rose twelve stories to assail his nostrils. He moved under the awning where Judkins sat, but remained standing, looking across the river.

"Sorry to bring you out here," Judkins said, "but I don't want the cook hearing what I have to say. He doesn't seem to understand much English, but you never know."

Judkins was in his early fifties, Kwame estimated, with graying hair surrounding a bald spot, tired eyes, and an expression of resignation that bespoke a career spent mainly in Africa dealing with crises, large and small. He had settled himself into one of the peculiarly African chairs that graced the balcony. It was formed of tree branches steamed and bent into chair-like shapes. It offered seat cushions and back rests made of foam rubber covered with mammy cloth bargained for in the markets. Beside the chairs stood a collection of drums on which guests could rest drinks. A gathering of African sculptures, weathered by rain and sun, clustered in one corner of the balcony as if to welcome benevolent spirits and ward off evil ones.

Quietly and without looking at him Judkins spoke the words the servant was not to hear. "Embassy's guessing that Mobutu's all but finished," he said. "After stamping his image across the entire country. After renaming the Congo Zaire and the river too. These days he's almost never seen." Judkins scanned Pool Malebo as if searching for Mobutu's yacht. "We're betting he's sick, very sick. We could be wrong." He shrugged. "You never know out here. In any case, we're not offering him medical treatment. We're thinking of what comes next."

"What does?" Kwame asked.

"Things fly apart," Judkins said. "Isn't that the title of one of the books you lecture about?"

The title was, in fact, *Things Fall Apart*, but Kwame would not be pedantic. "There's also one called *No Longer at Ease*," he remarked. "Same author."

"Achebe knew the territory," Judkins said. "But things flying apart doesn't serve our interests. Or anyone else's. Look at what's happened up at the Lakes. I've seen footage of Hutus and Tutsis opening each other's heads with pangas as if they were melons. Hacking up pregnant women. Smashing babies against walls. Slicing heads off. Stuff that makes you sick."

Judkins acknowledged that this was not a phenomenon unique to Africans. "But what happens," he asked, "if disruptions start popping across this entire country?"

Kwame said nothing, watching a ferry leave its wharf and start across the Pool.

"Chaos is what happens," Judkins said. "With a capital K. We've already got it in eastern Zaire after the Rwanda massacres."

Kwame nodded, feeling the sun's heat, the drag of time, the lethargy of Kinshasa in the early afternoon.

"Hundreds of thousands of Hutu refugees, both innocent people and thugs, fled into Zaire. The refugee camps, ostensibly managed by the UN? They're actually controlled by Hutu gangsters, the *génocidaires*, determined to wipe out the Tutsis. Mobutu's tried to turn them to his own purposes. With French help."

Kwame wished he were holding a cool drink, a gin and tonic chilled by ice. He remained standing in order to stay alert. But his throat was dry.

"Europeans have fucked with this place from the very beginning," Judkins said. "Most royally the Belgians. Now the French are playing their game."

After a moment Kwame said, "My impression is that the blame for Mobutu rests with us." He was surprised to find himself expressing this opinion. Perhaps heat and drowsiness were lulling his wariness. He cautioned himself, let Judkins do the talking.

"For a long time Mobutu seemed the best way for us to further American interests," Judkins said. "That's why we're out here after all."

Kwame said nothing.

"What happens once Mobutu goes," Judkins asked, "if the eight countries surrounding this one all reach out to 'eat' Zairean territory? And start massacring tribal rivals? We could face an unimaginable catastrophe."

Kwame saw that the ferry was now well out onto the Pool, cutting through clumps of water hyacinths that floated on the current like islands.

"What you've got in Zaire," Judkins continued, "is Kinshasa, a modern city of the sort you'd visit in a nightmare, and behind it a huge hinterland that once boasted a bit of development, but has now collapsed back into something almost primeval. What infrastructure there was has been eaten by tropical vegetation. It's jungle now, wilderness, a vacuum of spongy plant life." He gave an ironic smile. "And we're determined to preserve its territorial integrity. That make sense?"

Kwame was feeling so drowsy that he was afraid he might yawn. "Do you suppose I could have some water?" Kwame asked. "My mouth feels like cotton."

While Judkins was gone, Kwame tried to shake himself awake. He peered down at the street life twelve stories below him. Some of Conrad's *Heart of Darkness* had happened right down there. Kinshasa was a village then. Jungle grew down to the beach, to the shacks where Belgian King Leopold's Free State freebooters lived.

"You know *Heart of Darkness?*" Kwame asked after he had drunk some water.

"I do," said Judkins. "Some of it took place right here."

Kwame felt fully awake now, even quietly excited.

But Judkins was not thinking about literature. "We have no idea what the hell's going to happen here," he said. "But if Mom and Dad and Buddy and Sis see a humanitarian tragedy on their TVs, they'll insist we clean it up. When we can't do the job in two weeks, the barbs will fly. The media will love that."

Kwame saw that the ferry was now almost all the way across the Pool.

"We don't know what'll trigger the explosion or when it'll occur," Judkins said. "But we want to be prepared. Ambassador wants an American presence in every part of the country. Not an embassy presence, not a consulate. That shows our hand too obviously. And it's too damned expensive. An Information Service presence. In the early sixties we had cultural centers in the six capitals of the old colonial provinces. We're going back to the same places, reopening the centers."

Judkins watched him in what struck Kwame as a curious way. He started to speak several times, but didn't. Finally he rose and came to where Kwame stood. "Ambassador thinks you should see one of these field operations before you get too involved in lecturing," Judkins said. "He wants every one of our people to visit one."

The ambassador sounds very gung ho, Kwame thought.

Judkins said, "We're sending you out to do that tomorrow morning. A place called Mbandaka."

"Tomorrow?"

Judkins put his hand on Kwame's shoulder. "The attaché plane flies up there every week. On its way to Kisangani. We got you a ride on that. Kent Mason, our man up there, meets the plane. He's opening the center, been up there a couple of months, just long enough to receive equipment. He'll be glad to have another American around. His French isn't as good as it ought to be," Judkins confided. "How's yours?"

"*Pas mal*," Kwame said. (Not bad.) "*Je peux me débrouiller.*" (I can untangle myself.)

"*Bon.*" Judkins patted Kwame's shoulder. "Got any problems with that plan?"

"Not at all," Kwame said. "Most of my African experience has been in cities."

Judkins grinned. "Then Mbandaka's just the thing for you."

AT THE USIS library Kwame discovered that Mbandaka lay virtually astride the equator at the confluence of the Congo and a tributary called the Ruki. He learned that a branch cultural center consisted of a library and a film service. Patrons could borrow works of American literature and books about America, most in French translation, and, more importantly, videos. They could watch videos at the center. Once the film service got set up, African staffers of the center would take films into the bush to give village audiences a glimpse of America and the world beyond the jungle. Kwame wondered if it might not make more sense to offer books and videos about Africa. Wasn't that what center patrons wanted to know about? But he held his tongue. He and Kent Mason could hash that one over. He e-mailed Mason that he would arrive early the next afternoon. But e-mail, he learned, was unreliable. Welcome to Zaire. In any case, Mason would meet the plane.

Livie had not yet replied to Kwame's earlier message. He sent her another, saying he was going to Mbandaka and might be out of touch for a week.

TWO

Like a tiny insect droning above an enormous snake, the plane flew low over the Congo. From the air the river, curling out of Africa's heart, resembled a broad, flat boa with an island-dotted hide. A great eater of tributaries, it had gorged itself on them and now moved as a huge, unstoppable force.

From the copilot's seat Kwame looked toward the horizon. The land spread below him with unrelieved flatness. To his left it stretched to the Atlantic. To his right it extended beyond the range of his vision; it reached to the backbone of Africa, to the Rift Valley Escarpment and Lake Tanganyika, to the Mountains of the Moon and the refugee camps where Tutsis and Hutus were killing one another.

"I love flying at this season," the pilot said. He was the embassy's military attaché, an army colonel named Kelly. "These days during the rains the air is clear as a lens." He veered away from the river and flew over jungle growing out of swamp. Below them lay a dense, green sponge of vegetation. It extended like an endless thick-napped carpet over a space whose walls were the sky.

Watching below, Kwame saw the patternless intertwine of plant life give way to textured design, to oil palms set out and tended in neat rows. A plantation. It was as if a referee had

stopped the struggle among the trees for space. Along one edge
of the tree rows, buildings hugged the water's edge. Corrugated
roofs glinted in the sun. Then abruptly the pattern of trees
ended. The chaos of jungle resumed.

A mission station appeared: a shabby school, a steepled
church in the Italian style, a dormitory and refectory, all
roofed in rust-pocked corrugated iron, all rotting into the
orange-brown ground. Kwame caught sight of a black priest
in a white soutane walking in the garden, holding a breviary.
He was gaunt, otherworldly, a man out of place, out of time.
Kwame watched him.

"That's your friend Mason in another month," said Kelly
with a grin.

Kwame studied the priest. Why was he gaunt? From disease? Malnutrition? From realizing that Christianity was irrel-
evant in the jungle? Or from needing a woman? But many
African priests considered celibacy an unimaginable arrogance.
The *Bon Dieu* gave men an obligation to procreate. The mission
station disappeared. Kwame gazed out at the endless jungle and
did not envy Mason his assignment.

"Just shittin' ya," Kelly teased. "You're going to *love* Mbandaka. The Las Vegas of Zaire." He gave such a full-throated
cackle that Kwame could not help laughing. "Casinos on every
corner. Pimps and drug dealers to shine your shoes. And girls,
girls, girls! They all want to marry a Yank."

"You think I'll have a bride when you come for me next
week?"

"Two or three. With babies in the ovens." Kelly added, "Ol'
Mason's making out okay."

"Yeah?"

"He gave me that feeling." Kelly winked.

Below the plane a dilapidated collection of buildings
appeared. "Here's home," Kelly announced. Mbandaka spread

below them, a once-town where nothing moved except the sluggish river. Kwame could make out potholes on streets that had once been paved. Two streets paralleled the river. A third led into the jungle. A paddle wheeler with "ONATRA" painted on the pilothouse rode at the docks. Mbandaka was a toehold of civilization clinging to the riverbank. A place engaged in a struggle against heat, jungle, and an endless succession of days, a struggle it was not winning.

Kwame looked for the house leased for Kent Mason. But he saw nothing that fit the description Pilar Cota, the cultural officer, had given him.

KELLY BROUGHT the plane in low over the jungle and set it down on the tarmac of Mbandaka's airport. He taxied the plane close to the terminal. The paint on the building was peeling; the terminal looked blighted, deserted. Once he cut the motor, Kelly climbed out of the cockpit, scrambled across the wing, unzipped his fly, and urinated on the pavement. "Oooh! That feels good!"

When Kwame emerged from the cockpit, heat assailed him. He dragged out his two duffels and stood on the wing to survey the landscape. Jungle lay all around the runway: silent, eternal. The shimmer of heat made it seem to dance. Nothing stirred but insects; they buzzed. Kwame watched the wall of vegetation, plants fighting each other to survive. He thought: Well, you wanted to connect with Africa. There it is! Embrace it!

"Where the hell's ol' Mason?" Kelly asked. "Probably dallying. I shoulda buzzed the house." Kwame said nothing. "That Mason," Kelly said. "Seeing a lot of action with spike heads."

"Spike heads?"

"Two weeks ago he was late coming out here. Had one with him. She couldna been fourteen. Her head looked like a field of radio antennas. He know you're coming?"

"I guess not," said Kwame.

"He's probably in bed with her right now. Forgot what day it was." Kelly looked about the airfield. "Shit. Where is he?"

"I'll go check the terminal," Kwame said.

But the parking lot beyond the terminal was empty. The terminal itself was locked. No flights this afternoon. By its smell Kwame found a men's room. Its toilets contained such a collection of filth that he fled. To Kwame it did not seem quite the thing to arrive in a new place and immediately piss on it. But he felt the call of nature and relieved himself as Kelly had in the open air.

When he returned to the plane, Kelly glanced pointedly at his watch. "I'm supposed to be in Kisangani," he said. "It's two hours up there. I better get flying."

Kwame choked down the uncertainty he felt.

Kelly examined him. "You be okay?"

"No problem," Kwame replied, his face a mask. "This is Las Vegas in Africa."

"Why are we putting people into this place anyway?" Kelly stared at the decaying terminal and cocked an ear to the silence. "Listen. The roar of silence." They listened for a moment. The weight of the absolute stillness did seem a kind of roar. "We put all this faith in technology," the colonel said. "Our Father which art in technology. But our phones don't work here. E-mail doesn't work. If I were living here, I wouldn't be praying to Our Father which art in technology." He gazed at the jungle, the terminal, and the road leading to it. "Where the fuck is Mason?"

"I'll be okay," Kwame said.

"They got plans to get you and Mason out if this place implodes?"

"That's not on the sked for this week," Kwame told the colonel.

"When it goes, there'll be a giant whoosh!" Kelly tufted his lips and sucked inward. "Whoooosh! You'll have twenty minutes to get out. Then it disappears. It'll whoosh you down with it like a toilet." Kelly grinned. "You got a will?"

"And I got a way. I'm a can-do guy." Kwame hoped it was true.

Kelly climbed onto the wing of his plane and stared at the jungle. "That stuff's alive," he said. "There are people watching us right now."

Kwame looked where Kelly was staring at the wall of vegetation.

"Out there." Kelly gestured toward the jungle. "After a while they'll come out and stare at you."

Kwame examined the jungle. People were out there, in that immense silence, watching him? He didn't think so. "I'll ask 'em for a lift."

"Good idea." Kelly offered his hand. They shook and the pilot climbed into the cockpit. "Good luck," he said.

When the plane hurtled down the tarmac and lifted into the sky, Kwame waved. He watched the plane move out of earshot and become a mere speck in the sky. When it finally disappeared, he was conscious again of the heat and of the immense silence of the jungle.

KWAME STOOD on the tarmac, wondering what to do. Would Mason be along? If not, what? He couldn't leave his gear. It would be hell to carry into town. He had no idea how far the town was.

He turned slowly, scanning the jungle. He looked at the sky, at its varying shades of blue: azure and aquamarine, cobalt on the flat undersides of clouds that rode the heat shimmer like whipped cream. He marveled at the stillness, at the slow stir of the air and the cleanness of its smell, not like odorous Kinshasa. The stillness seemed to have a kind of music. He realized that he was responding physically to the jungle and its atmosphere. He did not feel frightened; he was elated. Goose-flesh had risen on his arms.

Finally he sat on the tarmac. The sun beat down. Sweat and heat fogged his sunglasses. Thirst dried his mouth, thickening his tongue. He looked about him. He asked himself: What's wrong with this picture? The terminal. The monument to tech-nology. He thought: Get rid of the goddamned thing! Then the picture makes sense. With the terminal trying to dominate the jungle it all seemed wrong. Give it time, Kwame thought. The jungle will reclaim its own. Even the terminal.

He waited. Got up to stretch his legs. Sat down again. That damn Mason.

"I thought he was just the sort of officer we'd want in a branch post." The words were those of Pilar Cota, the cul-tural affairs officer. A tall, chain-smoking Latina in her forties, number two at USIS Kinshasa after Judkins, she had taken Kwame to dinner the previous evening. "He was good-looking, a little arrogant, bit of a macho edge. Maybe too good-looking for government service. A guy to make the ladies swoon and conscious of it."

"Did he make you swoon?" Kwame asked with a grin. He felt comfortable with Pilar because like him she lacked the standard Foreign Service background.

"He was a little young for me," she admitted. "Like you. But I'm not immune. What interested me was Mason's sense of adventure. You felt you could plop him down in the jungle and he'd make something of the experience."

"Is he doing that?"

"We assume so. We don't know." Pilar looked steadily at Kwame and asked, "What about you? You have a sense of adventure?" Kwame assumed being in Kinshasa answered that question. "How does a Boston professor happen to be in the USIS Foreign Service?"

"I took the exams," Kwame said, "just like you did. I was in grad school, wondering why the hell I was there. So I sat for the exam. Passed it. Aced the oral. And," Kwame added, "I was a very junior professor."

"They took one look at you in the oral and knew you'd work in Africa."

Kwame shrugged. "My name got added to the list of candidates. Then I got a spot teaching at Boston University. When USIS offered me a job, I asked if they could wait till I got some teaching under my belt and they agreed."

"Is this a career for you? Or— Whatever."

"I'm interviewing careers," Kwame said. He laughed heartily and Pilar smiled. Whether she was amused at the line— he'd used it before—or at the self-confidence, he couldn't detect. "My career may be this. Or teaching. Or maybe I'll be a rock star."

"There are too many rock stars."

"This work does have satisfactions," Kwame acknowledged. "I'd like it better if we were trying to help the people in the countries where we serve instead of trying to manipulate them for our advantage."

"Mutual advantage."

"There are also satisfactions in teaching. But in an era of consumer education—which is what we've got now—a professor has to think about marketing himself, especially if he's teaching African literature. So my marketing strategy is: really know Africa. I've watched South Africa shed apartheid. Now if I watch Zaire shed Mobutu—"

"You'll be a regular rock star among professors."

The derision in Pilar Cota's voice was unmistakable. "Actually," he admitted, laughing boyishly, "that sounds more calculating than I really am."

"Let's hope so," replied Pilar. "Is the French serviceable? Can you explain American positions on world affairs?"

"If I have to. Will there be a lot of that in darkest Africa?"

"You never know. You might run into Mobutu."

"And shit my pants!" They laughed together. "The truth is," Kwame said, "I used to feel a little dumb when students asked if I've lived in Africa and I had to admit I hadn't. So I'm living in Africa."

Pilar finished her chicken and pushed the plate away. Kwame set his knife and fork on the plate at four o'clock. Pilar watched this evidence of home training and allowed herself a private smile. "You done much reading about Zaire?"

Kwame shrugged.

"Americans have a lot to answer for in this country."

"And a lot of others."

"CIA destabilized the country about three months after its independence. Connived to chase the first premier—Patrice Lumumba—out of office. Then the Belgians and their minions in the Katanga had him killed."

"At least we didn't do that."

"Our hands aren't clean. We brought in Mobutu and paid him well to be our puppet all these years." After a moment Pilar added, "It makes you wonder if a foreign policy designed solely to advance our own interests really serves our purposes. We were obsessed with the Cold War in those days. But a strong unitary country, which is what Lumumba was hoping to build—" She stopped, shrugged. "But that's all water under the bridge."

Kwame looked intently at her. Since she was articulating what was on her mind, he would raise the questions that were on his. "You say you don't know how Mason is doing up-country. Why is that? Can't you contact him?"

"The mail sometimes works. The phone and e-mail almost never." Pilar gave a shamefaced smile. "Truth is communications with Mban are shit."

She took a cigarette from her pack and lit it with the one that was merely an ember in the ashtray. She took a deep draw and released the smoke so that it became a gray curtain before the upper half of her face.

"What does Mason think about being up there?"

"I'm sure he knows it's great for his career," Pilar said. "He's very junior and he opens his own post."

Kwame studied the woman as she smoked. Why in the world, he wondered, was the embassy sending people for whom it was responsible into the out-of-reach emptiness of back-country Zaire? Into jungles that had reverted to a primeval state unknown since before the colonial era?

"Fill me in on something." Kwame spoke in a tone he would not have used with Judkins. "Why is the US government putting people into places where it can't communicate with them? This is the last decade of the twentieth century. Has the embassy never heard of radios?"

"If we were some big news organization," Pilar began. "Say CNN. Or if this were still the Cold War when we had money for such things, we'd load up the guys we send into the bush with all kinds of electronic gadgetry. Hell, they could relay TV pictures of themselves every afternoon at five." She smiled with the same resignation to bureaucracy that had put lines in Judkins's face. "Unfortunately," she continued, "we're not a big outfit. We're just the world's only superpower. Whose citizens feel overtaxed. Africa is a part of the world that Congress doesn't care about. So . . . No commo. Still, we've got a job to do. And we think putting officers into places like Mbandaka is the best way to do it.

"It's only a week." She smiled, teasing him. "Unless the plane misses its regular run."

"Does that happen?"

"Happened last week. The ambassador had to fly to Lusaka." Kwame's nervousness amused Pilar. "Don't worry. We'll get you back next week."

Kwame poured the last of the wine they shared into Pilar's glass and asked the waiter for coffee. As soon as the waiter brought it, a man appeared out of the darkness. He was Kwame's age, pleasant looking in shorts and a tank top, his arms and shoulders well muscled from moving on his hands. His deformed, matchstick legs were folded before him. He skittered to the table and tapped a finger on it, looking up at the diners. Pilar offered him a couple of her cigarettes. He placed them in a pouch worn about his neck and waited while she fished through her handbag for zaires. Kwame asked, "Should I give him some?"

"No, no," Pilar said, "I'll take care of it. He's an old friend."

"Merci, M'sieur-dame," the man said. He moved off to other tables.

"What happens to a guy sent off to a post like Mbandaka?" Kwame asked. "He get any special training?"

"Some guys go crazy," said Pilar, "feeling as half-whole as that beggar. Others go native. Some flee. But most just do their job and get on with it."

"Which kind is Mason?"

"You tell us when you get back," Pilar said. "He'll have changed a bit. We sent him into a rundown part of this derelict country. Put him into a town where he knew no one. Poor guy has great confidence, but not great French. We rented a house for him, told him to live in it and open a post." Pilar glanced over at the man to whom she'd given money. "Mbandaka's a great professional opportunity. Also a helluva challenge."

Kwame noticed that, as the man wove his way through the tables, he harvested more money from Europeans than from Africans.

"Mbandaka's not dangerous," Pilar said. "The challenge is boredom, not violence." Her eyes held Kwame's as she drew again on her cigarette. "The sky, the river, the jungle: that's all that's there. Boredom can be a killer. Don't think it can't."

Kwame nodded.

Pilar said, "I just hope he doesn't say, 'Fuck it!' and take off."

Sitting now on the airport tarmac, Kwame wondered if Mason had done just that.

AFTER A while—he was not sure how long—he saw figures emerging from the jungle. Four young men appeared out of the heat shimmer that rose from the tarmac. They wore khaki shorts, tattered and patched, and plastic sandals. Pangas—long, sharp-edged machetes—dangled from their hands. They had been watching him, Kwame realized, just as Kelly had said, and they were watching him now. They halted ten yards off and stared. Kwame rose. *"Bonjour, mes amis,"* he tried, realizing that he must learn Lingala greetings. He felt sweat pouring off him. He nodded. They stared.

He saw other figures emerging along a road that led out of the jungle, half a dozen African women moving through the haze of heat. They were barefoot, cloths wrapped about their bodies and tucked in at the armpits. Some carried on their backs loads of kindling so heavy they staggered under the weight of them, their legs moving forward as if in labored dance. Other women walked erect, large logs balanced on their heads. Seeing Kwame, the women did not break the pace of their march. Despite the weight of their loads, they all stared at him.

Kwame stared back. He spotted a teenage girl, her upraised arms holding a log positioned on her head. A cloth was wrapped about her hips, swaying as she moved. Her torso was naked, her breasts firm. The girl locked eyes with Kwame. They stared at one another. He gazed at her body: her grace, those breasts, the rolling hips.

"What a pretty girl you are," said a voice in his head. It was the voice of Mister Johnson, Joyce Cary's outrageous Nigerian clerk, praising Bamu at the ferry over Fada River on the first page of the novel that bore his name. It was a novel that Africans generally loathed, but Kwame rather liked. "What pretty breasts," Johnson's voice continued. "God bless you with them."

Kwame smiled at himself, the literature professor, his head still in books. Suddenly he heard a motor. It revved, shattering the distant music. His brain stopped indulging professor-type ideas. Instead it spun, dizzied by the jungle's silence, the humidity, the heat, the afternoon sun on his skin, the dryness in his throat. He swallowed at the sights before his eyes: the procession of women bearing wood, the quartet of men still staring at him, the girl's nakedness. Again the motor. The sound came from the road the women had used. Kwame forgot the men staring at him. He hoisted the duffels to his shoulders and hurried toward the sound.

A Peugeot sedan appeared out of the vegetation. Kwame ran across the parking lot toward it, flailing his arms despite the duffels. The driver was white, a woman. A white woman? Here? He ran toward her car. Startled, fearful, she swerved to miss him. She sped across the parking area and raced onto the road that led toward town.

Kwame dropped his duffels and watched the Peugeot disappear. Sweat poured off his body. He wiped his neck. Silence. Heat glistened off the jungle. A white woman. USIS had rented a house to serve both as Mason's dwelling and the cultural center. The landlord was the only white man in town, Pilar had said, a man named Berton who owned small-scale rubber holdings south of town. The woman must be his wife. Kwame looked in the direction her car had taken.

There seemed only one thing to do. Kwame picked up the duffels and started in the direction the Peugeot had taken, moving toward town. He had hardly left the airport when behind him he heard the sound of another vehicle. He turned to see a Land Cruiser approaching. He tossed down his duffels and ran into the vehicle's path. The Land Cruiser stopped. A tall, large-boned African in an agbada and woven cap climbed down from the driver's seat. He grinned behind dark Ray-Bans with lenses that were lighter than his black, lustrous skin. He said, "An American, right?"

"Yes, I'm Kwame Johnson." Kwame offered his hand.

Erect, but nonchalant, the man stood taller than Kwame. He had broad shoulders, large hands, and enormous feet shoved into sandals that stuck out below the yellow trousers that matched his agbada. The bright yellow of that garment, undoubtedly chosen with care, contrasted perfectly with the darkness of his skin. The garment immediately identified him not only as Nigerian, but as both a professional and a man with a developed sense of self-possession.

"Mister. Johnson," the man said. The tone was satiric, challenging.

"You know *Mister Johnson?*"

"Do *you* know it?" the man asked.

Kwame shrugged.

"That execrable tract. Had to read it in school. Author seemed to think that all Nigerians are twits." He added, "I'm a Nigerian."

"I hope you won't hold that name against me," Kwame replied as they shook hands.

"Not at all," said the Nigerian. "I've been to the States. I know that one black in every five is called Johnson. But rarely Kwame Johnson."

"My distinction."

"I'm the witch doctor, old man," said the Nigerian. "That's my distinction. Olatubusun Odejimi at your service."

The doctor spoke an English so impeccable and with a voice so beguiling that Kwame grinned. "Could you give me a lift to town?" he asked. "Kent Mason was supposed to fetch me, but I guess he's been delayed."

Odejimi cocked his head. "Does he expect you?" he asked. "Or did you drop out of the sky? I heard a plane."

"He was supposed to meet the plane. Have you seen him around?"

"Not for a few days. Or his vehicle. I expect he's in the bush."

As THEY drove into town, Kwame watched the frond-thatched huts at the roadside. Some had walls of woven sticks; others were made of scrap metal. Outside the huts old men sat chatting on carved wooden chairs. Boys played with toys bent out of wire. Women worked at mortars; they yakked to one another, pounding manioc tubers into powder, babies tied to their backs.

"How do you like this place?" Kwame asked the doctor.

"Better than some places, worse than others." He laughed with a musical voice. "Not so nice as Los Angeles, but so much easier to park."

Kwame laughed. "How did they deal with your first name in LA?" he asked. "What is it again?"

"Olatubusun," the doctor said. "What could be easier than that?"

"Yoruba?"

"It means 'wealth increases.' You know, another son. Not that it mattered. I was my mother's first son. But she was my father's third wife."

Odejimi was not handsome in any conventional way, Kwame felt, but he was undeniably attractive. His manner offered good-humored acknowledgment of that fact. His eyes gleamed with joyfulness, even when shaded by sunglasses. His laughter boomed from his mouth. His wit pricked in a way that was both wicked and so soft that it gave no offense.

"They called me 'Jimmy' in LA," the doctor said. "But I never felt like Jimmy. How is it that you're Kwame?"

"My parents went to Ghana before I was born and never got over it," Kwame explained. "If they'd gone to Ibadan, I might have had your name."

"And everyone would call you 'Johnny,'" the doctor said. "Johnny-Boy Johnson." The doctor's voice spilled out in a full-throated, musical laugh.

The Land Cruiser passed an open-air market. Kwame noticed women selling merchandise from cloths laid out on the ground, haggling with their patrons. Some of them were huge with rolling shoulders, breasts, and buttocks and a laughing joyfulness. Beyond the market, mud-and-wattle huts gave way to neighborhoods the long-ago colonials had built for work-ers. "The *cités indigènes*,'" Odejimi noted. "Where our friends, the Belgians, put their 'boys.'" Kwame nodded as they passed dilapidated two-room cement-block houses standing in rows. By the roadside children played in the picked-clean hulk of a 1960s Peugeot.

"You accomplishing great things here?" Kwame asked.

"If you mean: Am I spearheading a health care revolution in this part of Africa, the answer is no." Odejimi beamed a great grin on Kwame. "But I am surviving. Some might call it 'hiding out.' My government does not want me in Nigeria; our dictator is even worse than this one. So surviving is no mean accomplishment."

They passed the larger, better-built homes originally designed for Belgian colonials. Inhabited by Africans now, they had become rundown. Chairs had been set outside. Washing was spread over bushes to dry. Chickens pecked in the yards.

The Land Cruiser arrived at an intersection of two streets, the town center. Young men loitered around the badly maintained government buildings on three of the corners. Some slept on the steps of the post office. Beyond these buildings lay a stretch of open ground, the colonials' town *place*, now a market square.

The vehicle passed the Mongo, the town's bar-restaurant, and parked before an abandoned house, an unadorned, apparently uninhabited structure set in a yard of dirt and weeds. "Mason lives here," Odejimi said. "Doesn't look like he's around." Kwame studied the building. The Nigerian watched him. "Want some advice?" he asked. "Take a room at the Afrique. Other hotels are brothels."

Kwame gazed at the house. "I better check out this place first."

"I'm at the Afrique," Odejimi said. "There's a room available. The Air Zaire bloke who was renting it got transferred back to Kinshasa."

"Maybe I'll see you over there," Kwame said. "Thanks for the ride."

As THE Land Cruiser drove off, Kwame heard a rhythmic pounding coming from the rear of the building. "Mason?" he called. "Hey, Mason, you've got a visitor." The pounding stopped. "Mason?" he called again and waited for a reply. The pounding started again. Advancing uncertainly, duffels strapped over his shoulders, Kwame moved to investigate the sound.

Behind the building stood one of the two-room cement-block houses Kwame had seen in the *cités*. Before it a woman, no longer young, stooped over a wooden mortar. Naked to the waist, she was pulverizing manioc tubers with a pestle. As she hurled the pestle into the mortar, using her hips as a fulcrum, her breasts, soon to be mere nippled flaps, swung to and fro. Kwame did not think: "What pretty breasts—God bless you with them." He thought: This woman is that teenage girl in twenty years.

Glancing farther into the yard, he heard a shriek. The woman had seen him. She stood frozen, the pestle motionless at a height above her shoulders. She cast it aside, covering herself with her cloth, and rushed inside the small house.

Soon a man emerged from it, a gray-haired, benign-looking African. Kwame recognized him from the description Pilar had given him in Kinshasa: Tata Anatole. He carried a baby in his arms. A naked boy of perhaps three years followed at his feet, a thong and a charm tied around his waist.

"*Bonjour, M'sieur,*" the tata said. He handed the baby to the child and offered his hand, bowing deferentially.

"*Monsieur Mason est là?*" Kwame asked if Mason were around.

The tata said not. Kwame introduced himself, explained he was from the center in Kinshasa and expected to stay a week. As Kwame shook the tata's hand, the man brought a key from the pocket of his trousers.

"*Où est Monsieur Mason?*" Kwame asked. "*Savez-vous?*"

The tata did not know where Mason was. He had gone with the vehicle some days before. The man was not certain just how many days. Kwame nodded that he would enter the house. The tata took a duffel, mounted the steps of the rear porch, unlocked the door, and pushed it open.

The house that the embassy expected Mason to convert into a cultural center had a large central room. Smaller rooms led off on either side, one to serve as Mason's office, another as his bedroom. As Kwame entered the large room, a musty smell assailed his nostrils. Mason obviously intended this room to be the library. Tables, library chairs set atop them, had been pushed against the walls. On the dusty floor lay metal shelving, unopened crates of books and videos, and piles of circular cans, the beginning of a film collection. All were still boxed for shipping.

Surveying the room, Kwame tried to imagine young Africans in the library. Some would sit at tables. Some would scan titles on the shelves while others lined up at a charge desk to be helped by an African employee not unlike themselves. That was how USIA, the parent agency of USIS in Washington, would describe the place when justifying its mission to Congress. "Our Cultural Center in Mbandaka is filled with eager Africans, hungry for education," the report would chirp. "USIS Mbandaka is giving them the chance they've never had before to learn about the world." Kwame knew that in the short time Mason would be here none of this would be realized. Mobutu would die or be assassinated and whatever followed would occur.

In a smaller room that overlooked the barren front yard, Kwame found a table and chair of local manufacture that Mason had bought before the library furniture arrived. Unopened mail sat on the table. Files spilled off the table onto the floor. Others had been stored in boxes against the wall. Kwame blew onto the table, raising a thick cloud of the dust. He wondered how long Mason had been gone.

In the bathroom, soap film clothed the tub. A used bar of pink soap lay on its edge. A broken lid covered the toilet; above and behind it stood a cistern emptied by pulling a metal chain. On the windowsill beside an accordion strip of condoms lay a toothbrush. A cockroach napped on its bristles.

Entering a back room, Kwame encountered a screen of mammy cloths hanging from a rope. Pushing these aside, he discovered a lone chair and a metal cot. On it rested a thin mattress covered with bedclothes; they were rumpled and spotted with semen. Boldly across one wall were scratched the words: "The horror! The horror!" Kwame smiled. Mason had a sense of humor. He'd like to meet the dude.

Kwame examined the books that Mason had stacked against the wall: Lawrence of Arabia's *Seven Pillars of Wisdom* about his World War I exploits leading an Arab revolt against the Ottoman Empire; biographies of Gordon of Khartoum and Lord Lugard, the great colonizer of Nigeria; a reprint edition of Henry Morton Stanley's *In Darkest Africa;* Saul Bellow's *Henderson the Rain King,* and even two titles in Edgar Rice Burroughs's Tarzan series. Interesting, Kwame thought. Opening the cover of the Stanley reprint Kwame found this inscription: "To Kent. Superior men create the world. Dad."

On the floor beside the cot lay a reading lamp. Kwame turned it on; at least it worked. Beside it were an ashtray, a half-smoked, hand-rolled cigarette, an envelope of tobacco, and a box of cigarette papers. Kwame sniffed the tobacco: a strong

scent, hemp probably, African marijuana. Beside the tobacco
lay girlie magazines with pictures of nudes, a surfing magazine,
and a copy of *A Burnt-Out Case,* Graham Greene's novel set in
colonial Mbandaka, then called Coquilhatville.

When Kwame picked up the novel, photos fell out of it.
They showed African girls. None of them wore clothes, yet none
were nude. All were artlessly naked, standing matter-of-factly as
children might, devoid of allure. Another photo showed a grinning white man, late twenties, in shorts and an orange sport
shirt sprinkled with blue asterisks. Was this Mason? Kwame
studied the man. He was good-looking.

The final photo was a portrait of a young African woman,
beautiful and dignified, a woman, not a girl. Mason's taste in
women had obviously improved. The young woman posed
wearing a mammy-cloth bodice with a cloth of a different pattern wrapped about her hips. Kwame gazed at the photo. How
lovely she was! She gazed at the camera from a world it could
not penetrate.

Tata Anatole shuffled into the room. Kwame showed him
the man's photo. "*Ce type,*" he asked. "*C'est Mason?*"

The tata nodded.

"When did he go off?"

The tata shrugged. "A week ago. Maybe two."

Two weeks! Where the hell had he gone? And why hadn't
he informed Kinshasa? Or had he tried? Maybe communications really were so crude out here that Mason was basically out
of contact with Kinshasa.

Kwame tossed the photos and the novel onto the chair.
He went outside and walked about the town, heading past the
market square devoid of the hubbub of trade for this was not
a market day. A few women sat on stools, wares laid out on
cloths, babies tied to their backs. Boys dribbled a soccer ball in
one corner of the square; old men in ancient, wide-brimmed

hats watched while gossiping and smoking. Moving toward the Onatra docks, Kwame smelled fresh-baked bread and saw a line of customers buying loaves at the bakery's kiosk window. The dock gates were shut and padlocked; the place seemed closed even though a riverboat was moored to the dock. Kwame returned to the town center, noticed young boys climbing on each other's shoulders to harvest a papaya and drifted by stores with goods on display outside.

By the time he returned to the center, Kwame felt extraordinarily alone. Black, but not African. He was used to living in the world of white men. Used to their culture. Used to manipulating that culture to his advantage. Could he function without white men to measure himself against? To hide from in protective coloration? He had not seen a single white person during his walk about the town. He had a strange feeling of being disconnected, even from himself. These people were not his black people. It shook him to feel so out of place.

Why had he let Judkins send him here without confirmation from Mason? Or had Judkins suspected that Mason might not be here? Kwame recalled Judkins's strange hesitancy just before he told him that he was being sent to Mbandaka. Calm down, he told himself. What could Judkins have suspected? You're getting paranoid.

What would he do here for a week? He had always functioned in urban environments, mainly academic ones. Face it, he thought, in elitist environments. Mbandaka was a mere speck of a town, remote, isolated, unconnected. Without an academic infrastructure. Were there elites to connect with? Maybe a teacher or two? Where would he find them? Would they welcome him? Since Americans supported Mobutu and Mobutu had ruined the country, would people want to embrace an American? Had Mason said, "Fuck it!" and taken off? Kwame paced across the library, past that haunt of cockroaches, the bathroom, through the bedroom with its semen-stained bed-sheets, its books about superior men and its frantic heart-cry on the wall: "The horror! The horror!"

Kwame did not want to ask himself again: What am I doing here? Often he had escaped into books. Could he do that here for a week? Could he prepare another of the French language talks he was to give at universities? Would he go a little crazy? This was not the heart of darkness. It was too banal and somnolent for that. Even so, he had to admit he felt ill at ease.

A YOUNG Zairean, no older than twenty-five, strode into the reception from the terrace. He wore a business suit, pointed shoes, rather scuffed, and a shirt open at the neck, also steel-rimmed glasses and a scraggling goatee. He was the hotelier. He introduced himself merely as Tombolo and immediately recognized Kwame. "Monsieur iss de new américain, n'est-ce pas?" he asked with an unctuous grin, proud of his English. "Le Docteur Odejimi say you come. I have magnifique chamber for you, M'sieur. With bath—for de américain."

When Kwame had written his name on the ledger, Tombolo handed him a room key. "Upstairs," he said. "End of passage. You want I send La Petite?" The hotelier gestured toward the African girl sitting nearby. She lifted her skirt; she was not bur-dened with underwear. "She has no SIDA. At other hotels in Mban you find SIDA, but here jamais." Tombolo snapped his fingers. The girl hurried from her seat to stand beside Kwame.

"Just the room for now, thanks," Kwame said, speaking French. He took his duffel so that the girl would not take it and set off.

THREE

Carrying his duffel and a tall, brown bottle of Primus beer bought at the hotel bar, Kwame found his way to the corner room at the far end of the open-air passageway on the second floor. He entered a large room, darkened by dust-spotted curtains drawn to keep out the light. He found two beds with mosquito nets hanging bundled above them and a sitting area with a table and two chairs of dark, heavy wood, Belgian-style furniture from the colonial era. Corkboards adorned the walls. Stuck to them were photos, cut from magazines and newspapers, of Zairean entertainers in performance. Kwame yanked off his shirt and used it to wipe sweat from his chest. Crossing the room he pulled open a floor-length curtain. Behind it stood a glass door that opened onto a balcony overlooking the river. He gazed at the moving water, speckled with floating islands of water hyacinths. He turned on the air conditioner. It coughed into action and began the rattling that accompanied its operation.

In the bathroom he snatched a hand towel from the rack. He wet it in water that ran red-brown from the basin tap, washed away his sweat, and wiped himself dry with a second towel. He found a glass and washed it. He opened the bottle of beer, poured out liquid that ran golden from the bottle and rewashed the glass. He poured beer into the glass, now almost clean, and drank it down. Warm, but not bad. He refilled the glass.

He opened the duffel and, almost as if performing a ceremony, removed a large padded envelope. From it he withdrew a framed photo of Livie—Olivia Carlyle—whom he expected to marry at Christmas. He gazed at her longingly. Christmas was four months away. An eternity. He set the photo on the bedside table.

In midsummer Kwame had left Cape Town where he had served for two years as a cultural diplomat. He and Livie, who was there with him, assumed they were leaving the continent for good. Kwame expected to resume teaching at Boston University.

Returning to the States excited them both. When their plane landed at JFK, Livie was wild with joy. She began chattering nonstop to her father, Jack, as soon as he greeted them.

Kwame had met Jack Carlyle when he visited the couple in Cape Town. He had come through for two days on his way somewhere else. Jack had never made Kwame feel that he disapproved of his daughter's living with an African American, especially not one who had survived the Foreign Service exams. Since Kwame and Livie were together, Jack wanted to approve of Kwame. Jack gave him every indication, not only of liking him, but of seeking his regard, even his friendship. Kwame, of course, applied protective coloration, masked his wariness. Livie did not sense how uncertain he felt. Protective coloration also provided him with a means to give Jack the pleasure of self-esteem for now he had a good black friend. At JFK the two men greeted each other warmly although Kwame understood that the warmth meant different things to each of them.

As Jack drove the couple into Manhattan, Livie told him that South Africa had fascinated her; the country was so diverse and cruelly beautiful. It had been intriguing to watch the final dismantling of apartheid, to be present for the long-awaited elections that saw patient Africans standing in seemingly endless queues to exercise a right many of them had thought they would never possess: the vote. "Kwame felt exalted for days," she told Jack. "He was so moved that he went along the lines, congratulating people. Didn't you?" she demanded. Kwame acknowledged that he had walked among the newly enfranchised citizens, shaking their hands. "I've got a photo of him doing it," Livie said. "He was really emotional. I carry it in my wallet."

Kwame was amused to see Livie's exhilaration, to hear her chatter. He was also pleased to be home. If the collapse of apartheid and all its structures of oppression provided a burst of freedom, that burst also involved a dark side. Crime rose. Burglaries soared in the Sea Point section of Cape Town where Kwame and Livie had their apartment. Carjackings became frequent. As Africans felt free to wander the city, the disparities between the way elites and the majority of blacks lived became more apparent. Livie often felt unsafe. Whites who had silently tolerated the sight of a tall, blonde American girl of rather patrician beauty paired with a black man now began to mutter obscenities when they passed the couple in the streets.

These incidents occurred even though Kwame did not look Bantu. He had a pointed nose, thin lips, and an educated man's demeanor and confidence. His movements possessed an athlete's grace; his carriage suggested quiet, unassuming self-possession of a kind that few South African Bantu had achieved in a society that sought to destroy their self-respect. Kwame looked white men straight in the eye. He wore clothes reflecting educated taste, so recognizably expensive that any Afrikaner *rooinek* could tell in a glance that he was American, that he belonged in South Africa by virtue of achievement.

"We are through with Africa!" Livie exclaimed to Jack and his third wife, Amanda, when they arrived at their apartment on Sutton Place. "Kwame will teach again and I'm going to law school." Kwame was not at all sure how her plan for them would work out. It envisioned him as a black man who would make a success of living in white culture. Was that such a bad fate: an attractive and affectionate woman, her supportive father, a tenure-track position at an important American university, the respect of colleagues for his experiences overseas? He would have to play certain roles, but everyone had to do that. He would be a black white man only if he chose to regard himself as one. He would not fall into that trap; he'd be grateful for what had come his way.

When they were alone together in the apartment, Jack asked Kwame, "And you? Are you through with Africa?"

"I suppose I am," Kwame said. "But Livie can be through with Africa in a way that I never can," he observed. "Can I?" He smiled wryly, held out his hand, and looked at the hue of its skin. "I have to deal with it at a different level than she does."

"But not necessarily there."

"No," Kwame acknowledged. "Not there. I carry it with me."

An attorney, Jack specialized in securities law; Amanda described herself as an "arts advocate," doing volunteer work in arts education. "It is so wonderful to be back in a real city!" Livie kept saying. "So exciting! Cape Town is lovely—as beautiful as San Francisco. Truly. But there are no real cities in Africa. There's urban crime, but no urban life. Believe me, this place never looked so good!" Jack Carlyle smiled at this news. Kwame saw that he wanted his daughter living nearby.

Kwame and Livie had met in a modern African literature class he taught. He had been twenty-seven then. With a newly accorded doctorate—his dissertation examined emerging indigenous voices in French and British colonial Africa after World War II—he was in his third year of teaching. Livie was twenty-one, an international relations major. In her final term of college she considered reading novels about an improbable part of the world a fitting way to declare her readiness to be done with schooling.

She had not, however, anticipated the instructor's effect on her. From the first class session, she felt a magnetic attraction to Kwame. And he was drawn to her—at least partly because he sensed that he intrigued her. At first he told himself that he responded to her because she listened more attentively than other students; an instructor always appreciated that. But when Livie visited his office in the seventh week of the term to discuss a paper she was writing, they both found it difficult to concentrate. The paper dealt with Wanja, the troubled but alluring prostitute heroine of Ngũgĩ wa Thiong'o's *Petals of Blood*. Livie saw Wanja as a metaphor for Kenyan society and its embrace of the West's corrupting capitalism. She sought out Kwame ostensibly to test her interpretation. Was her notion, she asked him, a plausible reading of Ngũgĩ's artistic intention? Kwame shrugged. He was interested in what she thought, he said, not what he thought. They looked at one another. Sexual tension filled the small office. The point of the paper, Kwame explained, was to argue an insight, her insight. She nodded. Silence engulfed them. Kwame felt his blood pounding and could not look at her. Instead he glanced at his watch. He stood, saying that he had forgotten an appointment and must leave.

"Don't be afraid of this," Livie said.

Kwame frowned at her—as if to signal that he could not believe what he had heard.

"Are you seeing anyone?" she asked. "I'm not. Not since last winter."

"I look forward to reading your paper," Kwame said. He turned away to stuff books into a backpack.

When he tried to leave the office, she stood in the doorway blocking his path. "You do feel this," she said. "I know you do. We don't need to pursue it now."

"I have no idea what you're talking about," Kwame said primly. They looked at one another. He laughed, embarrassed, excited. "I'm an instructor; you're a student. For the record I have no idea what you're talking about. None." Then he added, "And pursuing it is not a good idea."

Livie grinned at him. "We won't pursue it till the term is over." She cocked her head as if awaiting his agreement, still blocking the doorway, and he would not trust himself to touch her to get past. "Are you seeing anyone?"

"No. And I'm escaping this place immediately after exams."

"Don't be afraid," she told him.

To his surprise Kwame felt jangled by the directness of this approach. A young lecturer hitting on a student was an excellent way to doom an academic career, particularly if the lecturer was a tenuously middle class black and the student a very patrician white. But the girl intrigued him; he had to admit to being fascinated by the prospect of mating with that blonde self-assurance. But no! He was off to Africa; he would not pursue it.

By the end of high school Kwame had decided that circumstance had made his head American, educated by whites, while birth made his body African. At university and grad school he avoided African American women. They were seeking husbands. He'd had a relationship or two with white girls, but they drained away the essence of his black manhood. He sought women from Africa. They empowered his body, deepened his essence. Leaving their beds, Kwame wondered what it would be like to become African.

Some African women flirted charmingly. The sparkle in their eyes, the laughter in their voices, caused stirrings in Kwame's groin. But moving forward with them in love-play proved disappointing. They did not know how to kiss. They brought no passion to foreplay. None of them screamed or bit him or scratched his back in climaxing. Still he felt empowered by touching something deeply African in them.

After grad school he had concentrated on establishing himself at Boston University, especially since he wanted a two-year leave of absence to work in Africa. He had no time for women.

Then Livie Carlyle returned to his office late the afternoon he filed his grades. He was emptying shelves, packing books into crates. He was disconcerted to see her. "Is this about the final?" he asked, dissembling.

"I don't think so," she said, grinning. He went on packing books. "I came to take you to dinner." She smiled mischievously. "Because . . . your course meant so much to me. Because . . . you made Africa come alive for me." She began to laugh. He smiled. "Because . . . I think you are going to be one of those teachers I'll always remember."

"And I'm not to be afraid of this."

"That's right." Then: "Why are you packing?"

"I leave for Washington day after tomorrow. Then on to Africa."

"No!" She seemed genuinely distressed, but he nodded. "Then you really must come to dinner," she said. "My place first for a drink. Then we'll go out. My treat."

He examined her and shook his head. "We'll meet and go Dutch."

She looked at him a long time. "You have been with a white girl before."

He nodded. She shrugged: So?

"And you've been with black guys?"

"I don't think of you as black, Kwame. May I call you Kwame? I think of you—"

"Please don't." He agreed to meet at her place for drinks.

When he turned up, she served champagne. Her father, she said, had sent her a magnum to celebrate her finishing her exams. To the surprise of neither, they snacked on hors d'oeuvres and went to bed. Her lovemaking pleased him. Livie knew how to kiss. Her foreplay was inventive, passionate. She moaned at climax and held the skin of his back as if she would rip it from his bones.

Then as moonlight splashed in from the window, they lay side by side and got acquainted. Livie said for now she wanted to get as far away as possible from school. Kwame was to take no offense, but she might never read another book. "How long are you going to be in Africa?" she asked. When Kwame explained that he would be away two years, she rose to an elbow and said, "You can't!"

He felt like a fake, he told her, teaching African literature when he hardly knew the continent. He had spent two weeks each in Nigeria and Senegal, three days in Ghana; that was all. His department chair had agreed that by living in Africa he would more effectively teach African literature. She had okayed a leave of absence. Now he'd be living in Africa. That excited him.

"Why?" Livie asked.

"Why not?" He pulled the sheet off him. "When you look at that, what do you see?"

"Something splendid." She slapped his chest.

"See something African. Going back generations."

"I'm content to see something splendid."

Livie rose from the bed. Kwame watched her walk through a slice of moonlight and return from the living room with the magnum of champagne. They drank from it and again made love. And talked once more. He explained to her that he had grown up, the son of proud parents, in western Massachusetts, in Amherst, the country's premier college town. In the midsixties his parents had gone to Africa, to Ghana, at the high-water mark of John Kennedy's "rising tide of expectations." They returned with the name Kwame. When he was born, they gave it to him. Yet somehow he always felt compromised, always an outsider, neither African, nor American.

From his youngest years, Kwame told the darkness and the girl whose hand lay on his chest, his mother had drilled into him that his people had never worked in the hot sun of the South. His people had been Northerners, freemen well before the Emancipation Proclamation; they had worked on the underground railway. He said, "My mother never stops reminding me that 'our people'—it's always 'our people'—worked with their minds, not their bodies. We were never plantation slaves. Never minstrel show performers or field hands, musicians, or athletes. We used our heads." Livie moved against him. She put her hand to his cheek and kissed him. "I sometimes want to say, 'Mother, why must we always be different? I don't want to be a black aristocrat.'"

"But you are one!" Livie exclaimed. She began to caress his body.

He left before dawn while she slept. He never expected to see her again.

Six weeks after he arrived in Cape Town, Livie appeared in the USIS library. "I told you I intended to get as far away as I could from school," she told him. She needed a place to stay for a week. He had already begun dating African women, but he agreed to let her camp in his apartment. In the context of South Africa, it was edgy and cool for a black man to be

living with a white woman. She was with him for the rest of
his tour.

KWAME SPENT a week in New York with Livie and the Carlyles.
At the end of that week he felt all ajangle. For seven days he
had been force-fed art. He was surfeited with culture. Over-
stimulation exhausted him. Images saturated him. Theatre,
concerts, and gallery openings, films (they were never called
"movies") and dance recitals: these had been stuffed down his
gullet. Now a physical malaise afflicted him. Seeking refuge
in television (was not banality an antidote for high culture?)
he found it to be a neighborhood of brothels. Each network
seemed a whorehouse. Both America's TV and its high culture
made Kwame yearn for the deprivations of Africa.

Kwame became convinced that the work of art that Amanda
most vigorously advocated was Amanda herself. He saw her as
a piece of sculpture: nose job and face lift by Myron Saperstein,
MD, plastic surgeon; breasts by Dow Chemical; waist and hips
by liposuction and Jazzercise, thighs and ass by StairMaster;
hair styling by Monsieur Pierre; hair color by Clairol; makeup
design by a consultant called Ariel; perfume by Lanvin; clothes
by Doris Klotz, a seamstress with "fantastic talent" for copying
Paris fashions.

Amanda also sculpted her opinions. She assiduously
scanned the *New York Times, Vanity Fair,* and *the New York
Review of Books.* A sense carefully honed at cocktail parties told
her when to agree with cultural pooh-bahs and when to scorn
their insights.

By contrast, Livie's mother, Consuelo, had become a thera-
pist. She did not need the money, but wanted to help people
less fortunate than herself. She was certain that she herself had
not been abused as a child; neither probably had Livie. But she

discovered that most of her patients had been. Kwame never felt comfortable with Consuelo. She seemed always to inspect him as if he were a specimen. When she asked about his background and childhood, he concocted excuses to flee.

Consuelo lived with Marcus, a computer genius and self-confessed, time-obsessed chrono-maniac. Unfortunately Marcus suffered from stress. He lived so much in his head that some of his motor skills had atrophied. He sometimes fell off curbs or stumbled on uneven paving. He had taken to wearing a safety helmet and even kneepads when he went for a walk. Having recently fallen in the shower, he was now wearing a helmet while bathing.

Livie had a sense of humor about the two couples; she was going to study law in Boston partly to keep her distance from them. Even so, Kwame wondered if she would turn out to be like them. She accepted the premises of the two couples' lives with such little question—and by now took Kwame so for granted—that she did not sense him watching them. And watching her. And feeling out of place. Even so, he told himself, "Suck it up! You've got a good thing going here."

AFTER A week in Manhattan, they escaped the city and the exertions of "keeping up." Kwame and Livie went with Jack and Amanda to spend a country weekend in Darien where the Carlyles owned a home.

Late Sunday evening when the women craved delicacies, Kwame was sent in Jack's BMW to fetch sherbet from a market. He drove slowly through the quiet, unpeopled streets, dark under heavily leafed trees, and noticed a police car pass. He glanced in the rearview mirror. The car made an abrupt U-turn. It advanced on him. It flashed its lights and pulled him over. Kwame felt a hollowness in the bottom of his stomach.

As the officer sauntered toward him, he knew an apprehension deeper than anything he had ever felt in South Africa. So deep it made him feel dizzy. He tried to calm himself. Hey, he told himself, you're in Connecticut. Even so, he knew that he must be careful.

"Good evening, officer," he said when the cop arrived at his window. The man inspected him with suspicion. He brought a flashlight from behind his back; for an uncertain moment Kwame thought it might be a club. The cop directed its beam onto Kwame's face. He flashed it throughout the interior of the car and brought it to rest, almost touching Kwame's nose.

The cop asked quietly, "What're you doing in Darien?"

Kwame explained that he was an American diplomat, presently on home leave; he was visiting friends. He mentioned Jack Carlyle by name and noted the street where he lived.

The cop inquired, "This your car?"

The car belonged to Jack Carlyle, Kwame explained. He was on his way to get ice cream.

"Get out," the cop said. "Stand behind the car, hands on the roof, feet spread."

A flush of fury swept over Kwame, but he obeyed. He was wearing a tee shirt, jeans, and sandals and the officer patted him down, the truncheon swinging off his hip. He slid his hands down each of Kwame's legs and checked his crotch. A car approached, slowed. Kwame turned his back against the headlights, feeling the car's occupants watching him. Humiliation and anger raged in his blood. But he must be cautious. He stood in silence, feeling outrage, but even more deeply feeling fear. The hollowness in his stomach expanded. Kwame was afraid it might swallow him. The car passed and moved on. Kwame knew that he must maintain his self-possession. "Careful, careful," pounded his pulse. "Always be respectful, play the inoffensive black boy." He must give the officer no reason to employ the truncheon, to hit him where the bruises would not show.

"Driver's license," the cop now said. Kwame surrendered the license. The cop examined it. He instructed Kwame to drive to the local station house, following him through the silent streets that now seemed full of menace. The officer called Jack Carlyle from the station house, employing his own carefulness, using an inoffensive white boy tone of voice. It turned out that Kwame was indeed Jack's friend; his use of the BMW was authorized. When the officer put down the phone, he told Kwame that he was free to go. "My apologies for any inconvenience, Mr. Johnson," he said. He spoke Kwame's name for the first time. The men looked at one another. The cop added, "But none for pulling you over. The people of this community want a certain kind of protection and that's the kind I give 'em."

"Thank you, officer," Kwame said. "Have a good evening."

Outside the night did not seem quiet and gentle, but raging and shredded. Kwame wanted to shout profanities. Instead he went to the market, looking no one in the eye. He got the sherbet and drove around. He tried to unwind, but could not shake the fear that yet again some cop would pull him over. When he returned to the house, Amanda had gone to bed. Jack apologized for the incident. "These things happen," he observed. "Roll with the punch." He said good night and went to bed.

"What the fuck's he mean?" Kwame demanded. "Roll with the punch."

Livie made a face. "Hey, baaad dude!" she teased. "You got danger written all over you." She sashayed around the living room, twitching her behind. Kwame made himself smile at her antics.

Livie tossed off her clothes, one item at a time, leading him to their room. When she had shucked off her panties, but not yet her tee shirt, he slammed her against the wall, intending to take her from behind, to release his fury on her. "Ooooh, such a baaad dude!" Livie teased, shaking her hips. But he felt no desire and walked away.

She turned toward him, pulled the tee shirt below her hips and said, "Everybody has to roll with things, Kwame."

"Do they?" he asked. "What's Jack Carlyle roll with?"

"You think everything's perfect for him?"

"He has to roll with the fact that a nigger's fucking his daughter. And in his own house. Right?"

"Racist fuckhead. He doesn't care that you're black."

"But what?"

Livie went to where she'd dropped her shorts, turned her back, and put them on.

"But what?" Kwame demanded a second time.

"He thinks I ought to marry you. Or move on."

"Oh, great!" Kwame said. Livie took refuge in the bathroom and shut the door.

Later when they were in bed together, Kwame could not perform. He wondered: What's happening here? This doesn't happen to black guys.

"Hey, hey, hey," Livie reassured him. "Forget it. It's not important."

Kwame said nothing. Livie patted his groin. He pulled her hand away, his humiliation deepening. His cock lay shriveled and as inoffensive as a worm.

By morning Kwame's humiliation had abated. The anger was gone, his virility restored. Over breakfast he asked her, "You coming with me to Massachusetts?"

"They don't want to meet me yet," she said. "Wait till they've had a good visit with you. We can arrange it over the phone."

And so it was left that Livie would meet his parents some other time.

ON THE drive from Darien to Amherst Kwame was alone for the first time in days. When he arrived and embraced his parents, Bob and Shirley Johnson watched him keenly. They could sense decisions being made even before he himself was aware of it. But he was aware of it now. At their first dinner together he announced, "I'm going back to Africa."

"Why?" his mother asked, exasperation in her voice. "Your future isn't there. And don't think you'll find some mystical connection with the people."

"That's what we thought when we went to Ghana," said his father.

"But there is no mystical connection," his mother declared. "Our forefathers may have been Africans, but we're Americans."

"Are you testing yourself?" his father asked.

"God, no!" Kwame assured him. "I've taken so many tests I don't ever want another one." He added, "I do teach African literature."

"You don't teach it there, son," his father said.

"Don't go there," his mother said. "It's the uttermost parts of the earth."

"Oh, c'mon," Kwame replied. "There aren't any 'uttermost parts' anymore. If you wanted, you could hop a plane and visit me."

His parents looked at one another, upset. As people of the mind, they preferred to boast that their son taught literature at Boston University than to say that he was an American diplomat living in an African country no one had ever heard of. "Is Olivia going with you?" his mother asked.

"I don't know."

"You said once she was going to law school," his mother remarked. Kwame nodded. "Is it serious with her?" she asked. "Do you love her?"

"Don't question the boy," his father said.

"I wouldn't if we saw him oftener." His mother scrutinized him. "Are you going to marry this girl? Or are you going to Africa to get away from her?"

Kwame said nothing.

His mother asked, "Do little bells go off when—"

"When we fuck?" Kwame laughed. His mother raised her hands to her ears.

"Don't talk that way in front of your mother," his father admonished, although he, too, was laughing.

"Bells sound then," Kwame told his mother, "only if the phone is ringing."

"Are we going to meet her?" his mother asked.

"Will you stop this!" his father demanded.

WHILE LIVIE thought he was with his parents in Amherst, Kwame drove to Brookline to visit his professor colleagues. To the chair of his department he broached the idea of extending his leave of absence for another two years. "If you want to teach here," she told him, "you can't keep putting it off. But okay. This is your last extension."

He flew to Washington—Livie still thought he was in Amherst—and told the USIS personnel officer in charge of Africa that he had decided not to resign; he'd like another assignment. "Someone who wants to serve in Africa!" she whooped exultantly. "Watch out! I may kiss you." The officer typed commands into her computer. The manning chart for the entire continent came up on her screen. She scrolled through it, Kwame looking over her shoulder. "The Number Two Cultural Officer slot is open in Kinshasa," she told him.

"Is it dangerous in Kinshasa?"

"Of course, it's dangerous. It's Zaire. The old Congo." She grinned. "I'm kidding. It's safe in Kin. There's a 25 percent hardship duty differential. And not much hardship. You could come out of there rich." She gave Kwame an impish look. "We need someone out there in less than three weeks," the officer said. "So if you want the slot, let me know. I've gotta fill it." They shook hands. As Kwame opened the door, she called, "Zaire's a good name on your personnel record. Or a résumé. It's not Malawi or Burkina Faso. People have heard of it."

"That hard to fill, is it?"

After the interview Kwame strolled through downtown Washington, wondering how Livie would react. Would she come with him? Did he want her to? Homeless people seemed stationed on every corner, their hands out, crudely lettered cardboard signs at their feet. Most were black. They would see Kwame approaching, look at him with special pleading and murmur, "Hey, Bro—" Then, taking a closer look, they would stop, realizing that he was not one of them, not a brother. It unnerved Kwame that fellow blacks sensed that they need not appeal to him.

HE AND Livie spent two weeks together at a rented cottage on the north shore of Cape Cod. At the end of the first week Kwame broke the news that he had signed on for another tour in Africa. Within ten days he would be in Zaire. He did not ask her to accompany him and she did not offer to go. She did keep asking, "Why do you insist on this?" He would shrug. "Don't keep shrugging," she would say. "You're a person of the mind, remember? Why do you have to do this?"

He would say, "There's something I have to connect with in Africa."

"That is such bullshit!" she would cry. "What about us?" Then she'd say, "Fuck it! I swore I'd never say that to a man."

On the second evening before he left they lay holding one another under a blanket, lying on a dune that sloped down to the water. A scattering of stars shone brilliantly above them. "The stars must be fantastic in Zaire," Livie said. "Less pollution—at least out in the boonies. Less ambient light. Shall I come watch the stars with you out in the middle of nowhere?"

After a moment she turned toward him. "We've been together all this time, Kwam. And yet—" She shrugged. "You're going back to Africa to break this off, aren't you?"

"No. There's something out there—"

"Like hell." Then for a long time she said nothing. Finally she asked, "Do you love me?"

"Yes, I do."

"Have you thought about marriage?"

He shrugged.

"Fuckhead!" Neither spoke. "I hate it that you always make me bring this up," she said. "Have you thought about us getting married?"

"Yes. I'd like that." The words found their own way out of his mouth. He realized that once he left her, he would probably never see her again. Suddenly he did not want that to happen. Them married: he would like that. "But not if we eventually get divorced."

"What about children?"

"Not if we get divorced."

"You shit. Why do you keep saying that?"

"Your people divorce. Mine don't."

He held her close and looked up at the stars, wondering if a marriage between them would work. It would be wonderful for a few years. Could one ask for more than that of an American marriage these days? But the time would come—fifteen, maybe twenty years down the road—when there would be concerns about money: about salary, retirement, and investment accumulation. He would come up short there; the women Livie had grown up with would have married entrepreneurs and international lawyers, arbitrageurs and investment bankers. Even if he did well as a cultural diplomat or in the academic world, he could not compete with them. Livie's friends would be wealthy. She might inherit money, but never wealth. She might even make a good bit of money as an attorney. But they would always be behind. Kwame wondered how that would be.

And he understood that her intention was that he should enter her world of privilege, her white world. Her friends would accept him in his protective coloration glow: always affable, no jarring opinions, Republican small talk. He would be one of those tiny drops of black in the can of white paint that Ralph Ellison had written about in *Invisible Man*; those few black drops made the white even whiter. But what about Livie's moving into the black world from which he came? Could she do that? She had promised to meet his parents—his mother wanted very much to inspect her—but she was never quite able to make time for the trip. Would she accept him, but deny where he came from?

He held her and looked at the stars. "You're going to marry some church-going black girl," Livie said. "I know you will. And she'll always feel good about herself because she beat out the white chick."

"And you're gonna marry some WASP with Mayflower ancestors and more money than I'll ever see."

While he was packing the evening before he left, he looked up and saw that she was watching him. "We've been together almost two years," Livie stated. "Haven't we?" Kwame nodded and went back to sticking socks into odd corners of his duffel. "And they've given us great times, haven't they, those two years?" she asked. He glanced up at her and smiled. "And we get on well."

He zipped the duffel closed and set it on the floor. He wondered: What was he doing? The Congo seemed an enormous black hole. Already he was missing her.

He went to where she sat on the bed, her back against the headboard, a pillow in her lap. He took her hands and gazed at her.

"I love you," she said. "If you love me, would you say it please?"

"I do love you. Kwame loves Livie." She smiled. He asked, "What if we had Christmas together in Paris?" She grinned and leaned forward to kiss him. "You'll have a break from law school and I'll get leave."

"We'll find a little hotel that caters to lovers."

They kissed. Kwame turned off the light and came back to the bed. Was he crazy to go to Africa, he wondered. If she found someone else to love, that WASP with the Mayflower heritage, would he ever forgive himself? They kissed again and looked at each other in the darkness. "What if we got married in Paris?" he asked.

She held him close. If they married, he wondered, what would happen to them? Would they be together? Would she abandon law school? Or would he leave Zaire?

"We won't tell anyone what we're planning to do," she said. "We'll just do it, get married in Paris at Christmas."

But when they made love that last night, they both wept as if they would never see each other again.

KWAME GAZED at Livie's photo on the bedside table and wished he could talk to her. He could not expect to e-mail her. He sat down to do what he had never done: write Livie an actual letter. As he began, he found that this was not so easy to do. Until recently people had written letters for centuries! Amazing! What would he write on? His mother had stationery in various colors and sizes, some with her name printed on it. She even used it—which he had laughingly told her made her a relic of a bygone era. Kwame had no stationery. He took a piece of computer paper and his ballpoint and began— But how did one begin? And was this a love letter? He could not recall ever writing a love letter. He had read them; that had been part of his education. But to write one? To lay naked longing and overwrought emotion on a piece of paper? "My darling, each whisper of the wind brings me thoughts of you— Livie, I long to touch—" He could not do it!

He started out, scratching away— My god, but this writing by hand took a lot of time! He told "Hi, Liv" that he was in Mbandaka for a week, in the only non-brothel hotel in town, scribbling these odd curlicues of handwriting, hoping the town's uncertain electricity would not shut down and hoping even more that Kent Mason, who might be more ghost than man, might show up. He read over what he had written. Labored. Stilted. Penned by an unimaginative drone used to writing academic monographs. My god, he thought, is my diss as dull as this?

He plugged away, crafting what was more an amplified grocery list than a letter. He finished with a line about missing her, obsessing about Paris and Christmas, wondering how he'd last till then. These lines embarrassed him when he read them over, but he knew she would like them.

When Kwame finished the letter, he really was missing her. The light had gone from the sky. He turned on the television, hoping to find out what was happening in Livie's world. The

TV set did not work. It was a reminder of the larger realms beyond Mbandaka, but not a means of access to them. He decided not to bother with dinner. He got another beer from the bar and ate crackers he'd brought in his luggage.

FOUR

The next morning while he had coffee and rolls on the hotel terrace, Kwame saw a man appear on his balcony to examine the day. His skin was as white as ivory, as spectral as a cadaver. After only a week in Zaire, Kwame's eyes had grown accustomed to seeing only dark-skinned people. Whites looked sickly, ghostly. He wondered if that was how Zaireans regarded Mason. The white man quickly returned to his room. So there were at least two of them in town. Kwame wondered who he was.

After mailing his letter to Livie, Kwame walked to the center. In Mason's bedroom, he pulled the sheets off the bed and towels from the rope tied across the room and tossed them by the door. He searched for Mason's laptop; certainly he had one. In the armoire he found a lone sport shirt draped over a hanger. That was all. No trousers, no boxers, no tee shirts, no shoes. And no laptop. Had Mason gone somewhere taking his clothes and his computer?

When Tata Anatole shuffled into the building, Kwame told him to have his wife wash Mason's sheets. As they attacked the crates of library shelving and furniture, Kwame asked if anyone had come to fetch Mason's clothes. "No one," Anatole said. To check the response, Kwame rephrased the question.

Anatole gave the same answer. Kwame said, "You always lock this building, right?" Anatole nodded that he did. "Especially when you're not here."

"*Oui, M'sieur.*"

The men worked steadily throughout the day. Whenever a vehicle passed on the road, Kwame looked up, hoping to see Kent Mason appear. But he did not.

At the end of the day, Kwame had Anatole show him where the mail was collected at the post office: in a large locked drawer below the smaller lock boxes that most patrons rented. Kwame estimated that Mason had not collected mail for about two weeks. He gathered it and started across town.

Ordering a beer at the hotel, he took a table on the terrace to sort the mail, hoping to make contact with other residents. But no one joined him. He nursed the beer for an hour. Finally Odejimi crossed the terrace, leaving for a swim. "Come along," he suggested. Kwame collected the mail, fetched his suit, and joined him.

As they were driving through the old colonial quarter of town, Kwame said, "I saw a white man at the hotel. Who's he?"

"Moulaert, a Belgian school inspector."

"What's he doing here?"

"Escaping his wife." Odejimi laughed. "She must be something, eh? If he's come here to escape."

The pool had been built in the colonial era. Its tiles were green with moss, but the water, a golden color, looked at least as clean as the river. Like something out of Gauguin, a girl of perhaps fifteen lolled beside the pool on a towel. She wore only a bikini bottom and had remarkably attractive breasts. She waved to the men across the pool.

Odejimi said quietly, "For a few zaires you can have her."

"I've never needed to pay," Kwame observed.

"Neither have I," said Odejimi. "But it's always part of an exchange, *n'est-ce pas?*"

Kwame dove in and started swimming sixty laps in a three-lap rotation of breaststroke, backstroke, and freestyle. During one of the backstroke laps watching the phalanx of clouds march across the sky, Kwame noticed Odejimi and the girl disappear into a dressing room.

As he was finishing his laps, doing sidestroke, the doctor swam up beside him on his back. "How was she?" Kwame asked.

"I can't stay away from those tits," Odejimi confessed. "She puts them on display and waits for me."

"Is she clean?"

"I've tested her. Warned her. These children need so much training." The doctor sighed. "It's not good for my health to go without."

"A man must be careful about his health."

"I'm taken care of now," the doctor said. "My friend just returned from Bikoro." He glanced at the teenager, shook his head, and expelled a deep-throated laugh. "I should be more disciplined."

Kwame observed, "Discipline always becomes a man."

The doctor guffawed. "What a load of shit! You're a post-modern, feminist Yankee, aren't you? You think I exploit that child." Kwame laughed and kept on swimming. "This is Africa, my friend. She loves being a magnet for older men."

KWAME SPENT the next couple of days at the center, arranging materials, looking through files. Once again he spoke to no one except Anatole. Walking across town from hotel to center, center to hotel, he had mental conversations with Livie. In them he confessed that she had been right; he never should have come to Zaire. He did math exercises in his head: how many hours until Kelly returned with the plane. Kwame often thought of Mason, living at the center, speaking indifferent French and no African language. Could he have been so lonely he just took off?

WANTING FRESH fruit, Kwame walked out to the town's largest market. Drifting past the yabber of bargaining and the radios tuned to competing stations, past offerings of food-stuffs and spices, apparel, plastic sandals, fishnets, and oddments, Kwame noticed something curious. Whenever merchants and patrons caught sight of him, they fell silent and stared. He was wearing jeans, a polo shirt, sandals, and dark glasses. He looked no different from other men in the market. But he seemed to exude an aura that hushed the surroundings. Everyone knew that he was a white man. The silent stares unnerved him.

He bought a pineapple and bargained for short, yellow bananas. As he crouched before gold-orange papayas, a market woman tapped him on the shoulder. When he turned, she unfurled a pair of chino trousers, labeled Dockers. Another market woman held out short-sleeved sport shirts. "Good price! Good price!" she jabbered. "You like? How much?" Kwame studied the garments. Light blue asterisks fluttered across an orange shirt. Hadn't Mason worn such a shirt in a photo stuck in *A Burnt-Out Case*?

"Where did you get these?" Kwame asked. The market women looked confused. "Who gave you these clothes?" Kwame demanded.

The women did not understand. They yakked in Lingala. Kwame made an offer on the orange shirt. Bargaining began.

Kwame walked away. The women followed, lowering prices. Eventually he bought the shirt.

At the center he checked Mason's photos. He found the one of Mason wearing the shirt he had bought and wondered what to think.

THE NEXT morning, dragging Tata Anatole along as translator, Kwame took the shirt and the photo to the Commissariat de Police. The commandant listened to Kwame explain about Mason's disappearance and concluded that he had not disappeared; he had merely left town. He had probably sold the shirts himself. If it was theft, well . . . Such things happened.

At the headquarters of the gendarmerie, the commander, who spoke some French, confessed that he had no idea how to trace Mason. But as a blood relative of the president, for a hard-currency consideration—say, $500—he could bring Mason's disappearance to the attention of Mobutu Sese Seko himself.

Kwame went alone to the military camp. The major in charge handed Kwame over to a captain. The captain asked how he might get to Fort Benning, Georgia, for parachute training of the kind Mobutu had received. He explained that an inquiry about Mason would cost money. When Kwame failed to offer any, the captain referred him to a lieutenant. The lieutenant speculated that Mason had gone swimming off a sandbar and had been eaten by crocodiles. "That is how such a man would disappear," he said. When Kwame thanked him for this opinion, the lieutenant said, "I give you information, but you give me nothing. How can we be friends?"

At the Air Zaire office the *chef de service* assured Kwame that no European travelers had flown out of Mbandaka in recent weeks. But, he said, his twenty-year-old son had a long-time interest in America. Might Kwame employ him at the center?

THAT AFTERNOON when Kwame went out on the Afrique terrace, carrying a bottle of Primus beer and a glass, he found Dr. Odejimi at a table overlooking the river. The Nigerian was smoking sweet-smelling hemp, a bottle of whiskey and a glass before him. Inviting Kwame to sit, he laid out a game of *mankala*, placing large seeds into two lines of circular cups carved in a board. "What's going on?" Kwame asked. "Mason was here for a couple of months, but no one will tell me anything. What kind of guy was he? I've seen his photographs," Kwame admitted. "I know he got girls to take off their clothes."

"Don't we all try that?" The doctor smiled.

"Would angry fathers have chased him out of town?"

"You could ask around."

"Ask who?" Kwame enumerated the people he had seen. He complained, "Doesn't anyone do his job here without getting tipped? What kind of country is this?"

"An African country," Odejimi replied. "The only way these blokes make it in Zaire is to exploit people like us. But you'll never learn anything if you pay for information," he cautioned. "Everybody will string you along."

"Is that what's happening? Or is there some code of silence?"

"Who are you?" Odejimi asked bluntly. "Why should anyone speak to you? Especially anyone in the military."

"Is the military involved?"

Odejimi shrugged. "Who else is taught to kill?"

"You think he's dead?" Kwame asked, startled.

"Soldiers plunder from their own citizens. So why not murder Mason for his truck?"

Kwame considered this possibility, sipping beer and staring at the river. Suddenly the atmosphere on the terrace changed. It was as if electrons had started crackling and dancing about.

"*Eh bien!*" exclaimed Odejimi, looking behind him. The men had been speaking English together. Now Odejimi switched to French. "Finally you've come."

Kwame turned. He saw the woman who appeared clothed in Mason's photos. He had heard her called *Femme d'un Blanc,* white man's woman; she had apparently been married to a Belgian who abandoned her. Barefoot and in European clothes, she moved toward them across the terrace. Odejimi turned back to the *mankala* board to demonstrate that he was tired of waiting for her. Kwame rose from his chair and watched the woman approach him. She seemed to exude a force field that caused his skin to prickle.

Words tiptoed into his literature professor's head. "A wild and gorgeous apparition of a woman." Conrad describing Kurtz's woman. The passage surprised Kwame for it did not seem to fit this woman. Still the words were there: "She was savage and superb, wild-eyed and magnificent." The woman was more beautiful than in Mason's photo, more inscrutable. Even so, strangely, Kwame had some inkling as to why Conrad chose those words.

He set his beer on the terrace railing and offered the woman a chair. "*Merci, M'sieur,*" she said, her voice soft and melodious.

"Van, this is Kwame Johnson from America," Odejiimi said to her. He nodded at Kwame. "Madame Vandenbroucke, wife of a Flemish asshole who took her to Belgium, then left her high and dry. His family sent her back here. Lucky for us, huh?"

The woman did not react to this recitation of her personal history.

Turning back to the *mankala* board, Odejimi ordered, "Begin." Madame Van picked seeds out of a *mankala* cup and proceeded to distribute them around the board.

"Would you like something to drink, Madame?" Kwame asked.

"Thank you." She glanced at him with the slightest of smiles. Electrons started crackling; his skin prickled. "A beer, if you please."

Kwame brought Madame Van a bottle of Primus and poured some into a glass. Again she said, "*Merci.*" Kwame poured himself some beer and positioned his chair so that he could observe the game and at the same time without seeming to he could watch the woman. Fortunately he wore dark glasses; where he looked would be hard for the others to discern.

Madame looked at him occasionally, her gaze as enigmatic as a sphinx. Her eyes disclosed nothing; he had no idea what she was thinking. Still he decided she epitomized grace. Embodied a dignity that was deeply sensual. Or was it a sensuality that was deeply dignified? He wasn't sure. She had married a Belgian. She had known Mason and was a friend of Odejimi. So she was a woman who welcomed outsiders. That would be unusual in a place like Mban. Kwame tried not to stare at her. Odejimi would be watching too.

The doctor studied the board and the seeds, shaking his head, his mouth tufted with perplexity. Madame Van glanced at him, amused. She picked up the seeds from one of the cups and, hardly watching the board, distributed them counterclockwise. She dropped the last seed into a cup on the doctor's side containing two other seeds. She scooped all three from the cup and tossed them idly into a saucer at her end of the board.

Kwame watched the game and the woman, wondering what the story was about Vandenbroucke. If he had, in fact, taken her to Belgium, she was no village girl. The *mankala* game ended when Madame Van scooped all remaining seeds from a cup and tossed them idly into a saucer at her end of the board. "Fuck all," Odejimi muttered in English. Then he complained in French, "This woman is a master at *mankala*. I dream of beating her and I never do." Amused at her dominance at *mankala*, Madame smiled mysteriously, rose from the table, and left the terrace. Both men watched her go.

"I saw you couldn't stop watching her," Odejimi said.

Kwame laughed, feeling caught out. He had not expected either of them to notice. "Is that why she left?"

"She's a woman. She left so we could talk about her."

"Was she really married to— What was his name?" Kwame asked.

"Vandenbroucke. A Belgian adviser. He needed a woman while he was here, asked nuns at a secondary school to find him a companion. They selected her. Lucky Van. He got a looker who was also bright."

"He married her?"

"Paid some cash for her. An African marriage."

"He took her to Belgium?"

"When his tour of duty ended, she wanted to see Europe. He claimed she was his wife and the Belgian government paid the fare." After a moment Odejimi added, "A way of saying farewell, I think. Something he could do for her at virtually no cost to himself." Odejimi stared off across the river. "But maybe he intended to live with her. No woman her equal in Belgium would have him." Odejimi threw up his hands. "But who knows? Van took her to Ghent to meet his family. They were shocked. They never realized he had a woman in the Congo, much less a black one. His mother and sisters refused to be in the same room with her."

"That's nice."

"He took her back to Brussels, put her in a hotel, and returned to Ghent, apparently to work it out with the family. Then his brother arrived in Brussels to tell her it was over. The family would refuse to receive her if she returned to Ghent. The brother put her on a plane and sent her back. The family paid her fare."

"How did she become your woman?"

Odejimi cocked an eyebrow at Kwame and guffawed. "Stop thinking American, old boy. You sound like a slave owner. She's not my woman."

"She lives in your room."

"When she came back here, what was she to do? Return to her father's village? I invited her to stay with me."

"But you didn't pay cash or goats."

"God, no! I've got two wives in Nigeria. I play sex with other women and she's free to have other men. Are you interested?"

Kwame laughed. "Are you a pimp?"

"I'm a doctor. Celibacy is not good for your health in the tropics."

Madame Van returned to the terrace and resumed her place with the men. Without speaking they gazed across the river. Huge orange clouds moved throughout the sunset sky. They tinted the river's surface silver, orange, red. Two dugout canoes—pirogues—floated in the still water off the bank below the hotel. In one a man in worn khaki shorts patiently fished. Time after time he threw a circular net into the water and pulled it back on board. In the other pirogue a naked man stood, lathering his dark, well-built body with soap.

Odejimi stretched and gazed at the man bathing in the pirogue. "Nice movement with the soap, eh, Madame?" He nodded toward the naked African, getting his own back for having lost the *mankala* game. Madame Van slapped his arm. "Every afternoon Madame comes to watch the fishermen bathe," Odejimi told Kwame. "This one here: you like him?" Madame Van giggled. "Shall I get him for you?"

Odejimi was speaking English, as if to taunt her. "Do you speak English, Madame?" Kwame asked. She gazed at him uncertainly. He sensed that his American speech and Odejimi's high-class British must sound very different to her ear. Again he asked, very slowly, "You speak English, Madame?"

"Un leetla," she said, holding her index finger and thumb barely apart.

"Where did you learn English?" Kwame asked, again slowly.

"*A l'école du couvent.*" (At the convent school.)

"And from me, old boy," said the doctor.

And from Mason, Kwame thought. "Did you know Mason, Madame?" he asked in French.

"Un leetla," she replied in her English, a tease.

"Do you know where he's gone?" Kwame asked in French.

"He's disappeared," Odejiimi explained, continuing in French.

Madame Van absorbed this news, surprised, upset. She gazed again at Kwame and slowly shook her head.

His skin began prickling again. Kwame thought it might be wise to leave Madame and the doctor to *mankala*. Odejimi was already laying the board for another game. "*A bientôt,*" Kwame said. "I need to write some letters."

But as he settled down to write Judkins, it proved difficult to shake Madame Van from his head. Even so, he reported that Kent Mason was not in Mbandaka; that he had not been seen in more than two weeks; that the center film truck and Mason's laptop were missing; that items of Mason's clothing were being sold in the market. He listed the people he had talked to and noted that he was doing what he could to get the center ready to open.

The letter finished, he rose to examine himself in the bathroom mirror. He decided he was better looking than Odejimi, not as tall, but younger, fitter.

Madame Van made him realize how much he missed Livie. He put Van out of his mind and wrote his law student. Well, not entirely out of his mind. He did not mention her in the letter.

When he went to bed, he lay awake wondering: Had Vandenbroucke really taken his Congolese woman to Europe, outraged his family, then left her on her own? Had she really wanted to see Belgium? Maybe. Probably he would never know.

FIVE

Late the afternoon of the following day, his sixth in the Equateur, Kwame paced the library, wondering if he were stuck in Mbandaka. How could he leave the next day when the attaché plane arrived? Hadn't he better try to telephone Judkins to inform him that Mason had disappeared? He realized that he would be instructed to remain where he was until another officer could replace him. Shit! Fuck! Well, it might not be for too long. If the ambassador truly intended that every officer have a stint in the bush, someone else could probably be sent to Mbandaka in a couple of days.

As he paced, a tan Mercedes parked before the house that was to become the *Centre Culturel Américain*. Kwame watched the driver leave the car and stride up the steps of the entry: a stocky white man of medium height who wore shorts and the rimless glasses of a businessman, but had a deep tan, strong legs, and big hands that worked in the open with plants. He approached the building with an air of ownership.

Anatole hurried to the entrance and opened the door, his head lowered with deference. "'*Jour, M'sieur*," he muttered. The man entered the building. He surveyed the stacks of books on tables still pushed against the walls. He inspected Kwame with an expression that asked: What's a black man doing here?

"*Bonjour, Monsieur,*" Kwame greeted the visitor.

"You're the new American?" the man asked, speaking French. The visitor was Jean-Luc Berton, the center's landlord. "I've been out of town," he explained as he and Kwame shook hands. "Someone told me a new American had arrived." Berton did not smile. He inspected Kwame and surveyed the room as if something smelled bad. Kwame sensed that Berton had come, not to meet him, but to measure him, and that he did not pass muster.

"Are you assisting M. Mason? That's the talk around town."

"I was to be here a week. Leaving tomorrow. Do you know what's happened to Mason?"

"Has something happened to him?" Berton asked.

"He's disappeared."

The two men examined one another. "I only met the fellow once or twice. I have an interest in a rubber plantation on the road to Bikoro," the Belgian explained. "It is very difficult to keep any concern running these days, but we try."

"I'm very anxious about Mason," Kwame remarked.

"Maybe he's chasing girls in the bush." Berton said nothing more about Mason. He looked about the room. "I take it this is to be the library." Berton's tone of voice turned cynical. "Mbandaka's American library." Kwame gave a modest gesture toward the stacks of books. "The latest outpost of the American empire." The planter's tone dripped sarcasm. Kwame did not know how to respond. "The great globe-girdling empire." Kwame tried to smile. "Before we know it, there may be an American air base here."

"Here?"

"Why not here?" Berton asked. "Don't you want to protect your friend, our president?" Berton surveyed the furniture and books. "Is this a CIA operation?" Kwame cocked his head, surprised at this question. "You can trust me with a confidence," Berton told him, suddenly smiling. "Since you are in my building, we are coconspirators."

"I'm here to dispense information," Kwame replied. "Not gather it."

"But you keep your eyes open, eh? For the CIA?"

Kwame laughed. "Let's give CIA more credit than that."

"What does that mean?" asked Berton. "CIA does not hire blacks?"

The man was beginning to irritate Kwame. "I'm in Zaire to lecture about African literature."

"A perfect cover," suggested Berton. "Especially since there is no African literature. And Mason's cover? That would be chasing girls, eh? Although he has no affection for them."

"No affection for them?"

"He humiliated them." Kwame wondered if this were merely Berton's manner of expressing dislike. Or was there more to it than that? The planter continued, "You think Mason's come to harm, don't you?"

"In this quiet place?" Kwame asked. "Why would I think that?"

"Because your culture is full of violence. People are gunned down in American streets every day. Isn't that so?"

"Has something happened to Mason, M. Berton?"

"If I were to guess I'd say he offended someone. Perhaps soldiers killed him." The planter broke away and stuck his head into a couple of the other rooms. "But maybe he's dead of malaria or SIDA. Those are the killers here. We hope not, of course." He moved to the front door and stuck out his hand. "A pleasure to meet you, M. Johnson."

Watching the Mercedes drive off, Kwame wondered how Mason had antagonized Berton. Or did the man feel a generalized hostility to Americans and their dominance in the world?

He must make sure, Kwame thought, that people in Mbandaka understood he was trying to benefit the town.

KWAME WENT to the post office, hoping to telephone Kinshasa. The operator was doubtful that the call would go through. Kwame pestered him to keep trying. After two hours he reached Warren Judkins. He explained that Mason had disappeared. Judkins could not immediately absorb this news. Kwame restated it several ways. "This is extraordinary," Judkins said. He instructed Kwame to remain in Mbandaka until he himself could fly up to take stock of the situation. The plane for the next day would be canceled.

ON THE terrace of the hotel at the close of the day Kwame joined Odejimi and Madame Van. "It looks like I'm here for a while," he told them, using French.

"Good news!" enthused Odejimi. "At the end of the world a new face is always welcome." Madame Van regarded him in her mysterious way. Was she pleased?

That possibility warmed Kwame. "Until Mason returns," he said. "Or we find out what happened to him."

"Maybe you can learn to play mankala," the doctor suggested.

"I don't imagine I'll be here that long," Kwame said.

Odejimi and Madame Van continued their match, the doctor cursing to himself, the woman smiling quietly as she won successive games. The doctor again drank whiskey. Kwame brought beer for himself and Madame. He glanced at two army officers drinking with La Petite and Tombolo. What might they know about Mason? He gazed off across the river at the far horizon. He felt the African sense of time encompass him. Or was it timelessness? Clouds drifted across the sky. The river gentled along its freight of water hyacinths.

"M. Berton came to inspect me this afternoon," Kwame said.

"Charming fellow, isn't he?" commented the doctor.

"Is it that he doesn't like Americans?" Kwame asked. "Or just Mason?"

Neither of the others spoke, playing their game.

"Did you know Mason more than 'un leetla,' Madame?" Kwame asked.

She smiled enigmatically. Kwame returned the smile, as if to encourage a response—and because it was a pleasure to behold her. Before she could speak, Odejimi said, "Berton certainly did not like Mason."

"Mme Berton and Mason, friends," offered Madame Van.

"All very platonic, I'm sure," remarked Odejimi. He laughed in a way that suggested otherwise. "Mme Berton needs someone to talk to. Monsieur is often away. Mason comes to town; he's a white man. Madame cultivates him. They talk about books. Berton supposes they become lovers because he cannot imagine what a man does with a woman besides fuck her."

"I understand your husband took you to Europe," Kwame said, addressing Madame Van. She did not reply. "Did you like Europe?"

Madame smiled enigmatically.

"No!" Odejimi exclaimed. "Madame did not like Europe!"

Now a white man in a safari hat joined the group. He set a bottle of Primus and a glass on the table and pulled up a chair. He was the man Kwame had seen fleetingly his first morning at the hotel. The man was stocky and bearded with an upturned nose in which the nostrils were predominant. His nose and pinkish complexion made Africans whisper that he resembled a pig. Removing his hat, he revealed russet hair and a face covered with freckles.

"*Salut*," Odejimi said in greeting. He pointed at Kwame and gave his name, then told Kwame, "Say hello to School Inspector Moulaert. From faraway Flanders."

"Johannes Moulaert," said the man. "Johnny around here." Kwame and Moulaert shook hands. Moulaert grabbed Odejimi's bottle of whiskey and poured himself a drink. "Since you're a newcomer," he said, addressing Kwame in French with a guttural Flemish accent, "let me warn you that La Petite is not worth paying for. You'll have more fun with your hand."

"How long have you been here?" Kwame asked.

"Not long enough." He poured himself some beer and drank a long swallow. "I'm on an erotic quest," he explained. "That, of course, would be news to my wife and two sons." He chuckled at his naughtiness. "They suppose I am here for the money, which is better than in Belgium. And that I have some noble feeling about wanting to help the world." The Fleming grinned at this deception and pulled from the breast pocket of his tunic a leather pouch. He opened it, withdrew a color photograph, and handed it to Kwame. It showed a tall, slender, almost breastless girl with blue-black skin. She wore a thin strand of leather about her waist—that was all—and seemed totally unconscious of her nakedness.

"If you see her wandering about," Odejimi said, "grab her for our friend."

"What will you do with her?" Kwame asked Moulaert.

"Worship her," he replied.

"With that white worm of yours," cried Odejimi, laughing. "It looks like death, but you'll make it stand, eh?"

"Everyone worships in his own way," answered Moulaert with a grin.

Kwame returned the photo to Moulaert. He gazed at it fondly. As he rubbed his thumb across the picture, Madame Van watched him with contempt.

THE NEXT morning, resigned to be in Mbandaka for a while, Kwame visited the Bomboko Congo School, the town's only secondary school with instruction in French. The school's director, a Zairean named Joseph Badeka, did not at first believe that Kwame was American, not with both black skin and decent French. "Every American I have known has white skin and struggles with French," the man said. Once convinced of Kwame's nationality, he embraced him.

Badeka had served at Bomboko Congo since the days immediately following independence. "A terrible time," he said. "One day I will tell you about it." He introduced Kwame to his wife, Théa, also a teacher. Originally Senegalese, she had met Badeka in Europe when they both studied there in the middle sixties. Together they took Kwame to the house where they lived on the school grounds. While they drank Orangina beneath a pergola behind the house, Kwame discovered that the Badekas knew little about the cultural center. Apparently Mason had not contacted school officials. Kwame told them about the center and his hope that it could make a contribution to education in Mbandaka. Feeling comfortable with fellow teachers, he explained his interest in African literature, mentioned his dissertation, which he assured them was, like most dissertations, very boring, and insisted that more and more American students were learning about Africa by reading African writers. The Badekas were charmed.

"We have a great deal in common, *Monsieur*," Mme Badeka said. "I teach African literature myself. Students in one class are reading Camara Laye's *L'Enfant noir*."

"One of my favorite books," Kwame said. "It gave me a sense of the African soul!" He enthused about some of his favorite passages. "I love the vignette about his schoolboy awakening to girls. To—" He focused his memory. "To Fanta. Wasn't that her name?"

Mme Badeka grinned with pleasure. "Yes," she said. "Fanta."

"He just reports the behavior and explains nothing. And how his mother—that strong, lovely woman!—cries when he goes off to France."

"My mother cried when I went off," Mme Badeka remembered. "Of course, she wanted the opportunity for me. But she knew that she would lose me, that I would come back changed."

"Actually," Badeka said, "she married me and did not go back at all."

"I'm about to teach that class," Mme Badeka said. "Would you join us?"

As the class began, Mme Badeka asked Kwame to tell the students why he enjoyed Camara Laye. He intended to speak briefly. But, in fact, he spent the entire class rhapsodizing first about *L'Enfant noir*. Then about *Le Regard du roi*. "After *Heart of Darkness* which we all read in America," he said, "it's refreshing to have Africans lead a European to a discovery of Africa!" Of *Le Maître de la parole* he noted, "It brings the history of this continent so vitally alive!" He realized that Mobutistes might find his opinions objectionable, but he plunged ahead. The class over, Kwame told Mme Badeka, "I proved I'm a scholar by talking too long."

"Please come again," she said. "It made my students proud to think that an American knows so much about African writing." She lowered her voice to confide, "I loved hearing things said that I can never say!"

Théa Badeka was probably twenty-five years older than Kwame, but he found himself quite charmed by her. She reminded him of his mother; they were both women of the mind.

IN THE afternoon Dr. Odejimi took Kwame to call on Jean-Luc and Joelle Berton. "I sent a note to Madame to let her know we were coming," he said. "One has to do things à la française with Madame." Kwame was amused to see the Nigerian so eager to engage in Western social customs. Mme Berton was obviously the only person in Mbandaka with whom this was possible.

A servant led the two men through the house and onto a terrace overlooking the river. There they found Mme Berton sitting rather theatrically on a chaise à la Madame Recamier. She was thumbing through a copy of *Paris-Match*. Her tailored slacks and blouse, chic and expensive, were designed for the Cote d'Azur. Her face carried an inordinate freight of makeup and for someone who resided in the jungle her hair was over-dressed. Kwame understood immediately that the Bertons did not live in Zaire. Their furnishings, their clothes, their manner: all these were of Europe. The Bertons were the wealth of Mbandaka. They dealt with the town by denying that it existed.

When she saw the two men, Mme Berton tossed her magazine aside and assumed a queenly posture. She measured Kwame. As she glanced at Odejimi, her cheeks assumed a blush that would please a peach.

"*Madame*," Odejimi began, "*je voudrais presenter—*"

Mme Berton gave a flirtatious pout and covered her ears. "*Non!*" she cried. "For Monsieur l'Américain we speak Engleesh. And for le docteur du Nigeria." She glanced at Odejimi, coquettish, and gestured to chairs, patting one beside her.

Odejimi took it just as the stocky, stolidly Teutonic Berton entered the room. The men shook hands.

"Nice to see you again, *Monsieur*," Kwame greeted the planter.

Berton ignored him. He surveyed Odejimi with distrust. "We speak Engleesh," Madame Berton declared to her husband. She turned to Kwame, all charm, and added, "Le Docteur Odejimi! Intelligent man, but he speak execrable français. Mon Dieu! It hurt our ears. So: Engleesh." She smiled at Odejimi. Kwame noticed that it disturbed Berton to see his wife so flirtatious, so exhilarated by the Nigerian's presence.

"Américains always drink cocktail, no?" said Madame, flirting with Kwame. "Nigerian, too, I tink." She sent her husband to prepare drinks. Once he was gone, she grinned conspiratorially at Odejimi. Kwame understood she and Odejimi had almost certainly been together when she raced the Peugeot through the airport parking lot the day he arrived. Odejimi had emerged from the same road only minutes later.

Berton returned with cocktails. Madame presided over the foursome as if she were the patroness of a salon. "Zees Américains," she chirped cheerily, speaking about Kwame, but casting eyes on Odejimi, "so reech! Why they come to our leetla corner of Afrique? We do not understand."

"To line their pockets," her husband replied in French. It was clear that he would not ingratiate himself to an American, especially not an African American, by using his visitor's language. "Who blames them?"

When Kwame asked Madame about Mason, Berton turned to him, a testiness in his voice. "Why are you Americans here?" he asked.

"Yes, why ees zees?" said Madame. "Tell us, please."

"To help these people build their country," Kwame told Madame. Berton eyed him with open scorn. "The overdeveloped world and the underdeveloped world need to help each other," Kwame offered lamely.

"Such hypocrisy," Berton declared. "Such cynicism." He switched to English so that the two men could not mistake his meaning. "You Americans are here to steal the country once again, having made a mess of it the first time you did it at independence."

"I admire your blouse, Madame," Kwame said, studiously avoiding her husband. "Is it from Paris?"

"Madame always wears Paris couture," Odejimi noted.

Berton said, "I don't imagine you will kill all these Zaireans the way you killed your Indians, but when Mobutu goes, you will steal their country."

Kwame said nothing, thinking that if he wanted to steal a country, he would not choose this one.

"I do not think you are a Jesuit, Monsieur," Berton said. "So you must be CIA. Of course, you deny it."

"Do you have any idea what's happened to my predecessor, Mason?" Kwame asked Madame. "He's disappeared." Then he repeated in French, "*L'américain Mason, il est disparu. Où est-il, savez-vous?*"

"*Mais c'est pas possible!*" said Madame. She glanced at her husband for an explanation. "Disappeared? We talked books."

"He's off chasing girls," Berton said.

When the visitors rose to leave, Madame took Kwame's hands in hers. "*Notre pauvre Mason!*" cried Madame. "At last a white man in Mbandaka and now he iss gone? No! It cannot be!"

When the two men drove back along the river toward town, they were silent at first. Odejimi observed, "Joelle Berton does not have an enviable life out here. Théa Badeka takes pity on her now and then, but they are not really friends. How could they be? And who else can she talk to? If something's happened to Mason, she really will miss him."

They drove on for a while in silence. The road along the river was not paved. Potholes dotted it, growing deeper with every rain. In some places Odejimi drove onto roadside vegetation in order to pass. When once again they hit pavement, Kwame asked, "What in the world are they doing out here?"

"Their entire wealth is in his plantations," Odejimi said. "Poor her. She has a good mind, but out here she's got no way to use it. Except to flirt with black men to make her husband jealous."

"Does she have lovers?"

"Find out for yourself."

"Does he?"

"He must have women at his plantations."

When they parked before the hotel, Odejimi said, "Madame Van was asking about you last night." Kwame looked at the doctor, uncertain what he meant. "'*Il fuck, n'est-ce pas?*' I think that was her question."

Kwame looked surprised. "Bullshit."

"Maybe it was: '*Fuck-t-il?*' I'm not sure which."

Kwame laughed. "You trying to get me killed? Just like Mason."

"She was never Mason's woman."

"I don't think I'll play that game here," Kwame said, laughing.

"I tell you, my friend," said Odejimi, "all the things your mother told you not to do—drink, drugs, sex—they're the keys to survival out here. You don't believe me now . . ." He paused for effect. "But when you're climbing the walls, drink, sex, drugs, they're your friends away from home."

Kwame wondered how soon he'd be climbing the walls. It occurred to him that the doctor was seeking friendship. Maybe men bonded at the Afrique by sharing toys.

"You'll want to taste the Equateur while you're here," commented the doctor.

"Is there a lot of SIDA here?" Kwame asked.

"Nothing like eastern Zaire. When I lived up there, I slept only with a white woman."

"It's rampant there?"

"A lot of men moving around: truck drivers, itinerant merchants. They're in bars every night looking for women. In this little godforsaken river town we don't have that. There's not even a road that goes through." He looked carefully at Kwame and shrugged. "But there is some here. Van is clean. She's careful too."

"I'm spoken for," Kwame said. "Good thing."

"So am I," said the doctor. "Two wives. That didn't keep me from living with a Belgian woman in Gisenyi and a girl from Georgia at UCLA. Van is married too. But our spouses are far away. So is yours."

"My spouse is a fiancée."

"Ah," Odejimi sighed. "Fiancées demand promises. That is a problem."

"All I've got to do is be a good boy till December."

"One day can be forever," Odejimi remarked. "Especially in Mban. But women are very understanding."

"Not white women. My fiancée is white."

"She would be," Odejimi said. "From one of the first families, I suppose."

"Something like that."

The Nigerian doctor gazed at Kwame and shook his head. "For an African American, my friend, you are very American."

He shrugged. "But it is hot here. Very boring. Not much to do. When you want Van, we'll arrange for the test."

AFTER DINNER at the Mongo Restaurant Kwame returned to the center. He wrote Livie a letter. "It's astonishing that I think these letters may really reach you. I miss you something crazy," he wrote, using words he could hardly imagine himself using when he started writing the letters. "I'm losing weight, eating African fare three times a day. I feel okay—except for being completely out of touch with you. Have your classes started? How are they? Mason hasn't reappeared. When I see you in Paris, I'll be the most unshakable little lap dog. Won't let you out of my sight."

Kwame could not believe he was writing such drivel. Livie might chuckle over it and think it sweet that he missed her so.

While writing the letter Kwame kept thinking of Madame Van. He had a very strong urge to look at Mason's photo of her. He resisted the urge. Livie was his ticket out of Mbandaka. He was getting married at Christmas. He would refuse to stay in Mbandaka beyond then. Even if Madame Van was the African woman he kept looking for in college, he understood that thinking of her now, looking at her photo, would only lead to trouble.

When he finished the letter, he went into the library. He needed a book that would take him out of Mbandaka, a book that would put him back in America. But he couldn't read for pleasure any longer. His education had destroyed that capacity. He found nothing he wanted to read.

He walked back through town, past the fires of night guards whose dogs barked and challenged him and nipped at his heels, out along the river, whistling in the darkness, to the Afrique.

He strode along the outside corridor to his room and felt the force field of Madame Van. She was living with Odejimi in the room next to his. Passing their door, he heard her voice. He wondered: would she ever come to his room? He pushed that notion from his head and thought, "Livie, Livie! How much I miss you!"

WHEN THE embassy plane next arrived at Mbandaka, Kwame and Odejimi were on the tarmac in the doctor's Land Cruiser. They watched Warren Judkins scramble out of the plane. Behind him came two men in short-sleeved white shirts, ties, and sunglasses; they carried small metal valises. Their ties, the valises, and the way they scanned their surroundings gave them a distinctive look. "CIA," said Odejimi. Judkins introduced them only as Joe Gianni and Karl Pedersen, nothing more. The plane would return in four days.

At the center Kwame showed the orange shirt and the photo of the man wearing it to Judkins and the CIA men. "That's Mason," confirmed Judkins. While Gianni and Pedersen studied the photo, Judkins pulled Kwame aside. "You surviving okay?" he asked. Kwame nodded that he was. "Looks like you been busy," Judkins said, surveying the library. "Good work."

THREE DAYS later Kwame and Judkins had attached shelving to the walls in both the library and the storage room where the film equipment would be kept. Gianni and Pedersen had traced the center's film truck to Ingende, a town with a ferry across the Ruki, and had repossessed it. The Zairean who claimed to own the truck insisted that he had bought it from a military officer. He could not remember the officer's name and would not provide a description of him. Gianni and Pedersen assumed Mason's laptop was somewhere in the military camp. Their report would officially list him as missing. They feared, however, that he was dead.

"We assume army people, probably officers, arranged a rendezvous with Mason someplace where he'd take the truck," said Pedersen. "They killed him there."

"We think they came back here for the clothes," Gianni added. "The old tata probably let them in."

While Judkins and his two associates went off to see the commandant of the military camp, Kwame uncrated the last of the books. He began to order them by classification numbers already printed on their spines. His thoughts were not focused. He kept finding 800 books on the 400 shelf, 200 books on the 600 shelf.

When Judkins returned, he told Kwame, "That was a crock of shit. Commandant said it couldn't be his people. We'll make representations in Kinshasa." Kwame continued to put books on shelves. "You can be sure the ambassador will pursue the matter at the highest levels."

Kwame said nothing.

"Not that anything will happen," Judkins added. Kwame appreciated this candor. "Out in the bush these army commanders are kings. Even Mobutu won't challenge them."

Orange light poured into the library, giving substance to motes of dust. Kwame continued to work, waiting for what he knew Judkins would say.

"I know you're here to do a specific cultural job," Judkins began at last. "A job we really need done. But we also need someone up here. At least until we can find a person to man this post." Kwame continued to shelve books. "Why don't you come sit here with me?" Judkins invited.

Kwame took a chair across the table from him. When he looked at him directly, Judkins averted his eyes, staring at his hands. "We've told the Congress this post is open. With an officer staffing it. We don't lie to Congress." Kwame heard a car go by outside. After a moment Judkins added, "I can't order you to stay here. And I wouldn't if I could."

Kwame smiled. That would make it tempting to refuse, he thought.

"You're a straight shooter," Judkins told him. "I won't say your country would appreciate it if you'd stay. Because that's bullshit."

"My country doesn't know anything about this place, does it?"

Judkins shook his head. "I won't tell you that it'll be easy to find another officer to come here. Once word gets out that Mason's gone missing, we won't have a lot of sign-ups for Mbandaka."

Finally Kwame said, "You haven't told me I'm in less danger here because I'm African American. Thank you for that."

"Am I doing something right here?" Judkins asked.

"I'll make a deal with you," Kwame offered. "I'll stay till Christmas. I'm getting married then. I'm not bringing my wife to this place and I'm not starting married life living alone."

"It's a deal," said Judkins. He stretched his hand across the table.

"But . . ." Kwame said. "The first time anyone takes a shot at me? Or pushes me into the river? Or comes at me with a car? I'm outa here."

Judkins laughed. "Escape clause accepted." The men shook hands. "You want my hunch?" Judkins asked. "Boredom's your enemy. Much bigger challenge than a killer. Mason was dallying. Be smarter than he was. Don't get into drinking, drugs, sex."

Kwame grinned. "You sound like my father."

THE NEXT afternoon after he put his visitors on the plane back to Kinshasa, Kwame found Odejimi and Madame Van on the Afrique terrace. Once again they were drinking whiskey as they played *mankala*. Kwame got a beer and joined them.

"Your visitors gone?" asked Odejimi.

"All gone."

"And you're here?"

"I'm here." Kwame shrugged, feeling relaxed, and poured himself some beer. He slid a chair before him and plopped his feet onto its seat. Madame Van was watching him as if she really did not see him. He saluted her with his beer.

"What did your visitors conclude about Mason?" Odejimi asked.

"It's a real mystery," Kwame said. He smiled at Madame Van and asked in French, "What happened to Mason, Madame?" He studied her. She glanced over at Odejimi. "Did he drown, do you think?"

She shook her head as if she did not understand.

The doctor pushed the mankala board toward Madame Van. She began to lay another game, dropping four seeds into each of the twelve cups. "You know what the real mystery is, my friend?" Odejimi asked. "Why Mason was here. Opening a library in the jungle? Showing films about America to villagers who've never seen a two-story building? Does this make sense?"

"Does anything in this country make sense?" Kwame said. He took a sip of beer. "I mean: what are you doing here?"

"Hiding from my government," Odejimi replied, laughing. "And trying to have a good time doing it." He and Madame Van started a new game.

Kwame watched the river and kept tabs on how *mankala* was played, how gently and deftly the woman handled the seeds, picking them up and placing them in cups. When the doctor fumbled over them, spilling some onto the table and muttering curses when he did, Madame Van watched Kwame. He gazed at her. Odejimi noticed this byplay. He poured whiskey into his glass, took a sip, and rolled it on his tongue. "Take this, my friend," he said, offering Kwame the bottle. "You'll need it."

"Why's that?" Kwame asked. He took the whiskey almost reluctantly. Was the doctor really helping him survive?

"Why will he need it, Madame?" Odejimi asked.

"To forget Mason," she said. "Until he comes back."

Something about the way she said these words made Kwame understand that Mason would not come back. He shrugged and accepted the whiskey. "Thanks. We'll have a party when he returns."

SIX

Kwame spent his days ordering the center, reading procedure manuals, establishing a system for library books and videos, and devising one for lending items he hoped borrowers would actually return.

Job seekers began to stand outside the center, hoping he would notice them. At first he greeted these young men, told them about the center, gave them handouts, and insisted he was not yet ready to hire a librarian. They continued to loiter outside. Waiting for Kwame to hire them seemed their only occupation. He stopped distributing handouts.

Girls, ostensible job seekers, also came to the center. A few actually seemed interested in books. From the manner of most, the way they hung around talking to Anatole's wife and playing with her children, the longing looks they threw him and some of their gestures, Kwame realized that news of Mason's interest in teenage girls had circulated in town.

Occasionally he went to the Badekas' Bomboko Congo School. He showed the students movies about world affairs. He began to team-teach African literature with Théa. These sessions were the highlight of his days; they gave him great pleasure. Now and then he taught classes by himself. On these occasions he enjoyed challenging students. "Why do you come to school?" he would ask them.

"To learn," they would say in an almost sing-song unison.

"To learn what?" he would ask.

That would cause the students to pause. Didn't he know what they came to learn? Occasionally one of the braver students would suggest, "mathematics." Or "history." Or "language."

"You come to learn to *think*," Kwame would say. "To *THINK!*" This idea surprised the students. "What does it mean to think?" Kwame would ask. "It means to wonder about everything, including what people tell you." The students would fall silent. What did he mean?

Kwame would point through the open windows to the sunlight making the leaves of the banana trees intensely green. He would say, "Those leaves are certainly red." Students would gaze at the leaves. Kwame would say, "If you are a thinker, first you look outside at the leaves. If I say, 'Those leaves are certainly red, aren't they?' what do you do?"

Silence would fall across the students. Some giggled. Others stared at their desks, embarrassed by his ignorance. "If I say that, what do you say? Do you say, 'Yes, Teacher. Those leaves are certainly red'?" Kwame looked about the class. The students had been raised not to contradict their elders. "You may not want to say, 'No, you're wrong. Those leaves are green.' But you want to *think* it. Do you understand?" Kwame examined the faces of his students. Some nodded slightly in agreement. Others frowned. "If I say, 'Look how hard it's raining outside.' What do you think?"

Silence. The students looked out the window at the sunlight on the banana leaves. "Kabenga, if I say that to you, what do you say?" Kabenga smiled and shook his head. He looked down at his desk. Kwame looked again through the windows.

"If I say, 'Look at the rain out there! I'm glad I brought my umbrella!' what do you think? Bileke, what do you think?"

Finally Bileke replied very quietly, "I do not see it raining, Teacher."

"Good!" exclaimed Kwame. "Excellent! Because it's not raining, is it?" He grinned at the students. They seemed relieved to be assured that, in fact, it was not raining. "Now here's something more complicated. If I say to you, 'Colonialism is the best way to develop this country.' What do you think?" The question puzzled the students. "Or if I say, 'Capitalism is the best way.' Or if I say, 'Communism is the best way.' Or if I say, 'A one-party government is the best way.' What do you think?" The students stared at him with wide eyes. "There were people in your country fifty years ago who insisted, 'Colonialism is the best way to develop this country.' Was it true?"

Some of the students shook their heads.

"Why was it not true?" Kwame asked. "Because the colonials took your wealth and put it in their banks. Because colonials said, 'People with black skins are savages. They are stupid.' Is that true?" Kwame asked. Before the students could digest the question, he exclaimed, "No! It is not true! I have a black skin. Am I a savage? No! Am I stupid? Only if I agree with what they tell me. If someone says to you, 'This is the best way to develop your country.' Or that way is. Then you have to ask yourselves: Is what he's telling me really true?"

Kwame would grin at the students, realizing they needed time to think about what he said. While they did, he would move to the academic material he intended to teach.

Kwame loved to watch his students' faces, their expressions generally eager, their eyes sometimes skeptical or amused, baffled or intent. He loved holding the students' attention in his palm, leading them to wider visions of themselves and their world. He loved their coming to the library. He loved seeing them on the streets of the town when some would behold him with awe, too shy to speak, and others, the bold ones, would crow, "Hello, Teacher!" They would jump with jubilation when he returned their greeting.

If he found the teaching fulfilling, when he returned to the center, it was often with a sense of frustration. Everything seemed to take forever. So much of the time he worked alone. He often felt lonely. He looked each day for letters from Livie, but none came. He continued to write her.

One afternoon the Peugeot sedan he had seen his first day at the airport parked before the center. Mme Berton left the car, climbed the three steps to the entry porch, and knocked coquettishly on the panes in the door. "*Entrez, Madame! Entrez!*" Kwame greeted her.

"Eng-leesh, please, sir," she requested. "I am determine to ameliorate my Eng-leesh."

She had come, she claimed, to see the library. She moved around the room theatrically, the jacket of her pantsuit flaring at her slim waist. She enthused about Kwame's progress and studied the books on his shelves. "With *mon ami* Mason," she said, "we deescuss book. Also news. Rwanda, zee terrible massacre there. *Mon Dieu*, how horrible! What happen there now? I do not get news. Never."

Madame floated into Kwame's office. He apologized that he could not offer her refreshment; he was still getting organized, he explained. "My husband, he iss away at zee plantation. And me, I need someseeng to read." Her glance fell on a dozen paperbacks Kwame had brought with him, novels by African writers, volumes he might lend to special library patrons. "What zees?" Madame asked. She examined the titles.

Kwame showed her his copy of *Things Fall Apart*. "You might like this," he said. "The novel about Africa everyone should read. Beautifully, but very simply written. You could read this without a French-English dictionary."

She smiled and took the book. "I read. We talk." She cocked her head beguilingly at Kwame. Her perfume wafted about him. She looked him over. Found him attractive. Kwame felt flattered. Sexual opportunity vibrated in the room. Mbandaka was a place where affairs relieved boredom. "Tomorrow night?" Madame suggested. "You come to dinner? I read all day."

The prospect of European food tempted him, but Kwame sensed trouble.

"You busy?" Madame asked. She giggled because no one was ever busy in the evenings in Mbandaka.

"Let's do this as a class," Kwame suggested. "When you finish the book, we'll talk about it in the library. The center's first cultural event." Madame made a pout. Kwame smiled and shook his head. "Here in the center. Invite your husband."

IN THE late afternoons Kwame returned to his hotel room, worn down by the heat. In Cape Town he had rarely had cocktails with Livie when he returned from the office, but by day's end in Mbandaka he wanted a drink. He looked forward to chatting in French, to the companionship of *mankala*, watching the sunset and the fishermen bathing.

"You tried the local weed?" Moulaert asked one afternoon. He and Odejimi were smoking. A dark layer of cloud was building across the river, promising rain.

"Smoking's bad for you," Odejimi said.

"What isn't bad for you?" Moulaert asked. He sat with his broad safari hat protecting his face. "Mama said smoking bad. Also sex. Papa said drinking bad. Also dope. Also Africa!"

"Africa's the worst," said Odejimi. Madame Van smiled her silent, enigmatic smile. Kwame wondered what she was thinking.

"Whanging off very bad," Moulaert continued. "So the priests said; they should know. Unnatural. Jig-jig? Natural, but also bad." He winked at Madame Van. "Erotic quest by married man. Verrrry baaaad. But it doesn't hurt me any." He guffawed. "I like smoking this stuff," Moulaert went on. "It makes everything mellow."

Odejimi offered a joint to Kwame. "You're trying to send me straight to hell, aren't you?" Kwame asked.

"How else can you be happy in Jungleville?" Odejimi inquired. "We don't want you to go crazy and run off into the bush."

Moulaert leaned forward and lightly touched Madame Van's knee. "Come to my room, eh, Madame?" he begged. "*Je t'en pri*e." He fell to his knees and implored her as if in prayer. The men laughed at this buffoonery. Madame Van paid no attention. Avoiding Moulaert's eyes, she began to prepare the *mankala* board. "I will give you a present," Moulaert implored.

"The bite of a white snake," said Odejimi, laughing heartily.

Madame Van's eyes narrowed. She did not look at Moulaert.

Blushing at the rebuff, Moulaert stood and flicked his cigarette off the terrace. "Her Flemish husband abandons her," he complained. "And because I'm his fellow countryman, she takes her revenge on me." Moulaert moved off toward the reception.

Madame Van observed, "A toad does not run in the daytime for nothing." Kwame thought: a proverb. To what did it refer, he wondered, to her refusal to go off with Moulaert? That was the thing about proverbs. You were never certain. In a moment or two Moulaert crossed the terrace; La Petite trailed behind him. Hmm. Did the proverb refer to that?

They watched the couple move toward the stairway. Moulaert placed his hand on the girl's behind.

"*Il est dégoûtant*," remarked Madame Van. (He's disgusting.) She gazed at the clouds over the river. Her eyes drifted to Kwame. Her weightless glance caused a stir in him. He smiled slightly. She smiled back. Odejimi caught this exchange.

"She loves your being a WASP with a black skin," he teased in English.

Kwame flicked his eyebrows.

"She would like to be your friend," he continued. As if by letting her be his friend he would join their family of pals. Odejimi was offering him membership. He remarked, "A man cannot eat celibacy and stay alive."

More proverbs, thought Kwame. He shrugged.

"Maybe some places," said Odejimi. "But not in Mbandaka."

Kwame glanced at Madame Van. He wondered how much she understood of the English he and the doctor were batting back and forth. Perhaps she wasn't even listening. Kwame felt her eyes lift off his skin. She looked back at the clouds.

"She doesn't want to be everyone's friend," Odejimi continued. "You saw with Moulaert."

If he did not join the family, Kwame wondered, would he become, like Moulaert, a kind of outcast, depending on La Petite for friendship?

"The whiskey holding up?" Odejimi asked, switching to French.

"Yes, thank you." Kwame poured a mere splash of it and some soda into a glass every night and raised that glass to the photo of Livie. "I have a taste before bed."

"A good friend, whiskey." Odejimi turned to Madame Van and suggested, "Roll our friend a cigarette." Then to Kwame in English: "It'll make you feel mellow, old boy." Madame Van took tobacco from Odejimi's pouch and shook a line of it into a cigarette paper. The doctor said, "Madame wonders if you are circumcised."

Kwame laughed with surprise. "I know why Mason disappeared," he said. "To stop listening to you." He knew he should go inside. But he did not want to sit alone in his room.

He watched Madame Van prepare the cigarette. She was really quite beautiful. Maybe twenty-three, no older. Her skin was like silk, like a flowing, liquid chocolate. Whenever she moved, her shoulders were held level, her back erect. Her posture displayed a straightness borne of loads carried on her head since early childhood. She had a classic African face: broad forehead, prominent cheekbones, the features not delicate, but strong. Her nose was slightly flattened. Below it were a well-modeled chin and mouth with lips that were sometimes poignant, often open in laughter and showing teeth that were even and brilliantly white. She had expressive eyes. They communicated her moods without ever betraying her essence; they did not disclose her mystery. Her mystery intrigued him. It made him feel hungry for a woman.

When Madame gave Kwame the cigarette, their eyes met. They touched. Kwame felt a tiny electric shock. Madame smiled. She struck a wooden match and lit the cigarette. Kwame inhaled and let the smoke move into his head and lungs. And, yes, he did feel suddenly mellow.

THE RAIN came at nightfall. From the balcony of his room Kwame saw huge flashes of lightning throw gray-white light across the endless expanse of sky. Cool winds rose. The river grew dark. The winds pushed clumps of water hyacinths in toward shore. Dogs barked. Birds circled in the pre-rain winds. Lightning revealed heavy clouds far across the river. Thunder cracked so close that Kwame shuddered. He smelled the fresh, wet air surge toward him, saw the first raindrops stipple the water and heard their delicate patter on the roof. Then with a crack of thunder the patter became a pounding. Torrents beat on the building. Gusts of wind blew the rain in patterns. It fell heavily, persistently, with an occasional rushing energy that made the roof shake. Outside on the street coconut palms bowed against the wind and flailed their fronds.

By two A.M. the rain had fallen for eight hours. Kwame could not sleep. He wished he had another of the cigarettes Madame Van had rolled for him. He set the photo of Livie before him. He stared at her image for long moments and tried to talk to her. But the words did not come. What came was a mosquito. Kwame heard its buzz and slapped it into oblivion on his shoulder.

He'd been drinking off and on all evening. Now he splashed two fingers of Odejimi's whiskey into the bottom of his glass. He added soda water and stirred the mix with his finger. Wearing only boxers he went out onto the balcony. He stared at the wall of rain and the river beyond it. The drumming of the rain was like a curtain of sound surrounding him. Beyond it he heard music. It came from Odejimi's room, Kinshasa rock 'n' roll. Rain droplets beaded the hairs on his arms and chest.

The door to Odejimi's room opened. Madame Van rushed out, giggling, on a blast of sound. She was dancing in the rain, her body swaying, her arms outstretched, her hands gyrating on her wrists, the fingers rolling enticingly. She was naked. She saw Kwame and stopped giggling, stopped dancing. She moved to cover herself, but the music captured her. She began to dance again, her hands waving to him on her wrists. She did nothing to hide her nakedness. She stood erect, moving her weight from foot to foot. She lifted her arms above her head, her breasts rising, and smiled at him. "*Bonsoir, Monsieur,*" she said. "*Quelle pluie, hunh?*" (What rain!)

They stared at one another. Then an amorous Odejimi ran onto the balcony. Madame continued to dance. Also naked, Odejimi flicked a towel at her rump. When he saw Kwame, he grinned and flicked the towel at him.

Kwame raised his glass. "Good whiskey you gave me."

"When the rain falls, the frogs dance," said Odejimi. "Join us."

In his tipsiness Kwame felt African. Why not join the family, he thought. Why not have a go at Madame Van? She cocked her hips, shifted her weight from side to side in time to the music, kept her arms raised above her head, lifting her breasts. She flung a hip provocatively. Kwame laughed; they were all laughing. He raised his glass again. "One vice at a time," he said.

Madame Van gazed at Kwame, laughing, still dancing, and Kwame could not take his eyes off her. "When the moon shines," she said in French, "the cripple becomes hungry to dance." Kwame nodded, moving toward her into the rain. Yes, he was hungry. Odejimi jumped onto Kwame's balcony and danced beside him. He grabbed Kwame's boxers and pulled them to the floor.

Odejimi really wanted to be friends, Kwame thought. He glanced at the doctor's nakedness. He shrugged. So be it.

Kwame undulated his hips as the rain hit his skin, feeling himself grow erect. Odejimi pointed at his groin. Kwame danced. Draining his glass, laughing, he waggled his hips, waved his flag. Madame Van inspected him. Her laughter transformed into impish interest. She saw that of the two men he was much better hung, at least for the moment. "Elephant!" she cried. She pointed at him, applauded what he displayed.

The rain fell harder. Odejimi returned to his room. Dancing, Kwame and Madame Van drew closer together. Laughing, she touched him. A caress in the rain. An invitation. He lifted her off her feet. He took her across the porch, pushed her against a wall. She coiled her legs about him. He entered her. Their hips moving, they clasped each other so tightly they could hardly breathe. They exploded, held on. And on. The rain pounded down on them. Finally they kissed, their mouths open, their tongues joined as their bodies were. Kwame felt himself swelling once more. He had not withdrawn, and moved inside her again. They clutched each other, panting, swooning.

Oh, how I needed this, Kwame thought. Livie, Livie, please understand. I really needed this.

Across a great distance he heard the flicking of a towel. Odejimi was back. Madame Van slid away. Odejimi led her off. Kwame stood in the rain, eyes closed, a grin on his face.

He slept soundly, his body refreshed by its exercise. Waking, he saw the photo of Livie looking down on him. Oh, how I needed that, Kwame told the photo. Livie, Livie, please understand. I really needed it. It won't— He turned away from her. Happen again.

He rose, put on boxers, and went out onto his balcony. He stepped into pools of rainwater that had not drained away. The sky was clear and brilliantly blue, the air fresh. He talked in his head to Livie, trying to explain himself. On Cape Cod they had talked about being apart, but not about how they would deal with it. "What're we going to do about this?" he had asked her. They had made love and were lying together on their bed. "We've been doing a lot of this."

"I like it with you," she said. "I like our bodies joined into one body."

When they had first been together in Cape Town, they would sometimes come together inside the doorway when he first got home, she naked under her hoisted-up skirt, his trousers flung down, him pressing her against the dining table. Sometimes in the kitchen on weekend mornings she would sit on the counter, her legs wrapped about him, while they ate cereal from bowls, feeding it to one another.

He thought of how needy he'd felt. He wondered: Can she have any idea what this is like for me? But he could not tell her. Especially not in letters.

She had turned toward him in the night. "Do you like it with all girls? Or just me?" He had not answered. "I guess it's different for men," she said. He stared at the ceiling he could not see. "What's going to happen out there?" she asked finally. He said nothing. "You can take care of it yourself, you know."

"You think that's the answer, do you?" She said nothing. "What about you?"

"I don't want it with anyone but you. Ever again."

He knew that wasn't true. Or wouldn't be once he was gone.

"Be good, Kwame," Livie whispered. "For me. For the kids we're going to have."

For her and the kids they would have. He stared at the river. After the rain the air was so clear he could see the opposite bank. He paced. Fuck, he thought, she's got the same problem. He could not bear to think of her with other men. He vowed not to think about Madame Van. What had happened in that rain had been an aberration.

SEVEN

Although Kwame possessed little talent for writing letters, he had a bureaucrat's facility with reports. The
morning after the storm he crafted a memorandum to his
bosses in Kinshasa. He reported no progress on Mason. He
was, however, forging ahead with preparations for the cultural
center. He asked for advice about opening it. Should he hire
staff—a librarian and possibly a projectionist—and open as
soon as feasible? Or should the official opening be the job of
his permanent replacement? He awaited instructions.

In the box at the post office he found an envelope from
Livie. He opened it on the post office steps. She was now in
Boston, but she knew no better than he how to write a letter.
She sent a collection of e-mail-style messages, little snapshots
of where her head was at the moment of writing. But no
exposition about her law classes or how she was readjusting
to law school or how she liked Boston or her new apartment.
And nothing to say that she missed him. Perhaps the messages
themselves were supposed to prove that. But they gave Kwame
no sense of being with her.

He returned to the center to find Anatole sitting on the
front stoop, studying the clouds. The tata seemed to live completely in the present. And to do everything in slow motion. A

watchman he certainly was. He always watched, stared: without self-consciousness, without speaking, perhaps even without curiosity. Now as Kwame returned, Anatole got to his feet and deferentially said, "*Bonjour, patron.*" Then he simply stared. Kwame felt self-conscious. He had to discipline himself not to react.

"Tata" was a term of respect conferred on a man of years. But how old was Anatole? Kwame had no idea. What hair Anatole had was gray; his unhurried pace suggested age. But he was still producing children. His figure comprised a series of interlocking circles: the nearly bald head, the eyes behind round lenses, the cheeks that smiled shyly when Kwame greeted him, the globes of his buttocks, his stomach hanging over the waistband of his trousers. He was certainly forty. Was he sixty?

Inside his office Kwame asked himself: How could Anatole sit for hours staring into space? At times he seemed as rooted as a plant. Was this what it was to be African? Was this the mantle of wisdom? A state of nature? Self-awareness? Serenity? Should he admire it? Even try to emulate it, he whose culture told him activity was everything?

Kwame tried to answer Livie's bundle of messages, to write her the sort of letter he would like to receive. He started on his laptop. But the writing went poorly. Words refused to flow. He closed the laptop and began to write longhand. He had hardly started when he stopped. He would write Livie a real letter that evening.

He went back to the Afrique, got some lunch, and found Madame Van on the balcony adjacent to his own. She regarded him without emotion. With the memory of her body still very strong on him, he felt awkward. "*Bonjour, Madame,*" he said.

"*M'sieur.*"

"*Enchanté de te revoir.*" ("Happy to see you again.") They both laughed because his voice was like a recitation from one's first French class. "*Il fait beau, n'est-ce pas?*" ("Nice day today, yes?") They laughed again. That observation came from the same lesson.

The awkwardness vanished. They smiled at one another. Because Africans did not kiss the way Europeans did, Madame did not expect Kwame to bestow on her mouth a kiss of thanks for their rain dance.

"I'm glad I found you. I need some help with shopping."

They drove together to an African market. As they walked about the stalls, Kwame addressed Madame in English, testing her fluency. She regarded him flirtatiously, recognizing the words, but unwilling to bother decoding the sentence. He tested her twice more. She shook off the English, as she might a mosquito, and demanded, "*Parlez francais!*" So that was settled. They would communicate in French.

"*D'accord,*" he said.

With Madame's help he palavered for a broom, paint, and, failing to find any brushes, a sponge to apply it. As they were leaving, Madame took him to a section where ancient women sold items spread out on faded cloths. She began to bargain with them. Kwame could identify none of their wares. As he examined the objects, Madame pulled curls of hair from his skull. "Ouch!" he exclaimed. "What's happening?" Madame gave him an enigmatic grin and continued her bargaining. He realized suddenly that the women were selling magic ingredients. He took Madame by the wrist and demanded, "What're you doing?"

She held the hairs in her opposite hand, well out of his reach. "I will make you a charm," she said.

"*Merci beaucoup,* but I don't want a charm."

"It will protect you. You will not end up like Mason."

They looked at each other a long moment. Kwame did not want a charm from her; that suggested a relationship. "How did Mason end up?"

She smiled, shyly at first, then more boldly. "If you tempt the spirits," she said, "they make you disappear."

He wondered: Was that a proverb? Or something concocted to sound like one? "Do you really believe that?" he asked. She looked at him for such a long moment that it was almost as if, behind her forehead, he could see her pondering: What does he want to hear? What am I supposed to say? Finally she said, "When the spirits cause someone to disappear, do not ask questions."

Another proverb, Kwame thought. Were they true proverbs? Or did she make them up as she went along? "You believe the spirits made him disappear?" he repeated. She did not have to consider that; she nodded. Yes, she did believe it. Kwame shook his head, baffled, and released her wrist.

She bought the ingredients for the charm and placed them and Kwame's hairs into a woven bag she carried. As they left the market, Kwame said, "I owe you a drink for helping me so much."

"*D'accord*," she said. Okay.

WHEN MADAME Van joined Kwame on the Afrique terrace, she arrived carrying her *mankala* board and the seeds. She announced, "Odejimi is coming down. He's received some bad news so he won't play *mankala*. That means I can teach you." While waiting for their drinks, she prepared the board. After receiving their beers, she explained the game, watching Kwame with eyes that lacked expression, yet sent across the small table between them a soothing sense of her presence. That presence so engulfed him that he hardly concentrated on the rudiments of the game. She easily won the round they played.

"You're too good for me," Kwame said. "I'll never beat you."

"You will beat me," she said simply. "The doctor won't, but you will beat me." She said the words as if telling his fortune.

Dr. Odejimi joined them at sunset. "Will it depress you to listen to the news?" he asked. He made room on the table for a Grundig shortwave radio. "I stopped when I first arrived. Who needs news in a place like this?" He poured whiskey from a bottle he had brought with him. "We're totally cut off from the world here. We're asleep in an island of tranquility, and that's the way I like it."

The doctor turned on the radio and tuned to a station. "But now and then we're shaken awake. I just heard from a Nigerian friend doing humanitarian work in Goma," he reported. "Across the border from Rwanda. We can be glad we're in this pisshole instead of where I used to live in Gisenyi, in Rwanda."

"You've moved around," commented Kwame.

"In Gisenyi I lived in a house overlooking Lake Kivu. A gloriously beautiful place. But so tragic."

"Pourqoi tragique?" asked Madame Van.

The doctor did not reply. He peered across the river as if staring at Lake Kivu from Gisenyi.

They listened to the BBC's Africa Service. It reported continuing tensions at the refugee camps around Goma. "Continuing tensions," scoffed Odejimi. "That's British understatement for you." Odejimi turned off the radio.

"What happened in Gisenyi?" Madame Van asked in French.

Odejimi watched a pirogue move across the surface of the river. "Gisenyi is set on the very backbone of Africa," he said, speaking as if to himself, but in her language. "With Rift Valley escarpments all around. The town stretches along Lake Kivu. Luckily I had a friend, a Belgian woman, a very generous person. She took pity on a doctor who found it inconvenient just then to return to his home country." The doctor spoke without looking at either of his listeners, as if in a trance, reminiscing of the generous Belgian woman. "She was a widow. Her dead husband had had pyrethrum plantations in the backcountry. She gave me a room in her house." He paused, as if thinking of that room.

"For generations there had been what the BBC calls 'continuing tensions' between the two main tribes, the Tutsis who were the traditional rulers and the Hutus. Now and then you heard Hutus say that they were going to get the Tutsis. Hutu radio broadcast virulent anti-Tutsi talk. The widow and I took comfort with each other. We were outside of this tension— although, of course, we felt it. Sometimes we spent the night together. Then the Hutu president was assassinated. His plane was shot down.

"We learned about this from the houseboy. He'd been with my friend for years, a Hutu, a Christian, married to a Christian Tutsi. They had three children. When he told us this news, he warned us that trouble was coming. He was afraid of what might happen."

Kwame and Madame Van glanced at one another. Odejimi who so often monitored their glances seemed totally oblivious of them.

"The next day," he went on, "there were soldiers in the streets. People were hurrying to cross the border into Goma. Into the Congo. The border's just outside town. People at the hospital didn't show up. Nurses pulled me aside to whisper that Tutsis were being murdered. People I knew were being killed."

Odejimi stopped talking. He reached over to grasp Madame Van's forearm in order to anchor himself in Mbandaka and prevent a drift back to Gisenyi. "You've stopped playing *mankala*," he said.

"Don't stop your story," Kwame said.

"I shouldn't have read the letter. I shouldn't have brought the radio. What's so wonderful about Mban is that nothing happens here."

"In Gisenyi," Madame Van said. "What happened?"

"Gangs of Hutus were killing Tutsis. Any way they could. We could smell blood in the air. Tutsis would take refuge in churches and Hutu priests would set their own churches on fire. They would kill Hutus sympathetic to Tutsis."

Odejimi sipped his whiskey and stared at the river. "The Hutu servant came running to us that very afternoon. 'You must leave,' he cried. My friend had a boat. The servant begged her to take his family. She told him to fetch them. We would leave immediately, meet them on the boat. We packed. Went to the boat—" Odejimi looked off again and stopped speaking. Madame Van and Kwame glanced again at one another. Madame Van put her hand on the doctor's shoulder. Odejimi put his hands to his face. He rubbed his eyelids with his fingertips. The eyelids were wet with tears.

"I tell you," he scoffed, putting on his man-of-the-world persona. "You can see vicious stuff on this continent."

Madame Van pushed her chair beside the doctor's. She reached her arm around his shoulders and laid her head against his. The doctor pushed her away, as if to demonstrate that he had not lost control of himself.

"From the boat we saw Hutu thugs chasing the servant and his family as they came racing into the yard. They hurried toward the boat, running as fast as they could. They were carrying cloths filled with belongings. Hutu thugs got into the yard. The parents dropped the cloths and picked up the children. As she ran, the wife stumbled. Dropped to the ground. The thugs fell on her with pangas. Cracked open her head. Severed her neck. Whacked the child almost in half. Oh! The wails! The blood on those pangas. On the grass. The jubilation of the thugs.

"The husband, the Hutu, he looked back. Stopped for a moment. The thugs came after him and the two kids he carried. Oh!"

After a long pause he went on. "The widow and I were on the boat. When I saw what was happening, I put my hand over her mouth and pushed her to the deck. I lay on top of her. I whispered, 'Don't make a sound! Not a sound!'

"Finally it was over. After the thugs ran off hunting others, I went down to the yard. To see what I could do. They were all dead." Odejimi poured himself whiskey and drank it. "My friend and I got out of that place as fast as we could."

For some moments they were all silent. Sunset reddened the sky and the river.

LATER THAT afternoon while the trio still sat on the terrace, Moulaert appeared, escorting a girl in a school uniform. Kwame and Madame Van watched the pair move across the terrace. Odejimi did not notice them; he still stared at the river. The girl was slimly well-shaped and very pretty. Moulaert paid her elaborate attention. Following the Belgian's instructions, Tombolo led her to a table removed from the others and took the order for refreshment, inspecting the girl carefully. "The erotic quest," commented Madame Van. Only then did Odejimi examine the new arrivals. He watched the hotelier appraising the new morsel.

"Tombolo wonders if she's a *femme libre*," Odejimi remarked, happy to anchor himself once more in Mbandaka. "If she is, he'll want his cut. If not, he'll want some of her himself."

When Moulaert glanced over, Odejimi saluted him. "Join us?"

"Not today, thanks."

After a time Kwame asked the doctor, "When you and your friend left Gisenyi, where did you go?"

"To Bukavu," said the doctor. "At the south end of the lake. She had a sister-in-law there with a large house. Ten miles from the Rwanda border. One day refugees started pouring in. They huddled on open ground around the town. Three days later they were camping in our garden. Not just a few of them, dozens. You couldn't tell them to push off. There was no place to go and more were coming."

Kwame tried to imagine the exodus.

"They were wretched. Cold. Terrified. Starving. The women realized they couldn't stay. Some of those people in their garden were murderers. They'd killed Tutsis in unthinkable ways. Who else might they kill?" Odejimi said nothing for a moment. Finally he added, "My friend and her sister-in-law were able to get out. I went to Goma. To be of assistance. I'd taken the Hippocratic oath, after all.

"By that time Tutsis living in Uganda had formed an army, a real army. They invaded Rwanda. Hutus, whether they'd done any killing or not, assumed they'd be slaughtered. So they fled to Zaire. A refugee camp—500,000 people—suddenly appeared on an old lava flow just west of Goma. Soon there were outbreaks of dysentery and cholera. Bodies stacked up at the roadsides. Black flies so thick you could hardly drive through them. A stench that made you wretch." Odejimi smiled sardonically. "There was plenty of work for a doctor."

He reached down to pinch Madame Van's toes. "Don't I wish you'd been there, my lovely!" he laughed. "Do you wish you'd been there?" She shook her head. "No curiosity about eastern Zaire?"

"How long were you in Goma?" Kwame asked.

"Too long. The *Interahamwe*, the Hutu thugs, the *génocidaires*, were no match for the Tutsis' Patriotic Front. So they also fled to the refugee camps. They were the only group with any organization. They took over the camps. Demanded that all food be handled through them. All medical care. So they stopped being refugee camps. Became concentration camps.

"Relief workers didn't know what to do. Refuse to let the *Interahamwe* handle the food, you'd get killed and people would starve. I told myself I would not get involved. But being there involved you. I was threatened again and again. I was haunted by what I'd seen in the yard of the house in Gisenyi." The doctor shrugged. "Then I heard the hospital in Mbandaka could use me. *Voilà!* Here I am."

For some minutes none of the threesome spoke. Odejimi took his bottle of whiskey and poured some into Madame Van's glass and into Kwame's. "After that story," he said, "you need something stronger than beer." Kwame swallowed his whiskey and was glad for the taste of something strong in his throat. Madame Van did not drink her whiskey. Instead she inspected the girl Moulaert was entertaining on the terrace. Kwame and Odejimi joined the inspection.

The girl sat erectly, enjoying her moment on the Afrique terrace and the obvious effect she had on Moulaert. While he settled the bill, proud of himself and avoiding the eyes of his friends, the girl glanced around the terrace with a boldness that missed nothing.

"Moulaert's found love!" whispered Odejimi.

"And the girl, she has found freedom," added Madame Van.

"He's in for a ride!" said the doctor.

When the girl's eyes met Madame Van's, the older woman nodded to her. "This is a girl who wants never to return to her village," she said. "I think we will not see her again in that uniform. I would guess that Moulaert has bought her clothes." Madame Van gave the girl an ironic look and left the terrace.

Kwame watched her go.

"That's Van eight years ago," said Odejimi. "A village girl thinks a white man's attention makes her special."

"Did you ever meet Vandenbroucke?" Kwame asked.

"Another Moulaert." The doctor laughed. "Moulaert can thank his juju Van won't sleep with him. He might wake up dead." The doctor dragged on his cigarette and scrutinized Kwame. "A bee visiting many plants makes the honey sweet," he said. "And causes flowers to bloom." He grinned. "I'm glad you had her."

Kwame shrugged.

"I speak to you as a doctor, a humanitarian." He laughed. "Let Van help you out." Kwame did not answer. "Or Joelle Berton. Or this girl of Moulaert's. She'd rather have you than that Belgian."

"Perhaps," said Kwame. "But why break Moulaert's heart?"

"Even if you marry at Christmas," Odejimi said, "it's not exploitation to sleep with Van."

Kwame wondered if the doctor had talked this way to Mason.

"Sleep with her and you exalt her status. That's not exploitation. And it's important for your health."

"You sound like a pimp."

"That's what you get trying to help a pal," Odejimi remarked. "Relax. You're in Mban. Poor Berton. Consumed by fears that someone's cuckolding him. Afraid that if I'm alone with his wife, or you are, she'll want to jig-jig." He grinned. "Which she will." He cocked an eyebrow. "She knows the secret: 'Once they've had black, they never go back.'" Odejimi laughed. Kwame joined him. The two men played the game of *mankala* that Madame Van had set up. Odejimi won. They pushed the game aside to watch the sunset. Finally the doctor said, "The Americans will get drawn into that business in Rwanda. When that happens, will you go there?"

EIGHT

Kwame found that his days passed more quickly if he had a whiskey to sip at work. Odejimi helped him buy a supply. Sometimes in the evenings he would work late at the center. He would reread through the e-mail jottings Livie had sent him, many written on her laptop in classes she found boring. Since he had kept Mason's tobacco and cigarette papers, he would roll a cigarette and smoke. The tobacco made him feel mellow. When he returned to the hotel, he would smoke another cigarette and have a nightcap. In the glow they created, it bothered him less—although he was still bothered—to hear the sounds of Odejimi and Madame Van making love in the next room. Or to know that across the courtyard Moulaert was enjoying the schoolgirl he had brought to the hotel.

Sometimes at work he would both sip whiskey and smoke. When this happened, he moved through the workday in a haze. He accomplished little. In moments of clarity he realized that the haze was a negative. On the other hand, he felt less frustrated at being in Mbandaka; that was a positive. The haze seemed appropriate to this place seemingly outside of time, outside of connection to the forces and the people who had hitherto shaped his life.

KWAME RETURNED to the center after dinner at the Mongo Restaurant. It could not have been later than eight o'clock. Walking across the dark center toward his office, he bumped into an obstruction on the library floor. It took him a moment to realize that he had stumbled over Anatole making love to a woman. Embarrassed, Kwame muttered, "Excuse me!" The tata was unruffled. In his deliberate way, he climbed to his feet, hoisting his trousers to his waist in his slow, methodical way. He bowed and gravely said: "*Bonsoir, patron.*" His woman grabbed a cloth and covered herself.

"Excuse me, Anat," Kwame repeated. He felt mortified. He did not want to fuck up anybody else's fucking. He lurched into his office and closed the door. He leaned onto his table, laughing, his head in his hands. The odor of sex, that dangerous perfume, was in the air. Lucky Anatole! He fanned the air in front of his face. He did not emerge until he was certain the fortunate tata and his friend were gone.

BACK AT the hotel Kwame poured himself some whiskey and paced the room. I better get out of here, he thought. How will I ever make it to Christmas? A knock came at the door. When he opened it, Madame Van stood at the threshold, her hands behind her back. The way she gazed at him set off a tingling in his body. Time suddenly vanished. Whether he beheld her for seconds or minutes he did not know. He knew only that his mouth was suddenly dry.

"You are not with the doctor tonight?"

"Monsieur Berton has gone to Kin." She smiled, rather shyly. Her smile gave him an overpowering impulse to touch her. He sensed himself as being outside of time. Whoa! he told himself. He thought of Livie. He consciously dragged himself back into the pull of minutes, hours. When neither of them spoke, Madame Van brought her hands before her body. They held a laptop computer. "For you," she said.

It was as if Mason had entered the room. Kwame's body no longer tingled. Moisture returned to his throat. "Where did you get this?"

"Mason give it to me," she said.

No, Mason would not give away his computer.

"He gave it to me. I give it to you."

He watched her. How mysterious she was. How beautiful! Standing there, holding a computer she did not know how to use. She offered it to him with the same ceremony, the same solemnity, with which a girl might offer her virginity.

"When the spirits offer presents," she said, "take them."

"Thank you, Madame. What a gift!" She extended the computer. When he took it, touching her, a buzz sounded in his head. The tingling returned to his body, stronger now. He stepped back into the room, a little dizzy, thinking only that the room was mainly dark now, that Madame had shut the door and that she was close beside him. Blood pounded so strongly in his head that he could hardly see, hardly think, hardly—

Suddenly he was holding her, kissing her, pulling away her cloth. Then they were beside his bed. Then together, holding each other fiercely. Then inside her, blood pounding in his head. They grasped one another, cried out together as convulsions shook them, as the end of the world might shake them. Time stopped. They hurtled through space, clinging to one another, going farther and farther until—

They loosened their grips. Collapsed into one another. Laughed. "Oh!" whispered Kwame. He gazed at her, her eyes closed, light sweat on her upper lip as it curled in a smile. "What was that? An earthquake?" She opened her eyes. They seemed those of one dead until they came alive, watching him.

Smiling, she groaned with pleasure. "Thank you for the laptop," Kwame said. They laughed again.

When their body heat subsided, Kwame covered them with a sheet and lay, holding her. He drifted in and out of sleep. He wondered, what's become of me: adrift at work, smoking and drinking more than he ever had. And now this.

He thought finally of Livie. Please understand, he told her. Then he slumbered. Van moved beside him. He woke. He thought of Odejimi. Would he discover what they'd done? Would Van report to him: *L'américain et moi, nous avons fucké?* Would he laugh? Would he care?

Of course, he would care. A man might offer his woman to another man, but usually the offer was designed to produce their bonding. The man would expect to grant permission. The permission giver became a patron, the receiver a vassal. So that the relationship between the men was redefined, deepened, and the woman served merely as an agent in that deepening.

But maybe Odejimi wouldn't care, Kwame thought. He might be pleased. They lived side by side at the hotel; they drank together. Odejimi was his only friend in Mbandaka. Now they had become buddies, sharing the same toy, this woman.

And what did Madame Van think? Did she care? Apparently not. Hadn't they all conspired to have this happen?

Madame Van shifted her body toward him. They kissed. Their tongues touched. His hands caressed her. Suddenly she was astride him and he inside her. He thought: Are you crazy? Oh, this is good! What are you doing? Oh! He turned off his thinking. He wouldn't think. Like the tata he would just be. Just be in his body. In her body.

STANDING ON his hotel balcony the next morning in a tee shirt and boxers, smoking the first of the day's cigarettes, Kwame watched the river pass below him. After a time he returned to the room, reached beneath his mattress and pulled out Kent Mason's laptop. He beheld it for a time. He knew that, if Mason had left Zaire, he would have taken the laptop with him. Had he truly given it to Madame Van for safekeeping? Was that credible? It suggested more of a relationship there than he— Hunh.

Finally Kwame opened it. Would it operate? He pushed several keys. The laptop greeted him with a tone that cheered him. It did work! A screen-saver image spread itself across the screen. A wedding party stood on the lawn of a country club somewhere in America.

Kwame bent close to the screen, surveyed the bridal party, and studied the groom. He shook his head, trying to clear the haze induced by the cigarette. Was that Mason? The bride-groom bore a striking resemblance to the man in the photo wearing the orange sport shirt with the blue asterisks. Was Mason married? No one had mentioned Mason being married.

Kwame closed the laptop. He felt superstitious about tres-passing on Mason's life. Even people who disappeared had rights to privacy. And Madame Van? The feel of her was still on his body. She was still in his head. He slowly sipped the whiskey. Why not believe her story?

When he arrived at the center, Tata Anatole shuffled into the building. "*Bonjour, M'sieur.*"

"*Bonjour, Anat,*" Kwame replied. "I'm sorry to—" He found himself at a loss for words. "To have interrupted you, you two, last night."

"My bush wife," the tata explained. He evinced not the slightest embarrassment.

"You have two wives, eh?"

"*Oui. C'est bon, ça.*" Anatole explained, "She's here for me to give her a baby."

Kwame nodded. "Excuse me for disturbing you." He turned back to the laptop. Anatole watched him, as if awaiting instructions. Kwame sent him to fetch the mail.

LATE THAT afternoon Kwame watched the Berton Peugeot park before the center. Madame emerged, wearing dark glasses and a tennis outfit, a large fiber carry-all dangling from her arm. Her shirt, unbuttoned almost to the waist, showed the swell of breasts unrestrained by a bra. The tennis outfit displayed nicely tapered legs. Madame moved toward the entry on those good legs and flashed Kwame a smile.

"*Bonjour, Madame*," Kwame greeted her at the door. "I was just leaving for the day."

"No leave," she commanded. The smile turned sultry. "Zees book." She drew Kwame's copy of *Things Fall Apart* from the carry-all. "We talk book, no?" She patted his cheek and brushed past him into the center.

Kwame again made his excuses that he could offer no refreshments. "Zees center," Madame said. She moved about, leaving a trail of perfume. "I hear so much about zees center." She praised Kwame's transforming her husband's building into a palace of culture.

In addressing Kwame she leaned forward in a way that caused her unbuttoned tennis shirt to reveal delightful glimpses of breasts.

If she had come only a few days earlier, Kwame thought, he might have found her hard to resist. Her cleavage and perfume would have inflamed the liquor haze in which he moved. But Madame Van had taken possession of that haze.

"You finished the book?" he asked.

"Yes, I fineesh." Madame observed him in a way that caused a silence and a tension to fall across the room. It seemed as if they were the only people in the world. His mind's haziness vanished. A caution alarm sounded in his head. He gestured Madame to a library table and sat out of reach at the end of it. She took a seat next to him and placed the novel between them.

"What did you think of Okonkwo?" Kwame hastily inquired. Okonkwo was the novel's hero.

"Difficult man," Madame replied. "Terrible husband." After a moment she added, "I know for difficult husband."

"Were you moved by the ending? How the mighty have fallen?"

"The man is all impulse. No self-control. He did not please me." She watched him as if maneuvering to entrap him.

Kwame discussed the structure of the novel, noting that Chinua Achebe had consciously arranged his material to present a portrait of the traditional life of Nigeria's Ibo people, their festivals, their marriage practices, their values. Madame never took her eyes off him. "An African view of African life," Kwame expounded. "Did you find that interesting? There's more to Ibo life than most Westerners realize."

Mme Berton gazed deeply into Kwame's eyes and leaned closer. "It make me feel alive to talk book with you," she said. Her knee slid against his. Kwame moved his leg.

"Were you aware of the Ibo proverbs? I've always loved them." Kwame began to thumb through the novel, looking for proverbs.

"Mostly in this swamp-town I walk around dead. You understand me, *Monsieur*?" Madame placed her hand on his thigh.

"Here's one," he said quickly. "Only a fool pours grain into a bag full of holes."

Her hand slid to his groin. "Meet me somewhere."

Kwame slipped from his chair and walked about the room, searching for more Ibo proverbs. "Here's another," he said. "Eneke the bird says that since men have learnt to shoot without missing, he has learned to fly without perching."

Mme Berton put her head in her hands and stared at the table. "Forgive me," she whispered. "Forgive me for touching you the way *une Congolaise* would." Kwame slid onto an adjacent table and regarded the woman with sympathy. "Not easy for me to come here. To beg. My husband . . . *Difficile* like Okonkwo."

Kwame put his hand on Mme Berton's.

"I want to stop being dead," she whispered. "*Tu comprends?* We could laugh together. I am charming companion." She implored him with her gaze. "Forgive me. I move too quickly."

"Madame," Kwame said, withdrawing his hand, "I would love to talk books with you. We may be the only people in this place who read. This other?" He shook his head. "I would never compromise a woman's marriage."

"Boy scout!" She gave him a scornful smile. "You understand nothing yet, do you, about Mbandaka? There is no culture here. No sauce for the mind. The only thing that gives interest to my life is to walk in the moonlight with a man. Most men want companion. I know about love. Unlike African girl who merely open her legs."

Probably she would be an interesting companion, Kwame thought. "Madame," he said, "I'm flattered that you—"

"We could meet at house by the airport. Friend let me use it." She examined him slowly from head to toe. "Without woman you cannot survive in Mbandaka."

"Madame, please."

"Or do you . . . Have I come too late? Tell me."

Kwame looked back at the novel. He thumbed through pages.

"You have woman, isn't it? I make fool of myself." She inspected the table as if hunting for her dignity there. She glanced up at him. "If man of promise come to this town, woman must move fast."

"You are beautiful, Madame," Kwame said. "And I am awkward. I'm engaged to be married. At Christmas. My fiancée and I agreed that— I am a boy scout."

For a long moment neither person spoke. Finally Kwame asked, "Would you like to take another book?" Madame sat staring at the table. He was sure she would not return. "You might like *Une Si Longue Lettre.* A Senegalese woman looks at her life."

Madame finally regained her dignity. She rose and stood erect. She went to the door. She turned back to him. "You have not been here very long, *Monsieur,*" she said. "If you change your mind, bring me another book. My husband does not object to my discussing book."

KWAME AND Odejimi sat on the terrace together. Odejimi drank whiskey. Kwame was content with beer. Odejimi said, "Van tells me she gave you the computer." Kwame nodded. "I hope you thanked her."

Kwame chuckled. "Yes, I did."

"She was keen on having the thanks."

"How did she get the computer?"

"Took it from me." Odejimi shrugged as if this theft were a matter of no concern. "I didn't want it."

That wasn't Madame Van's story. Kwame wondered what to believe. "How did you get it?" he asked. "Mason wouldn't have given it away."

The doctor sipped his whiskey. "Mason was going through a crisis, you know."

"No, I didn't. I don't think Kinshasa knew."

"Who am I? Why am I here? What am I supposed to do?"

"How American! Asking such questions."

Odejimi shook his head in bafflement. "Strange behavior. He'd pick up teenage girls and give them a ride in his truck. For that they'd take off their clothes and he'd photograph them."

"I've seen some of the photographs. Why did he take them?"

"To send to friends in the States perhaps? You tell me."

"Did he fuck the girls? That would have been risky."

"I don't know. He was careful about AIDS. In fact, he made an appointment to see me professionally. I wondered what it was about. When he didn't turn up, first day, second, third, I went round to the center. The tata had no idea where he was. I sent him on an errand and took the computer. Before anyone else could."

"You open it?"

"Oh, no. Afraid I'd jig it."

"This crisis. Think he took off somewhere?"

"I doubt we'll ever know."

THE SCHOOLGIRL moved into Moulaert's room. Odejimi would tease him. "The ancients contended," he would say, "that for any marriage to work one party must be a fool." The Nigerian would laugh while Moulaert blushed as red as his beard. He seemed to think that naming the girl would bind her to him and so he called her Marike. He hoarded his treasure and would not share her with others. He did not even introduce her. Odejimi was amused. "Haven't the ancients always said," he asked, "that the best husband eats his wife completely and swallows her with alcohol?"

"This husband does not need alcohol," Madame Van observed. "With this child he is already drunk."

Moulaert asked Madame Van to find clothes for Marike to wear when she was not in school. After their shopping expedition, Van reported that Marike knew the season she was born, but not the year. Van estimated that she was fifteen, plenty old enough by the standards of her people to begin a life of pleasing a man. Odejimi shook his head. "Moulaert's broken the cardinal rule of erotic quests. He's fallen in love."

At first Marike behaved with schoolgirl modesty. But the greater her success in bewitching Moulaert the bolder became her curiosity about the men from whom he quarantined her. The more determined became her resolve to attract their notice.

Sometimes in the mornings, after showering, Marike would emerge onto Moulaert's balcony. She would gaze at the river. Wearing a cloth about her hips, she would towel the tight coils on her head. Kwame and Odejimi would be having coffee and rolls on the terrace. Marike would nod to them. She would display her smooth, chocolatey skin and show her taut and firmly rounded breasts. Having a weakness for breasts, Odejimi would mutter, "I'll take the pair."

When Moulaert caught Marike on the balcony—she would go there while he was showering—he would scold her: "Get in here! We're late for school!" When she did not obey, he would shout: "You hear me!" Ten minutes later she would walk modestly across the terrace, her eyes lowered, nunlike and virginal in her school uniform, Our Lady of Education.

ONE MORNING at the center, Kwame set up Mason's laptop to examine it. He had decided that he must learn more about the man. The hard disk held folders labeled USIS Kinshasa, USIS Mbandaka, and USIS Quebec, the post where Mason had served before coming to Zaire. A folder labeled Pers. Corresp. caught Kwame's eye. He opened it and found a folder labeled Dad. In the folder he found files of letters. Kwame remembered that Mason's father had inscribed one of his books, something about "superior men remake the world." He wondered what kind of letter Mason wrote to his father.

He accessed the most recent one. It started simply: "Dad, you miserable dude." Could this be Mason's father?

The body of the letter stated: "Mbandaka's a jewel of a place—at least it will be when I finish with it. It's a shit-hole town where a guy with a sense of humor as big as his sense of adventure can really make his mark. I'm gonna build a surfing resort here. How many American multibillionaires would like to Windsurf the Congo River? Supremo adventure, right? Steph was probably right to pass, the bitch. I wish I had my gear here to see if it's as great as I think it will be.

"Not much to do just now. I've chased some tail. There's a white woman here who offers delights whenever her husband leaves town. And plenty of African girls so eager to ride in a white man's truck that it's hard to keep them clothed.

"I've gotten to know the local governor. He's stoked about having an American to try ideas on. He'd heard of Harvard so I told him I went there. I'm over at the 'Residence,' as they call it, several times a week. My French is getting *meilleur*. The more Guv trusts me, the more I'll accomplish here. I feel like Gordon, Teddy Roosevelt, and *Henderson the Rain King* all rolled into one."

The letter made Kwame laugh. Could this be the same "Dad" who inscribed the book. No. "Dad" might be Mason's pal-father. More likely he was a surfer-mentor who enjoyed kidding Mason about remaking the earth. Or just a buddy. Who was Steph, "the bitch"? His wife? Kwame hoped Mason turned up. He'd like to meet a guy who saw Mbandaka as the site of a surfing resort.

Kwame poured himself a splash of whiskey—he never drank more than a splash—and settled down before the laptop. Mason's letters proved amusing. He read some of the letters to Dad, then investigated the folder called Steph. What might Mason write to her? Accounts of "tail chase"? The folder contained some twenty letters. After the early letters was the word "Sent." After the others: "Not sent." Kwame read the earliest letter that had been sent. It started:

"Oh, Fabbbbbbulous Steph!

"Jeeeeezusss! It's miserable hard here without you. Come to your fucking senses and get out here! Before I end up like fucking Kurtz.

"Okay. I shouldnta wrote that. Two fuckings in two sentences.

"As for Zaire? Different kind of sentence.

"Why'd I ever sign on for duty in any fucking place assigned? I could strangle the bastard that changed my assignment from Rabat to Congo. Depraved sadist.

"Sweet Steph. I haven't known how to write you. Or what to write. I feel like we were driving down the highway of life in a Porsche convertible that suddenly went off a bridge. You got out somehow and I landed in a chasm. Jeeeezusss, Baby! How can we get back into the Porsche together?

"I've been in Zaire two weeks now. I'm being sent to a pisshole called Mbandaka. State wants an American there, but not one of its precious FSOs so fuck me. It's midnight. I leave in six hours. Better cut this short.

"Have I lost you? Can't believe it. This has got to be a nightmare. Yes, it happened fast. But we were so close. We found such joy just being together. I've gotta believe that somehow this is going to be reversed. You can't pull out without giving this more of a chance.

"Shit! Gotta go. I'm getting horny writing this. More soon."

Kwame read over some of the letters to Steph that had not been sent. An entirely different person had written them. It was as if Mason were talking to himself in a manner he could not trust himself to use with her. No mask. No profanity. No affectation. One of them said: "Steph, my love, you let me feel the outpush of care, love, and sharing that goes into giving to a wife and a family. You made me realize how much capacity for love there is inside of me, and for loyalty and sharing and willingness to work to make my loved ones happy."

Kwame wondered, what's going on here? Who was Mason anyway? The incredible shitslinger who wrote to Dad and photographed and maybe even had teenage Congolese tail? The sad/exuberant guy who sent letters to Steph? Or the guy whose loss produced such gentle love-speak? Why hadn't he sent those letters to Steph? Was he afraid to let her see that side of him? Or afraid to acknowledge it to himself?

Mason's shy words astonished Kwame. Mason could write as if stripping his soul naked before a woman. Having such thoughts and being able to set them down! What a capacity! Kwame had never expressed to Livie feelings that the shy Mason put into words. Mason could express them, but then what? Was he embarrassed to send them?

Kwame could not help feeling the exhilaration of a gossip who has stumbled on a trove of juicy information. And he knew Mason better, that consummate shitslinger! How adroitly he fashioned letters for the expectations of his readers! He could be a Windsurfer buff, tail-chaser extraordinaire. Or a sharer of deepest thoughts. Being able to write such thoughts! This capacity astonished Kwame. He had never expressed such feelings to Livie.

WORKING IN his office about midafternoon, Kwame heard a vehicle pull up outside the building. A car door slammed. When he went to the window, he saw M. Berton leaving the Peugeot. Kwame hid the whiskey and the glass that usually sat on his desk. He grabbed the breath mints he kept in a drawer and popped several into his mouth. He left the office to welcome his landlord. After they shook hands, Kwame backed away and kept a hand over his mouth.

Berton glanced about, noticing changes to his building. "A lot of work yet to do," Kwame observed in French.

Berton declared, "We need to talk. In private."

Kwame showed Berton to his office, feeling apprehensive. "Your wife came by to discuss a Nigerian novel I lent her," he said.

"She told me."

"I'm not sure the novel was quite her thing."

"She gets bored in this town." Kwame cleared a chair for Berton and shut the door so that Anatole would not stand in the doorway watching them. "She would like to spend her life at fashion shows."

"I'm sorry I have nothing to offer you," Kwame said. "I could send the tata to the restaurant for beer."

Berton waved his hand no. "I have something to tell you," he said. He paused for such a long moment that Kwame felt uncomfortable. He examined Kwame, his eyes narrowing. "I have wondered if I should tell you. And decided yes. Can you hold what I say in confidence?"

Kwame said nothing. It was his turn to measure his visitor. "I can't agree without knowing what it is," he said at last. "But I think you can trust my discretion."

Berton finally said, "I am one of the few people in Mban who knows what happened to your friend Mason. I've made inquiries since we last spoke."

The two men studied one another. "I would very much like to know what happened," Kwame acknowledged. "So would my government. May I report what you tell me?"

Berton considered this request. "Of course," he finally replied. "But as a confidential matter."

Kwame nodded. Berton did not speak for such a long time that Kwame again asked, "Are you sure I cannot have the tata—" Again Berton waved his hand.

"Your friend Mason cultivated contacts at the Residence," the planter began. "He ingratiated himself with the governor. Gave him books, videos, recordings." Berton paused for Kwame's reaction to this information.

Kwame shrugged. "All part of the job," he said. "I haven't got around to calling on the governor, but I should."

"He also gave the governor advice," Berton continued.

"What kind of advice?"

"All kinds. Including unwanted advice."

Kwame wondered how much of what Berton said was true—even though Mason himself had boasted about cultivating such contacts.

"Mason had opinions about everything," Berton continued. "He also possessed that very American quality of assuming that all his opinions were valuable."

Kwame forced himself to smile. "That's not a quality peculiar to Americans, *Monsieur*." He was not liking this interview, but he determined to keep it light. "Although, of course, we thank you for the compliment."

Berton did not return the smile. "Some people at the Residence thought he aspired to be a *Conseiller du Gouverneur.* The governor himself thought so."

The idea seemed preposterous. Kwame made no reply.

"In short," Berton said, "Mason made a nuisance of himself. The problem was how to get rid of him."

"Is he alive?" Kwame asked.

"I am told he left here alive."

"Who are your sources?"

"They are well-placed. Reliable. At the Residence."

"Why not send him back to Kinshasa?"

"Ah! You Americans are so direct." Berton smiled. "No one knew what his support was in Kin. Or how determined the Americans were to keep him in Mban. Disappearance was much simpler."

Kwame nodded. "What happened to him?"

"He was invited to the Residence one night when the governor was away. The next day the army flew him to Lisala. I understand he went overland from there to Bangui." Bangui was the capital of the Central African Republic, several hundred miles to the north. "When he crossed the border, he received a small bit of money. He was told that if he ever returned to the Equateur, he would not leave alive."

The two men sat in silence. Kwame wished he could have a smoke of Mason's tobacco. And a splash of Odejimi's whiskey. Pleased to see him unnerved, Berton watched him with placid hostility.

Finally he added, "I tell you this because you say you've come to help these people build their country. You are less arrogant than Mason, thank God. We have a common interest. And we are both Europeans."

"No one would mistake me for a European, M. Berton."

"Only Zaireans," Berton replied. "We do not want them thinking that the way to handle Europeans is to make them disappear."

Kwame smiled tightly and gave his visitor a nod.

"Mason's fate should make something clear to you," Berton said. "In building their country these people do not want your help. They do not want Americans exploiting their resources. Or their women. Yes, they have made a mess of their independence. But it was not without a great deal of help from America. They want that help to stop."

"He thinks you've slept with his wife," Odejimi said. Kwame had told the Nigerian about his meeting with Berton. "He's playing with your head."

"Have you been to Bangui?"

"No. And neither has Mason. If someone actually took him there, the first thing he'd do is contact the American Embassy. Your people would know where he is. Berton is leading you astray."

"But why?"

"He's warning you off his wife. He's warned me. But when the cat is away, the mice dance. Madame Berton likes to dance." Odejimi grinned and poured whiskey into both their glasses. They were sitting on the Afrique terrace wondering when Madame Van would join them.

"Did Mason 'cultivate' the Residence?" Kwame asked.

"He went over there once or twice. But how could he offer advice? He hardly spoke French."

The doctor kept glancing at the portal through which Madame Van would appear. "That damn woman," he said. "She knows she's more interesting if she keeps us waiting." Kwame wondered what, if anything, she had told Odejimi about their being together.

"So Berton's story is not what happened to Mason?"

"No."

"What did happen to him? You must know."

Odejimi raised his whiskey glass to his lips and held it there. He looked out across the river at the huge clouds turning from orange to red. He finally said, "Honestly, old boy. I don't know."

As soon as Berton had left the center, Kwame wrote a report of the conversation for Kinshasa. Concluding the memo he felt he should offer some assessments of its revelations, but did not know what to write. His hunch was that Mason had gone to see Stephanie wherever she was and had not bothered to tell anyone. But Kwame did not want to reveal that he knew anything about her.

"Is there anyone at the Residence I could check out Berton's story with?" Kwame asked.

"No. You aren't here long enough yet to confirm rumors."

"Kinshasa will want to know I've done some checking."

"You Americans!" Odejimi sighed tiredly. "Why tell Kinshasa? It's bullshit. Why try to check it? You may never learn what happened to Mason. Is that so hard to accept?"

Madame Van appeared on the terrace. Odejimi gave a sigh of relief. "Thank God you're here!" the doctor greeted her. "This chap is almost as boring as Moulaert." Madame Van moved to their table without looking at Kwame. As she and the doctor began their game of *mankala,* he felt shut out as if he meant no more to them than did Moulaert.

THAT EVENING the sense of isolation he felt at the *mankala* game deepened. Perhaps work would assuage it, he thought.

At the center he opened Mason's laptop. He scanned the relevant files and found only one report of a meeting with the governor. At it Mason distributed books and pamphlets and offered English lessons. That was all. Since an ambitious young officer would certainly report—probably even exaggerate—his contacts with the governor, there seemed little to justify Berton's tale.

Kwame began to edit the report he'd drafted earlier during the day. The hell with it! he thought. He shut the laptop. This was like a curse. He had not felt this lonely since his first days in Mbandaka.

Write to Livie. Maybe that would help. But as he started, all he could think was: "Why are we writing these letters? We aren't going to marry. I know this even if I won't admit it."

Shit! He stared at the paper. Beginning again he would be blunt. "I am sitting in this office at night," he wrote, "missing you. God, I've never felt so lonely. I miss our sex. I miss touching you, your warmth in the night. I miss your fragrance, your taste, your voice. I miss my being wound about you." Reading it over, he thought, what crap! He sounded horny. But the problem was loneliness, the feeling that no one in the entire continent of Africa, maybe no one in the entire world, knew or cared that he existed. He wanted to withdraw what he'd written. But he would send it. Maybe Livie would like getting it wrong, thinking him horny for her in Mbandaka when he was really crazy lonely.

He gave it up, left the center. When he trudged across town, the *sentinelles* sitting before stores ignored him. The dogs that sometimes menaced him did not move. He walked along the empty road beside the river. He passed through the deserted reception of the hotel. As he entered his room, the loneliness felt like weight on his back. He paced, went out onto the balcony overlooking the river. By now his isolation seemed almost impossible to bear. He stared for long minutes at the river.

Finally a light illuminated the adjoining balcony. Without quite knowing what he was doing, he climbed over the railing onto that balcony. He went to the glass door and knocked on it. After a moment Madame Van opened the door and peeked out. "*Ah, Madame, bonsoir,*" said Kwame, greatly relieved to see another human being. "Come out and talk to me. Please. I need someone to talk to." Madame regarded him uncertainly. At this hour of the evening a man did not knock on a woman's door to talk. "Ask Odejimi to join us. We can tell each other stories."

Van smiled at him quizzically. "The doctor was called to the hospital."

"You come then." He reached out his hand for her. She moved uncertainly onto the porch. Kwame took her hand and led her to the balcony railing. They stood, looking at the river. "Are there village stories about the river at night?" he asked. "There must be."

Yes, there were many, she said: stories, folktales. She regarded him curiously and quoted some proverbs.

"Do people get lonely in the villages?" Kwame asked. He tried to explain what he meant by lonely. "I know they get lonely in towns. That's how I feel." He went on, "It's not wanting a woman. It's—"

She looked at him so strangely that he stopped talking. "You do not want me, *Monsieur*?"

Kwame realized he was not explaining himself well. "Yes, of course, I want you." He understood suddenly that he did. "But I also want us to talk."

Madame frowned, cocked her head.

Beholding her, he felt desire climb onto him, onto the loneliness that was choking him. Was it all merely desire for her? Was he fooling himself? No. He really needed some talk. "What have you done today?" he asked. "Tell me about your day."

It required several promptings, but eventually she recounted the ordinariness of her day. Kwame told her what he had done, the meeting with Berton. He had not gone to Bomboko Congo, he said; perhaps he would feel less lonely if he had. Then when she and Odejimi were playing *mankala*, they made him feel that he was nothing, a cipher, a zero.

"You felt that?" she asked.

The desire for her was great on him now. He kissed her.

She cocked her head again and laughed. "Are you sure you do not want me, *Monsieur?*"

He blushed. Perhaps she would not notice in the darkness.

She moved to the section of wall where they had been together in the rain and laid her hand against it. "I remember this place."

"A very good place," he said. Then he asked, "Will you come to my room, Madame? I have some etchings." He laughed at the little joke that she would not understand. He took her hand, led her to the railing that separated the two balconies, and helped her across it.

She spent the night with him and he could not get enough of her. Finally about dawn the loneliness drained away. They lay together in his bed, smiling, as the first light crept into the sky.

NINE

When he woke in the morning, Kwame lay naked and uncovered on his bed. Madame curled beside him, her back warming his side. Sunlight streamed into the room. Blinking, looking about him, Kwame saw Odejimi sitting on the other bed, watching him. When their eyes met, the doctor smiled. "Well, well," he said. Kwame felt a foolish grin spread across his face. That foolishness extended so deeply into him that he was not bothered by another man gazing at his nakedness. He did not cover his body with a sheet.

At the sound of Odejimi's voice, Madame stirred. She shifted her body, flowing like liquid, curling against Kwame. Then, seeing Odejimi, she sat up. She arched her back and raised her arms above her head. The two men watched her. Finished stretching, she snuggled back against Kwame.

"Have some breakfast," Odejimi suggested. He spoke in English, the language of the guys. He opened a pouch, brought out a large pinch of tobacco, stuffed it into his mouth, and then handed pinches to his friends.

Kwame asked, "What is this shit?"

"Breakfast of champions," Odejimi assured them. "Why smoke it when you can eat it?" Kwame and Madame giggled. "Really sets up your day."

"Pardon me for asking," Kwame replied before sticking a pinch into his mouth. "But do I swallow? Or spit it out?"

Odejimi laughed. "Suit yourself," he said. "I want it to stay with me. So I chew it well, then swallow." He took a swig of whiskey and demonstrated his technique. He passed the bottle to Kwame. He duplicated the process and gave the whiskey to Madame Van. "Have some more," Odejimi suggested. Kwame took the pouch and had more breakfast. He chewed slowly, letting the juice swirl in his mouth. He felt extraordinarily comfortable, his body spent, his mind benignly floating about the room as if detached from his body.

As his senses hovered, sharp but disconnected from the room, he saw Odejimi stand and shed his clothes. "Ah!" Odejimi enthused. "Family sex!" His arms flowed out from his body, as sinuous as snakes. They lifted Madame from beside Kwame; they carried her to the nearby bed and laid her lightly upon it. Madame giggled. The sound of her voice filled Kwame's head with tingling bells. Even as Kwame watched the ceiling, he saw Odejimi's dark chocolate snake arms lift Madame's dark chocolate knees and spread them. He observed teammate Odejimi stretch upon the dark mattress of Madame. They began to move together in waves. They floated—just as Kwame himself was floating. He watched them float and giggled and shut his eyes.

Later, when he got up for more breakfast, he saw Odejimi and Madame still levitating, but they were now side by side, both watching the ceiling. He floated over beside Madame and looked down at her and her arms snaked up toward him and he hovered above her and into her, their arms wrapped about each other, his hips moving and then they were all laughing and Odejimi was embracing them both, kissing Madame, licking her face, as Madame and Kwame clung to one another.

All three of them stayed in bed together that day, eating tobacco, drinking whiskey, and laughing, the two men sharing the woman repeatedly, each man showing off for the other his amazing staying power.

Late in the afternoon a very insistent Dr. Odejimi drove both Kwame and Madame Van to the hospital. "Only a formality," the doctor said. "But I insist on it." He took samples of their blood and reported two days later that, as expected, they were clean.

LATER IN the week Kwame sat in his office, staring at the street outside, sipping whiskey and smoking Odejimi's hemp. He thought about the Nigerian. He seemed happy to share Madame Van; he even offered to have her spend nights with Kwame. Odejimi offered Madame to cement the friendship between them. They could be pals because she was mutually their toy.

Their relationship was not competitive. They were teammates now, pals. With a language that excluded her. Eventually they would vie with one another for dominance, for the position of starting quarterback on Team Van.

In that inevitable competition Kwame assured himself that he would command the inside track. Why? Because Van interested him as a person. For Odejimi she was merely a toy, amusement, diversion. Just as he and Mme Berton were merely play for one another. While the Nigerian took Van for granted, her beauty and mystery truly fascinated Kwame. He would beat out Odejimi by probing behind Van's beauty and mystery as soon as an opportunity offered.

THE NEXT day at the post office Kwame ran into the British missionary doctor he had met at the mission station he had visited outside of town. The doctor's child had been ill. "Is your daughter better?" he asked.

The missionary glanced at Kwame with a look of pure anguish and shook his head. "We lost her," he said.

"Oh, god!" Kwame exclaimed. "I'm so sorry." The missionary nodded and offered a stiff-upper-lip smile. "If there's anything I can do," Kwame said, his voice trailing off. The doctor nodded again and hurried off.

The child's death devastated Kwame. He spent the rest of the day and most of the following one sitting on his balcony, staring at the river. He thought about the missionary and his child and the cruelty of this country.

KWAME READIED the center for business. Every day young men and a few women waited outside the building, seeking jobs. Since Kwame's assignment was temporary, he did not want to hire Zairean assistants or hold an opening celebration. This was not a matter of indolence—or not entirely that. Those tasks, those pleasures, he felt, rightfully belonged to the officer permanently assigned to Mbandaka.

But because he wanted townspeople to enjoy the resource the center represented, he began to hold evening video shows in the front yard. He erected a video projector on the steps of the center and projected images onto a translucent screen. He put Madame Van in charge of a CD player that provided music before and after the videos. He invited guests: Odejimi, the Badekas and other teachers from the Bomboko Congo school, Moulaert and Marike, Tombolo and members of the Afrique staff and, since he wanted good relations with his landlord, he also included the Bertons. Most guests brought their own chairs. The center had only a few to offer and Kwame saw that those went first to Madame Van, Odejimi, and the Badekas.

Anatole's two wives and children attended. Having seen Mbandaka, the tata's bush wife, now pregnant, refused to return to her village. Anatole moved about the property, keeping order among the young people; they watched the images from both sides of the translucent screen and danced joyously to Madame Van's music.

After the first of these *fêtes*—Madame Van referred to them by no other name—the Badekas, Madame Van, and Odejimi took Kwame to a Zairean club where they danced to the music of a local combo. It was a place, Kwame thought, where the blonde, slim, very white Livie could only be a tourist. But he blended in; he was almost an African.

When the Badekas and the doctor left at midnight, Odejimi bestowed an elaborate wink on Kwame. The Nigerian now made no objection to Madame Van spending some of her nights with Kwame. This arrangement was never actually discussed. They both found themselves stuck in Mbandaka. Madame Van made Mbandaka easier to endure. Their sharing her was as simple as that.

Leaving the nightclub, Kwame and Madame Van drove to a place overlooking the river and watched it flow in the moonlight. Stars surrounded the moon. Suddenly one of them shot across the sky. Madame laughed elatedly. "A spinning star," she exclaimed, using the French expression. She asked: "How do you call them in English?"

"We say a shooting star."

"In the village," she said. "we call such stars 'a child.' Each star that races across the sky carries a child to its mother. Some woman is very happy tonight. She will become the mother of a star-child."

Madame Van watched the night like a schoolgirl, looking for more shooting stars. She spoke the proverb of her people. "A spinning star brings some woman happiness." Kwame watched her, touched her cheek. When she turned to look at him, he pulled her toward him. He kissed her tenderly. They made love on the front seat of the van. Toward dawn they returned to the hotel and slept wrapped about one another.

AT THE nightclub Kwame complained to the Badekas that he was under-occupied. They suggested that he teach more classes at the secondary school. "Teach modern history," Badeka urged. "Or geography. Tell about America, South Africa, West Africa." The music began again, loud and pulsating. Dancers crowded the floor.

"What about curriculum?" Kwame asked. "What about books?"

"Come dance with me?" Madame Van whispered, close to Kwame's ear. He held up a finger to say he was coming, but gave his attention to the Badekas. Madame went off to dance with Odejimi.

"Books?" Badeka asked with a laugh. "We have no books, except ones that are out of date. And very few of those."

"We understood that schools in American inner cities do not use books," Mme Badeka teased. "We assume this is the latest method. We are imitating it."

Early the next week Kwame sought out the Badekas, bringing beer and peanuts, and asked about teaching at Bomboko Congo. Madame Badeka, who now insisted that he call her Théa, brought glasses to the table outside their bungalow and announced that Kwame must teach African literature to the students.

"What about history?" Kwame asked. "Or world affairs?"

"Too controversial," Badeka informed him. "Do you suppose 'Our Friend'"—meaning Mobutu—"and his people want students to learn about Western politics: fair elections, an independent judiciary, the right to express ideas freely? It's dangerous enough that you encourage the students to think for themselves."

Kwame shelled peanuts for his hosts, tossing the nuts into a bowl and the husks into a cardboard box on the ground.

"Teach literature as history," Théa urged. "The Equateur has seen unbelievable change in the past century."

"Tradition used to be everything," Badeka said. "Now it is nothing. Before every African was anchored to a community and knew his place in it. Now the person who seeks to advance himself is the one who succeeds."

"Do tatas still remember the times of gathering wild rubber?" Kwame asked.

"Let's find out," suggested Théa.

"So you agree?" said Badeka. "You'll teach for us?"

"Why not?"

"I think this is more important than the work you do at the center," Théa declared. "Prepare the students for change. There is more change coming."

On the Afrique terrace Kwame told his friends about the classes. He wanted students to ask questions, he said, to challenge received truth. "Get different clothes," Madame suggested. "You look foreign."

"I am talking about their minds," Kwame said, a little miffed, "and you are talking couture?"

"If you do not dress so American—"

"I dress American?" Kwame asked, surprised at this charge. The others nodded.

"If you dress Zairean," Madame Van suggested, "you won't be so terrifying."

"Terrifying?" Kwame was offended.

"Students might even ask you questions," Odejimi teased.

"But they will never challenge you," said Moulaert. "Forget about that."

"I want them to challenge me," Kwame insisted. "Why won't they?"

"The fart of a rich man never smells," observed Odejimi. Kwame frowned. The others laughed. "You are the American," the Nigerian explained, "rich in money, in property, in experience. Your shit doesn't smell."

Madame Van took Kwame shopping. The selection was limited and the quality of the merchandise inferior, but she selected two long-sleeved shirts for him, a belt, sandals, and a pair of khaki trousers. These Kwame rejected. They fit badly over his behind and through his crotch. But to please Madame Van he bought them. He would wear them only when he taught.

KWAME'S LETTER thrilled Livie. "Have those words been inside you for months," she asked, "and you've never let them out? Maybe it's not so bad, once in a while, for us to be apart."

Livie said that she missed Kwame terribly. She could not wait to see him at Christmas. As for their time together in Paris, Kwame looked forward to it eagerly. If it sometimes seemed improbable that they would marry, he still intended to go through with it.

KWAME DID not write Kinshasa about his waning attempts to discover what had happened to Mason. That no longer seemed to matter. Kinshasa now had more concerns than the whereabouts of Kent Mason. By the middle of November eastern Zaire had begun to collapse. Kwame and Odejimi tried to follow what was occurring in the region of the Lakes. Despite nightly radio reports of African news from London and Brussels, however, they found it difficult to keep track of events so far away. It seemed that Zaire's dictator, Mobutu, was in no hurry to cleanse the Goma refugee camps, where Odejimi had served, of the Hutu *génocidaires* terrorizing them. In fact, Mobutu had teamed Hutu militants fired by a passion to kill Tutsis with Zairean troops more skilled at looting than at warfare. These troops had now expelled Tutsis long resident in Masisi, west of Goma.

On other fronts, however, Tutsis put up surprising resistance led by the very Tutsi troops of the Rwandan Patriotic Front that had pushed the Hutu refugees into Zaire.

This much Kwame and his friends had been able to follow in Mbandaka. But eastern Zaire seemed even more remote than America. So when Kwame learned that Pilar Cota, the cultural officer who was his boss, was to visit Mbandaka and brief him on the region, he was relieved. He and his friends would learn what was going on. Pilar was hitching a ride to Mbandaka in the embassy plane. She would spend three hours in the town before flying on to Kisangani.

KWAME WAS waiting at the airport when the plane arrived. He had come straight from teaching early classes at Bomboko Congo and was wearing a Zairean outfit Madame Van had chosen for him. Pilar scrambled from the plane, looking harassed, a cigarette hanging from her mouth. She strode toward the terminal, Kelly the pilot close behind her. Kwame went to greet them. As he neared the pair, Pilar turned back to Kelly and yelled, "Where the hell's our guy? Do the phones work in this place?"

"Your guy's right here," Kwame said.

Pilar glanced at him, then examined him carefully. "My god, it's you!" she said. "You could pass for a goddamn Zairean." Kwame smiled at this. Pilar stopped walking. "You're not going to take offense at that, are you?" she asked. "I got enough problems without being called 'insensitive.'"

Kwame dropped Kelly at the military camp and escorted Pilar to the center. After a bathroom stop she inspected the building, her boots sounding on the cement slab floor with a hollowness that made Kwame aware of the silence, the emptiness. The air was dead. The rooms smelled close; they had been locked up since late the previous afternoon. "It looks great," Pilar said at last. "But where are the people? Why aren't they here?"

Kwame reminded her of his memos.

"It oughta be open," she said.

"Okay," Kwame replied. "I'll hire a library assistant and have it open by the end of the week."

"Good. We're a can-do outfit." Pilar examined the center again and asked, "You don't have anything to drink here, do you?"

In the office Kwame poured her some whiskey and apologized for having no ice. Pilar took a hefty swallow and began to pace. "Looks like we may commit US troops in eastern Zaire," she said, giving him a situation report. "This stuff is secret, by the way."

Kwame nodded.

"The idea scares us guys in Kinshasa fucking shitless."

"Does Washington know that?"

"The White House feels guilty that we stood by and let 800,000 people be massacred in Rwanda. It's a hellish problem. Clinton sees TV coverage of starving kids in the refugee camps. He knows it's good politics to save them." She shrugged. "But bad politics to lose American kids doing it. Or getting stuck in

Africa. The Canadians are willing to carry most of the burden if we support them with troops."

Kwame watched Pilar move: three paces in one direction, three paces in the other. And always the cigarette.

"We say: 'We're with you the whole way, Mr. President, but you must understand that there are Hutu thugs in those camps. The starving kids aren't refugees; they're hostages. You can't get food to them until something's done about the thugs.'" She paused. "So the idea is, fine. We'll limit our mission. We'll secure the airport in Goma and let somebody else deliver the food."

"Will that work?"

"Shit, no. If we go in, we'll get sucked into this mess just like everyone else has. Only worse cause we're bigger." She stopped pacing and asked, "Is there a restaurant in this town? Can we get something brought in?"

Kwame sent Anatole to the Mongo. While they waited, Pilar spoke frankly about her worries: mission creep, the moral nullity of Mobutu, the impossibility of a right US policy when serious objections could be raised to every option, the chaos toward which the country was edging.

"We hate all this," Pilar said, "every one of us. Because we want to help these people. But if we stop the killing, we'll have to run the country. And ethnic hatred will still be there. We all know if we go in we'll get our asses burned."

Anatole and two other men returned with tilapia sandwiches and Primus beer. Kwame tipped them all. "This stuff is shit!" exclaimed Pilar. "Do you eat this way all the time?"

Kwame shrugged. He would not knock Mbandaka. "What about the branch post policy?" he asked. "Does that still seem—"

"I don't know what to tell you. Your center should be open. We could also close it next week. We know the Mobutu era is ending. Hell, it's over. We just don't know what the death throes look like. Or exactly when they'll come." She pushed her sandwich aside and drank her Primus. "It's a pretty good guess that there's going to be chaos."

They said nothing for a time. Finally Kwame told her, "I think maybe Mason just took off. To go see his wife. You know about her?"

"How do you know?"

"Why didn't you tell me?"

"What business was it of yours? If you needed to know, Mason would tell you." Pilar lit another cigarette. "Some Foreign Service wives choose to stay home."

"That's all you know?"

"That's all. When he was assigned to Rabat, she expected to be with him. When the assignment was changed—" Pilar shrugged. "She didn't come. That's all I know."

"Did she back out of the marriage?"

"If it's any of your business, you better ask Mason."

As THEY shook hands on the tarmac, Pilar said, "I know you've requested leave over Christmas."

"My deal with Judkins was that—"

"Judkins left a month ago. I'm in charge until a new bossman arrives. With this place about to explode, I can't let you have leave. I'm sorry."

Kwame felt as if hit by a blow. He gritted his teeth. But he merely nodded.

"We aren't having any luck getting an officer out here to replace you. You may be staying here for a while."

"How long?"

"Could be a year."

As he watched the plane disappear over the jungle, Kwame said to himself, "You fuckhead! You asshole! They'll fuck you as long as you let them." He understood why Mason had taken off. Every night he spent with Madame Van he wondered if he really wanted to get married in Paris. Now that he couldn't, he was certain that he did. As he drove back to town, tears of frustration swam into his eyes.

TEN

When Kwame had drinks late that afternoon with Odejimi and Madame Van, he was in a foul mood. "What's the matter with you two?" the doctor asked. "Madame's in a tizzy and you're ready to hit someone."

"They canceled my Christmas leave," Kwame said. "I was going to Europe." He glanced at the woman. "What's the matter, Madame?" he asked. She abruptly left the hotel terrace.

"You better sleep with her tonight," Odejimi said. "I don't want her in my bed."

It turned out that Madame was irritated that a woman from Kinshasa had come to visit Kwame. By the time the story reached her, Pilar was a white woman of extraordinary beauty. Rumor claimed that Kwame and Pilar were seen making love in the center.

It had been a very long time since Kwame had encountered jealousy. He had never seen Livie inflamed by the green monster. Yet here was Madame Van raging that he had paid attention to Pilar Cota. Despite his anger about the canceled leave, he could barely suppress his amusement.

He took Madame to dinner at the Mongo. He explained that the woman who had come to see him was his boss, his "*patron*," his "*chef*." Madame Van frowned; Kwame was bossed by a woman? He described Pilar Cota as a kind of ogre, breast-less and foul-smelling, a man in a woman's body, a creature no man would touch.

"How can she be your '*chef*?'" Madame Van asked.

"It is our way," Kwame said.

She gazed at him and shook her head. When he told her that Pilar had instructed him to open the center, she begged him to give her a job there. If he employed her, he explained, he could no longer see her. See her? She did not understand. He could no longer sleep with her. Her brow clouded with confusion. He explained that in America it was not acceptable—in fact, it was a crime—for a man to sleep with a woman he employed.

Madame Van laughed. He must be joking. Any man who gave a woman a job expected to sleep with her. Why else would he give her the job? And if a woman wanted the job, she would accommodate her boss. This was simply a condition of the employment, nothing to get excited about. She asked Kwame to promise that he would not give a job to any other woman.

"No, I won't," Kwame assured her. "There's only trouble for me in hiring a woman."

"Americans are strange," Madame Van observed. She asked if it were true, as she had heard, that American women killed their babies during pregnancy. Kwame explained that American women had that right; they had won it only after a difficult struggle.

Madame Van frowned. "The right?" she asked, clearly perplexed. Kwame nodded assent. "But why would they want that right?" Kwame realized that he could not say they wanted it in the name of freedom, to show that they were the masters of their own bodies. She would not understand that. "Why would a woman want to kill her baby?" she asked. "Here not to have a child is—" She shrugged. How could she untangle the verities of African life to an American?

"You want babies?" Kwame asked.

Madame Van nodded. "It is very sad that I have no babies by now." In a whisper she admitted, "Something is wrong with me. I sleep with men, but I don't have babies." Kwame reached across the table to take her hand. It often worried him that he did not use contraceptives with her. The experience was better without, but it did seem irresponsible. He did not want to give her a child and then leave her. He wondered if she cared who gave her a child. She looked at him strangely. "And American women kill their babies. I will never understand Americans."

He asked, "Will you try to understand me?"

Saying nothing, she reached for the fiber bag on the chair beside her, pulled away its crown, and reached inside it. "Close your eyes," she instructed. "Open your hands."

Kwame watched her. What was she up to?

"Close," she repeated. "Open."

He followed her instructions. He heard her fumble in the bag. Then she placed something—he had no idea what—into his cupped hands. He opened his eyes. In his hands rested a whatsis of fur, hair, and God knew what, a magic charm, the sort of thing he had seen tied around the waists of Anatole's children. "This will protect you from your *chef*," she assured him.

He did not know what to say.

"Wear this and it will give you long life."

"Thank you," he said. "How do I wear it?"

She took the charm, knelt beside him, and tied it to his ankle. His impulse was to kiss her, for she was not so much protecting him as safeguarding her interest in him, shielding him from the sexual witchery of his boss. But to publicly kiss a woman in the Mongo? That would have sullied her reputation.

The charm felt awkward on his ankle, but he wore it the rest of the evening.

AFTER DINNER Kwame drove Madame out beside the river and told her—quite truthfully—that she was the most beautiful woman he had seen in Africa. She laughed. "'You cannot eat beauty,'" she commented. "That's what the men of my village say. 'Beauty is no use to a woman working in my fields.'"

Kwame was fascinated. "Tell me about your village," he said. She shrugged and said nothing. "Tell me about yourself. I know nothing about you." She looked at him strangely as if he were the first of the men she had been with to ask about her life, to see her as more than a diversion. "What is your village called?" he asked.

"Bolobe," she said. "Near Bikoro."

"Tell me about Bolobe. About you."

When she realized that he was genuinely interested in answers to his questions, she explained that she was a Mongo, of the people who inhabited this part of the Equateur. She spoke Lonkundo. Bolobe lay on the banks of Lake Tumba, south of Mbandaka. She had attended secondary school at a convent run by French nuns at Bikoro.

"Going to secondary school: that's unusual, isn't it, for girls? And it must have cost. Your father must be rich."

"You are full of questions," she said.

"I want to know you," he told her. "As more than Odejimi's girlfriend."

"I am more than this doctor's girlfriend," she said. "I am your girlfriend."

As they watched the river flow past, Madame Van explained that her father was Bolobe's teller of stories. When she was younger, he had a friend, also a storyteller, older, more experienced and richer. He helped with the school fees. In Bolobe it was the custom for people to form special, lifelong friendships and for friends to help each other. When she achieved marriageable age, her father's storyteller friend had also become her friend. "A friend of this kind," she said, "helps to instruct a girl in matters pertaining to marriage."

"You mean—"

Madame Van smiled. Of course she meant that.

Kwame felt a sudden, Puritan sense of outrage that this trusted friend of her father, a man certainly more than twice her age, had seduced her.

She smiled indulgently and Kwame felt that she regarded him as very foreign, very American. "We met secretly," she said. "I felt grown-up. Like a woman."

"But little is secret in a village," Kwame said.

"Better to learn from a man who knows such things," she said. "I had been with boys. They knew nothing." Kwame made no reply. After a moment she commented, "It is our way." He nodded.

When young men and their fathers came asking for her, the father's friend insisted that she was too young to marry. He was a Christian, a Catholic, and arranged for her to have a place at the convent school in Bikoro. He even agreed to pay the fees. She had stayed at the school four years. In the final year when the nun in charge of the refectory fell ill, she helped the sisters run the kitchen. She ordered food, prepared menus, and cooked; she enjoyed the work, but did not know where it would lead. In her society cooks and chefs and eating place owners were men—although in his home a man never prepared food; that was a woman's work.

Then Vandenbroucke had appeared at the convent, a young, Catholic Belgian in his late twenties. He was seeking a wife he could take to Mbandaka. The sisters suggested several candidates; he chose her. She'd been uncertain about him and about going to Mbandaka. One of the sisters, however, was his distant cousin; she vouched for the family. Moreover, her father wanted to take a second wife and needed money. He persuaded her that Vandenbroucke represented an extraordinary opportunity.

When her father's friend endorsed her father's advice, she agreed to marry the Belgian. She assumed that, as tradition required, bridewealth would be given in livestock. But Vandenbroucke offered only cash. That humiliated her; she was not being sold, after all! She objected, but her father accepted the cash, deepening her humiliation. She must be a modern woman, he told her. More and more these days cash was being offered and accepted as bridewealth. She must not take offense. She made no public objection and was married to Vandenbroucke.

"He took you to Europe?"

She smiled. "I wanted so much to see it. I studied about it at the convent. Van took me there to live with him."

Kwame wondered if this were true. Odejimi had termed the trip Vandenbroucke's farewell gift to her. He also claimed that Vandenbroucke had passed her around. That seemed not to be true. "You didn't like Belgium? Was that the problem?"

"His family objected." She shrugged. "I could have lived in Brussels. There were many Congolese."

"And in Flanders. Could you—"

"Not with people like his family." They smiled together. She went on, "It's different from here, you know. I was always cold. The air smelled bad. They call it—pollution?" Kwame nodded. "The food had no taste. And the noise. Always, always noise, never silence." She put a finger on Kwame's lips. For a moment they listened to the silence. "And it was so crowded. Everywhere you looked—"

"White people," Kwame said.

She laughed. "When they looked at me, they saw only black."

"Not beautiful. That's what I see."

"Now and then a man saw something. If he had money, he would whisper, 'Let me take you to a hotel.' If he had no money, he would grab my arm and pull me toward an alley. 'Come in here with me,' he'd say. 'I'll make you happy.'"

Kwame observed, "Men are men." Madame shrugged ironically. "I'm sorry."

"When Van's brother came to put me on the plane, it was the same thing. It was hard for him to ask, but he did. 'Will you show me why my brother is so fond of you?'"

"At least it was graceful."

"He was sweet. So young. Embarrassed by the way his mother and sisters treated me. I kissed him out of gratitude. That's when he looked at me so shyly and asked. So eager for me."

"You weren't offended?"

She shook her head, remembering the difficulty the brother had getting those words out. "I couldn't help liking him," she admitted. "And I needed a friend. If I'd suggested it, he would have come to the Congo with me. Instead I kissed him."

"Lucky him."

"He spent two nights with me." She gazed at Kwame for a long moment, put her hand on his cheek, and drew a line there with her finger. She no longer wanted to talk about Belgium. "Tell me," she said. "Are there villages in America? Where do your people come from?"

"Originally from Africa," Kwame told her. He did not know precisely where, would never know. They had been enslaved; he did not know under what circumstances. From what he had been told, his people were always in the northern part of the United States. They had never been plantation slaves. "That is very important to my mother," he said. "She always insists that we are people of the mind. The BaBrainy." Madame Van laughed. Kwame felt witty and pleased that she had gotten his joke. She seemed more attractive than ever.

Holding her, her back against his chest, Kwame had an impulse to kiss her. It was the same impulse he had often felt with Livie. The difference was that Livie would have shared the impulse and would have expected to be kissed. Madame Van did not expect a kiss and, as he held her, did not seem totally relaxed. He told her once more how beautiful she was. "In America," he said, "a man eats a woman's beauty—with his soul. A beautiful woman never has to work in a field. She has others do that kind of work for her."

When he took her to his room, he wooed her with more compliments. He untied the charm and placed it carefully in the ashtray beside his bed. He forgot his anger that he would not be marrying Livie at Christmas. They made long, slow love in the night and when he brought her to a climax, she cried.

To Kwame's surprise he was moved. He held her gently and the thought occurred to him that he would like to have a child with Madame Van. He would like to be the man to give her the gift of full womanhood among her people. His male vanity would be pleased that his Power Loins had done what no others had managed.

Then he thought, what! These ideas startled him. Where had they come from? They were not his! He did not want a child. Not now. Certainly not with Madame Van! She was just a toy he shared with Odejimi. He did not want to leave a child behind in Africa.

THE NEXT morning Kwame tried to telephone Livie. He could not get through. He felt oddly relieved that nothing in the middle of nowhere seemed to work. He cabled Livie: "Leave denied. Impossible phone you. Letter follows. I love you."

Kwame began a letter to Livie about Pilar's denial of his leave and the panic she manifested over growing American involvement in the chaos at the Lakes. The words read like a report; they conveyed little emotion even when he felt it, when he expressed regret and frustration that they would not be marrying at Christmas. He wondered if this lack of emotion would raise a question in her mind: Had he found a woman in Africa?

KWAME TOLD the Badekas about Pilar Cota's instruction that he open the center. He asked if they could recommend a student to serve as a library assistant. He would open the center provisionally at first, he said, from three to five in the afternoons. It was a time when a student could learn the work without compromising his education. The Badekas suggested several candidates. Kwame remembered one from the lecture he had given about Camara Laye and Théa called him out of class.

Kwame interviewed Lofale. He explained the work: enrolling members into the library, checking out books and making sure they came back; showing one video documentary every afternoon in a room where Kwame would set up a video monitor and some chairs. Kwame himself would introduce the films. Once Lofale became familiar with them, he could introduce them himself. The young man seemed overjoyed at the prospect of a job. Kwame hired him. Immensely proud to be employed at the American center, the young man began his work.

Good to his promise to Pilar, Kwame had the center open by the end of the week.

KWAME SPENT most of the following Monday at the post office trying to get through by telephone to Pilar Cota in Kinshasa.

Late in the day he succeeded. She was just leaving for a cocktail party. "I'm calling to tell you the center's open," he reported.

"You're a marvel," she said. "Want to make that a permanent assignment?"

"You sound more relaxed," Kwame hazarded.

"There's been terrible fighting around Goma," she reported in a voice that was oddly lilting. "The humanitarian catastrophe we've all been dreading may be in the making."

"Are we involved?" Kwame asked. The shortwave radio reports he had heard did not make it clear exactly what the American role was. A puzzled silence came from the other end of the line. "The Americans," Kwame repeated, "are we in—"

"Oh, you haven't heard," exclaimed Pilar. "We're off the hook. Our guys aren't coming in after all. We're all so relieved."

"What happened?"

"I'm on my way out. There's an embassy cocktail celebrating our release. I'll send you a report of what happened." Pilar signed off.

The promised report never arrived.

ELEVEN

Kwame found Madame Van and Odejimi, Moulaert, and his Marike on the Afrique terrace. "I've just done the impossible," he boasted to his friends. "Talked to Kinshasa by telephone." A cry of astonishment greeted this news. "Of course, I had to threaten and cajole—"

"And bribe!" added the doctor.

"And bribe," agreed Kwame. "All day long to do it. I announced to Kinshasa that the American library is now open. I hope you will all come borrow books." The friends applauded this news. Kwame turned to Marike, the newcomer to the group. She sat primly in a European woman's jeans and top. "I hope you will borrow a book, Mademoiselle. I'm sure we have one that would please you." Marike smiled shyly at Kwame.

"I will look for her," said Moulaert.

"Bring her along," Kwame urged. He turned again to Marike. "Please tell your school friends that the library is open."

"What news from Kin?" asked Moulaert to shift attention away from the possession he intended to share with no one.

"Terrible fighting around Goma," Kwame said.

"I heard the news at noon," said the doctor. "Tutsi soldiers and irregulars invaded the refugee camps. The innocents are returning to Rwanda. The *génocidaires* are fleeing into Zairean jungles. And good riddance to them!"

"The Tutsis did this?" asked Moulaert.

"Yes, Tutsis!" exulted Odejimi. "Africans did this! Not Canadians. Not Americans!"

"What happens to the people who flee to the jungle?" asked Madame Van.

"They die," said Odejimi.

"Women and children too?" she asked.

"The *génocidaires* have this choice, Madame," Kwame explained. "They can go back to Rwanda—"

"Where they will be killed," interrupted Odejimi.

"Or they can take their chances in the jungles."

"But many who flee to the jungle were never killers," she protested.

Kwame looked at the doctor. "Are you sure there were no outside troops? No Americans?"

"Tutsis did it," said the doctor. "And hats off to them!"

If this was true, Kwame thought, no wonder the embassy staffers were so exhilarated. They dreaded the prospect of American involvement at the Lakes. Kwame himself felt ashamed that Americans, with all their power and protestations of goodwill, had done nothing to right the wrongs of the Rwandan massacres.

ONE AFTERNOON Kwame beat Madame Van at *mankala*. When Odejimi heard this news, he did not believe it. Kwame insisted it was true. "She let you win," Odejimi said. When Kwame began to win consistently, Odejimi warned, "Be careful, my friend. She gave you a charm for who knows what purpose. Now she is submitting to you. You will never escape from her."

How ridiculous, Kwame thought. All he had done was to win a few *mankala* games. Fair and square. How could Madame entrap him? He did not believe in charms. It was true that his victories over her, so long in coming, flattered his masculine vanity. They meant that she preferred him to Odejimi. That idea pleased him.

But at the same time fearing that Odejimi might be right, that he could not escape from her now, Kwame began to avoid *mankala*.

WHEN KWAME's friends gathered again to watch videos at the center's library, they sat around afterward, drinking whiskey and beer, and discussed the situation at the Lakes. Madame Van once again bemoaned the plight of innocent Hutu refugees, moving without food or shelter ever deeper into jungle. "What will become of them?" she asked.

"They better not be headed here," Mme Berton said.

"Keep the thugs out of the Equateur!" agreed her husband.

"It's a thousand-kilometer walk," said Odejimi. "If they come this far, their feet will be sore."

They began to debate the dangers posed by those among the refugees who were militants. "Do they kill people for food?" Marike asked.

"Probably," said Badeka. "Most of them are armed."

"And desperate!" added his wife.

"Poor Zaire!" Moulaert said. "Nothing but troubles these past forty years."

"The Americans were going to do something," said Badeka. "Is that finished?"

"What is there to do?" Odejimi asked.

"The Americans are so rich," said Théa Badeka, "but they help only themselves."

"Americans want to help Africa," Kwame said. He paused. Should he try to explain how his countrymen thought? He plunged ahead. "Most Americans honestly believe that—with goodwill, hard work, and money—practically every problem can be solved." This assertion produced looks of perplexity. His listeners glanced at one another.

"Even the massacres?" asked Madame Van.

"Most Americans—many of them anyway—think that life is fair," Kwame continued. "That generally bad things do not happen to good people."

The others snickered, as if Kwame had said something preposterous. He felt conspicuous and tongue-tied.

"It's your job to tell us that," Odejimi challenged. "Do you believe it?"

"Americans are well-meaning people," Kwame went on. "Most of them work very hard. But they are fortunate and comfortable and life has been good to them." He shrugged. "They want to help—but not if it hurts them."

The others glanced at one another again. "Do you believe that life is fair?" Odejimi asked a second time.

"How could I?" Kwame asked. "I'm a black man."

"But you are rich," said Madame Van.

"No, I am not rich."

"But, of course, you are," insisted Badeka.

"Things are getting better," Kwame admitted. "Especially for those who work hard." He realized in saying this he sounded very American. "It is not so much a white man's country anymore. And really—I am not rich, not in America." The Badekas and Madame Van stared at him with genuine surprise. They glanced at Odejimi who had studied in America. He nodded, confirming the truth of what Kwame said. "I'm not poor either," Kwame added. "And I've had good jobs, the jobs I wanted."

"Have you ever had a white girlfriend?" Badeka asked.

"Of course," Kwame said.

"Could you marry this white girlfriend?" Madame Van asked.

"Of course," Kwame repeated. "We lived together for two years. That's not marriage. But we were a couple. We are a couple."

"Do you have a photo of her?" inquired Madame Van.

Kwame withdrew his wallet. He removed a photo taken in New York of Livie and him, arms about one another, and passed it around. The Africans examined it carefully. When Madame Van took it, Kwame sensed that she was comparing herself to Livie feature by feature. "She has no breasts," Madame Van remarked.

"I can assure you," Kwame said. "She is not a boy."

"American women starve themselves to be thin," said Odejimi. "Impossible to sleep with them. Their bones keep you awake."

"And you could marry her?" Madame Van asked again.

"Of course. You married a white person. So could I." Madame folded her arms across her chest. "And I could divorce her. And have all the problems and unhappiness that stem from that." The others watched him; America seemed inexplicable to them. "It is mainly white people who think that life is fair," he tried to explain. "That all problems can be solved. Life has been good to them."

LATER THAT night Kwame sat alone on his balcony, annoyed that he had been so inarticulate about Americans. He was also distressed about the refugees, about frightened people plunging ever closer to the privation that awaited them in the jungles. He heard Madame Van enter the room. She came out onto the balcony and took the chair beside him. At last she asked, "Will you marry this white woman?"

Kwame shrugged.

"Does she believe that all problems can be solved?"

"Probably," he said.

"And you?"

They were quiet for a moment, both of them staring at a river they could not see. Finally he replied, "Americans are by nature optimistic. And everything changes over time."

He thought again of the refugees. He supposed—how American of him!—that most of them were innocent of participating in the genocide. But not all of them. Genocide: that was a problem that did not solve itself over time. It disturbed him that embassy people in Kinshasa had cocktails to celebrate the fact that American troops had escaped duty in Zaire.

Yet what could troops accomplish? If there was ever a quagmire, Rwanda was it. Still it unsettled him that American policy seemed always to seek only its own advantage, that Americans, besides being rich and fortunate, also had to be comfortable, that they were willing to help others only if no American got hurt. He knew, too, that most Americans did not see things his way. They would ask: "Why should Americans sacrifice their blood and treasure for an ungrateful world?"

A voice woke Kwame during the night. He opened his eyes and listened. He lay naked, Madame's back warm against his side, and stared at the ceiling.

Then the voice spoke to him once more. "Get out of here!" it said. It was a man's voice, one that Kwame did not recognize. Again it demanded, "Get out of this place!" Kwame suddenly understood: it was Mason's voice. Mason, calling him from wherever he was, telling him to leave.

But how could he leave? He had a job to do. Mason's voice kept repeating the warning: "Get out of this place while you can!"

Kwame turned his body toward Madame Van, his chest against her back. He caressed her hip, slid his hand up under her arm and cupped her breast. He took the nipple between his fingers; he pinched it until it became taut. The woman murmured. Kwame slid his hand down around her, turned her toward him. Only half-awake, she embraced him. He felt engulfed by her, safe. He no longer heard Mason's voice, warning him.

LATER LYING awake, grateful for Madame's rescuing him, he could not help thinking that his relationship with her was contrary to nature. At least to his nature. He had grown very fond of her. He had come to want exclusive sexual rights to her. So how could he share her with Odejimi?

He wondered if his desire that she be exclusively his stemmed from macho acquisitiveness. From ancient genetic programming that made men want to possess women as mere objects as he and Odejimi possessed her. If not, had he become trapped into thinking the way his mother did? Was his mother's morality haunting him? After all, why object to sharing her? He and the doctor were both transients. They were pals, all of them friends. There could be no intellectual objection to the arrangement.

Strangely he again wished that he could give Van a child. That would make her so happy. But how could he? She seemed unable to conceive. That relieved him from any annoying obligation to use contraceptives with her. Still this wishing disturbed him. It even frightened him a little. Where did it come from? Why did it keep popping into his head? Was it genetic too?

He mentioned the recurring thought to the Nigerian doctor. "She gave you a charm, didn't she?" Odejimi asked, laughing. Kwame admitted that she had. "Did she take hair from you?" Kwame acknowledged that she had. "And she has access to your semen." Odejimi mocked him, shaking his head. "She has a charm working on you, old boy."

"I don't believe in that kind of thing."

"Of course, you don't. You're an educated man." Odejimi guffawed. "But you keep thinking about it."

"So what do I do?" Kwame asked.

"Burn the charm."

Kwame nodded. He would do that.

Odejimi scrutinized him. "Next you'll tell me you want exclusive access to her." Kwame shrugged. "In America, old sod, this is called 'falling in love.'"

"I'm not in love with her."

"You need to sleep with other women," Odejimi said.

"Is that a medical diagnosis?"

"I didn't have to go to medical school to know that," said the doctor. "What about Marike? She's ready."

"I don't even much like Marike."

"You have to like them?" Odejimi laughed.

"It helps. Van has such sweetness—"

"Oh, blimey! You're in—"

"I am not!" Kwame insisted. Then he asked, "How could it possibly happen with Marike? He watches her."

"She might come to the center. Borrow a book. You have some place to do it there? Cushions or something?"

Kwame shook his head. He would not turn the center into a site for assignations.

"Marike's not impossible," Odejimi assured him. "I've had her."

Kwame burst out laughing. "You've had her? When?"

"Moulaert sent her for a test. So I tested her." Odejimi howled with laughter and raised an eyebrow. "She needs variety. And she doesn't like it that Moulaert wants her to do things Africans consider abominations." He stared at Kwame. "You better do something there if you think you want a child with Van."

"She's Moulaert's plaything," Kwame said.

"You Puritan!" Odejimi laughed. "You could try La Petite. Be sure you wear a condom. Or two or three."

Kwame smiled. The idea was completely preposterous.

"I hope you won't ask Van to live with you."

Kwame shook his head.

"Good. I'd get lonely."

As Christmas approached, Kwame's friends made plans to escape what Théa termed "the hubbub of Mbandaka." The Badekas would leave town. Moulaert was driving Marike to her village. Dr. Odejimi invited Madame Van to accompany him to Kisangani where friends he had known in Gisenyi were working. That she had accepted the invitation distressed Kwame. It seemed certain that the Nigerian would gain ground in their unspoken competition for her favor.

Kwame's feelings for her had deepened. He thought of her frequently during the day, wondering what she was doing, whom she was with. The nights when she was with Odejimi Kwame did not sleep well. He mused, too, about what Livie would do for the holidays. Perhaps she would simply catch up on her law courses. And what would he do? Suffer Mbandaka without friends.

Lying in bed one morning, watching reflected dawn light move across the ceiling, Kwame realized that he must get Madame Van something for Christmas, something very special for she, after all, had given him Mason's laptop. She was leaving the next day for Kisangani. There she would surely be impressed with the large city, with Odejimi at ease in it, this place where he had friends. There Odejimi might begin to win at *mankala*.

But what to get her?

Unless he got her something striking, she would not think of him the entire time she was gone. His gift would need to signify that their relationship was different from the one she had with the doctor. She must know that, while she was a mere plaything to Odejimi, with him she had a deeper bond, even a kind of romance. Probably she did not see it that way; Africans seemed not to think in those terms. But he treated her with respect; their times together were sweeter. He was not fooling around, as Odejimi was, with Mme Berton. Madame Van was certainly aware of that dalliance.

In midafternoon he drove to the communal market. He walked through aisles of offerings: plastic shoes, cheap mammy cloths, cheaper videos, throwaway trinkets, items for fashioning fetishes. He saw nothing that rose to the level of a gift fit for this special friend. He bought her a gold chain—which was probably not gold—because he had to give her something. But the chain did not satisfy him. It was something a man gave a woman whose body pleased him. Madame Van might like that, but he must get her something significant.

At the edge of the market he came upon a curious display: carvings sculpted apparently from tree trunks about the width of his outstretched hand. The pieces exhibited rude artistry. Kwame found himself drawn particularly to the head of a woman, perhaps a foot tall. She had almond eyes, a flattened nose, full lips, and hair coiffed in tight rows, trimmed at the back of the neck. The wood was dark brown and lustrous like the skin of a woman. The wood's grain was clearly visible on the forehead and cheeks. The head possessed an innate dignity. Although it did not resemble Madame Van, it made Kwame think of her.

A gift of art! Not merely a merchant's gift of gold. He doubted that any of the men she had known had given her such a thing. He hoped she would understand that the artist in him, the poet, was giving her something finer than gold.

When he saw her later that afternoon on the hotel terrace, he asked her to accompany him away from the others. At the door of his room he said, "I have a Christmas gift for you." He led her into his room. Standing on a table was the head. She beheld it and stood stock still.

"That's it? For me?"

"*Oui. Pour toi. Joyeux Noël.*" She gazed at it, not knowing what to say. Kwame laughed. "It's a gift of art," he said.

"*Mais comment?* What do I do with it?"

"You admire it. As I admire you." She glanced at him to see if he was joking. "You gaze at it and see a woman's dignity, her quiet steadiness. Her mystery. That's what I see when I look at you. You keep it forever and always think of me."

Madame Van glanced at him, perplexed. "A man gives a woman a cloth," she said. "Or a bodice. Or a head scarf." He realized that what he had given her, this head, could not be worn before other women, to demonstrate his regard.

"I'm not any man. I give you art."

"Am I to take it with me to Kisangani?"

"No, it's too heavy. You keep it here."

"In your room?"

"If you like." He started to tell her that it would make him think of her while she was gone, but he did not say that. Neither did he say that a woman kissed a man when he gave her a present.

"You keep it for me," she said. He realized the present had been a mistake. Livie would have been pleased; Madame Van was not. Odejimi would have her to impress during the entirety of their trip. Perhaps when she returned, she would no longer want to sleep with him. He reached into his pocket, pulled out the gold chain and gave it to her. She was delighted. She draped it around her neck where their friends would see it and assumed the head was a joke. She kissed his hands. He pulled her to him and kissed her mouth.

THE NEXT morning Kwame was to drive Odejimi and Madame Van to the airport. He fetched the center's truck. Odejimi left the hotel, carrying a duffel. "We all set?" he asked.

"Where's Van?" Kwame inquired.

"It turns out she doesn't like planes."

"She's not going with you?" Kwame's heart jumped with delight.

"She's gone to her village, Bololo or something."

"What a bummer for you," Kwame said.

"No matter," replied the doctor. "There are women to amuse a man in Kisangani."

When Kwame returned to the hotel after a swim, he saw Moulaert placing a footlocker into the back of his Land Cruiser. "What have you got in there?" Kwame asked. "You moving to the bush?"

Moulaert grinned and opened the lid of the footlocker. Inside it were tens of bundles of zaire notes. "Bride price money," he said. "You think she's worth it?"

"What if they want hard currency?"

"I give them the vehicle. And rent it back in zaires!" He laughed heartily. The transfer of notes would signify for Moulaert the fulfillment of his quest. It would establish for him more or less exclusive rights to his beloved—at least until he returned to his wife and two sons in Flanders and sent her back to a life of pestle and mortar.

"*Ay, copain,*" he called. "What a gift, eh? My best *Noël* ever!"

ON CHRISTMAS Day Kwame felt depressed. When he woke, he lay staring at the ceiling, missing Madame Van. They sometimes made love in the morning, neither of them fully awake, and he missed her. Missing her would persist all day. He drank some whiskey. He ate some breakfast of champions. He went down to the terrace, had rolls and coffee, and stared at the river. Back upstairs he tried to call Livie, mainly to be able to say he had. He could not get through. He wrote her a letter. He said he missed her—which on this day at least he did.

He made a pact with himself that he would not go to the center. He thought about his students and what he was trying to impart to them. He thought, "I ought to read something." All his life reading had given him pleasure. Now, although he had a library, he had not read a book in weeks.

He took a skiff with an outboard out onto the river. He maneuvered it behind islands to block off his view of Mbandaka and beached it on a sandbar. He stared at the tracks made in the sand by crocodiles, visitors to the place at night. He stripped and swam in the river, careful of the current. Drying off in the sun, watching clouds, he thought: "What's happening to me?" He drank whiskey nowadays, not excessively, but nonstop. He chewed dope for breakfast and smoked joints every day. He liked the woman he was fucking, liked her very much, but was sharing her with another man, treating her like a whore. And what was he doing in this shit-hole town? Running a library for illiterates, offering books in languages people couldn't read. He was achingly lonely and achingly bored. And the sun was burning him alive.

Back at the hotel he watched the river from his balcony. Perhaps Odejimi was right; he needed to be with another woman. He went to the pool, half hoping to give himself a Christmas present of the Gauguinesque girl. But she was not there. He swam lap after lap to wear out his body.

When he returned to the hotel, he found La Petite lounging in the entry. "Come with me," he said. She followed him upstairs and along the passageway to his room. It was Kwame's intention to drop his pants to his ankles and have her worship at the altar of his masculinity.

When she approached him, smiling salaciously, he noticed that her teeth were filed sharp. He also saw the sculpted head he had given Madame Van. It was watching them. He pushed the girl away. A voice behind him distinctly spoke. "My friend, what's the matter with you?" it asked. "You are missing Madame Van. Thinking all she is to you is a fuck. Give her some respect. And notice, too, this sida bug's teeth."

Kwame looked behind him. He saw the charm Madame Van had given him, lying in an ashtray. It spoke again. It said, "Tombolo will know you were with La Petite." Kwame did not believe in talking charms. Odejimi had advised him to burn it. The voice warned him, "These people talk. Van will know who you've been with half an hour after she gets back." Kwame gave La Petite zaires and some bananas, said, "*Bon Noël*," and pushed her from the room.

HALF AN hour later a knock sounded at his door. He trudged to it grumpily and opened it. Madame Van stood at the threshold.

Kwame was astonished. She smiled at him. "Madame, it's you!" he exclaimed. "I've been missing you all day and here you are!"

When she stepped into the room, he kissed her. She pushed him away, teasing.

"I thought you went to Bolobe."

"I was thinking," Madame said. "You are alone at Christmas. Maybe tomorrow you would like to drive me to Bolobe. You could show films for my people."

The invitation flattered Kwame. So she had never intended to go to Kisangani. He understood that he was now starting at quarterback on Team Van.

As they lay in bed that night, their Christmas being together, Madame Van was sad. "Those poor refugees in the jungles," she said. "It's Christmas and I cannot stop thinking about them." Kwame kissed her forehead. "Terrible things happen in the jungle. The ghosts of the dead live there."

Kwame did not want to tell her that there were no ghosts, only psychological projections. If he did, she would not believe him. And anyway how did he know? "Do they?" he asked.

"Some ghosts are as tall as trees," Madame said. "Others are as tiny as ants. Some of them have nothing but skulls. No bodies. When they go into the world they take on body parts from other creatures. So as not to frighten the living. They put them on like clothes."

Kwame smiled at this thought. He moved his head away from her so that she would not feel him smiling.

"Some ghosts live in the ground," she continued. "They come into the world through tiny holes. If you are not careful, they will lure you down a hole."

They were quiet for a time.

"Those refugees in the jungles," she persisted. "They have nothing to eat and no place to live. The ghosts are watching them. When they are weak and tired, the ghosts carry them off. They take their spirits into their holes in the ground."

Again they said nothing for a time. Kwame thought: How curious that I once wondered about becoming African. I could never think like that.

Finally Madame said, "You do not believe me, do you? About ghosts."

Kwame put his arms about her and kissed her forehead again. "The ghosts in America are different," he said.

"You will go back there, won't you?"

"Eventually."

When he kissed her cheek, he realized she was crying.

"What is it?"

"I would like to have your child," she said.

Kwame said nothing. She must have sensed that because of the charm he had been considering this. Was that the cost of starting at quarterback?

"Some of you is African. Leave part of you here."

"I am doing nothing to prevent you having a child. You know that."

"You are withholding permission."

"Am I?" he asked. "I thought the seed was permission enough?" After a moment he said, "Maybe it's the babies. They look down at this country falling apart and they do not want to come."

They were quiet again. He did not want to tell her that she was the person withholding permission. That without her knowing it, her body had erected a psychic barrier to conception. Why? He suspected she resented her lovers, not so much because they would leave her. But because they did not respect her; they considered her only a toy that gave them sex. Kwame himself had been guilty of that. But was no longer. Conception might happen when they truly trusted one another. Surely

Odejimi would scoff at this notion as poetry, not biology. Let Odejimi scoff.

"If a child consented to come," he asked her, "could you raise it alone?"

"I will never be alone. In a village a child has many parents."

The darkness lay all about them. Finally Kwame said, "The *Bon Dieu* gives a woman a child. Let's leave this in His hands."

He wondered: Could he truly withhold permission? No! In his society a man gave permission with his seed.

Madame Van wanted a child in order to gain admittance into that category of adulthood that in Africa a woman could achieve only by producing offspring. For his part the deeper their emotional bond grew, the more concerned he became that they used no contraception. Trust was blooming between them. If they grew to love each other, he feared that she would conceive. He would leave her with a child he would not participate in raising. An affair, Kwame thought, should not produce a child. In that sense she was right; he truly was withholding permission.

If the emotional bond between them continued to deepen, Kwame wondered, would whatever was blocking conception dissolve? And would he have a responsibility in that? Should he break with her now? No! That was impossible! He liked her too much. So perhaps, he mused, it really was best to leave the matter to the *Bon Dieu*.

Kwame thought of Livie. She disapproved of male irresponsibility. She also opposed using condoms, but for reasons of aesthetics. Sex was better without latex; that was her strongly held opinion. In any case, she was on the pill. Aesthetics in sex were important to her. Often in their postcoital mellowness she would analyze the performance that had just occurred. She would contemplate ways to improve it, to heighten their sensations. Kwame hated these debriefings. He fell asleep—or pretended to.

There had come a time in South Africa when Livie grew moody and depressed. When Kwame asked her what was wrong, she could not pinpoint the malaise. "I've been here more than a year," she complained. "I need to go home for a while." Kwame was not the kind of man who kept track of his lover's menstrual cycle. But he wondered if she were late. Livie did not approve of abortion—although, of course, she approved of a woman's right to have one. In fact, she had one night tearfully, regretfully admitted to Kwame that she had had an abortion her second year at BU.

Then one day she called him at the office to say that she was at the airport. She was about to board a plane for New York; she would be back in a couple of weeks. When she returned, she was happy again and overjoyed to see him. "Oh, how I've missed you!" she told him repeatedly. "I don't want us to be separated ever again."

More than once Kwame felt himself on the brink of saying, "You went home for an abortion, didn't you?" But he never spoke the words. What was the point? He knew what she had done. Asking for a confirmation she did not want to acknowledge would only damage the relationship. They handled the matter in a very WASP way; nothing was ever said. Kwame sometimes thought, I am not a WASP. But this woman is turning me into one.

He wondered the same thing now. Was Madame Van's charm working its magic on him? How else could he explain the fact that he sometimes wanted her to have their child—even when he knew that he would not be around to parent that child?

He had also been wondering something else. If abandoning her was what he must do when he left Zaire, why didn't he marry her? Take her with him? Impossible! he would tell himself. Even so, the idea was often in his thoughts. But these were not his ideas, he reminded himself. They were placed in his head by Van's charm.

"I would like to have a child," Madame said again, caressing him. "I know you will go away. All men go away."

When they made love that night, Kwame wanted Madame to feel fulfilled. As they climaxed, he thought, "I give my permission." Would the *Bon Dieu* hear him? They would see what the *Bon Dieu* did.

TWELVE

Kwame and Madame Van set out in the film truck at midmorning. Kwame carried two jerricans of gasoline, another of drinking water, a projector, gasoline generator, portable screen, cans of film, and a couple of changes of clothes. Packing for the trip, he recalled the morning he and Odejimi and Van had enjoyed their threesome together, drinking, fucking, and chewing the breakfast of champions. A reprobate moment, the lowest he had sunk to on the downward path to gain Odejimi's friendship. He had enjoyed it, but now felt corrupted by it. And so in packing he did not take whiskey or hemp. He wanted to test Odejimi's contention that these were crucial to his survival. He did, however, take a case of Primus beer for Madame Van's father.

The road followed the Congo River. It proved to be in good repair as far as Wendji about twenty miles west of the town. Beyond it they headed south into an area of swamp, some of it open water, very shallow, with the road a ridge above it, some of it moving through scrub jungle. Kwame drove carefully. Madame Van watched him. Neither spoke.

In the silence between them Kwame felt comfortable. He realized that this was almost the first time he had been with Madame when their being alone was not about sex. He glanced over at her and recognized her not as an object of competition with Odejimi, but as a person in her own right. Who was she anyway?

Finally Kwame said, "Shouldn't I know your name? What do people call you in your village?"

The question seemed so unusual that she did not immediately respond. Finally she said, "Kalima."

"May I call you Kalima?" Kwame asked. She looked at him carefully. "It's not improper, is it, for an American to call you Kalima?"

"You may call me Kalima," she said gravely. She glanced at him ironically and added, "*Monsieur.*"

"*Monsieur*! Stop calling me *Monsieur.*" He grinned at her. "Can you say Kwame?"

"*Oui, Monsieur,*" Kalima replied, teasing him.

He laughed. "Quoi-mee. Say that?" Kalima shook her head. "It's an African name, Ghanaian. Kwa-mee. Can you try that?"

"Kwa? As in *pourquoi?*'

"*Oui.* And mee as in *moi.*" She laughed. Kwame explained the origin of his name, good teacher that he was. His companion listened with the intensity of his best students. "Will you call me that please—" he hesitated, then for the first time, addressing her, spoke her name. "Kalima?"

"I will call you Kwame," she agreed. "*Monsieur.*" She laughed.

Although they teased each other, Kwame had a strange feeling that something significant was happening. He and Kalima were exchanging not merely names, but—what? He would not allow the word 'vows' to form in his mind. Kalima seemed virginal to him, not a woman men had used. Men like Odejimi and Vandenbroucke and possibly Mason— And he himself, he acknowledged. Now that Madame Van was Kalima, she acquired a purity. Kwame smiled at her. He stopped the truck and kissed her with such tenderness that she gazed at him with a kind of radiance.

Moving south over swamp, the traveling was very slow. They could see remnants of the road that had existed in colonial times, but it had not been maintained. Kwame drove where he thought the road must be. When they crossed through swamps, he left the truck and walked the road before driving over it. Kalima walked with him and sometimes they would see women bathing or soaking manioc tubers.

The farther they advanced from Mbandaka, the harder the road was to follow. Now and then they lost it all together. Several times Kwame stood on top of the truck to scout where they should go. They arrived in Bikoro as the sun was setting. They discovered that the road to Kalima's village of Bolobe had reverted to being merely a trail; vehicles could no longer pass over it. They found a guesthouse to lodge in and Kalima sent a young man to inform her people that they would arrive the next day. Kwame would show films to the entire village if her people could provide porters to carry his equipment.

After dinner Kwame and Kalima went to their room. With a single candle alight on the bedside table, they crawled onto their bed, got cozy inside the mosquito net, and leaned against the wall at the head of the bed, pillows wedged behind them. Kwame took Kalima's hand in his, a gesture to which she was not accustomed, and told her that inside the mosquito netting it was as if they were in a little house all their own. He told her about little houses he had made as a child out of cushions on his parents' couch. He told her about growing up in Amherst, Massachusetts, about snow and cold, about first beginning school, and autumn leaves. He asked her to tell him about Bolobe. She started hesitatingly—how could her childhood in a village interest a man from great America?—but every time she faltered he asked questions to keep her talking. Eventually the candle burned out. "You are very beautiful," he said. "Do you know that?"

She laughed. "It is easy to tell a woman she is beautiful in the dark."

"Ka-li-ma," Kwame said, tasting every syllable. "My Kalima." Instead of lighting another candle, Kwame moved toward her and held her, his cheek against hers. "Your eyes sparkle when you laugh. Did you know that? You have an extraordinary mouth."

"How are my ears?" They both laughed.

"If I had never come to Zaire, I would never have held you."

They held each other a long time. Finally each went to the bathroom and came back to the bed to help the other undress. They kissed and caressed without hurry. They made love quietly, slowly, and Kwame was aware less about the sensations in his groin than about the woman in his arms. Before they slept, Kwame whispered, "I have never known anything like this."

"I loove oo, Kwa-mee," Kalima said. Kwame kissed her, pleased that she had attempted English, even if not with complete success.

The next morning when they were still in bed, some thirty people from Bolobe appeared at the guesthouse where they lodged. Their songs of greeting made Kalima rush from the building in a frenzy of delight. She shook hands with every person who walked over. Not wanting to emphasize the difference between him and her people, Kalima advised Kwame to dress casually. When he appeared in shorts, a tee shirt, sunglasses, and sandals, the visitors grew quiet, inspecting him with a mixture of curiosity and respect. Kalima introduced him to each of the visitors. He said, "*Mbote*," the local greeting, but understood little of what they answered. When he offered his hand, many of them took it in both of theirs and bowed to him with deference.

There was not equipment enough for everyone to carry, but Kwame spread the gear as widely as possible. Most of the villagers lofted the loads onto their heads, whether they were single video cassettes or the gasoline generator which Kwame himself could not imagine carrying on his cranium. As they walked, they sang.

They arrived in Bolobe about noon. The village was a long string of huts, mud-and-wattle walls with banana frond roofs, on two sides of a rutted and unpaved road leading to Lake Tumba. There large pirogues had been pulled up onto the beach. It was clear when Kalima introduced Kwame to her father that she admired and respected him. In Bolobe Bonanga had great *mpifo*, prestige, as the village's primary teller of stories. He struck Kwame as a man of great presence and dignity. If he was not one who possessed the charisma and theatricality that Kwame assumed might attach to a storyteller, he sensed that Bonanga expected a certain deference. He seemed very aware of his position as an elder.

"I hope to hear you talk about your people and your village," Kwame told him. When Kalima translated his words, Kwame detected only the slightest flicker of reaction across his eyes. Bonanga measured him with a sadness that stemmed, Kwame assumed, from his disappointment with Kalima's failure to choose men whose ways he understood. Kwame also met Bonanga's two wives. Kalima claimed both women as mothers, an assertion which Kwame realized he must accept until the time came to get it straightened out.

He was presented to Bolobe's leading citizen, a small-time politician who represented both Mobutu and his political party, the *Mouvement Populaire de la Révolution*. This dignitary and Bonanga walked Kwame around the village. A train of young men followed them, carefully deferential to their elders. They watched Kwame as if he were an alien prince. Together he, Bonanga, and the dignitary selected the site for the film showing. No one in the village seemed to speak French; everyone who had mastered that language had moved beyond Bolobe. Kwame found that he could offer greetings in Lingala, the lingua franca of the area, but could not make himself understood otherwise.

He spent the early part of the afternoon sitting on a stool outside the dignitary's hut. With this host, Bonanga, and several younger men, Kwame drank the Primus beer he had brought with him. He listened to the music of the talk, which sometimes fell into silence.

Occasionally Bonanga or the dignitary would send one of the young men off on an errand. This person unfailingly jumped up at the slightest request, performed it speedily, and seemed honored to be in the elders' presence. Kwame could not help thinking how different was the African reverence for elders from the casual disregard of young Americans for theirs. Now and then he would see Kalima; she was preparing dinner with her birth mother. Sometimes he would catch the sound of her voice. He did not feel entirely comfortable. But for reasons he did not understand neither did he feel ill at ease; in America he would have been antsy, wanting to flee.

Late in the afternoon two young men took the duffels and led Kwame a mile or so from the village to a house overlooking the lake. Apparently once a European's home, it had a floor of concrete and walls of cement. Once it had possessed a roof of corrugated iron, most sheets of which had now been hauled away. It was devoid of furniture except for a large bed and a mattress stuffed with local fibers.

A pirogue lay pulled up to the shore. The young men took Kwame for a paddle on the lake. Out on the water the stillness possessed an almost tangible weight; Kwame could feel it pressing against his skin. The air was clear, free of pollutants. The sky began to turn yellow, then orange. As they walked back to the village, the orange darkened into red.

Kalima had prepared a dinner of goat meat and manioc greens. She served it to Bonanga and Kwame with great pride and deferential bowing. While they ate, young people danced in a circle, clapping their hands and following the steps designated by a leader. Meanwhile villagers gathered for the films, men carrying lanterns, women approaching with infants tied to their backs.

After praising Kalima's cuisine, Kwame showed USIS informational films. In preparing for the trip, he had decided that it would be impractical to take to Bolobe the projection equipment required for showing the Hollywood entertainment videos he screened at the showings he hosted outside the center. Hollywood products—romantic comedies or action movies, full of gunfire and car chases—might prove more incomprehensible to villagers than the usual USIS fare. What he was really offering the villagers was not movie narratives so much as the opportunity to witness light show technology they had never seen before. The audience applauded and whistled at the conclusion of each selection. Youngsters danced excitedly, flailing their arms and throwing their hips. When the show ended, young people, not yet initiated, formed a circle again; drummers provided music. This time they danced excitedly, with a kind of frenzy.

After a time a cry arose. It was started by men of what would have once been the warrior class, then taken up in a slow, rhythmic clapping, by women. Young men who had undergone initiation built and lit a fire. Kwame watched Kalima clap, a grin on her face. "We are calling for my father to tell a story," she explained. Kwame mimicked the clapping, as if asking her permission. She nodded and he joined the villagers.

Beginning his performance Bonanga shuffled out before the fire, moving like an ancient although he was clearly in the prime of life. The villagers settled around the fire. Bonanga hobbled toward children clustered at his feet. He reached out to take their hands. He spoke to them in a quavering voice. Kwame looked to Kalima for a translation. "I have already forgotten more than you have seen in your life," she translated, a look of delight on her face.

Now Bonanga, very much portraying an old man, hushed his listeners as if to begin his story. Then he looked around, as if perplexed. He peered into the fire. He searched among the listeners, delighting the elders among them. One of his wives passed something to Kalima. She ran out to him and passed him a pipe. He took a fiber, leaned into the fire to light it, and then brought it to the bowl of the pipe. He puffed on it; the tobacco caught.

Suddenly as if transformed, Bonanga became a young man, strutting around the fire. The children watched him with awe. He produced the sounds of animals and birds, began to fashion snares and traps out of thin air. He caught an animal in a trap, then another and another. Kalima put an arm around Kwame's back, drew his ear close to her mouth and explained, "This is the story of our forefather, Nkundo. He invented snares before our people ever had them."

"Nkundo?" Kwame asked. "He gave his name to your language?"

Kalima nodded that the words were the same.

Bonanga feigned sleep, then suddenly woke, beholding something magical. Kalima explained. "He dreams that he catches the sun in his snare." Then in the way Bonanga moved, both as Nkundo and his prey, Kwame understood that the snare had caught a beautiful woman. "Ilánkaka," Kalima whispered to him, "the daughter of a king. He takes her to his village—"

"And they live happily ever after," Kwame said.

"This is not the story of a European," Kalima whispered. "*Attends!*"

Kwame watched Bonanga start out again on other journeys, but lost the thread of the story. Was he hunting? He seemed to capture four animals. Then went out with Ilánkaka and brought more. Kwame released the plot line of the story and simply wondered at the artistry of Bonanga. He captured the audience and held them fast, as if his voice, gestures, and movement were snares too.

As KALIMA led Kwame through the warm darkness to their house, he reviewed their time together: the sweet closeness they'd felt, shedding their old identities and becoming new people to one another, Kalima and Kwame; that closeness given physical expression the night before; the walk to Bolobe, her village people carrying his movie projection gear; his long afternoon with the men . . . His review faltered there. He had wanted to feel welcome, but had not. Nor entirely comfortable. That was a contrast to the comfort Kalima had so obviously felt, back among the people from whom she'd sprung. Had her comfort with them pulled her away from him?

As they walked, each carried a lantern. The whisperings of crickets and cicadas accompanied them. As they passed, frogs croaked in their pools. Owls hooted in the darkness. "I liked seeing you so happy," Kwame said. He could tell that brought a smile to her face. "Your father's an extraordinary storyteller."

He placed his hand on the back of her neck and gently caressed it. He hesitated before asking the question plaguing him. Then he inquired, "What did your parents think of me? I couldn't tell."

Kalima said nothing as if she had not heard the question.

Oh-oh, Kwame thought. We have a problem. They walked a bit farther. He raised his lantern and glanced at her. "I take it they didn't like me. Is my skin too white?"

Kalima kept walking. She pulled so far ahead of him so that his hand dropped from her neck.

Kwame decided to play it lightly, to charm her if he could. "A nice guy in town. Not so good in a village? Is that it?" Frogs sang at them. "The wildlife likes him: croak, croak." Kalima walked on as if she did not hear him. Kwame raised his voice just a bit. "Not such a bad fellow. Gave your father beer. Showed films. Applauded your papa's story." Then: "Loves his daughter. Treats her well."

Kalima did not respond. She led him along the path, saying nothing. They did not speak for several minutes. Kwame felt very alone. If she were still Madame Van, he could have asked her what went wrong. But she was now Kalima. Whatever was wrong was much more serious.

Finally he said, "Your father's so amazing. I got a lot of his story without understanding the words."

That made them friends again. Kalima said, "Bolobe is so proud of him."

Carefully they chatted about her father's story. "What exactly was Nkundo doing at the end?" Kwame asked. "I got lost."

Kalima turned toward him and walked backward. "You expected him to be Prince Charming, didn't you?" she said, suddenly scornful, dismissive. "Like in a white man's story."

Careful, Kwame thought. He asked, "Didn't he marry the daughter of a king?"

"You wanted Ilánkaka to be Cinderella, didn't you?" The same tone of voice.

"Ilánkaka?" Kwame repeated. "Can I call her Caca for short?" Kwame doubted that she would get his little joke. That was just as well. He hid his amusement.

"ILÁNkaka," she emphasized, aware that he was joking. "Our ancestor, a real person." She turned to walk forward again.

Kwame thought it charming that Kalima supposed the king's daughter, looking like a sun goddess, might get caught in a snare, that she might be an actual ancestor.

"They are happy for a time," Kalima explained. "Then Ilánkaka wants Nkundo to take his proper role. That means finding more wives."

"First he was hunting animals. Then he was hunting wives?"

"He brought home four wives and Ilánkaka said, 'That's not enough. Get one hundred.'"

Kwame laughed. "Wow! Some ambitious wife!"

Kalima's tone became impatient again. Kwame realized he would not reconnect with her unless he took the ancestor story seriously. "She wants people to respect her husband," Kalima said. "To see that he is a man rich enough to have many wives. Each of them will give him children."

Kwame recalled such stories in anthropology readings. In most of the African fiction he had read, however, women were distressed about husbands wanting multiple wives. Kwame could see how a man might want a mistress. But several wives—to say nothing of one hundred—all living in the same compound? Impossible.

"You understand that those wives will do Ilánkaka's bidding," continued Kalima. "So she also becomes very rich."

"She doesn't care that he sleeps with the other wives?"

"How else will they give him children?"

"Doesn't he miss sleeping with her? If it were me—" He stopped her walking, turned her to face him, and kissed her. "I don't want to sleep with anyone but you."

"I'm not even giving you children," she said.

"What would I do with children?"

They walked on in silence. Finally Kwame asked, "Your parents didn't like me because I don't give you children? Is that it?"

A sapling had fallen across the path. Kalima stopped. Kwame came up behind her, put an arm about her neck, and kissed the side of her head. "Is that it?" he repeated.

She shook his arm away and pulled the sapling off the path. "My father, he says: 'Why always a white man?'"

This remark surprised Kwame. He laughed. "I am not a white man."

"A white man does not have to have white skin," Kalima said.

"My ancestors were African," Kwame replied.

"My mother says: 'Where are your babies? At your age you should have babies. Why are you with these men who do not give you babies?'"

Kwame said nothing. Kalima's parents did not approve of him; that was distressing. "I thought you couldn't have babies."

Kalima gave a shrug. "I will not be a real woman until I have them. It seems I don't have them with white men."

They walked on in silence. Finally Kalima said, "There is a man in Bikoro that my parents want me to marry. He wants a wife with education."

Kwame wondered: Who was this guy? Was he real? Village Africans didn't wait around for women with education. Or would she be his second wife? "Will he give you babies?"

"My parents think so."

WHEN THEY reached the house by the lake, Kwame began to shed his clothes. "Don't," Kalima said.

"Let's go in the lake. Cool off. Wash off the day." Kwame had already kicked off his shorts and sandals and was standing in the lake in his briefs. Kalima seemed distressed that he had shed his shorts. It was as if someone were watching them.

"I'm going back to the village," Kalima said.

Kwame walked out of the water and came to her. "Why is that? I'll come with you." He put his shorts back on.

She shook her head and glanced down the path they had crossed.

"We're here together," Kwame said. He put his arms about her. "Last night was so—"

Kalima pushed him away. She continued to shake her head.

"What's happened?" Kwame asked.

"My father says it's finished for me in Mbandaka."

Kwame was astonished. "That's not his right," he said. "You live there. Your life is there. I'm there."

Kalima shook her head.

"Stop shaking your head!"

"My father says I belong in Bolobe. My mother is sure the man from Bikoro will give me babies."

"Don't let them run your life!" Kwame exclaimed, as if she were an American girl from western Massachusetts. "You're not a child. You left them for the convent. You left them for Vandenbroucke. You don't belong in a village."

"My parents disapprove of my life in Mban." Again she glanced toward the path. "They say I must come back here, marry, and have children."

"I'm not going to let this happen!"

"It doesn't concern you."

Kwame felt the words, "I love you," clamoring up his throat. But even if she did not know what they meant, he was not going to say the words. The relationship was not there yet. Finally he asked, "Are you just going to do what they tell you?"

"In Africa we do what our elders tell us."

"Even when they sell you to Vandenbroucke?" He went to her, tried to take her hands in his. One was still holding a lantern. She thrust the other angrily behind her back. He looked deeply into her eyes. Quietly he said, "You're your own person. You have your own identity, your own destiny."

Kalima shook her head.

"Let me walk you back. You can't go alone. I'll talk to your father."

"He will walk me back. He's waiting for me down the path."

What? Kwame felt betrayed. Had Bonanga followed them from Bolobe? He moved to embrace Kalima. She moved away. "No!" It was as if her father must not see them embrace. She hurried down the path. Kwame started after her. Suddenly Bonanga appeared, holding a lantern. His expression brooked no opposition. Kalima moved past him. Bonanga watched Kwame as Kalima disappeared. Then he turned and followed her into the darkness.

KWAME SLEPT badly. He woke in the night, wondering if he'd lost her, Kalima. But what had he really lost: a woman he shared with another man. He could understand her father's concern. Shortly before dawn he left the lonely bed, grumbled at his fate, and went outside to piss. He stood naked, the cool air of the morning clothing him. Despite his sadness, he watched the light change, the clouds turn orange against the scarlet sky. The way things had turned out, he wished he had followed Odejimi's advice and brought hemp and whiskey. They would have helped him get through the night.

On the ground beside the back door he found a gourd and a piece of soap. The water was cool. Kwame waded in above his knees, then squatted into the water, soaped himself, then ladled water into the gourd and over him. By the time he dressed, young men from Bolobe appeared, carrying the film equipment he had left at the village. He packed the duffels and verified that all the film equipment was accounted for.

He told the *chef* of the "porters" that he wished to return to Bolobe to thank Bonanga. The man seemed not to understand. Kwame indicated his intention in gestures. The young man shook his head. Did he still not understand? Or was he blocking the way? Kwame managed a smile, raised his arms as if to ask for patience, and started toward the path to Bolobe. The porters blocked his way. The *chef* respectfully shook his head, said something that might have been "*Bonanga dit non,*" (Bonanga says no) and gently put his hand on Kwame's arm, restraining him. Kwame realized that the young men were endeavoring both to show their respect, but also to prevent his returning to Bolobe.

Kwame suddenly realized that he might never see Kalima again.

Reluctantly Kwame followed the young men to Bikoro. After they replaced the equipment into his truck, he thanked them, entered the small guesthouse where he and Kalima had stayed, and got a breakfast of coffee and an omelet. As he ate, he could not quite believe what had happened. In their room in this very guesthouse he and Kalima had grown closer together than they had ever been. Although he was not entirely sure what the words meant to her, she had said she loved him. He had acknowledged to himself that he loved her. If she felt true affection for him, wanted to be with him, how was it that she would submit—cave in!—to her father's demands? Obviously he did not understand African life!

Leaving the guesthouse, ready to start back to Mbandaka, he found the "porters" waiting beside his vehicle. Had they been instructed to make sure he left Bikoro? Bonanga certainly meant to see the last of him. Kwame took control of himself, opened his arms expansively, and exclaimed, "*Ah, mes amis! Merci!* Thank you for your help! *Merci!*" He shook the hands of each man and grinned at them. As he drove off, he hoped they would return to Bolobe, singing his praises.

DRIVING BACK to Mbandaka, Kwame stared at the road without seeing it. He functioned in a kind of limbo. The road was as empty as Kwame felt inside. There were no pedestrians, no traffic. He felt as alone as he had ever felt in his life. In the place inside him that Kalima usually filled, there was only hollowness.

He stopped the film truck at a bridge. He got out, the motor still running, checked the soundness of the bridge, returned behind the steering wheel and sat. He loved her. So what? What did his love signify for her family? Apparently nothing—except that he was yet another white man using her for his pleasure. He became aware of the motor's sound. He drove forward.

American fathers might disapprove of their daughter's boyfriends. But generally they did not oppose them, certainly not in the way that Bonanga was opposing him. In America opposition generally allied the daughter more strongly with the boyfriend. Jack Carlyle had tried to make Kwame his friend. If he opposed Kwame, it was because he and Livie had not married.

Kwame crossed a section of swamp where the surface of the road lay underwater. He told himself to pay attention to the driving. But he hardly saw where he was going. He kept thinking about the threesome with Odejimi. He could not blame Bonanga for determining to put a stop to shenanigans like those.

But he had intended to tell Kalima that he wanted an exclusive relationship with her. He expected to tell Odejimi that the competition between them was over. He had won. Kalima was his. He had been set to instruct Odejimi to find diversion elsewhere. But he had not yet informed Kalima of that. He had not yet sought her permission to take that step.

Kwame parked and left the truck. He walked the road in front of him. It was a decent section, needing no reconnaissance, but he had to stretch, had to think. What most haunted him was the prospect of Kalima's future in Bolobe.

In Bolobe there was no role for a woman of Kalima's age except as someone's wife. With every step he took Kwame thought marriage, marriage, marriage. Bonanga would almost immediately try to set up a marriage for Kalima. That would not be easy. At twenty-three, which Kwame supposed her to be, she was past prime marrying age. Moreover she had some education and was accustomed to urban living. In the village, both of those, he supposed, would make her less attractive. She had beauty and presence, but as she herself had explained to him they counted for little in village life. They might even be seen, not as advantages, but as negatives. However the crucial negative was that, despite the earlier marriage to Vandenbroucke, despite relationships with other men, she had produced no children. Producing children was the focus of African marriage, the purpose of African life. Who would agree to marry a barren woman?

Walking back to the truck, Kwame wondered if she were destined to become the second or even the third wife of a man in middle life. Perhaps the man in Bikoro, about whom she had spoken, was older, well-established, and interested in a woman who could serve, less as a producer of children, than as an ornament of his success. This was the African version of the toy she had been for him and Vandenbroucke and Odejimi.

When he resumed driving, he tried to make peace with having lost her. When he returned to the Afrique, he thought, he would get drunk, smoke hemp, and wait for Odejimi to return from Kisangani. But as he rolled along, mile after swamp mile, he decided, "No!" As a penance for treating Kalima as he had, he would swear off whiskey and hemp, reduce his association with Odejimi, stay celibate for a time, and spend more work hours at the center.

It was late afternoon by the time he reached Mbandaka. He went to the center and replaced the film equipment on its shelves. When he entered the office, the whiskey bottle in his desk drawer called out to him. He marched himself out of the center and over to the post office. He collected the mail. He returned to the center, settled down at his desk, and fiddled with correspondence until the Mongo opened and he could get some dinner. The bottle in his drawer kept enticing him; he thought repeatedly of pouring its contents down the toilet. But although he had sufficient resolve to resist the bottle's call, he lacked the strength to rid himself of it.

After dinner he drove back to the Afrique. He shut himself up in his room. If he had the force of character to forgo whiskey and hemp, he could not resist the items of Kalima's clothing in his armoire. He took them delicately in his hands, fondled them, smelled them, carried them in his fist as he paced back and forth across the room, missing her, overcome with the sadness of losing her.

THIRTEEN

Following the plan for his post-Kalima life, immediately after he returned from Bolobe, Kwame spent long days at the center. Most of his work, however, was for his classes at Bomboko Congo. He avoided the Afrique terrace in the late afternoon.

Kwame did run into Moulaert. He had returned from Marike's village so besotted with his teenage bride that he did not care about having spent all his zaires. He smiled incessantly. His skin glowed. His delight in Marike only made Kwame increasingly conscious of what Kalima's defection to Bolobe cost him. He avoided the man.

Finally one afternoon Odejimi knocked at his hotel room door. When he opened it, the doctor urged, "Come have a drink with me, old boy. Where have you been keeping yourself?"

They repaired to the terrace. Kwame got a beer. Odejimi had his usual whiskey and a smoke. "How was Kisangani?" Kwame asked.

"Too close to that mess farther east. But I must say pleasant to be in a place larger than this. Mban is hardly more than a village, you know?"

"Tell me," Kwame said. "I've been here all by myself."

"What's become of Van?" Odejimi asked.

"She's gone to her village."

"All this time? What's happening down there?" Kwame wondered if by this time Bonanga had married her off. "You miss her, old chap?"

Kwame smiled sardonically and took a sip of his beer. "Don't you?" he asked.

"Berton has gone to his plantations. So things are not so bad."

KWAME GOT an urgent communication from his bosses in Kinshasa. Had he forgotten to submit the year-end reports congress wanted? Could he please indicate the number of people using the center; the number of books, videos, and films borrowed; contacts made; plans for future activities? How did he expect to increase book and video usage? Kinshasa needed the report ASAP.

Kwame knew that honest reporting would fail to impress Washington bureaucrats or congressmen. True numbers would prove disappointing. He would look ineffective in his job. So he stalled. He soon received an urgent nudge from Pilar Cota. He fretted about his predicament just as he had done to Kalima the last time he had been pestered for a report.

"Tell them what they want to hear," she suggested.

"I can't do that," he told her.

"Why not?"

"It's not the American Way." Kalima frowned. It was obvious that she had no idea what he meant. He did not want to explain that her suggestion was contrary to all his training. That in America truth was Truth. It marched with a capital T and even if unpalatable it must be stated. On the other hand, he reminded himself, it was also the American Way to massage the numbers.

He sat in his office, having a mental conversation with her.

"Why would you tell them something to make them unhappy?" she asked in his head just as she did one evening in his room. "They are far away. Tell them what gives them pleasure."

Mulling this advice, Kwame wondered what he would accomplish by reporting true numbers. If Kinshasa were unhappy with them, people there would feel a need to do something. Check up. Visit. Give him a bad report. But he did not want to be checked or visited. At least for the moment, he wanted to be forgotten. So why not tell them what they longed to hear?

"I have been so busy with the program," Kwame began his report, "that it has been difficult to find a moment to prepare the requested post assessment." He exaggerated the figures for attendance, borrowings, showings. He reported his plans to present village film showings and gave a glowing account of the visit he had just completed to Lake Tumba. The roads were bad, he reminded Kinshasa, but he had managed to spend a night both in Bikoro and Bolobe, where he had shown films and met the local *chef* of Mobutu's *Mouvement Populaire Revolutionaire.*

ONE AFTERNOON shortly after his return from Marike's village, Moulaert joined Kwame and Odejimi on the hotel terrace. Bestowing wife-besotted smiles upon them, he poured himself a beer and attacked a pile of accumulated mail. He opened envelope after envelope, glanced at their contents, and tossed them into a box he used for trash. Finally he picked up an envelope, scanned the handwriting, and giggled shamefacedly. "My god," he muttered. "This is from my wife."

"Madame Marike Moulaert?" asked Odejimi. "A love note from her honeymoon?"

Moulaert did not reply. He looked at the letter.

"My darling husband," Odejimi teased, doing a riff on what Marike might write. "I am so blissfully happy with you! The exquisite pleasures of your white worm—"

A cry leapt from Moulaert's throat. Odejimi stopped his teasing. Kwame reached forward and took Moulaert's arm, "You okay, *copain*?" he asked.

Moulaert slumped forward in his chair. His head fell into his hands. Kwame and Odejimi watched him carefully. He sat up. His eyes once again moved across the letter. "No, this can't be! The *Bon Dieu* wouldn't do this to me!"

"What's happening?" Kwame asked.

"My wife is coming to visit."

"Your Belgian wife?" asked Odejimi, unable to resist taunting him.

"She's bringing my two sons." He groaned as if wounded. "If it were only her, I might have the courage to tell her, 'We're finished. I've married an African woman and I've never been happier.'" He groaned again. "But my sons admire me. I care what they think of me." He stared out at the river. "I will go to hell for this," he whispered.

Marike now appeared on the terrace. Wearing a new cloth and bodice, new headcloth and sandals, she bore herself with supreme self-confidence. She walked across the terrace, her eyes lowered, with a seductiveness reflective of that confidence. Odejimi stood for her. "Madame Marike," he said, "please join us." Kwame rose to fetch a chair. Moulaert remained slumped in his place, staring at the river. Kwame held the chair while Marike sat.

"*Merci, messieurs*," the young bride whispered, smiling with a trace of flirtation.

"Your husband finds his mail tiresome," Odejimi told her. "The news from Europe is upsetting."

"My little cabbage," Moulaert purred to the young woman, the ecstatic smile returning to his face. "Nothing is upsetting when you are beside me."

KWAME'S YEAR-END report with its fictitious numbers was so happily received in Kinshasa that Pilar Cota sent Kwame an attaboy. The rebellion in the east was preoccupying everyone in the capital, she reported. *Génocidaires* and Hutu refugees were still fleeing into Kivu jungles, moving toward the Congo River. At the same time Zairean rebels and Tutsis were both chasing the fleeing Hutus and heading south toward the Copper Belt. That a collection of ragtag rebels could mount effective actions against Mobutu's army seemed improbable, but embassy analysts assumed that Tutsi Rwandan Patriotic Front officers were leading the rebels. There was a feeling that Mobutu, gravely ill in France with prostate cancer, might be all but finished.

"Keep up the good work," Pilar encouraged. "This rebellion might end things for Mobutu. We are so busy in the east that we trust you to do the best you can in the quiet part of the country."

In a postscript she announced that Kwame was now permanently assigned to Mbandaka.

ONE AFTERNOON Kwame was at work at his desk in his office at the center when a strange sense of Kalima's force field enfolded him. A very welcome sensation, but one that carried sorrow. A knock came at the door. "*Entrez,*" he said. The door opened. He did not immediately look up from his computer. When he did, he saw Kalima.

She smiled. He leaped from his chair, knowing she had come back, pulled her into the office, closed the door, and wrapped her in his arms. They kissed so passionately that dizziness swept over them. Kwame kept them from falling by holding onto the wall. "God, I've missed you!" he said.

He led her to the film truck and took her to the hotel. They made love with eagerness and passion. They slept. When they woke and held one another, Kwame said, "I want you staying with me. Don't tell Odejimi you're here."

Kalima stared at the ceiling, a shy smile on her face. "*D'accord.*"

Kalima put her arms around him as if she would not let him go.

"We should look for a house," he said. "Get out of this hotel."

"I would like a house."

"When Odejimi finds out, can you get him another woman? Someone who's clean?" Kalima nodded. Kwame kissed her. Had she left her parents for him? What did that mean?

They lay, staring together at the ceiling. Finally Kalima said, "The day after you left, my father had his great friend from Bikoro come to call. His son was with him. It was the beginning of marriage negotiations."

Kwame said nothing.

"I refused to welcome them," Kalima said. "I told my parents that my life was here. They did not stop me leaving." After a moment she continued, "I did not want to insult our visitors. The man from Bikoro: he is also a friend. His wife died last year."

"You know him?"

She nodded. "He was willing to take me although I may never have children."

"He had children with the wife that died?"

Kalima nodded again. She added, "He worries what will become of me."

Kwame felt exultant. She had chosen him. Was it a wise choice? Her parents thought not.

"I will try to make you happy," Kwame said. He did not speak the further words that were on his tongue, "While I am here."

THE NEXT morning Kwame went to the hospital and waited outside Odejimi's office for the doctor to arrive.

When Odejimi saw Kwame, he asked, "Are you sick?"

Kwame followed the doctor into his office and closed the door. Odejimi looked surprised. "Anything wrong, old man?" he asked.

"Kalima came back from Bolobe yesterday." Odejimi frowned, uncertain what Kwame was talking about. "She will live with me."

Confusion passed across the doctor's face. Then he grinned. "Kalima?" he asked. "You mean Madame Van?" When Kwame nodded, the doctor guffawed. "Did you burn that charm she gave you?"

"I don't believe in charms."

"Except 'Kalima's.'" Odejimi could not suppress his laughter. "Lovesick. You're as bad as Moulaert."

"Never."

"Yes. And you do not want me to—" Odejimi turned away to spare Kwame his amusement. When he turned back, he went on, "—to 'see' her. Is that right?"

"You can look at her," Kwame said, laughing now himself. "Just don't touch."

"You are so American!" the Nigerian said. "You can have her. Fine. But you know, old chap, it may happen that we—'touch,' as you call it." He grinned, delighted by this improbable conversation. "We're programmed that way."

"Kalima will find you another girl," Kwame said.

"I find my own women, thank you," said the doctor. He studied Kwame rather seriously. "Don't be too disappointed if—" He shrugged. "Remember where you are. African men are used to having any women they can get. They often test their luck. Taking another man's woman can be a very amusing game. Be warned, old boy."

Kwame nodded.

"I hope nothing happens to ruin our friendship." Odejimi patted Kwame companionably on the shoulder. He declared, "I knew this would happen the day you beat her at *mankala*."

Kwame went to the center and paced back and forth across the library. Was he being a fool? An American fool? Did Africans never feel this way? Did Kalima herself not feel something for him? He was sure she did. She had defied her parents for him, hadn't she? What more did he want? Finally he was able to calm down. You aren't getting married, he told himself. You're just going to live with her. And if she can't stay away from other men, you better know about it.

That afternoon Kwame helped Kalima move her belongings from Dr. Odejimi's room into his.

KALIMA PROVED to be a very different sort of companion than Livie had been. With Livie Kwame discussed everything: books, movies, sex, life intentions, American foreign policy, domestic politics, social problems, and on and on. He talked with Kalima, but they rarely had probing discussions. While he enjoyed having an intellectual companion with whom he could bat ideas around, Livie's opinions, her intellectual pretensions, often annoyed him. He would feel that she was stuck in the perspectives of her privileged background and tell her so. She would reply that he was mocking her, not because of the strength of his ideas, but out of macho defensiveness, out of an expectation that because he was older, male, a doctor of philosophy, and could claim a background of deprivation, his opinions had more validity than hers. When things got rough, she would call him a WASP dressed in blackface, an Oreo, white at the core, a professional Black Man.

He would call her a privileged and pretentious twerp. She would retreat to their bedroom and lock the door. He would leave their apartment and walk around Sea Point until his temper cooled. When he returned, they usually made love. The arguments became a sexual/intellectual game that both intrigued and fatigued him.

With Kalima, Kwame felt a strange contentedness, a glow of satisfaction that he had never known with a woman. She exuded a kind of harmony. It gave him pleasure to be in her presence, to inhale her fragrance, to feel the warmth of her body in the chair next to his, to let his eyes rest on the symmetry of her features, on the rich dark glow of her skin. There was mystery about her. Livie tried to grasp everything intellectually, to define and categorize all aspects of their relationship. Kalima simply existed.

During the first days Kalima was with him, Kwame's pleasure in her company, in his closeness to her, in their rapport, deepened to the extent that, had he been in America, he might have acknowledged that he had fallen in love. But he was in Africa—and there only temporarily. The value of everything was not in permanence. He would enjoy Kalima now and let the future take care of itself.

As THE day of his wife's arrival approached, Moulaert's robust health gave way to panic attacks, sleeplessness, and depression. Dark circles appeared under his eyes. Worry assailed him.

"What will I do about Marike?" he asked Kwame in private meetings at the center. "I can't send her away. I know it sounds foolish, but I love her. She's my wife."

"Can't she stay at another hotel in town?" Kwame wondered.

"She must stay at the Afrique. I can't get through the day if I don't see her."

"Get her a room by herself," Kwame suggested. "Your wife isn't planning to stay, is she?"

"If I do that," Moulaert pointed out, "that rascal Tombolo will be after her the minute I turn my back." Kwame nodded that this was undoubtedly true. "You know African women," Moulaert went on. "Socialized to believe that they must oblige any man who asks."

"Could you put her under the protection of the doctor?" Kwame asked.

"Not that damn Nigerian!" Moulaert declared. "I've seen him gazing at her. He thinks she's a papaya ready to be plucked." He leaned across Kwame's desk, a look of desperation on his face. "*Copain*," he said, "you are the only man I can trust. I know that Madame Van is your special friend and I would do nothing to interfere. But I'm in a terrible kerfuffle. May I put my beloved Marike under your protection?"

"In my room?" Kwame asked, incredulous.

"Oh, I would be so grateful, my friend."

"You know I am living now with Madame Van," Kwame said. He rarely referred to her as Kalima, not wanting to share that persona with others. "How can I have Marike sharing a room with us?"

"It would only be while they are here," Moulaert said. "I implore you! I am going out of my mind."

Kwame was too flabbergasted to reply.

"Just let her stay in the room. She can sleep on the extra bed. My wife must think she's somebody's woman."

"Wouldn't it be best to come clean to your wife?"

"Impossible!" Moulaert assured him. "My family lives in a small town in Flanders. My wife's a village woman, pious but provincial. She must never know about Marike. And my boys— They're teenagers. They don't yet know what it is to need a woman. They've always looked up to me. Please! You're the only person I trust."

Kwame did not know how to respond. "I don't see how this can work. Perhaps she could stay at the center."

"Oh, no! I need to see her. Please," Moulaert implored. "Just let her have the extra bed. Let my wife see her at breakfast with you." The desperate husband grinned sheepishly. "And if you don't object, I might visit her sometimes. No more than half an hour. Would that be all right? I know you and Madame Van care for each other."

"I'm sorry to disappoint you," Kwame said, "but have Tombolo get her a room at the hotel."

Two days later in a panic at midafternoon Moulaert sought out Kwame in his room at the hotel. "I beg of you," he implored. "Take my Marike. I'm on my way to the airport. My family arrives in half an hour."

Moulaert went out onto the passage and returned with Marike. She wore her school uniform and carried clothes over her arm. Moulaert looked at Kwame, nakedly beseeching. "You won't touch her, will you? Eh, *copain*?" Kwame was nonplussed. "I'm the only man who's ever been inside her. She and I want it to stay that way. I love her."

"Moulaert," said Kwame, "she can't stay here. It's impossible."

Moulaert cried out with anguish. "Please help me! My wife and sons are due any moment." With that he hurried from the room. Marike stood watching Kwame with a frank and appraising look. Moulaert reappeared, dragging a footlocker behind him. Then he scurried away. Marike closed the door, moving with the dignity of a queen. Kwame wished Kalima were with him.

Like a child bereft of a loved parent, Marike went to the window to watch the road. Kwame heard Moulaert rev the motor of his Land Cruiser and listened to the vehicle move off down the road. Marike turned from the window and watched him, measuring him, her stance erect, challenging. She shed her sandals and slipped across the room to Kwame's radio. She turned it on and dialed to music. Swaying to the rhythm, she undid the buttons of her schoolgirl's blouse. Kwame raised his hands, gesturing her to stop. She removed her blouse.

Kalima suddenly appeared. Seeing Marike naked to the waist, she strode into the room. Gathering Marike's belongings, she hurled them outside the door. She returned, muttering in a tribal dialect, marched across the room, grabbed Marike by the front of the blouse she had now put back on, pulled her to the door, grumbling in Lonkundo, and shoved her into the passageway. She glared at Kwame. All he could say was, "Thank you! Thank you!"

LATER, KWAME, Kalima, and Odejimi were together on the hotel terrace, waiting to witness the Moulaert family's arrival. Suddenly Kalima left to make sure Marike moved into a room far from Kwame's. As she crossed the terrace, Odejimi whispered to Kwame, "Did you get a chance with Marike?" Kwame shook his head. Odejimi shrugged. "Be grateful for blessings." He cast his doctor's eye at the departing Kalima, at the way she walked. Sighing with nostalgia, he observed, "Ah! What hips."

A Land Cruiser pulled up outside the hotel. Soon, looking henpecked, Moulaert appeared leading across the terrace a tall, large-breasted Flemish woman in an enormous sun hat. Two red-haired teenagers followed them, the older one almost a man. Moulaert nodded to his friends. They raised their hands in salute. Suddenly they all heard a greeting, shouted loudly, "*Bienvenus, les visiteurs!*" An attractive young *Congolaise* waved from the balcony of the room Tombolo had assigned her, the voluptuous and very naked Marike.

Mme Moulaert cried out in astonished Flemish. She grabbed her sons and pushed them toward their lodgings. The young men resisted. Halting, laughing, they beheld the girl with obvious delight. "*Merci, Mam'zelle,*" they called back. Their parents hustled them away.

KWAME MET Mme Moulaert at one of the video evenings he hosted at the center. He learned that Moulaert had made peace with his African wife by giving her a bundle of zaire notes. He had told his Belgian wife that the pathetic young woman his family had seen the day of their arrival was a schoolgirl who had chosen to become a *femme libre*.

Mme Moulaert was a thick-waisted woman with a ruddy complexion and decided views about everything. She had the squawk and the imperious waddle of a mother hen, her arms akimbo on her hips, her back arched, her breasts protruding, her head rocking back and forth, her red hair waggling like a cock's comb. When she declared her opinions in a French roughened by her native Flemish, her tall, gangly sons regarded her with embarrassment. Mbandaka was a latrine, she asserted. The hotel was a brothel, run by a black *putassier*. Her sons were constantly accosted by whores. Zaireans were stupid. Educating them was noble, but pointless. Still, whoever undertook the task, especially Moulaert, deserved the highest admiration. She assured whoever would listen that her coming to visit her husband in this foul and immoral place and bringing her sons demonstrated the depth of her love for him. She railed against the young *putain* who stood morning and evening, displaying her naked body to hotel guests.

"But it's a delightful body," Odejimi told her at Kwame's *fête*. "You have to admit that."

Mme Moulaert cocked an eyebrow.

"Marike!" Odejimi called. "Is she here? Perhaps she will show it to us."

"Marike!" squawked Mme Moulaert. "Who gave her that beautiful Flemish name?"

But Marike was not there.

"Let's ask your sons what they think," suggested the Nigerian. "I'm sure they consider her body a work of art."

"The *putain* is disgusting!" said Mme Moulaert. "And a mere child. The man who exploits her should be run out of town."

"I agree," declared Mme Berton, challenging Odejimi. She wore a striking white gown patterned on those of ancient Greece, her dark hair atop her head. It was unclear whether she was agreeing with the visiting matron or mocking her. "The men I respect have nothing to do with such women." She raised a witty eyebrow and threw a glance at Odejimi that was half-condemnatory, half-flirtatious.

Odejimi bowed slightly to her. "You are beautiful tonight, Madame," he said. "An Aphrodite from Greece."

Mme Berton bowed in return, her eyes locked with Odejimi's.

"My dear Madame," the doctor exaggeratedly implored Mme Berton, "please don't belittle us. We are men without our families. I hope you would not let circumstances deprive us of both our families and the company of local women. We are not saints."

"No one mistook you for saints," she replied, enjoying the game.

From across the room Berton hurried to his wife's side as if to protect her.

"It is quite possible, is it not, Mother Belgium," Odejimi asked Mme Moulaert, "that the young woman is exploiting our masculine weakness? She displays her body to drive us to distraction."

"That American should keep her under control," said Mme Moulaert. She had decided that Kwame was responsible for Marike.

Kwame stepped forward. "I am the only American in Mban," he said. "Also your host. May I introduce myself? I'm Kwame Johnson." Kwame bowed to her and offered his hand. Mme Moulaert spat toward his hand.

The assembled partygoers gasped. Moulaert and his older son rushed to make sure that the woman's outburst did not get out of control. Kwame bowed again. The woman had spat air, not saliva, and his hand had not been soiled.

"You make our evenings lively, Madame!" Odejimi said. "For that we thank you. I want to say I admire your husband for his loyalty to his work here, for his love of Africans, and his devotion to his family. He's an example for us all." He turned to the Moulaert boys. "And, gentlemen," he said, "what do you think of African womanhood?"

The young men snickered and rolled their eyes. Their mother cuffed them. She advanced again on Kwame. "Your whore is a mere child." Moulaert tried to calm her.

"Madame," said Kwame, "the child you're talking about is a married woman." Mme Moulaert seemed surprised to hear this. "The man she just married paid a footlocker of zaire notes for her."

"She is married, Madame," Odejimi agreed.

"Are you that man?" she demanded of Kwame.

"No," Kwame said. "But you have seen him. He lives at the hotel."

"This is enough, my sweet," said Moulaert, gently touching her shoulders.

"Don't mock me!" the woman thundered. She jerked out of her husband's grasp and stuck her face into Kwame's. Her breasts touched his chest. She spewed Flemish invective at him. Having no idea what she was saying, Kwame nodded amiably. The Moulaert boys snickered at their mother. "Married or not, any man who would corrupt such a child is truly piteous," Mme Moulaert declared. She threw the remainder of her beer into Kwame's face. As Moulaert and his sons hurried her away, Kwame excused himself and washed up in the bathroom.

THE NEXT morning Adriaan Moulaert, the older of the two sons, appeared at the center. Kwame found him browsing in the library and invited him into his office. "I've come to apologize for my mother," the young man said. "She behaved badly last night."

"I hope she's all right this morning," Kwame said.

"This whole trip has been very unsettling for her."

Adriaan was tall with blond-red hair that stood straight up on his head, strangely dark eyebrows and rangy muscles in a body that was beginning to fill out. Kwame admired the young man for offering the apology. He had thought the Moulaert boys tied to their mother's apron strings. The apology made him reconsider. It was the action of a mature young man. Kwame decided that the sons, poor guys, were afflicted with too much Mama. Moulaert had escaped for his erotic knight-errantry; his sons had not yet been so fortunate.

Kwame asked, "How have you found the trip?"

Adriaan smiled. At first his eyes had avoided Kwame's out
of embarrassment over his mother's behavior. Now he fixed
Kwame with an alert, intelligent gaze. He declared how amazing he found Africa to be: the warmth of the African sun in a
season that was winter in Belgium, the brilliance of the colors,
the friendliness of the people, their gaiety despite poverty.

"Would you like some whiskey?" Kwame asked.

The young man was taken aback. "Morning whiskey?" he
asked.

"It moves the day along." Kwame took two small glasses
and a bottle from his desk drawer and poured a shallow bottom
in each glass. After Kalima's return he had reverted to occasional splashes of whiskey.

"I've never drunk much whiskey," Adriaan said, looking at
the glass before him. "But Africa's for doing things you haven't
done before, *n'est-ce pas?*" Kwame nodded. The young man
drank down the whiskey, his eyes bulging slightly, his mouth
open for a breath.

"Would you be willing to do something for me?" Kwame
asked. He poured Adriaan another splash of whiskey.

"Sure. After last night I'm indebted to you."

Kwame proposed that Adriaan accompany him to Bomboko Congo. He was teaching a class later that morning and
thought it might be useful for his students. "They've heard
about colonials," he explained, "and there's a white man in
town, but they've never seen a white person their own age.
Maybe you can tell them about your life and ask them about
theirs."

"There's nothing interesting about my life," Adriaan assured
him. But he agreed to meet some students.

Kwame took the young man to class. At first the students
stared at him and he stared back. Under Kwame's questioning
he began to relax. Kwame had him demonstrate how he would

greet a friend, complete with handshakes and gestures, in his native Flemish, then in French. He had African students do the same in their native tongues. In addition, he had them play a greeting on a two-tone "talking drum." The drum fascinated Adriaan and everyone relaxed. He was finishing school, Adriaan told the students. He wasn't sure what he wanted to do next. University? Maybe not. Travel. That sounded good.

He loved Africa, Adriaan assured the students. He loved the space, the enormity of the river. He'd like to take a boat all the way down to the mouth of the Congo. Kwame asked if any of his students would like to accompany Adriaan on the trip. Several raised their hands. When the class period ended, Adriaan decided to spend the afternoon at the school. He'd find his way back to the hotel on his own.

"Your mother may never forgive me," Kwame joked as they said good-bye.

Adriaan exclaimed, "This is the best day of the trip so far."

A few nights later Kwame walked back across town with Kalima. They had gone dancing at a club. The night air was cool. Now and then they heard a wisp of Kinshasa cha-cha carried on the breeze from a bar and danced a step or two on the road. Kalima was singing. The two of them danced side by side along the passageway to Kwame's room. He slid his key into the lock, looking more at his footwork than the lock. He guided Kalima into the room and closed the door to kiss her. Kalima's body went rigid. She broke the kiss. Kwame sensed something amiss. He flicked on the overhead light.

A gasp. A couple was entwined on Kwame's bed, brown arms and legs wrapped about a long white body. A brown hand held a blond-red head against her dark one. Marike looked up at them with a blissful, uncaring smile. Adriaan slid off her body. Squinting against the light, he stared at them, his hands masking his tumescence.

"Sorry," said Kwame. "Wrong room."

He turned out the light and pulled Kalima outside with him. They held each other to muffle the sounds of their laughter. Kwame knocked on Odejimi's door. When he opened it, Kwame said, "We need somewhere to sleep. The Great Quest, Part Two, is playing in our room."

Odejimi invited them in. "What's going on?" he asked.

"Marike's teaching Moulaert's older son what his father taught her," Kwame explained. "She intended us to catch them."

"She's very naughty," observed Kalima.

Shaking their heads at her behavior, the trio had some whiskey and retired for the night, all three in the same bed.

THE NEXT morning Odejimi and his guests listened to the news on his shortwave radio. The news reader announced that tens of thousands of Hutu refugees were still thought to be pushing west through the jungles of eastern Zaire. Aid workers were trying to locate them and get them repatriated to Rwanda. Tutsi troops were pursuing them.

"How do they eat?" asked Kalima. "How do they stay dry at night?"

MARIKE CONTINUED to lodge in the room Tombolo had arranged for her. She stopped appearing naked on the balcony in the mornings. She also succeeded not only in sleeping with both Moulaert and Adriaan, but in convincing each that he alone enjoyed her favors. Moulaert had to use great care to arrange rendezvous with Marike; his wife now dominated his existence. Adriaan had to be equally watchful; his mother did not want him tainted by Africa. Each man was so busy deceiving Mme Moulaert that it was not hard for Marike to deceive both of them. Nor for Tombolo to collect an occasional commission.

MOULAERT SEEMED such a buffoon with Marike that Kwame and Odejimi often laughed at him when they were together in the late afternoons

But when Kwame was alone—especially alone with Kalima— he would perplexedly reconsider their laughter. He himself felt an ever-greater attachment to an African woman. He had always responded to Kalima's beauty. Her mystery fascinated him. He enjoyed her body. Their lovemaking involved an exploration of the unknown; it brought Kwame satisfactions beyond the merely physical.

As the weeks passed, their enjoyment of being together had less and less to do with lovemaking. They spent hours together talking. Kalima was full of questions about Kwame's childhood in Massachusetts, about his schooling, the subjects he loved and those he hated, about his closest companions and especially about his girlfriends, about what it was like to be in Europe and West Africa. And what was it like to live in South Africa?

To help her understand his answers Kwame brought maps and magazines and picture books. She would pore over them as they lay side by side on their bed. She would study the photographs, asking questions about them: What was snow like? How could buildings rise forty or fifty stories? Why did people want them that way? Why did they not fall down? How did people find the rooms they were looking for in such buildings? An elevator? What was that? Was it not inconvenient, even dangerous, to have so many cars blocking the streets? What about the trash on the streets: how did it get there? What happened to it?

Kwame watched her examining the photos, asking questions. Weighing his answers, he could not suppress the emotion that flowed out from him.

He would also ask questions about her village and the people in it. She would delight in his amazement about things so simple she had never thought to question them. How could she keep track of all her relatives? What was it like to live in a family where a child had several mothers but only one father? Did she not ever want to flee the village community and be alone, by herself? Such questions made her smile. She tried not to let laughter show how preposterous they were. She would cover her mouth with her hand; sometimes she would cover his eyes. He would take her hand that covered them and kiss it.

There were other questions. Did she want to see the world he came from? Perhaps, but how could she? Did he want to see the world she came from? Of course! He had already seen some of it and wanted to see more.

In the enormous stillness that sometimes lay over the town, in the lassitude that allowed nothing to stir—not insects, not the air—in those moments when even the river seemed to slow its pace, Kwame would wait for this time alone with Kalima. It became the focus of his days.

One evening they talked until after midnight, then, feeling amorous, made love. Soon Kwame slept. After a time Kalima woke him. She whispered, "A spinning star visited me." Her expression was so luminous that she lit up the darkness. Immediately Kwame understood what she meant. She had conceived. Was it possible for her to know? Was she really so in touch with her body that she knew? Perhaps she did. He smiled, kissed her lightly, and put his arm around her. "The star was waiting for us to finish talking," she said.

He woke before dawn and lay in bed, trying to remember what had happened in the night. Kalima had wakened him. She had made an announcement: They had reached the necessary level of trust for permissions to be given. But, of course, she did not phrase it in that way. Could it possibly be true? Amazing! But was this really what he wanted, to father a child with a woman for whom he felt deep affection, but whom he hardly knew? He would not allow himself to think too deeply in terms of loving her. Still he wanted her happy. Now she would be. He thought of what Moulaert had done. But how could he possibly marry her? He decided to have confidence in what trust and the *Bon Dieu* had brought about. What else could he do?

AT BREAKFAST Kalima chattered about how to announce the good news to her friends. Kwame pleaded with her first to let the two of them absorb the news. "But I am a woman now. I want everyone to know."

"Wait a month. Please. Then you will know for sure."

"I know now. I want everyone—"

"Please wait."

"I will write to my parents. They will be so pleased!"

A couple of days later, Odejimi stopped by the center. Kwame invited him into his office and offered him a splash of whiskey. "You'll soon need another bottle," said the doctor.

"I may give it up entirely."

"I came to congratulate you."

Kwame was surprised to hear this.

"Your 'Kalima' tells me she's preggers." Kwame did not respond. He supposed she had to tell someone. "She's told you?" said the doctor.

Kwame grinned.

"That's your doing, I suppose."

"The *Bon Dieu*'s doing, I believe."

"With an assist from you."

Kwame shrugged.

The doctor glanced in the direction of Kwame's groin. "Impressive equipment you've got there."

"One doesn't like to boast."

"I should think not. Or every barren woman within a hundred miles will be calling for an appointment." Odejimi finished off his whiskey. "A lot of men gave it a try and weren't up to the job."

Kwame shrugged again.

"And when you leave?"

"Am I leaving?" Kwame laughed. "I guess the *Bon Dieu* will take care of that as well."

ONE MORNING Kwame was alone on the hotel terrace. Kalima had stayed in the room. Lingering over coffee and rolls, Kwame thumbed through the book he would present that day to his class at Bomboko Congo. He glanced up as Moulaert and his wife appeared on the terrace. Moulaert nodded a greeting, but the wife ignored him, the whoremaster. After they were settled at their table, Tombolo approached and handed them an envelope.

Kwame looked back at his book. He heard Madame speaking to Moulaert as she opened the envelope. She fell silent. Kwame glanced over at her. She stared at the letter, her face contorted with disbelief. A muted cry escaped her throat. She threw down the letter. For a moment she seemed poised between control and hysteria. Then she screamed. She pounded the table. Moulaert tried to calm her. She pushed him away.

She rose and marched toward Kwame. She hurled curses at him in Flemish. Kwame rose and moved off. Madame grabbed a chair and came after him. Kwame retreated across the terrace. Tombolo and two waiters raced to Mme Moulaert. They wrestled the chair from her. She collapsed on the terrace, weeping hysterically. Moulaert hurried to her. He crouched beside her, reading the letter. A look of silent anguish crossed his face. He waved the letter at Kwame at the same time comforting his wife. Madame sobbed uncontrollably.

Kwame moved carefully toward Moulaert, his expression asking if he could help. Moulaert shook his head and handed him the letter. It was in a schoolboy script in Flemish, which he could not read. It was signed Adriaan.

Mme Moulaert began to collect herself. "Married that whore!" she wailed, speaking her heavily accented French. "There is nothing in Zaire but chaos! Ruination! Oh, my son! My son!"

Kwame handed the letter back to Moulaert and left the terrace.

As he was leaving the hotel, Kwame learned that Tombolo was equally upset. A thief had stolen a sizable sum of money from his bedroom.

THAT AFTERNOON Moulaert appeared at the center. "I cannot believe this," he confided to Kwame. "I loved that girl. I know she loved me. Can a mere teenager take care of her the way I could?"

Kwame got Moulaert a drink and asked what exactly had happened. "I can hardly believe this," Moulaert repeated. "Yesterday afternoon Adriaan took my Marike to the Catholic fathers. They married them. But she was already a wife!"

"Have you talked with them?" Kwame asked.

"I talked to the priest who married them," Moulaert said. "I would not let my wife come with me. He said, 'They were so in love.' Idiot graybeard! My wife would have pummeled him." Moulaert shook his head in disbelief. "I had to walk over there. Adriaan took my vehicle. I walked here too."

"Where have they gone?" Kwame asked.

"God only knows." Moulaert removed Adriaan's letter from his shirt pocket. He slowly unfolded and reread it. "Adriaan says Marike has money. But how? From where? Enough to tide them over until they get established." He looked abjectly at Kwame. "Where would she get money?"

Kwame shook his head.

Moulaert stared at the letter. "I know there is opportunity here—" He stumbled, translating from the letter. "Opportunity? What can he mean?" He looked back at the letter, "Opportunity here for a man who will work," he translated. His voice broke. He bit his lower lip. "I love Marike," he read. "I will work for her as no man has ever worked."

Moulaert stared at the letter, his eyes glistening, and refolded it. "My heart cries out for my son! What will happen to him?" He gasped for air, his voice breaking with emotion. "My heart is breaking for my little wife."

Kwame sat beside him and put an arm around his shoulder.

Moulaert wiped his eyes. "I know it's improbable for a man of forty-five to love a girl of fifteen," he said. "But that's what happened. She made me realize that I never loved my wife. Oh, that witch! So ugly. So loud. So opinionated!" He laughed piteously. "While I was talking to the priest, she was writing a letter to the Pope." He cried out with disbelief. "That woman! I've never really known her."

He stared at the floor. "My little Marike! She made me so happy. I know she loved me."

Finally Kwame said, "What now? Can you find them?"

Moulaert shook his head. "Impossible to make any plans." He proceeded to lay out a provisional course of action. The younger son would return to Belgium. Mme Moulaert would stay in Mbandaka, living at the hotel, comforting her husband. She could trace Adriaan; she was sure of that! It would not be difficult to locate two teenagers, a European boy with blond-red hair and pale skin and a young *Congolaise*. After all, the jungle was not impenetrable. Once she had traced her son, Mme Moulaert would kidnap him if she had to. She would take him back to Belgium and get the marriage annulled.

"The names she calls Marike!" Moulaert moaned. "Always *putain*. I don't think I can stand it!"

"She'll calm down in a few days," Kwame assured him.

"I keep wanting to tell my wife that I know why Adriaan loves her," Moulaert whimpered. "I know the sweetness of her kisses." Moulaert finished off his drink. Kwame poured him another.

"She says she will kill Marike," Moulaert sniffled.

"She won't kill anyone," Kwame assured his friend.

"I wish she would kill me," Moulaert lamented. "I really cannot stand it."

IN THEIR evenings together Kwame and Kalima began to build a bridge across the chasm of cultural differences that separated them. Repeatedly Kwame told Kalima how beautiful she was, especially now that she was expecting their child. But what he felt on his tongue was the urge to say, "I love you." But he would not say those words. They were the impositions on him of a culture that was a world away. He wanted to declare them to Kalima, he knew, because his culture glorified romantic love, because it laid on those it influenced a hunger to seek romance, because he had seen too many movies, too many TV shows, where one person said those words to another and suddenly the light changed, soft, sweet music swelled, kisses were exchanged, and the world seemingly became a better place.

But Kalima did not come from that culture. She did not know what those words meant even if she might haltingly say them in an approximation of English. If he said them, she might cover her mouth to hide her laughter; she might cover his eyes so that he could not see how preposterous he seemed. What did "I love you" mean? Was he not going to be leaving her one day? Had he not acquiesced in her sleeping with another man?

So instead of saying the words, he waited through each day's stillness and watched her in the close darkness of his hotel room. They laughed together and let their emotion unite them in its embrace.

FOURTEEN

As the weeks passed, Kwame and Odejimi continued to drink together in the late afternoons. Kalima often sat with them, her chair drawn close to Kwame's. He would rest his hand lightly on her arm. Seeing such signs of affection, Odejimi teased them about being in love. They shrugged. He would ask Kalima when she would bring him the new girl Kwame had said she would find for him. Although he would tease about fixing assignations with her, he made no serious attempt to undermine their relationship.

Sometimes Moulaert would join them on the terrace. And sometimes even his wife, so worried was she now about Zaire's disintegration and so hungry for human contact. They would listen to the news. Madame Moulaert would worry that Adriaan and *"sa petite putain"* had headed in the direction of the rebellion. Tens of thousands of refugees were still said to be in the jungles. The rebels were advancing toward Kisangani. Zairean planes had bombed Bukavu on the eastern border. Mobutu remained in France. Would he return to mobilize a defense of Kisangani? If not him, who? Kisangani was the gateway to Mobutu's home territory. His support was strong there; he had Ngbandi ethnic allies. And surely he and his people would fight for Kinshasa, would they not?

Radio reports came that foreign aid workers had evacuated Kisangani. "The rebels will take it now without a fight," Moulaert predicted, partly to reassure his worried wife that their son would not be hurt. "Mobutu's troops won't hold Kisangani; they loot, but they do not fight."

"Adriaan cannot have been so stupid as to go there," his wife mewed. "But he got involved with that girl," she added. "So what kind of judgment can he have?"

"I suspect she is not as bad as you think," Moulaert mumbled.

"She's worse," said his wife.

The others kept their silence.

SOMETIMES IN the night Kwame and Kalima would hold each other or lie side by side, their fingers lightly entwined. Kalima would repeat the stories the ancients of her village told around night fires. About the evils and uncertainties of the impenetrable jungle. About creatures who lived there, some trapped in Nkundo's snares, spirits of the dead, ghosts of creatures who had never lived like people do. About fearsome creatures, large as hippos, strong as elephants, with beaks like birds and scales like lizards, creatures who ran fast and swam. They ate people, but never stopped being hungry. She would talk of people tall as trees. Others whose skin and hair and eyes were green or red or blue, some who were speckled or striped like zebras. Listening to her, Kwame would think how mysterious Kalima was, how lovable in her naïveté, in the beliefs natural to a prescientific mind. Kwame could almost feel the presence of ghosts and goblins in the room.

His old academic training would click in. He would think about Red Riding Hood and the wolf dressed up as the grandmother, lying apparently sick in bed, a story that had never before seemed credible to him. It had always been told to him as a send-up. "People used to tell children these stories," his mother would say because they were people of the mind and knew better. He thought about how science and rationality had stolen from people their imaginations and at the same time had given them reassurance about irrational fears.

Sometimes he wondered if he would ever know Kalima. Then, as if sensing his thought, she would confess that these were only stories. Her teachers in school assured her that they were not true. And yet, she would say, she noticed that none of those teachers would venture into the jungle.

A LETTER arrived from Livie, the first in more than a month. It was written in her characteristic style, in a single paragraph flavored with dashes. It read:

"Swami— I so want to e-mail you!— How've you been? Seems like forever since we talked. Since we touched. Since we— Just tried to call you. It's two A.M. here— God knows what time there and the phone just rang on and on and on— and I didn't know if it was ringing at your cultural center or at some operator station God only knows where or even if it was ringing in Africa— I miss you so much. Law school is such a grind—and I get so lonely!!!!! I wish you were around—wish we could talk—wish we could take out our frustrations—anyway my frustrations—with some good healthy fucking that would leave me breathless and exhausted and refreshed and renewed. Where are you? Why don't I hear from you? I'm so alone here. There's a guy here who wants me to live with him—he's the kind you always said I'd marry. But I want to marry you!!! I'm thinking of living with him only to stop the loneliness—but couldn't consider it unless I talked to you about it first. I keep thinking that I will just come out to see you and maybe that will make it all better. Sorry I haven't written more— Have zillions of cases about disputes you wouldn't believe and I suppose it's good for me and all that—but I would sure like to see you, touch you, hear from you, feel you inside me, hold you all night, and know what's going on in your life. Liv."

KWAME THOUGHT about the letter for two days. Obviously Livie was sleeping with the man who wanted her to move in with him. He felt no jealousy about that. He was pleased that Livie had someone in her life. He had always known their relationship would end.

He answered:

"Dear sweetest Olivia,

"I wish we could talk. Or phone. Or e-mail. I wish I were there to make the loneliness go away, but the grind of law school would still be there, wouldn't it? I don't know what to say about your moving in with this guy. Maybe it's okay. Being lonely is <u>not</u> a good idea—and melancholy and having to deal with it. I think you should do it.

"Strangely, I'm not lonely. I've told you about the two or three other expats here and the group we form. There's a Zairean woman too—very educated for a village girl, beauti . . ."

Kwame stopped writing. Should he acknowledge that a woman was living with him in his room? No. This would be his last letter to Livie. There was no reason to hurt her, to let her think that she had been replaced. He completed the word "beautiful" and added "married to a Belgian." The sentence now read: "There's a Zairean woman, too, very educated for a village girl, beautiful, married to a Belgian." She might wonder where the Belgian was, but he would leave it that way. He added: "She acts as a bridge for us to Africa and we are all half-infatuated with her." Why not let Livie think— Whatever she chose to think.

"Most Americans would probably hate this place," Kwame went on. "The pace of American life grows faster and faster. Here time stands still. In the States there's an underlying noise of hurry. It's technology clicking away, making our lives more convenient, more frenetic. Here, it's all stillness, a silence so great that sometimes the sky seems to press down on us. That huge sky wears different colors throughout the day. And the river is always slipping past. I must be vegetating. Because for the moment that's enough."

Kwame told Livie how much her love had meant to him in their years together. "The love we shared, it's something I'll always carry with me. Foolish, isn't it, to think of permanence as the only value?"

Kwame bid Livie succeed in law school. Perhaps someday years hence, he wrote, they would meet somewhere, have a meal together, and meet each other's children. He knew that he would not hear from her again.

LE TOUT MBANDAKA attended a party that weekend given by the Badekas and their Bomboko Congo instructors. Kwame, Kalima, and Dr. Odejimi arrived together, followed almost immediately by the Moulaerts. Mme Berton appeared alone in a dress of yellow chiffon, very Paris couture; her husband, she reported, was down at the plantations. The Badekas hoped their guests would dance to new CDs from Kinshasa, but most of the men gathered in a corner, beers in hand, to discuss events in eastern Zaire.

Both the BBC and shortwave broadcasts from Brussels had reported the Kisangani airport under attack by Kabilistes, so-called after their leader Laurent Kabila. At the time of independence in 1960 he had been a *Lumumbiste* and an opponent of Mobutu for thirty years. In addition, some 350,000 refugees were said to be roaming the jungles in the area.

"Will Mobutu's men be able to hold Kisangani?" Moulaert asked.

"No," predicted Badeka. "History is repeating itself."

"With a precision that is unnerving," remarked Berton. He had arrived out of nowhere, just in from the bush, and gotten himself a beer. He wore work shorts and a safari jacket, its pockets full to the brim. "These troubles will reach us here," he said. He scanned the guests with an edginess of manner.

Kwame wondered where Mme Berton had gone. He had seen her with Odejimi.

"In the midsixties," recalled Badeka, "Simba rebels came out of the Kivu to menace Kisangani."

"It was Stanleyville then," remarked Berton impatiently. "It fell like a ripe papaya." He quaffed his beer, surveying the guests.

Kwame also looked over the guests, searching for Odejimi.

"Will the rebels push into the Equateur?" asked Moulaert. "What do we do if these rebels come toward Mbandaka?"

"They never got this far in the sixties," said Badeka. "But here we are thirty years later. Mobutu is very rich; Zaire is very poor. Mobutu no longer works as a man; Zaire no longer works as a country."

"And the Americans are back," remarked Berton.

Kwame withdrew from the conversation. He sought out Théa Badeka, spun her onto the dance floor, and asked, "Where's Dr. Odejimi?"

"He slipped into the garden with Mme Berton," she said. Then, alarmed, she asked, "What's Berton doing here?"

"Madame thinks he's at the plantations."

Kwame went outside. He walked through the garden, whistling to make his presence known. At the back of the property he came to a hedge of bougainvillea. Through it he saw a flash of yellow. He declared in a loud voice, "Berton has arrived. Berton is here."

Returning to the house, Kwame danced with Kalima. Mme Berton appeared at the kitchen door. She smoothed the skirt of her lemony dress. Odejimi followed behind her. They walked through the kitchen and took the dance floor, playing the moment recklessly.

Berton stalked onto the dance floor. "Jean-Luc!" his wife exclaimed. "You're here!" She left Odejimi, ran to her husband. "I thought you were gone for another week! How good to have you here!"

"Indeed, old boy," said Odejimi.

Mme Berton kissed her husband. He pushed her aside. He drew a pistol from his safari jacket. He aimed it at Odejimi. Mme Berton shrieked. Odejimi said, "Easy, old chap." He raised his hands in submission. A shot rang out. Odejimi staggered. A second shot. Mme Berton howled. Odejimi fell to the floor. Guests fled. Berton shot again. Mme Berton dropped to the floor, her body covering the doctor's.

Guests rushed outside. They screamed. They whispered. They peered through the windows. They watched in horror.

Mme Berton lay embracing the doctor, wailing and blubbering. Blood pooled beneath her. Kwame saw Odejimi's eyes stare upward, trying to comprehend this incomprehensible event. The light in them went out. Mme Berton shrieked, feeling Odejimi's life ebbing away. No one spoke. After the explosions of gunfire, the silence had physical weight, broken only by Mme Berton's cries.

Berton shoved the pistol into his jacket. He grabbed his wife under her arms. With the strength of passion, he lifted her to her feet. He pulled her through the kitchen. No one tried to stop them.

Kwame knelt beside the doctor. He gently held his head. He looked into his eyes. Moulaert knelt down, took a wrist, and searched for a pulse. "Dead," he said.

GUESTS SCURRIED away. The Moulaerts vanished. Kalima took Kwame's hand and whispered, "We must leave." But when he saw how shaken the Badekas were, Kwame refused. "I will be at the hotel," she said. She disappeared into the garden. In the grip of panic, Badeka insisted that the doctor might still be saved. He and several students loaded Odejimi's body into a car and drove off toward the hospital.

After her husband departed, Théa grumbled, "White men are so stupid!" She stared at the pool of blood. "Could Berton not see that his wife was bored? That there would be trouble?" Standing over the blood, Théa vented her anger. "Now he's killed a doctor. We don't have doctors to kill." She shook her head. "Everybody knew what was going on."

"Berton must have known."

"Of course, he knew! He came here, hunting the doctor."

Théa went into the kitchen. Kwame picked up bottles and glasses and took them to her. She had removed her blouse and stood at the sink, an apron over her bra, filling a plastic pail with water. Handing Kwame another pail and old towels, she led him to the pool of Odejimi's blood. "If we don't clean this up, it will get sticky," she said. They dropped to their knees and mopped up the blood, wringing it out in one pail, then rinsing the towels in the other and wiping up more blood. Théa muttered, "I suppose the police will come."

Badeka returned. "We left the body at the hospital and hurried away," he said. He went about locking doors.

Kwame went to the kitchen and scrubbed his hands with soap. "I should go," he told Badeka.

"No, stay. It's good to have you here."

When the police came, Kwame thought, his presence might protect the Badekas. He could corroborate their report of what happened. He stayed with them until three A.M. But no police came. Kwame finally asked, "Where are the police?"

Badeka shook his head, almost with relief.

"Won't there be an arrest?" Kwame asked. "Berton was standing over him with the gun."

Badeka shrugged. "Maybe they'll try to arrest him tomorrow. When he's had time to flee."

"They'll let him flee?"

"They want to flee themselves," Théa said. "There are rebels in Kisangani. They may come here."

Badeka said simply, "There is no law here."

WHEN KWAME returned to the hotel, he sat for a long time in the film truck, remembering Olatubusun Odejimi. The doctor had showed him how to live in Mbandaka; in a sense he had saved his life. Now he was dead, he who seemed to know everything about survival. Poor doctor. Madame Berton was no woman to die for.

He glanced up at the hotel. A light shone dimly in the doctor's room. Someone was already there, looting his belongings. They did not wait long, Kwame thought. He hoped Kalima was safe in his room.

As he went along the passage, he stopped outside Odejimi's door. Anger welled up in him at the doctor's death. He felt an urge to take vengeance on the looters in Odejimi's room. He moved silently to the door, turned the handle, and burst inside. The looter gasped and slid into darkness.

"*Docteur?*" the voice asked.

"Kalima?"

"Kwame?"

Kwame shut the door. Kalima moved from behind the armoire into the dim illumination of the reading lamp. He embraced her, held her to him. "Oh!" she exclaimed, "I thought you were his ghost!"

But another ghost was suddenly with them in the room. Kwame took Kalima's arm and held it tight. "Is this what happened to Mason?"

"Why talk about Mason? Odejimi's dead."

Kalima pulled out of his grip. She cried, "Odejimi's dead!" She went back to looking through the doctor's belongings. Kwame went to the table beside the bed where she was working. On it he saw Odejimi's checkbook, a small stack of hundred dollar bills, and packets of nearly worthless zaire notes in bundles. The doctor must recently have bought black market currency.

Kwame saw that Kalima had forced open the armoire. Seeing his surprise, she said, "If we do not take these things, the police will take them. Or someone who did not even know him. His ghost is in the room here. He wants us to have these things."

She handed Kwame the cash and the checkbook. He stuffed them into his pockets. He went into the bathroom, searched the place, and took the toiletries. Kalima found his tobacco and whiskey. They transported what they could carry into Kwame's room. Kwame returned, gathered the rest, and closed Odejimi's door.

Back in their room Kalima poured Kwame a whiskey. He shook his head. She came beside him, gave him the drink, and took some of it herself. An idea had occurred to Kwame.

Examining it from every angle, he wondered if he had the cold nerve—the balls—to carry it out. Finally he finished off the drink. He took the bundles of cash and the checkbook. He sped across town to the center and hid them in a footlocker he kept above the ceiling.

He drove out along the river to the Bertons' house. He reckoned they would be awake, packing luggage to flee. He drove almost into the house. His headlights shone brightly into the front room. Kwame left the truck, moving slowly so that Berton would know who he was, his arms away from his body. Berton could see that he was not armed. The planter appeared out of a side door. He held his right hand behind him, obviously hiding a gun.

"I know he was your friend," Berton said, "but he defiled my wife."

Kwame said, "You'll want someone in your house while you're gone."

Berton moved closer. He peered at Kwame across the headlight beams.

"My companion and I would like to occupy it," Kwame said. "It's us or Zairean squatters."

Berton said nothing, studying him.

"We'll take good care of the place," Kwame assured him. "At least until rebels push us out."

"What can you pay?"

"You can't collect rent from anyone."

Finally Berton said, "You Americans never miss a chance, do you?"

"Never do," Kwame said.

"You want the cars, too, I suppose," Berton said.

Kwame had not thought of the cars. "Why not?"

Berton spat to show his contempt.

"If you agree to this," Kwame said, "put it in writing. That will give me some authority against squatters."

Berton spat again. He disappeared around the side of the house.

Kwame waited. He heard the river sliding past, just beyond the yard. The night was dark, densely black, even with the headlights. Kwame grew cold. He waited for what seemed forever, feeling strangely that Odejimi's ghost was standing just beyond where he could make him out. He was sure the ghost was chuckling. "This was worth a try," Kwame told the ghost—silently for if he were truly a ghost he needed no audible words.

Berton returned with a handwritten letter of authorization and a collection of keys.

Kwame said, "Have a good life." Then for the benefit of the ghost, he added silently, "It's more than you deserve."

He got back to the hotel, exhausted. Kalima was relieved to have him safe. He could see that she'd been crying. He lay down beside her, knowing he would not sleep, and said, "I got us a house."

KWAME LEFT the hotel at dawn. As he started down the passage, he discovered that Odejimi's room had been sacked, his clothes removed, and papers and books scattered by looters looking for cash. Among the debris he saw a book that bore Odejimi's signature. He took it, went to the center, and practiced again and again writing something that resembled the assemblage of curlicues Odejimi used in signing his name. Then he took the doctor's checkbook from the footlocker in which he'd hidden it. He wrote out a check to himself for a bit less than the amount remaining in the Nigerian's account.

He psyched himself up and attempted what he hoped would prove to be a passable forgery of the signature. His third try looked worth testing.

At the bank the manager was closeted with important patrons. The assistant manager told Kwame he could not be disturbed. The young man examined the check. He looked carefully at Kwame. He scrutinized the signature, compared the amount of the check to the balance in the account, and returned to Kwame. "It is remarkable," he said, "that the doctor should write you a check that is almost exactly the balance in the account."

"We had a wager," Kwame told the man. "I emptied my account to him if he won. And if I won—"

"And you did. Lucky you." Kwame nodded with a smile. The assistant manager stared at him. He had an accountant's manner. He wore gold-rimmed glasses, a white business shirt, and a tie and coat and clearly had ambitions beyond Mbandaka. "I suppose wagers do happen at a time when the world is falling apart," he noted. "Kisangani fell to the rebels last night."

"I hadn't heard that," Kwame said. "Will the rebels come here?"

"They are killing refugees in the camps," the assistant manager reported. Then he asked, "Can you help me get to America?"

"These days I'm not sure I can get to America myself," Kwame replied.

The young man looked again at the check, then back at Kwame. He glanced toward the door of the manager's office. "This is so unusual," he said. "This is quite a large check. I think the director should approve it."

"But he is so busy. I would appreciate it if—"

"Could Dr. Odejimi come to authenticate it?" the assistant manager asked.

"The doctor left town," Kwame ventured, his heart pounding. "As I think you may know," he added. "I suppose there is a service charge for cashing such a check?"

The assistant manager reappraised the check, then stole another glance at the manager's door. "Yes, there is," he said. "Ten percent. I thank you for reminding me." He smiled at Kwame, relieved. "If you'd like to wait, I can handle the matter now."

"Perhaps you'd like to put the money in there," Kwame said. He gave the young man a cloth duffel. He took it and went off.

As Kwame waited, the bank manager's door opened. He escorted M. and Mme Berton from his office. Apparently they had been arranging their financial affairs. From what Kwame overheard it seemed that they were leaving Mbandaka on the noon plane. He heard Berton say that they might be gone for some time.

Berton spoke quietly, in tense clipped phrases, his glance furtive. Madame, however, was expansive, her cheeks abloom with health, her voice lilting with melody. The fact that her husband would murder a man out of jealousy made Madame kittenish. She was as flirtatious as a new bride well-satisfied with her wedding night. Her voice trilled with merriment. Her perfume scented the room. She moved with a sprightliness, clinging to her husband. Berton caught sight of Kwame. He nodded. Madame danced up to him. She extended her hand. Kwame shook it. "*Bon voyage,*" he said.

She replied, "Have a good stay at our house."

As soon as the bank manager returned to his office, the assistant manager appeared with the cloth duffel, now stuffed quite full. "It turned out that the bank's service charge came to more than 10 percent," he said.

"I can't say I'm surprised," Kwame said. The two men shook hands.

AFTER HIDING the money in the footlocker in the center, Kwame returned to the hotel. The police were searching Dr. Odejimi's room. Looters stood watching from the road outside, waiting for them to finish. Kalima paced at the far end of the hotel property. As soon as Kwame appeared in the film truck, she stepped into the road and waved. They left quickly.

The house by the river delighted Kalima. She and Kwame explored the rooms and fantasized about what they would do in each one. Kalima would have a cocktail for the Badekas in the "grand living," followed by a sit-down dinner in the dining room and dancing on the verandah. "You will have to teach me how to live in this house," she said. "I have known of such places only in movies."

"Me too," replied Kwame. "I've never lived in a house like this in America." Kalima looked at him, surprised. A house in Mbandaka could be larger than the ones he occupied even in America? "We will learn to live in it together," he said.

Upstairs they found that Berton had locked off most of the second floor. He had left them a small bedroom that over-looked the river. It contained an ancient bed frame on which frayed ropes held the mattress. Kwame lay down on it. Kalima sat beside him. "Police are searching the hotel," he said. "But we are safe here."

She smiled at him, but shook her head. "Safer in Bolobe," she said.

Kwame fell asleep. He woke he did not know how much later—maybe an hour, maybe only minutes. Kalima was watching him. She said, "The rebels have taken Kisangani. There is turmoil everywhere." She added, "There will be many strangers coming into Mban. Some of them will be dangerous."

"If the rebels come this way," Kwame said, "and there is fighting, I may have to leave. Evacuate to Kinshasa. Will you come with me?"

Kalima looked through the window toward the river.

"Wherever I am," he said, "I want you with me." But, of course, if he left the country, she would not be with him.

After a long moment she said, "Someday you will leave Zaire. When you do, I am not going to be alone in Kinshasa."

"What will you do?"

"Go back to Bolobe. With a baby I will be welcome there."

"And marry the man in Bikoro?"

She shrugged and did not look at him.

"Will you be happy with him?"

"Why don't we go to Bolobe? My father will like you better now that you have given me a baby."

Kwame said nothing. It was not an unreasonable request.

"You were happy there. I could tell how happy you were."

"My whole life has prepared me for something different."

"You think my life has prepared me for Kinshasa? Or America?" She laughed, with hurt rather than humor. "Will all American women be like Vandenbroucke's mother? Like Mme Moulaert? Will they think Kwame Johnson has brought his *putain* with him from the Equateur?"

"They will think how lucky Kwame Johnson was to meet a woman like you—a woman with education—in the Equateur."

Kalima smiled at this naive idea. "There is no place safer than Bolobe." She touched his cheek. "How can we be safe in Kinshasa? The rebels and Mobutu's people will fight for power there."

After a moment he said, "If we were married and things got dangerous, my people would take care of you." He paused, knowing that her interpretation of what "my people" meant would be different from what he intended. "Would you come to America?"

"For a visit perhaps. Two weeks, a month."

"No more than that?"

She said nothing. To go to America: it was something she had never considered. He saw that, as she considered it now, the prospect of America terrified her. It was an idea too big for her head to grasp.

"The doctor told me about America," she said. "It is very comfortable there. But also very hard. For black people, I mean." They looked at one another. "Was he wrong?"

"It is better than Nigeria."

"Come to Bolobe."

"There is nothing for me to do there. I've been trained—"

"Oh, you and your training!"

"You wear me out," he said, teasing. "Right now I need to sleep."

"You sleep," Kalima told him, rising from the bed. "I will go look at the kitchen."

LATER, WHEN he woke from his nap, Kwame went downstairs. He came upon Kalima sitting in the living room. She was staring sadly, thinking of Odejimi and the way he died.

"Odejimi brought me here once," Kwame said, startling her out of her reverie. "I had been in town only a day or two. He had already begun his game with Mme Berton."

"The dear doctor," said Kalima. "So like him to feel that if he sees a woman, he must have her. She herself means nothing. He is testing himself. His charm against her resistance. Showing off for his friends." She smiled ironically. "Mme Berton cannot have been much of a test. Of course, she was white. The jealous husband made it interesting. White men take things too far. They think shooting settles things."

She did not speak for a moment. Then she said, "I did not know there was so much blood in a body."

"Do you miss Odejimi?" Kwame asked. The question meant: "Did you love him?" And that, of course, meant: "Were you in love with him as an American woman might have been?" An impossible question. Kalima could not love as an American woman loved. A Nigerian doctor would not have wanted that. What Kwame really wanted—he was mostly aware of this himself—was an assurance that Odejimi had never been important in her life.

Her answer was a shrug. Which might mean: "I live in present time and he is no longer here."

"I fell in with him when I thought Vandenbroucke might still come back." She smiled self-mockingly. "I thought this was what education did to men. It made them pass around village girls like me." After a moment she added, "We loved him as a friend, but he was not serious." Kwame nodded. Kalima went on, "Odejimi's wives in Nigeria had lives separate from him. They had money and their own businesses. He resented this. Wives are an encumbrance when one wants to wander the earth."

"When he passed you to me," Kwame asked, "should I have resisted?"

"No. From the beginning I meant to have you." She gazed at the river without turning toward him. "If you are forced into that role, you want to play it well." She smiled at him. "Did you think I would allow you to resist me? Why do you think I gave you the laptop and the charms?" He grinned, relieved.

"Why do you think I let you win at *mankala*? I never let him win. He was not going to take that from me!"

A FEW days later the Mongo Restaurant closed its doors. Tata Anatole explained to Kwame that the *chef*, the owner, was a Mubinza who came from the hinterland behind the town of Bumba. It lay at the northernmost point of the great river's curve. Things were uncertain now. During the disintegration of the country some people thought it unwise to get caught in the territory of a tribe not one's own. The restauranteur consulted a *féticheur* three times, twice before the fall of Kisangani and once since. Each time the *féticheur* had counseled him to return home. Finally he had taken the advice.

KWAME BROUGHT the CD player from the center and set up speakers throughout the house. He and Kalima had music whenever they wanted it, often American jazz, sometimes music for cocktails: ballads by Gershwin and Rodgers and Hart. Kalima loved these. She would dance. Kwame would join her for the secret pleasure of watching her move. They would sing to one another: "Embrace me," Kwame would implore to strains of Gershwin, hugging her, "my sweet embraceable you." And Kalima would sing back, mimicking phonetically the lyrics: "Seeto mbarazolo-oo." Kwame had either to hold her close or dance away, hiding his laughter from her, for if she knew he was laughing, she refused to dance. And some-times she would sing one of her songs and he would reply in a Lonkundo that made her cry with laughter.

So they moved into their new house in song and laughter.

FIFTEEN

Two weeks after Kisangani fell to the Kabilistes, Kwame received a letter. It contained parts of a secret cable the American ambassador had sent to Washington. Even though now "virgin," edited for transmission through the public mails, the letter contained a message scrawled at the top of the text: "Destroy after reading." At the bottom a note was scrawled: "Kabilistes/Rwandan Tutsis hold Kisangani and Bukavu. Headed toward Copper Belt. If they push toward Mbandaka, your work for USEmb will be crucial." Another hand had written: "Rwandan civil war now being fought in Congo jungles. Tutsi soldiers hunt Hutu refugees. Thousands and thousands massacred. 'The horror!'" Again at the bottom: "Destroy after reading."

For the first time Kwame understood what he was really doing in Zaire. The embassy did not care about the effectiveness of its cultural program in Mbandaka. It merely wanted a presence in the town, a pair of eyes on the ground, and in case of trouble in the Equateur a building to use as a command post. If it needed that command post, USEmb would expect him to welcome its operatives, CIA types like Gianni and Pedersen; they would execute policy. If he showed "heroism and courage," if he helped advance American objectives in the new

Kabila-era Zaire, a commendation might be inserted into his personnel folder. If not, he would find the ranks of advancement closed to him. He destroyed the document as instructed.

Kwame could not truly say that he felt used. When they had talked at his apartment that first day in Kinshasa, Judkins had as much as told Kwame the purpose of the branch post in Mbandaka. Now that purpose had been made all but explicit. Reporting must continue, of course. Congressional monitors of USIS activities must still be reassured. So the elaborate game would continue.

Reporting would enumerate program goals that had no meaning. It would exaggerate post effectiveness. If necessary, in secret closed-door sessions, policy makers might reveal to selected congressional friends that the posts were deemed crucial to the achievement of US policy goals in Zaire at this time of crisis and flux: the maintenance of a unitary national entity; avoidance of war and national dismemberment in Central Africa; American access to Zairean resources; the promise of movement toward a democratic system with free and fair elections—despite the fact that the country was virtually without infrastructure.

A question, apparently not considered by USEmb, was this: What would happen if the Kabiliste/Tutsi soldiers attacked Kinshasa, totally disregarding Mbandaka? Wouldn't that throw all Kinshasa, including the embassy, into turmoil and panic? Might the embassy forget the Equateur?

Kwame now disregarded any guilt he might feel about misrepresentations. He keyed his reporting to policy objectives. He exaggerated the number of books and videos borrowed, the number of visitors to the library, the number of attendees at video showings, the breadth of his contacts with provincial leaders. He reported details of the fictional gala he had held to mark the center's official inauguration and mentioned the titles of local dignitaries who had attended.

"The provincial governor is particularly pleased with this new addition to our community," Kwame reported. Knowing his superiors' desire that he make influential contacts, he allowed them to believe about him what Berton had believed about Mason's contacts with the Residence. He enthused: "The governor and I have become friends. We sometimes breakfast together at a small bakery." In fact, Kwame had several times met the governor, a frustrated, out-of-favor Kongo politician rusticated to the region of the Mongos. The governor feared that his investments south of Kinshasa would be stolen from him during his tenure in Mbandaka just as he had plundered investments from a tribal brother sent out of the country as ambassador to Ethiopia. "The governor hopes to make himself useful to Mobutu," Kwame reported fancifully, "should the rebellion spread throughout the country, should Mobutu choose to make a stand in his home region." Kwame finished off by noting: "USIS Mbandaka is monitoring preparations for this eventuality."

Kwame fabricated accounts of film trips into the bush. He assumed that readers of his reports—if indeed anyone actually read them—would realize that roads in the Equateur were all but impassable. He noted he had employed a second local assistant, K. Vandenbroucke, on a probationary basis and was paying the employee from petty cash. Kwame kept careful accounts of these expenditures and reported them monthly, giving a weekly salary to Kalima so that she would have money of her own.

Kwame dutifully transmitted these reports on time. He would occasionally get a hurried note from his bosses in the capital. "Keep up the good work!" they would encourage him. "We know the lonely vigil's tough duty!" They reported that the Kabilistes had turned south and west, heading for Kinshasa. It looked as if the Equateur would be spared any excitement—unless Mobutu decided to make a stand there.

As THE days passed, Kwame took extraordinary pleasure in watching the transformation of Kalima. She changed almost daily, virtually before his eyes. Not solely because she was pregnant. That, of course, was a large part of it. The function of her womanhood was being fulfilled. At night as they lay side by side, she would whisper to Kwame, "I am carrying your child." He would look at her through the darkness. She would seem illuminated by joy. Kwame did not feel the white expatriate's annoyance that biology had sprung its trap. Instead he experienced a curious, almost African elation: A child was coming! The *Bon Dieu* had blessed them. Kalima would smile when she saw how pleased he was. "My first child," she would say. "Thank you for giving your permission."

Kwame began to have a different sense of who she was. It transformed her from the mere physical being into a kind of full-bodied womanhood, seen by herself as having value and individual identity.

And her sense of Kwame expanded. The father of her child was a man to respect: an American, virile, intelligent, educated, one of the world's grand men. She could not believe he was despised in his own country, as Odejimi insisted. This man accorded her dignity. Had he not balked at sharing her with others? Had he not visited her people? Had he not found a palace for them to live in, better even than the homes he inhabited in his own country? Did he not worry about what would become of her when he had to leave her? Eventually all men left their women, some to disappear, some to take new wives. Did he not give her money every week? Was it not the

American way for a man to make certain that his woman had adequate money to meet her expenses? Were there not feelings between them, which she had never felt with any other man? She knew this emotion would not last forever, but had she ever before shared such feelings with a man?

For Kalima it was not enough merely to bask in the pleasure of Kwame's feelings, to be an object of his delight. Instead she wanted to prove herself a woman deserving of his respect. She noticed that with the closure of the Mongo Restaurant the only food available in "downtown Mbandaka" was sold by street vendors and food stalls in the market. She decided that "downtown" should offer a place to eat. Using the money Kwame gave her, Kalima had workmen construct in the yard before the center a shelter of palm fronds. She showed them the roomful of usable wooden crates at the rear of Kwame's building, crates in which his center had received its supplies. She had the workmen build from them rude tables and benches at which her patrons could eat. When the work was completed, Kalima took Kwame to the center—he had not been there for days, spending his time instead at Bomboko Congo school—and showed him what had been accomplished. "You are amazing!" he said, impressed with what she had achieved.

At first "Chez Kalima" served only snacks: fried plantains, pineapple slices, sweet bananas and papayas, rice and beans garnished with onions. Except for the kitchen, it did not use the center building. Kalima located vendors who could supply her food and badgered them to keep their prices low. She spent long hours training the people, most of them from around Bikoro, who would prepare and serve the fare.

When *le snack* proved a success, she began to plan for a place that offered lunch. The enterprise was problematic. Few Zaireans ate more than snacks at midday. But Kalima hoped that there were enough men who wanted to be seen in the act of eating in the fashion of their betters in Kinshasa to make a lunch place viable, especially if music, played on the center's equipment, invited patrons to her tables. She decided to offer table d'hôte entrees according to what food was available: *poulet moambe* (chicken in a spicy peanut sauce, the national dish), *capitaine* if the river catch was good, *soso* (chicken stew), *saka saka* (manioc leaf stew), *fufu* (mashed manioc), or *loso* (rice). If the lunch place succeeded, then perhaps even dinner would be possible, she told Kwame, especially if it included entertainment: music and videos from the center.

Kwame was proud of Kalima—and pleased to provide the kind of support that enabled her to blossom. She proved herself to be so much more of a woman than he had realized.

By now everyone in Mbandaka understood that she was pregnant with Kwame's child. He himself regularly referred to her as "*ma femme*," a French usage that carried an ambiguous double meaning. "My woman" also meant "my wife." He wondered if they should marry. As far as the town was concerned, they already had.

As KALIMA took on a new identity, Kwame changed as well. The influence that Dr. Odejimi had exerted over him—an influence of which he was hardly conscious—dissipated. The Nigerian had so charmingly insisted that sex, drugs, and whiskey were the only routes to survival in Mban that Kwame had accepted his view as truth.

But it was not truth. Now that the doctor was dead, Kwame found that he had little desire—and no hunger—for hemp and hard liquor. And none for the compulsive and emotionless fucking that Odejimi preferred. Kwame began to see that through his charm the Nigerian had imprisoned both him and

Kalima in his vision of how life must be lived in the Equateur. His death set them free of that vision.

To PROTECT their household now that a child was coming, Kalima had a Bikoro artist carve them a doorpost. The figure was a watchful, large-breasted woman of childbearing age. She would protect everyone who entered the dwelling, especially if Kwame and Kalima were faithful in pouring a small libation of beer or milk at the bottom of the doorpost every week.

A Bolobe *nganga* came to throw bones to read the couple's future. He prophesied good fortune and gave Kalima charms that she asked Kwame to wear. He refused. "This is not just for you," she explained to him. "It is for our child." She spoke with certainty now that she was pregnant. She had already begun to act like a mother. She repeatedly badgered him to wear the charms. Because the matter was important to her, he hung them around his waist on a thong.

One AFTERNOON after teaching his classes at Bomboko Congo, Kwame was having tea with the Badekas. Without his planning to ask it, a question spilled out of his mouth. "If I wanted to marry Kalima," he asked, "would that be possible?" The inquiry was greeted with silence. The Badekas glanced at one another. "How would I go about it?" Kwame persisted.

"Why would you marry Kalima?" asked Théa.

"Why does a man usually marry a woman?" Kwame replied.

"There are many reasons to marry," Théa noted.

"But already she lives with you," said Badeka. "She keeps you warm at night. She prepares your food—or sees that it is prepared the way you like it."

"And she is giving you a child," Théa said. She nodded her head as if she understood and said, "Ah! You want the child."

Kwame laughed, a little frustratedly. "I want to know about marrying her. Is it possible? What has to be done?"

Again the Badekas glanced at one another. Badeka asked, "Would you take her to America when you leave here?"

"She doesn't want to go to America."

"But you will go back to America, won't you?"

"Maybe if we are married . . . When the time comes, she will agree."

"And if not?" asked Théa. "Would you want to take the child?"

All these questions! Kwame did not know how to answer.

"You would want the child, of course."

"I don't know," Kwame said. "I keep thinking about marrying her, that's all. I thought I should know something about it."

"It would not be right to marry such a woman and take her to America," Badeka said, "and then abandon her."

"Whether you take the child or not," his wife added.

"Why would I abandon her? I want to be with her."

"But would you want that in America?" Théa asked.

"You are all rich in America," said Badeka. "Everyone has his own car and a computer and fine clothes and everyone lives in a large house. But black people are despised there. Everyone has a gun and people kill each other in the streets, especially black people."

"Let's start again," Kwame said. "Tell me about marriage among your people."

The Badekas made no objection to a theoretical discussion. They enumerated four types of marriage-like relationships between a man and a woman. The first and most complicated was full and legal marriage, a union not just between a man and a woman, but between two families, two lineages, but never between a couple with genealogical links. Full marriage involved the exchange of gifts and commitments. The man and his family amassed bridewealth and transferred it to the father of the woman, preferably over a period of years. During that period the bond between the two families deepened. If the marriage did not work, if the woman failed to produce offspring, or for whatever reason returned to her family, the bridewealth—or at least part of it—was returned to the man and his group.

Anciently bridewealth had consisted of goats or bars of metal, not the Europeans' currency for that suggested that the woman was merely bought. But more recently money was given as bridewealth. Even today successful men in the Equateur, men with surplus wealth, took second or even third wives for they did not have to buy cars and fine houses and splendid clothes as successful men did in cities like Kinshasa. But a man with several wives was expected to treat them equally and impartially, providing each woman with her own living quarters, her own gardens, sometimes even her own kitchen. Among the Mongo people the offspring of these legal marriages belonged to the husband's lineage.

Two other kinds of union existed, only rarely now, but with some frequency in ancient times. In one case a man purchased a woman in a cash transaction, the money paid fully at one time. The woman worked for the man and served as his sexual partner. She was not quite a slave—for slavery had long been abolished—but neither was she accorded the respect due a legal wife. In the second case, a temporary situation, the woman served as security for a debt. She offered herself voluntarily as a gesture of assistance to her father or brother. When her relative had accumulated sufficient funds he bought her back. In both of these cases offspring from the union belonged to the child's father and his lineage.

In a fourth kind of union, now widespread, Kwame was told, a man kept a woman as his mistress, his concubine. No marriage agreement was entered into. No linkage was affected between two families, two lineages. Offspring of such a relationship belonged to the woman's lineage.

"I take it which lineage claims the children is very important," Kwame said.

Théa nodded. "This last kind of relationship is the one you have with Kalima," concluded her husband. "Assuming you do not marry, the child belongs to her lineage."

"We call that 'living together' in America," Kwame said. "Two people share their lives, but they choose not to marry." He laughed. "I can tell you that the woman I lived with before coming here would attack you for insulting her if you suggested she was my concubine."

"Maybe you were her concubine," teased Théa.

"We were equals," said Kwame. "Nobody's a concubine in America."

"But this is Africa. You are not equals here," Théa pointed out. "Kalima is dependent on you. She lives in your house. You give her money every week."

"You know a great deal about us," Kwame said.

"It is because you are fascinating," Théa said, teasing. "And Kalima tells us these things. Although we could see that she was pregnant well before she told us."

Kwame returned to his original question: "If I wanted to marry her—"

"Don't marry her," Badeka interrupted. "Europeans have a concept that is strange to us: *amour*. This *amour*, it comes and it goes. Americans, I understand, have a notion that is even worse, '*amour romantique*,' 'romantic love.'"

"Is that what you feel for Kalima?" Théa asked.

"She seems part of my life," Kwame said. "I don't want to think of her not being part of it. And if trouble comes to the Equateur," he added, "I want to have made arrangements that will provide for her."

"Her people will provide for her," Théa observed. "That's what African families do."

For a time they talked of other things: situations at the school, the hardships of the refugees in the jungle, the possibility that the fight between Mobutu's loyalists and the Kabilistes might spill into the Equateur.

After he announced that he should be leaving, Kwame asked Badeka, "If I were to approach Kalima's people, would you serve as my family? Could you attest for me—"

"Don't think of marrying her," Badeka said.

"You married Théa," Kwame said. "She's Senegalese. Is that so different?"

"The Senegalese are Africans," Théa reminded him. "And we married in Europe. We returned to Africa already married."

"Go home to America with happy memories of this woman," Badeka advised. "I have seen American movies. A man feels temporary pain at the loss of a woman for whom he feels 'romantic love.' But soon another woman enters his life. Let that happen to you."

"And let Kalima keep the child," said Théa.

"It's not about the child," Kwame said.

"It's always about the child," said Badeka.

Kwame returned home, irritated that the Badekas could not understand his point of view. The child was not the main consideration; the relationship was. But perhaps the child would always be the main consideration for an African. Kalima was not at the house. These days she seemed to spend more time at *le snack* than with him. She would be even less involved with him once the baby came. Well, at least he had checked out the possibility of their marrying. Clearly it was not a good idea. There would be other women; there always had been. He put the idea out of his head.

Every evening while the servant made dinner—Buta from Bolobe was being trained by Kalima to cook at *le snack*—Kwame listened on Odejimi's shortwave radio to news of Africa from London and Brussels. He learned that Mobutu had returned from France. Commentators speculated that this consummate political manipulator might yet engineer a peaceful solution to the conflict in Zaire. Even so, American troops landed in the old French Congo. Stationed in Brazzaville across Pool Malebo from Kinshasa, they stood ready to evacuate Americans in danger in Kinshasa.

Meanwhile there was concern about the fate of tens of thousands of Hutu refugees who seemed to have disappeared in the jungles southeast of Kisangani. Were they massacred by Kabiliste rebels? If so, what happened to the bodies? Some 80,000 bodies could not simply disappear. But helicopter overflights showed no evidence of either the refugees or their bodies.

Lubumbashi, the country's second city, the Elisabethville of the colonials, fell to the rebels; it was in Shaba Province, the heartland of the Copper Belt. A few days earlier Mbuji Mayi had fallen as well; it was the capital of the diamond mining area of Kasai. The Kabilistes were marching toward Kinshasa. Nothing could stop their advance. Some commentators warned of a bloodbath ensuing there. Others speculated that if Mobutu could not broker a settlement, he would take refuge at his palace in Gbadolite in the far north on the Ubangi River where he and his ethnic followers might try to make a stand in the Equateur. Perhaps they would negotiate for the region to become a separate republic, bounded by the Congo and Ubangi Rivers and their tributaries in the east. Or perhaps they would fight.

Speculation of fighting in the Equateur deeply disturbed Kwame. He tried not to let Kalima know how worried he was. They made love every night—with an intensity and pleasure he had never experienced before. Kalima gave herself to him completely. He responded with tenderness and patience. Nothing was hurried or urgent as it had sometimes been when they were first together. They moved in harmony with one another. In being joined together they seemed to become one.

After lovemaking Kwame would fall asleep, his hand resting lightly against Kalima. Later, still touching her, he would wake and stare at the darkness. How much longer, he would wonder, could they do this? Would there be fighting in Mbandaka? If there were, would she take refuge in Bolobe? Would he be ordered to evacuate Mbandaka while she was gone? Would he be with her when the baby was born? Or far away in another country never to see her again?

One night he slipped from the bed and walked naked through the house. He went out onto the terrace where a breeze blew so strongly that mosquitoes did not bother him. He let the air wash over him. Nakedness felt natural now. He drank in the warm night air; it carried the scent of the river. He stared into a darkness so black to his eyes that at first, he could hardly see the house he had just left. Then he made out stars and heard the whispering of the river as it passed.

He felt himself a tiny speck of humanity against the immensity of the night: its darkness, its solitude and silence. But even a speck of humanity had to consider its destiny. His woman was asleep upstairs carrying his child. Should he marry her? Could he abandon her? Abandon them? If he had to leave, would she come with him? If she would not, could he stay? And do what?

How could he stop whatever it was that was hurtling toward them? Could it be stopped? Not by pouring libations to a statue every week. Not by wearing charms tied to a thong. Was there nothing he could do? Was it his fate—their fate— simply to be overwhelmed?

The present course of his life seemed to offer three career possibilities: academia; US government service; and remaining, without a career, in Mbandaka with Kalima.

The academic possibility would involve jockeying for position and tenure, trying to maneuver into ever-better situations at ever-better universities. It would require churning out sham-intellectual articles about Third World literature for navel-gazing audiences of less than twenty souls. It would demand couching these "explorations" in polysyllabic obfuscatory jargon, the lingo of the priesthood of on-the-make academics. It would mean concocting arcane insights so esoteric that they bewildered—and thus impressed—colleagues so fearful of confessing puzzlement and confoundment that they would not acknowledge what any nonacademic could immediately see: that the "exploration" was all piffle, poppycock, twaddle, humbug, malarkey—in short, bullshit.

The academic life would mean playing political games, currying favor with the right people, seeking graduate students and grants for research. It would involve years of classes full of students who had little interest in the subject matter— although a few would, indeed, feel passionate about it. Academic life in the States would inevitably mean sometimes skirting, sometimes engaging, but never escaping the matter of race.

Kwame thought about Livie. Had she loved him? He was no longer sure what love in America meant or involved. He knew that what he and Livie felt for each other was based partly on race. That she enjoyed being different by living with a black man. Doing that made her special. A black man's regard oddly credentialed her. For his own part Kwame felt a higher level of self-acceptance because she was white. Her being white and pursuing him gave him a better sense of himself.

But he had also known that any marriage to Livie would end in divorce. In the long haul Livie would want comfort. She disapproved of divorce the way she disapproved of abortion: it was disagreeable, but it had to be done. One just didn't talk about it. He knew that at some time she would turn into her parents: having—or at least espousing—all the right liberal passions, but not experiencing any inconvenience in supporting them. She would want to be comfortable, which meant rich. Which Kwame would never be. He could not help thinking that her ultimate comfort would be achieved by marrying a wealthy white man, probably the man she had asked his permission to live with. Later she would startle her children by revealing that, yes, she had once lived with a black man; she had loved him desperately (that, of course, would be part of the myth), but she had finally realized that at least for now life was better with her own kind.

Of course, returning to academic life would mean renewed contact with women students who indulged fantasies about their professors. Or, in the case of Livie, acted them out. If students knew that he had had a serious affair with a Mongo woman—or that he had married her or had a child with her— that would make him even more intriguing. More desirable. Irresistible even. He would fill his classes. He did not look forward to any of that.

Standing in the night, he realized that he did not want to return to consumer society. Where people judged you on the basis of what you wore and owned and drove, not on what you'd achieved, given where you'd started. Nor did he want to return to a society where sex was a mere commodity of pleasure, where that commodity became an engine driving the entire society. The sex he now had was uncomplicated, hetero-sexual contact, deeply enriched by emotion and mutual respect and—admit it, he said to himself—with love. Kalima and he did not spend much time during the day thinking about it.

As for a USIS career, race would always be a factor there as well. Advancement would be facilitated by a mentor; he would need to find one of those. It would still be parsed out in terms of racial categories and slots. Sometimes this would help him, sometimes hurt. But he would never be free of it. And overseas he would be expected to defend American policy regardless of what it did to small countries that needed help in achieving not client status, but true independent nationhood. Too many American politicians and policy makers wore blind-ers; they could not see the other guy's point of view. Or look at America from a non-American perspective. The American obsession with American interests had led Zaire into its present condition of deprivation and crisis.

Kwame had genuine, perhaps idealistic, desires to help Africans achieve a better life. Did American policy have any real interest in that? If he agreed to play the game in order to achieve what he could—which would require all he could muster in terms of "protective coloration"—would he ever find a companion to share his life with him? Kalima had made him realize he wanted a family.

And what about Kalima? Would she ever feel American romantic love for him? They had mutual respect. Was that enough? Could it work? Anyway, he thought, if he tried a life with Kalima and it didn't work, he could always return home. He would deal then with the ambivalence he felt toward returning to America. "For an African American, you are very

American," Odejimi had teased him. Now he felt that for an African American he was becoming increasingly African.

As THE days passed, Kwame noticed people in Mbandaka and its outlying areas who did not look as if they belonged in the town. He was not certain what distinguished them as different. Perhaps he was simply antsy about the country's deterioration. But some of these newcomers appeared to be refugees. Were they Mobutu loyalists from Kisangani? Or Mongos returning to their home territory? It was not possible that they were Hutu refugees who had walked through hundreds of miles of jungle to come here.

But where were the Hutu refugees? Each evening radio broadcasts from Europe reported these refugees' plight. One evening commentators talked of insurgents cutting off access by aid workers to refugee camps southeast of Kisangani. The next night the early broadcast reported 55,000 refugees missing. The late broadcast confirmed that aid workers had reached the camps, but found them empty. Where were the refugees? Where were these people headed?

The next day a report announced that the American government had sent its ambassador to the United Nations to mediate a settlement of the conflict in Zaire. The rebels' Laurent Kabila had agreed to mediation; assent was awaited from President Mobutu. Meanwhile the rebels were asked to account for 80,000 missing refugees.

Two DAYS later a broadcast reported United Nations officers claiming to have found the bodies of slain refugees in Zaire. It suggested that the Kabilistes were murderers. But news came the next day that several army commanders had gone over to the rebels; this suggested that the rebels were seen as winners. Tombolo the hotelier confided to Kwame a rumor that the local army commander, who was from Shaba province where the rebels were already entrenched, would declare at the appropriate time—whatever that meant—for Kabila.

Moreover, residents of Mbandaka not native to the Equateur were continuing to abandon it for their home territories. When Kwame went to the residence to make an appointment to see the governor, he discovered that the governor, his *chef du cabinet* and his *chef du protocol,* all of them BaKongo, had returned to the Kongo heartland.

The governor was not alone in leaving Mbandaka. Moulaert came to the center one afternoon while Kwame was shelving returned books. "My wife and I are returning to Belgium," he said.

"What about the job?"

"At a time like this," Moulaert asked, "what can a school inspector accomplish?"

"And Adriaan?"

Moulaert sat down at a library table and put his head in his hands. "We are frantic. Every night my wife cries herself to sleep." The Belgian's voice grew thick with emotion. "I don't want to leave," he said. "But it's dangerous here now. We have our other son to consider."

"Can I do anything to help you?" Kwame asked.

"If you hear anything of Adriaan, let us know." Moulaert pushed a card toward him. It contained an address.

"You've heard nothing?"

"Not a word." Moulaert turned his body away from Kwame and began to weep. Kwame went to him, patted his shoulder, and stared into the tangle of red hair that crowned his head. Kwame returned to shelving books; that seemed the kindest thing to do. Finally Moulaert got himself under control.

He turned back, his large, raw-boned hands still holding his head. He stared off across the room. "You've always thought me a fool, haven't you?" Kwame turned toward him and shrugged, paying him the compliment of not mouthing social lies. "Odejimi thought I was a fool. He poisoned the opinions of everyone he met. Probably I was a fool to say I was on an erotic quest," he admitted. "I understand now that it was a quest for myself."

"Maybe we are all on quests for ourselves," Kwame said.

"May I give you some advice?" Moulaert asked. "Is it possible for you to take the advice of a fool?"

"Why not?"

"If you are happy with Madame Van," he counseled, "marry her."

They did not speak for a moment. "I've considered that," Kwame said, making an admission he would not have expected to utter aloud, certainly not to Moulaert. "But it's impossible."

"I'll tell you what's impossible," Moulaert said. "To bear the loss of a woman you love. To know that, during most of the time you have been together, you have treated her like a whore. Like something you can throw away."

"What happens when I leave here?"

"Take her with you."

"Impossible. She wouldn't be happy."

"Would you be happy without her?"

Kwame looked at the red-haired, red-faced, and now red-eyed man. Moulaert really was a fool, he thought. Now he was in emotional anguish and it was hard, even in his presence, not to laugh at him.

"If you can't take her with you, then stay here."

Kwame tried not to smile and shook his head. "Impossible," he said.

"Why?" the relentless Moulaert persisted. "I am trying to prevent you from making the mistakes I made. My father instructed me that, to be happy, I must marry a woman of the same religion, the same ethnicity, the same social class. I did as he told me and my wife is a horror. It was Marike who showed me the way to happiness."

Kwame said nothing. How could he tell Moulaert that what Marike had given him—whatever that was—was not the stuff of happiness?

"Why is it impossible? Because you come from a superior civilization?"

Kwame felt annoyed with him. Finally he said, "That's one reason."

"Because you are rational and she is filled with superstition?"

Kwame shrugged. Another reason.

"Because your civilization is rich and hers is poor? Because your civilization—if we can call it that—is rich and gives you the comforts of gadgets and entertainments—"

"I'm not uncomfortable here," Kwame said.

"Then it must be that you do not love her," Moulaert said. "That like Odejimi you are only using her body."

Kwame said nothing.

"Or perhaps you love her and cannot admit it to yourself," Moulaert suggested. "That makes you an even bigger fool than me."

Kwame remained silent

"We are fools, you know," Moulaert said. "To think that we are serving Africans when we are really pursuing the interests of our own countries. Of our own kind. To think that we are helping Africans by trying to turn them into replicas of ourselves. We are trained in rationality," Moulaert said. "But is that rational?"

Kwame nodded. It occurred to him that Moulaert, however lovesick he might be, was less of a fool than he thought. Or that Odejimi, whose advice he had so scrupulously followed, was more of one than he had realized.

"You'll be the only white man left now, won't you?" Moulaert said, rising from the table.

"I will keep an ear open for news of Adriaan," Kwame promised.

"Thank you," Moulaert said. He came to Kwame and gave him a hug. At the door he turned and said, "Marry her."

Kwame never saw him again.

SIXTEEN

One noontime when Kwame came from the school to have lunch at *le snack*, he found Kalima paying extraordinary attention to patrons she would ordinarily ignore. The couple were *tatas*, obviously rural people. The bustle of Mbandaka unnerved them, the occasional passing car. The ceremony of a midday meal at a restaurant baffled them. But Kalima had placed them in the shade of a palm frond canopy at *le snack's* best table; they sat on chairs brought from the center. Kalima hurried up to him. "My parents are here," she told him. "Come sit with them."

Kwame suppressed his knowledge of her father's disapproval. He hid his perplexity: Why had they come? Travel was not easy from Lake Tumba. He approached with deference and gave them a Lonkundo greeting, although he still knew very few words in Kalima's mother tongue. He sat with them. They ate together, lacking a common language, stumbling along for a time in Lingala, saying little except when Kalima joined them.

"My parents will stay with us for a few days," Kalima explained in their presence. "I will put them in our room," she continued. "We can sleep downstairs." If there had been a rupture between Kalima and her parents, her pregnancy had harmonized it. The parents had apparently come to Mbandaka to verify that a pregnancy had occurred and to rejoice with Kalima about it. Kwame smiled as if their presence were his dearest wish. Perhaps the parents were now reconciled to him.

After lunch Kwame returned to the house with Buta, who had finished cooking at *le snack*. Together they broke open the locked doors of second story bedrooms. Sheer perversity, Kwame felt, had caused the Bertons to lock the rooms. They contained little of value except clothes and linens that the couple was never likely to use again.

In the smaller bedroom stood a desk. How curious, Kwame thought, for Berton to lock a desk drawer he would probably never return to open. Animated by a perversity of his own, Kwame determined to open it. Since he had broken the locks of the bedroom doors, it was no challenge to force the one on the desk. As if he were taking a small act of revenge on Berton, he took pleasure in rendering the drawer unusable.

In it he found legal papers, keys, scissors, staples, and a pair of eyeglasses. At the back of it lay a leather wallet. Why a wallet? No matter, Kwame thought. He would have Buta toss it with the rest of the contents into the trash.

Together he and Buta prepared the master bedroom for Kalima's parents. While Buta finished up, Kwame took the desk drawer downstairs. As he pushed the contents into a trash bin, he examined the wallet. Strange. It had an American look. Then he saw the initials. Depressed into the leather were the letters KM. Kwame set the drawer onto the kitchen counter. He stepped backward and stared at the wallet as if it were an evil fetish, as if it might move.

At last he lifted it from the drawer. It felt almost hot in his hand. Kwame inspected its contents. The money it once carried had been removed. In one pocket was an expired Visa card. In a second Kwame found a California driver's license, the expiration date now passed. He recognized the photo on it. It showed the man who, in another photo, had worn the orange sport shirt he had bought in the market so many months before. In the plastic photo holder were an Automobile Club card, a mini calendar, a small portrait of a middle-aged couple and a photo of Mason, clowning in a tuxedo, bussing the cheek of a bride. Kwame thought: Stephanie.

He set the wallet on the counter and held his head in his hands. Why this now? Kent Mason had not tiptoed through his head for weeks. Kwame had hoped that Mason had vanished in a trek to get back to the States, back to Stephanie and the life that refused to follow him to the Congo. Now he knew that Mason was dead. Poor Mason, Kwame thought. Somehow he had gotten involved with Mme Berton. How lonely he must have been!

Before Buta came downstairs, Kwame threw the wallet and the drawer into the trash. He would not tell Kalima or anyone else what he had found. Mason's fate would remain a mystery.

KWAME AND Kalima did not talk privately until after everyone had gone to bed. If she had not been focused on her parents, she would have sensed that something was bothering him. But instead, while undressing, she said, "They are pleased about the baby. They knew, but now they see. At last I am a woman for my parents."

Kwame saw that airing his grievance against her father would only lead to dissension. They went to bed without further talk, lying side by side in the darkness. Finally Kwame asked, "Why are they here?"

"To see that the baby is really on its way. They are so pleased."

Kwame pushed behind him his grievance and the thought of Mason's wallet. He realized that the baby was not merely his and Kalima's. It was her parents' baby too. Its umbilical cord tied them all together. That cord bound Kalima more strongly to her parents. Although she had spent years away, the baby was already bringing her back to them. Kwame had not expected any of this to happen. An American mother might come for a week or so after a baby's birth, but the maternal grandparents did not move into their daughter's home.

Kalima sensed that something bothered Kwame. He seemed baffled, perhaps disapproving. "Also, they have heard stories of the rebellion," she said, reinforcing reasons for the visit. "Of fighting, people killed. They have heard of strangers coming into the Equateur." She took his hand. "They want me to come home."

The darkness fell into heavy silence. Kwame waited for Kalima's assurance that she had no intention of leaving him. But she said nothing. "You aren't thinking of going," he declared finally. Her silence persisted. In the darkness it possessed a kind of physical presence. It surrounded them, had weight. Kwame reached over and turned on the light. "You live here," he reminded her. "You have a house here, a man, a business. The last time you were in Bolobe, they tried to keep you there."

At last she said, "But now I am carrying a child. My father claims it is not safe here. Rebellions are always fought in cities."

Kwame sat up in bed and stared at her. "In cities like Kinshasa. Not in Mbandaka."

"This is difficult for me," Kalima said. "I cannot ignore my father's advice."

"Of course you can. You left Bolobe to live with me."

"He wants me to come home. He says the baby should be born among its own people."

"I am its own people," Kwame said. "They know it's my child?" She nodded. "The baby is with its people. You are here. I am here."

"You are here," she said. "But for how long?"

That was the problem, Kwame thought. Vandenbroucke had left her. Mason. Odejimi. Kalima and Bonanga, her father, were both sure that he would also leave her.

"I have no plans to leave you. Or the baby." She said nothing. "We are the baby's parents—together, its family. And you're a woman, not a child. You left your village long ago. Your father knows that."

"You talk to me as if I were American."

"No, I'm talking to you as if you were"—he emphasized the words—"*an adult*. You decide what you want to do."

"I want to do what my father asks."

"No!" Kwame said. "I don't agree to this!" He rose from the bed and began to pace. He found a *pagne*, a cloth, and tied it around his waist like a sarong. "I am your man now. Not your father." He waited for her to acknowledge this. But she said nothing. He continued to pace, feeling humiliated. She would not acknowledge that if any man had authority over her, it was he.

"Will you go?" he asked finally.

She said nothing.

"Will they take you back to Bolobe and marry you to the man in Bikoro?"

Silence.

"You defied your father once and refused this man. Why are you suddenly the obedient little girl again?"

Still nothing. He was sure that her parents had been at her, insisting that he would leave.

Finally he asked, "What if we got married?" A woman was supposed to look flattered, even excited, Kwame thought, when a man spoke to her of marriage. But Kalima only looked sullen. "In my society a man does not tell a woman what to do. But generally she attends to her husband's wishes."

"You forget. I have been married to a white man—"

"I am not a white man."

"But you will leave."

"I will take you with me."

The silence persisted, pressing down on him.

"Perhaps I won't leave," he said.

"You will leave," she said quietly.

Kwame mused that this was why ultimately it had been unthinkable to marry Livie: Because he knew the marriage would end in divorce, in their leaving one another. If they married, would he leave Kalima? Finally he said, "I talked to Badeka about our marrying. He said it was impossible."

"When was this?"

"Why is it impossible if we both want to do it?" He untied the pagne and lay beside her again. He realized that he should phrase the question differently. "I would like to marry you," he said. "Will you marry me?" She made no reply. "You would rather be married to the man in Bikoro?"

"No," she said. "But I am Mongo and he is Mongo. I am African and he is African."

"And before long you will tell everyone that my child—our child—is his."

"If he raises the child, it is his child."

Kwame sat up again, irked at her. She said nothing and stared at the ceiling. "Fuck you!" he said in English. He left the bed and headed for the door.

Kalima jumped from the bed and grabbed his arm. "Don't go!"

"I'll sleep downstairs."

"Wear something!"

"I'll do what I want in my own house."

"My parents are here!" she whispered. "If they see you naked, it is a great insult. They will be insulted and you should be too!"

"Fuck them," he said, again in English. "You can all go back to Bolobe." Kalima did not release his arm. He pushed her away, took the pagne, and left the room with it over his shoulder.

As he descended the stairs, he wrapped the pagne about him. He lay down on the couch, but he was too upset to sleep. He went outside, paced up and down the terrace, then went back upstairs, snatching the pagne from around his waist, and reentered their room. He threw the pagne onto the floor, put on jeans, a tee shirt, and sandals and started out again. "Where are you going?" Kalima asked. He did not reply.

THE BADEKAS were surprised to see him at the door. "I must talk to you," Kwame told them.

Badeka said, "With strangers infiltrating into town it is not a good idea to pay visits at midnight."

AFTER THEY talked, Kwame spent the night on cushions on the Badekas' floor. In the morning he made a stop at the center, taking money from the footlocker he kept hidden, and returned to the house with Badeka. Kalima heard the film truck arrive in the driveway. She met the two men at the door, an expression of concern on her face. "Are you all right?" she asked Kwame.

Badeka stepped forward, greeting her with a strange formality. "I come as Kwame's father," he said. He offered her two presents, placing them on the dining table. The first was an envelope; they all understood that it contained money. The second was a necklace that Kalima had once admired. Théa Badeka had presented it to Kwame the night before when she discovered his intentions and had been unable to dissuade him from them.

Kalima stared at the gifts resting on the table. She looked at Kwame, almost apprehensively. They began to move with unusual formality. They seemed to have entered a ceremonial mode. Kalima examined Kwame, as if wanting to be certain he understood what was happening. Kwame bowed to her slightly and tried to smile.

But he was so overcome with apprehension that she would reject the envelope that he could not manage the smile. She stared at the envelope for a long moment. At last she picked it up. "Excuse me," she whispered. "I will give this to my father."

Kwame and Badeka waited without speaking. Kwame paced back and forth. Finally Badeka said, "You did understand what I explained last night, didn't you? An African marriage is a union of families." Kwame nodded, feeling more nervous. "You understand that usually before the process goes forward, families send out— If you will, call them spies. They check out the person seeking a connection to the family." Kwame nodded again, realizing that the scrutiny he was about to encounter was much tougher than the one he faced for his doctoral exams or the Foreign Service orals. He needed to piss. Why hadn't he thought of that before? "It's fine for us to say that in this matter I am your father. But I know nothing about you."

"You know the kind of person I am."

"Do I? I have not watched you grow up. I do not know your parents, your grandparents. How do I answer when he asks about them?"

"Will he ask about them?"

"Of course."

"What else?"

"Is there insanity in your family?"

Kwame laughed. "You tell him, 'Of course!' I'm Exhibit A. Only a man of impaired intelligence would submit to this."

Badeka smiled and shook his head. "Ordinarily the two fathers speak together," he said. "In this case I must refer some questions to you. This is very unusual." Kwame swallowed. "We may have to pay more for Kalima as a result."

"Excuse me for a moment," Kwame said. "I must make a stop."

On the way to the bathroom Kwame saw Bonanga in the hall. The man turned his back as if Kwame had broken a ritual taboo. Kalima, who was with her father, looked aghast. Kwame gestured his apologies and ducked into the bathroom. He pissed as if he had not relieved himself since before he came to Mbandaka. When he left the bathroom, he peeked out the door. He saw the coast was clear and hurried back to wait with Badeka.

After some minutes Bonanga entered the living room. Kalima trailed behind him, her movements deferential, almost toadying, her eyes uncharacteristically lowered to the floor. "Please, sit down," she said to the men. "You must be hungry. I will prepare food."

The men sat down. While the two Africans spoke in Lonkundo, Kwame heard Kalima in the kitchen, speaking in a low, strained voice. She ordered Buta out of the room, for there must be no question but that she had prepared this meal herself. Buta went onto the terrace overlooking the river where the men could see him. He set up a table with three places.

After a time Bonanga and Badeka stopped talking. Kwame wondered if their silence portended difficulties. Perhaps, perhaps not. Kalima had told him that in social situations Africans did not feel a need always to keep talk flowing. He tried to occupy his mind by concocting correct Lonkundo praises for the meal Kalima was preparing.

The three men ate mostly in silence. In traditional Africa women did not eat with the men for whom they prepared food—although Kalima and Kwame always ate together. Now Kalima stood nearby, ready to serve or fetch if anything were needed. Kwame recited the Lonkundo phrases he had carefully worked out to praise the meal.

As they ate, Bonanga scrutinized his daughter's suitor. Kwame felt nervous under his inspection. His mother's etiquette lessons reverberated in his head. "Never eat with your fingers!" she had admonished him. Of course, she did not know that he would marry into a family where eating with one's fingers was customary.

When it was clear that the men would need no more food, Bonanga nodded to Kalima to leave. She disappeared into the kitchen. Bonanga surveyed Kwame once more and turned to Badeka. He posed a question in Lonkundo. Badeka turned to Kwame.

"He wants to know: Is this young man an outcast from his own society? He says all black people in America come from slaves."

The question surprised Kwame. His reaction—from embarrassment—was almost to laugh, but he suppressed the urge. No, he answered. He was not an outcast. In fact, the American government took great care in choosing people who represented it overseas. They had to be well-educated, well-spoken, and possessed of dignity. He acknowledged that the forebears of virtually all black Americans had been taken to America as slaves. But, like many others, he had worked hard, taken advantage of opportunities and gotten an education. It was these very qualities of hard work, perseverance, and adaptability that qualified him to be a husband for Kalima.

Badeka listened carefully and translated for Bonanga. The two men talked for a moment. Badeka turned back to Kwame.

"He wants to know: Why has this young man come to live in Mbandaka so far from his own people? What kind of relationship does he have with his own people that he should live so far away?"

He came to Zaire, Kwame said, because he wanted to know more about the people from whom his ancestors sprang.

Badeka translated this answer to Bonanga. Bonanga posed another question.

"Was Kwame a good son to his father and to his people?"

"Yes."

"To his mother and her people?"

"Yes."

"How could this be when he chose to live so far away from them?"

His family knew it was an honor, Kwame explained, for him to serve his country, to travel the world on its behalf, and meet the people from whom his ancestors had come. He had his parents' blessing for his time in Zaire.

"Had he left a wife and children behind in America?"

"No." He had no wife, no children.

When Badeka told him this news, Bonanga regarded Kwame carefully.

"How could this be? Had he divorced a wife?"

"No."

Bonanga's regard became suspicious.

"Had Kwame already deserted a family then?"

"Why this question?" Kwame asked.

"In our society," explained Badeka, "a young man seeks a wife as soon as he can. Having a wife is a badge of full manhood. That's how he enters into adult society. A man's father helps provide the bridewealth."

"Our society works differently," Kwame told him. Badeka looked perplexed. "Does he not understand that things are done differently in diff— Forget it." Kwame tried not to let his expression or behavior show his impatience. "What's he really asking?"

"A man of your age should be married," Badeka explained. "He wants to know why you are not married."

"Because I'm not."

"Is your family impoverished?"

"No."

"Do you have some ailment?"

"No."

"Is there a history of disease in your family that makes American women refuse to marry you?"

"No."

"Insanity?"

"No."

"Are you impotent? Or sexually defective?"

Kwame tried not to laugh. "Let him ask his daughter."

"You are a mature man. Mature men produce children. Why have you not produced children? If you have, what kind of care do you give them?"

"I am in the process of producing a child with Kalima right now."

Badeka turned to Bonanga and spoke at some length. Bonanga replied even more lengthily. Badeka turned back to Kwame.

"He has not specifically said so, but I think he cannot believe that a man of your age, education, and wealth has not married and produced children. Since you have deserted your parents and presumably also the wives and children you choose not to speak about, he worries that you will tire of Kalima and abandon her."

"I have no intention of doing that."

"To him desertion is the practice of white men from the West," Badeka said. "The first husband abandoned Kalima. He thinks it is logical to assume that you will eventually do the same thing. He doesn't want his daughter to be abandoned again."

"I love her," Kwame said, declaring what he did not ordinarily articulate. "It's as simple as that. Can he understand that?"

"No. We do not understand what you mean by love."

"Then tell him whatever you must to make it happen."

Bonanga and Badeka talked at some length. Then Bonanga rose from the table and left the room. "He doesn't agree, does he?" Kwame said.

"You are always so sure of yourself," Badeka observed. "Now you seem as nervous as a schoolboy before exams."

"He didn't go away happy, did he?"

"He is distressed that his daughter is interested only in marrying white men. I commiserated with him."

"Is it over?" asked Kwame. "Does it happen or not?"

"As according to custom, I invited him to my house. He is coming this afternoon." Badeka paused, pondering. "I must offer him a chicken. Could you go to the market and buy—" Badeka stopped in midsentence. "I suppose you know nothing about buying a chicken."

Kwame laughed, somewhat relieved. "Don't know how to buy one," he said. "Or how to carry it once I've bought it."

"I will get the chicken," Badeka said. "You can reimburse me later. Right now I have to get back to classes."

Kwame took Badeka back to Bomboko Congo. When they arrived there, he could no longer contain his nervousness and asked again, "Is it going to happen?"

"This is not what he wants for his daughter," Badeka said. "Still, she took your present. That's a good sign. Her father accepted the preliminary gift and is coming to talk."

"But," Kwame said, "I hear 'but.'"

"But regardless of what you think of yourself," Badeka said, "he considers you a white man. An American. From a people who have gone to the moon and have different customs. Kalima was married once to a white man and it didn't work. As they see it, Vandenbroucke deceived them. He entered into a legitimate Mongo marriage with Kalima. He transferred bride-wealth for her, then treated her like a *femme libre*. He did not give her children and he was careless with her."

"I'm not Vandenbroucke," Kwame said. "She's carrying my child and I've made it clear to her that I don't want her to be with other men."

"You're still white," Badeka said. "I will try to think of good things to say about you."

Badeka started to leave the film truck. "Don't go just yet," Kwame said.

"I've got a class to teach."

Kwame put his hand on Badeka's arm. "I've been thinking as we drove here. You must make Bonanga understand that if Kalima agrees to this, she must realize that the time may come when she must go with me to America."

Badeka closed the door of the truck, willing to arrive late for his class. "He will not agree to that."

"He's not marrying me. She is. It's her decision."

Badeka smiled with astonishment. Clearly Kwame did not understand how negotiations proceeded. "Is this marriage a good idea?"

"Yes. We both want it."

Badeka shook his head. "Kalima is an African village girl. She knows little English. She has almost no education."

"I know her better than you do," said Kwame. "She has talents that neither Bolobe nor Mbandaka have allowed her to develop. Look what she's done with *le snack.* "

Badeka continued to shake his head. "*Le snack* works here, but it's nothing in America. Nothing."

Kwame turned pleadingly to his friend. "My father," he said with a smile, "I don't pretend it will be easy. But she can do it. Millions of people have done it, even from Africa."

"I can't keep the class waiting any longer," said Badeka. He opened the door of the truck again.

"Be persuasive!" Kwame urged.

Badeka put his hands up as if to say, "Enough!" and hurried off to his students.

AT NIGHTFALL Kwame went to the Badekas' home with a case of beer, a present for Badeka. He reimbursed him for the chicken and inquired about the negotiations. "Were you able to say good things about me?"

Badeka did not smile at this banter. He reported, "Her father wants to be certain that you understand you are not buying a woman. You are negotiating a connection between two families."

Kwame nodded and asked, "You explained about America?"

"I explained. He listened."

Kwame felt relieved. Bantering again, he inquired, "What will it cost me to connect our families together?"

"Her father wants fifteen goats in good health."

"Goats!" Kwame began to laugh. "I can't even buy him a chicken! How am I going to find him fifteen goats in good health?"

"I palavered him down to twelve."

"Wonderful. Will you help me buy them?"

"Twelve goats is not much in terms of bridewealth," Badeka informed him. "I got you a pretty good deal on Kalima."

"Really?" said Kwame. He was not sure that he should be pleased to be getting a bride on the cheap.

"Bonanga said he figured she was already your woman. But he might as well get some money for the cost of rearing her."

"Money too?"

"Yes. Quite a bit of money." Badeka mentioned the sum.

Kwame swallowed, but nodded. "I can pay that," he said. "But I won't have much left. Kalima can live in a poverty that was brought upon her by her own people."

"He does not want it all at once. In fact, he insists that it must not be paid all at once. You pay it over time and the linkage between the families is strengthened." Kwame nodded again. "The two of you must also marry in a ceremony that is official, legal, legitimate, in your own society. He wants to be sure that you understand—"

"That I am marrying a woman, not buying her."

"Precisely," said Badeka. "When I spoke about America, he demanded that you agree not to take Kalima or your children out of the Equateur. I said that was impossible."

"Good! That is impossible."

"I said that you were an American, after all, and the time might come when you had to visit your people." Badeka added, "I also reminded him that it was his daughter's decision."

"He did not like that."

Badeka grinned. "No, he did not like that."

"I can agree not to take her away for eighteen months. Perhaps two years."

"We agreed on five years," Badeka said.

"I cannot agree to five years," said Kwame. "I work for people who insist I do their bidding. And there may be circumstances—"

Badeka shrugged. "He was adamant. And he opposes this marriage." Kwame said nothing, but this demand created an impasse. "If you want to have any rights to your child," Badeka advised, "you better agree to his conditions."

"What happens in two years if this matter cannot be resolved?"

"Perhaps it is not such a good idea to marry," Théa Badeka said.

"The father is a man of strong views," Badeka reported. "Traditional views. You might call him obstinate."

"That word will never cross my lips." Kwame smiled.

"He opposes this marriage. So you must not be obstinate."

"Why not enjoy Kalima now," suggested Théa, "and leave her when you must?"

"I've been with women I enjoyed," Kwame said. "I want to marry Kalima."

"If the marriage fails," Badeka explained, "it is possible that some of the bridewealth would be returned."

"That's fantastic!" Kwame said in English. "What am I going to do with a bunch of fucking goats?"

Badeka waited until Kwame calmed down. "But not all of it will be returned," he continued. "She will have presented you with a child, after all. If you leave the Equateur and desert her, you cannot expect that any bridewealth will be returned."

Controlling himself, Kwame nodded. He would not be another Vandenbroucke, but how could they ask him for a five-year commitment to stay in the Equateur? He wondered if not marrying Kalima would be the wiser course. "What happens next?" he asked.

"Her father makes one more demand," said Badeka. "He does not want her to stay in Mbandaka. He believes it's dangerous here. He and his wife are taking her back to Bolobe tomorrow."

"He makes those decisions for her?"

"Until she marries," said Théa. Kwame did not like this arrangement, but apparently he was stuck with it. "Or until she rebels," Théa added.

"She rebelled once before," remarked Kwame. Remembering that mollified him.

"Yes, but there would be no point in rebelling this close to marriage."

"Is Kalima committed to this marriage?" Kwame asked.

"She accepted your gift," Badeka said. "And she understands about America."

"Thank you again for the necklace," Kwame said to Théa.

She acknowledged his thanks with a smile. "A man's family helps him with his bridewealth."

"Thank you for being my family."

"Are you committed to this marriage?" Badeka asked. "It seems impossible for you to stay here and it will be very difficult for her to go with you."

"She has amazing resources," Kwame said. "I think she can get along almost anywhere."

"Do not go back to the house to be with her tonight," Badeka advised.

"I can't see her again?" Badeka shook his head. "Will they know I've agreed to these arrangements?" Kwame asked.

"I will tell her father tomorrow," Badeka said. Then he added, "We go to Bolobe in eight days."

"To buy goats," Kwame replied.

"When you have transferred the goats and the first money payment to her father, then she becomes your wife. And you can return here."

"Consider this carefully," Théa advised, "before you decide to do it."

Kwame drove to the hotel. He had a drink in the bar with Tombolo. The hotelier had been listening to news broadcasts from Brussels. The Kabilistes were approaching Kinshasa. Every commentator expected a pitched battle for the city. "They want blood, these commentators," Tombolo said. "After all, it is our blood, not theirs."

Kwame asked Tombolo if strangers were entering the Equateur, if he thought that Mobutu and his people might make a final stand in the region, perhaps even seeking independent nationhood for it. "People are coming into the Equateur," Tombolo acknowledged. "Unfortunately few of them have the price of a hotel room. And Mobutu is dying," he commented. "Who fights for a dying man?"

They talked like friends, citizens of the same town, from the same people. Finally Kwame asked, "Did you know Vandenbroucke?" Tombolo gave him a sideways glance and said nothing. Kwame smiled. "You think it's taken me a long time to ask." Tombolo shrugged. "You did know him."

"*Il n'etait pas méchant,*" Tombolo said. "Not a bad guy."

Both men drank from their glasses and stared before them.

Finally Tombolo said, "He never intended that Kalima, as you call her, should be more than his companion while he was here." Kwame nodded. "In a time of SIDA a man needs a companion who is faithful to him."

"Dr. Odejimi always talked as if he passed her around to his friends."

"That Odejimi," Tombolo said. "He was the one who passed her around. When she was with Van, Odejimi kept trying to seduce her. When Van was about to leave, he allowed it to happen." Tombolo gazed for a moment at Kwame. "Don't hate me for saying this. She was agreeable that it should happen. They saw that Odejimi would take care of her. That was what they both wanted. *Il n'etait pas méchant, Van.*"

Kwame stared into his drink for a time. Well, what else was Kalima to do? She could not return to Bolobe unmarried.

At last Kwame asked Tombolo if he could stay the night. Tombolo regarded him strangely, but said the room where he had first lodged was free. "My prospective father-in-law is staying at my house," Kwame explained. "I don't want to see him."

As he registered for the room, the child-woman Tombolo was now calling La Petite sidled up to Kwame and offered herself. "Practically a virgin," Tombolo assured him, recommending her services. "I guarantee you she is clean."

THE ROOM was unchanged since Kwame had first lodged in it. He could have sworn that the same sheets remained, unchanged, on the beds. He went out onto the balcony overlooking the river and thought of Dr. Odejimi and Kent Mason. Poor Mason, sent where he should never have been posted. As Kwame stood there, all of that seemed very far away, truly in a different life.

Kwame did not sleep well. He rose grouchy, missing the scent, sight, and presence of Kalima, her laughter, her voice humming, the pleasure of knowing that she was there. He slept best now with Kalima warm beside him. The rise and fall of her breathing animated the breath of life for him.

Kwame hung around the hotel most of the day, giving Kalima and her parents time to leave without seeing him. He thought of her constantly, his grouchiness increasing. When he went out on the balcony for a last look at the river, he told himself: You're in bad shape. You better get married.

SEVENTEEN

Kwame's grouchiness continued. He realized that Kalima mellowed him, brought sweetness and harmony to his life. To occupy himself he began to pay attention to the *Centre Culturel Américain.* He arrived early, looked through the accumulated mail, thought about answering it although he did not actually do that, and concocted fictional numbers for reports that were overdue.

One morning when he arrived early, he discovered Tata Anatole sitting on the front stoop, waiting for him with the patience that took everything as it came. He rose as soon as Kwame's film truck appeared. As Kwame left the truck, he saw not patience on the tata's face, but alarm. The old man led him into the center and pointed to a crumpled figure asleep on cushions in a corner. A white man. "He arrived in the night," the tata said.

As Kwame approached the figure, he caught the scent of dirt, dried sweat, and exhaustion. He heard short, troubled intakes of breath; they sounded like sobs. He noticed boots that had gone through at the soles, torn jeans, and bloodied scratches on the young man's arms, clumps of blondish hair that had not seen a comb in weeks, a stubble of red whiskers on his chin. As he knelt down, he recognized the young man as Adriaan Moulaert. Kwame and the tata carried him to the film truck. He was so thin that he seemed almost weightless. He stirred, opened his eyes without seeing, and submitted to being carried.

At the house Kwame and Buta carried him inside. They stripped off his clothes, noticing the rib cage prominent under his skin, the stomach flattened against vertebrae, and put him into the bed that Kalima's parents had used. Kwame covered his shivering body with blankets and left him to sleep. Buta made soup and washed those of his clothes that had survived his journey. Kwame looked through his belongings and Berton's for trousers and shirts the young man could wear. He laid them in the room.

Adriaan woke in the evening. He cautiously descended the stairs, uncertain of where he was. He slowly surveyed the living room. When his gaze fell on a mirror, he peered at his own likeness, finally touching the mirror to verify that it was his own image that he was trying to apprehend. When his eyes fixed on Kwame, reading under a lamp, he stared as if he had never seen him before. He spoke words—Flemish words—which Kwame could not understand. Kwame answered him in French, "Do you know where you are?"

"No," said the young man in a voice that was hardly a whisper. "I was trying to get to Mbandaka. Did I make it?"

"You probably need something to eat," Kwame said.

Adriaan nodded. He stared at his image in the mirror. He looked again at Kwame and pointed at the mirror. "Who is this?" he asked.

Kwame suggested that while Buta was cooking, the young man might want to shower. He led Adriaan back upstairs. He took him to the bathroom, showed him the shower, gave him a new toothbrush, and set out his shaving equipment. Kwame collected the clean clothes he had laid out for Adriaan to wear. When he took them into the bathroom, he found the young man staring at the shower as if he could not remember ever seeing such equipment before. "You can wash in here," Kwame said. He turned on the shower for Adriaan and left a towel on the counter.

When the young man came back downstairs, shaved, his hair washed, and in fresh clothes, he still seemed uncertain of his surroundings. Although he had showered, his eyes peered out of deep blue hollows. He asked again where he was. When Kwame explained, he listened carefully, then asked, "And who are you? Have we met?"

Kwame called Buta to bring dinner and promised to explain everything to Adriaan while they ate. Waiting for Buta, he reminded the young man that he was the American in charge of the cultural center. "You came there one day and we went out to a secondary school," Kwame said. The young man nodded, but Kwame was not sure he remembered. Kwame told him that his parents had returned to Belgium after waiting for weeks hoping for word from him. Adriaan nodded. He ate a dish of soup very slowly. A look of queasiness, then panic, came over his face. He clenched his mouth shut, pulled up the polo shirt Kwame had laid out for him, and vomited into it. Kwame hurried around the table to help him. "I need more sleep," Adriaan said.

He slept around the clock. Kwame stayed close to the house the next day to be of whatever assistance was needed. When Adriaan reappeared late the next afternoon, he still seemed unsure of where he was. Over a dinner, eaten very slowly, Kwame once again explained who he was and why Adriaan was at his house. He also mentioned again that his parents had returned to Belgium fearing he might be lost forever.

"Where have you been?" Kwame asked.

What Adriaan told Kwame was not always coherent, not always entirely audible, many of the details blurred and beyond recall. He had walked from Kisangani, Adriaan said, a distance of 600 miles. He had needed to keep ahead of other refugees moving in the same direction. Many of them were Rwandan Hutus who had been walking and starving in the jungles for months. All of them were exhausted; many, especially children, were sick. When he first left Kisangani, walking with the refugees, he would see people every day who lay down at the sides of the road, unable to go on. They would look at him with hollow, imploring eyes and he knew that if he did not move on, he would join their ranks.

Young men with guns threatened him. They would not allow him to beg for food. So he walked most of one night, determined to get out ahead of the refugees. This proved crucial because otherwise he would have had no hope of securing food. Some villagers were suspicious of him. Others were kind-hearted and hospitable, but they began to sense the hordes that were coming behind him. They gave to fellow Africans first.

"Why are refugees coming here?" Kwame asked. The Equateur was poor; much of the area around Mbandaka was swamp.

"It's where the road goes," Adriaan replied.

"The road ends here," Kwame said. "They'll be stuck here."

Adriaan shrugged and finished his food. When Kwame asked if he wanted more, he said he thought he should lie down again.

After Adriaan went to bed the second night, Kwame wrote a letter to Johannes Moulaert informing him that Adriaan had returned. He drove to the post office, mailed the letter, and went on to the Badekas to report the likelihood that strangers would be flooding into Mbandaka. "Maybe it's just as well we are getting out of here for a few days," Badeka said.

"Should we do something?" Kwame asked.

"What can we do?" Badeka replied. "The governor and his people have already fled. This sort of thing is their responsibility."

"What about the army?"

Badeka said nothing at first. They both knew that the army commander was thought to be sympathetic to the Kabilistes.

He would not welcome Rwandan Hutu refugees into Mbandaka. "If the army is doing its job," Badeka said, "the commander will have intelligence about refugees on the road. If they are not doing their job, we cannot do it for them." He added, "You better get young Moulaert out of here while the airport is still open."

Kwame drove out to the military base and spoke with the duty officer. Because he was "the American," he was finally taken to the quarters of the commander. He explained his business. After regarding him for a long moment, the commander said simply, "This is a Zairean matter. We will handle it in our own way."

"I would like to help," Kwame said.

"You Americans have already helped too much," the commander said. "Or too little. You could have stopped this problem in the beginning."

Kwame persisted. "If tens of thousands of refugees enter this town—"

"This is a Zairean matter," the commander repeated. "We will take care of it in our way." He added, "If you want to help us, go home. Solve the problems in your own country. We don't want you here."

On his way back to the house Kwame stopped at the center. He took his footlocker of money from its hiding place, set aside sufficient funds for Kalima's bridewealth, then took out enough cash to buy Adriaan Moulaert a plane ticket to Kinshasa. He counted what remained. The money from Odejimi's bank account was almost depleted. It was a good thing Kalima's father did not want the entire bridewealth at the time of the marriage.

At dawn the next morning Kwame listened to news reports on the shortwave radio. Then he went downstairs to discover Adriaan eating whatever he could find in the kitchen. "Do you have any plans?" Kwame asked. The young man shook his head. "Do you want to go back to Belgium?" Adriaan shook his head more firmly. Kwame saw that there were tears in his eyes.

"What about Marike?" Kwame asked, trying to be gentle. "Is she—" He did not finish. The question hung in the air.

"We got separated," Adriaan said, his voice thick with emotion. "During the rebel takeover of Kisangani, she went off in our vehicle. The rebels may have commandeered it." He added, "I tried to find her. They probably—"

Kwame nodded. It seemed probable to him that Marike, who had always wanted to advance herself, had become infatuated with the whole idea of rebellion. She had probably made contact with the rebels. Very likely she had delivered the vehicle and herself to them. Probably by now she had become a "friend" of a rebel commander. Probably she had gone with the rebels on their journey, leaving Adriaan Moulaert, her white-man husband, to fend for himself.

"What's happened to the rebellion by now?" Adriaan asked.

"I just listened to the news. Mobutu and Kabila met yesterday aboard a ship anchored off the Congo-Brazzaville port of Pointe Noire. Neither one gave an inch. Ten thousand Kabiliste troops are threatening Kinshasa. There could be a bloodbath."

Without hesitation Adriaan said, "I must get down there. Marike may be with them."

Kwame very deliberately poured himself coffee from the pot of it Buta had made. He wanted to put a brake on young Moulaert's enthusiasm.

"Can I get a plane to Kinshasa? Could you lend me the fare?"

Kwame stirred his coffee and examined the young man. Despite the rest, he was still tired and very thin. "Stay here a few days. Kinshasa is dangerous right now."

"It can't be worse than what I experienced coming from Kisangani. I hate to ask, but can you lend me the airfare?" When Kwame made no reply, Adriaan said, "I must find her. She's my wife. Don't tell me I'm not strong enough."

Kwame drank his coffee, feeling its warmth move down his throat and into his body. He wondered what, if anything, Marike had told Adriaan about her connection to his father. He wondered if it were possible that she felt some attachment to him. Neither seemed likely.

"If you can't give me the money," Adriaan declared, "I'll try to get there by road."

"I'll buy you a ticket," Kwame said at last. "But there are two things you must do for me. Take a letter to the American Embassy. And go to the Belgian Embassy. Tell them who you are, a Belgian citizen, and let your parents know you're safe."

Adriaan stood, grinning, his fatigue erased by Kwame's generosity.

This transformation pleased Kwame. "You must promise to do those things for me first, before you start looking for Marike."

"I give you my word."

Kwame wrote a letter to Pilar Cota for distribution at the embassy. He noted that he had received reports that starving Hutu refugees had entered the Equateur and were headed toward Mbandaka. He had tried to check the reports with local officials, including the military. He had received indications that they were probably accurate, but had been rebuffed by the military when he had offered American help. He pointed out that the road the refugees were traveling terminated in Mbandaka. The town did not possess sufficient resources to feed tens of thousands of starving, homeless people. If they actually arrived in Mbandaka, they would find themselves at the end of the line. Beyond the town lay only swamp and the river.

As he wrote, it occurred to Kwame that his report might never be read. In fact, this letter might not reach the embassy before Kinshasa collapsed into chaos. Unquestionably all American Embassy officers were trying to forestall the possibility of unimaginable bloodshed. Meanwhile their families would be making arrangements to flee. In that confusion a memo from Mbandaka would almost certainly be overlooked.

Even so, Kwame outlined his plans, noting that he intended to drive immediately to Ingende in hopes of confirming reports about the Hutu refugees. They would probably congregate across the Ruki from Ingende, waiting to be ferried across this tributary of the great river, in order to reach Mbandaka. He would report what he observed there without mentioning his immediate future plans.

With Tata Anatole's help, Kwame loaded the film truck with water cans and jerricans of gasoline and enough food for himself. Anatole said, "*M'sieur,* do not go to Ingende." Kwame assured the tata that he would be all right. He wanted only to verify the rumors he had heard. Still he wondered about the dangers he was inviting. Some of the refugees would be armed. Was it not likely that they would want the food he was carrying? Would they try to commandeer the truck?

At the airport Kwame stayed with Adriaan. The young man was still fragile. Shaking his hand as they said good-bye, Kwame wanted to advise him to return to Belgium. For one thing was certain: no matter how hard Adriaan looked, he would never find the Marike he cherished in his heart.

As Adriaan walked out toward the plane, a final passenger debarked from the incoming flight. Blonde, tall, lithe, she seemed like a golden figure. Light shimmered around her as it might for some white goddess out of Rider Haggard. She was Olivia Carlyle.

EIGHTEEN

K wame watched Livie walk hesitatingly across the tarmac, surveying the silent jungle and the decaying terminal with the same perplexity he himself experienced his first day in Mbandaka. He felt a stirring in his groin. As she came closer, he saw that she was thinner than when they were last together. Her face, always placid and unlined, wore an expression of strain. When she entered the building, he grinned at her. Their eyes met, but she looked away, not wanting to encourage the attentions of a Zairean hustler who hung around airports. Then she glanced back at him. He said in English, "Want a taxi, lady?" She screamed with surprised excitement, dropped her flight bags, and embraced him. She wore the same perfume she had always worn, a fragrance that swirled memories into his head. When he held her, he felt the bones of her ribs.

"What the hell are you doing here?" he asked. "This place is about to explode."

"Look at you!" she said, laughing. "Scumbag!" Her grin and the pleasure of seeing him erased the strain from her face. They kissed. She tasted as she always had, a taste that now made him feel a little dizzy.

"The embassy has commandos across the river in Brazzaville," he told her. "They're ready to evacuate American citizens from Kinshasa and you choose this time to visit."

"I came to Cape Town. So why not here?"

They examined one another. "You look fantastic," he said. "What's going on?"

"Swami, I read the news. I came to rescue you from the uttermost parts of the earth."

Kwame laughed, looked at her carefully, and saw that she meant it.

As THEY drove into town, Kwame told Livie, "Walking in from the plane you made me think of the title character in *She*. Rider Haggard hasn't crossed my mind in months."

"Your secret's safe with me," she said, grinning.

He asked, "Did you move in with that guy?"

"Are you kidding? When I was finishing up my first semester of law school? I had exams for god's sake." She scrutinized him for a moment, not actually having denied that she was living with the man. "Are you jealous?"

"Of course," he said. He realized that he was also relieved. He did not want her living with another man. "But I'm a long way away."

"Not so far I couldn't come see you." She grinned at him. "Who goes to Cancun when they can get to Zaire?"

"Who wants sun," he mimicked her inflections, "when she can get shot?" Livie stuck out her tongue at him. The gesture excited him. He had an impulse to stop the van and seize her. Shit shit shit! How damned inconvenient of her to appear out of fucking nowhere. Typical of her to come walking out of the jungle as if she were returning from a mall.

"How is law school?" he asked. "Other than being a great way to lose weight."

"Want to see how much I've lost?" She raised an eyebrow. "Is there some place where I can show you?"

What the hell was he going to do with her, Kwame wondered. He was certainly not going to touch her.

They regarded one another, each of them amused, both knowing he wanted to behold her unclad again, to see how thin she looked, to kiss the ribs that showed through her flesh and the points of her hips. Livie smiled. "You must have a bed," she said, "and a bedroom door we can lock."

Kwame looked away. He was not going to sleep with her. If he did, Kalima would never trust him. And how could he expect her to? He would not want her sleeping with Vanden-broucke if he walked out of the jungle.

"Let me show you the center first."

Livie examined him. He carefully watched the road. She surveyed the rear of the vehicle. "Were you going somewhere?" she asked.

Kwame told her of the rumors about refugees entering the Equateur and his desire to check them out.

"Isn't that dangerous?" she asked.

He guffawed. "Talk about dangerous! What possessed you to come here now? Kinshasa's a powder keg with the fuse lit."

For a moment she stared at children playing, at laundry spread to dry on bushes as they drove through the *cités*. She decided to risk the truth. "I realized I would never forgive myself if something happened to you and I hadn't seen you again." She smiled provocatively. "Things must be pretty dull if you're going looking for refugees. Can I come? I'd love to see the Africa tourists never see."

"Keep your eyes open," he told her. "This is it." He added, "I can go to Ingende tomorrow. Or the next day." He wondered how long she intended to stay, but he did not ask her. "One day or the other, it's all pretty much the same out here."

"Not if you're a starving refugee," Livie said.

"If they're really starving," Kwame told her, "if they're really coming here, then this is not a place you want to be. Or that I'll want you to be."

"Will you come back with me?" she asked.

He said nothing and watched the road. She said nothing and watched his face.

OUT IN front of the center *le snack* was beginning to serve lunch. Buta and the other Zaireans looked surprised to see Kwame with a slim, blonde *américaine*. He nodded to his friends and took Livie inside the center. He introduced her to Lofale, who had begun to work full days, and to Tata Anatole, showed her the film and video collection, and took her into the office. Kwame made sure the door stayed open. The tata stood in the hall outside as if waiting to be called. His presence made Livie uncomfortable. "Is he always there?" she asked.

"Always," Kwame said.

"Can't you send him on an errand?"

"That would set tongues wagging." They regarded one another. Livie scrutinized Kwame as if they had just met and she could not yet read his thoughts. "You'll find that you're an object of intense curiosity," Kwame said.

Livie waited for his move. He thumbed through the stacks of unopened mail. "Would you like some lunch?" he asked.

She examined him again, went calmly to the threshold, smiled at Anatole, and closed the door. She said, "I sort of thought you'd see me and want— To do something else."

"I do want to," Kwame said. He did want to. But he was not going to.

The assurance seemed to relieve her. "But maybe we should talk first, hunh?" she asked. "That's cool. It has been awhile."

Kwame felt her impulse to come to him and—damn his body's hunger!—he wanted to kiss her. He wanted to hold her, to be in bed with her, not to rekindle memories, but because she seemed like a stranger, as mysterious as Kalima sometimes seemed, a traveler from a distant land he had once known, but no longer knew. He wanted to go exploring, to know who she was. But he let the impulse pass.

She smiled, realizing that he was holding himself in check. "Still a person of the mind," she said.

"They're watching us out there," he said, nodding toward *le snack*. "If I kiss you, everybody will start looking in the windows."

"The 'American Presence' can't kiss his girlfriend?"

"Africans are extraordinarily—" He spoke the word that came to mind. "*Pudique*."

"'*Pudique*?' Chaste?" said Livie. " 'Modest?' "

"I speak so much French out here I forget—"

"You forget 'chaste'?" She laughed.

"Anyway," he said, "Africans never kiss in public."

"And we are in Africa," Livie said. "When in Mbandaka . . ."

They had beer and fried, salted plantains and papaya at *le snack* and sat where everyone could watch them. And everyone did.

"Did you come out here alone?" Kwame asked. "Things are—"

"Just a little dangerous?" Livie said, finishing his thought. "Refugees are about to swamp this place and Kinshasa is eerily quiet. It feels as if the entire citizenry is locked up behind shutters, waiting for the terrible battle everyone expects."

"You felt that?" he asked.

"It's as palpable as humidity," she said. Then she added, "No, I didn't come alone. Mike wouldn't let me."

"Mike's the man with room in his apartment?" Livie nodded. "And a thick wallet," Kwame noted, "if he escorted you all the way out here."

"He finished Harvard Business School a couple of years ago and is doing very well. He wants to be married to someone like me."

"To your type? Or to you?"

"We haven't figured out yet which," she said. "You always said I'd end up with someone like him."

Once again Kwame wanted her very much. He asked, "Where is Mike now?"

"In Kinshasa. I told him he absolutely could not come here with me today. I had to have time alone with you."

They looked at each other a long moment. Kwame felt the old life pulling him back. He glanced away because, with the first traces of maturity in her eyes and with the lines that would one day appear on her face already forming, she seemed more beautiful than ever.

"When's he get here?"

"Day after tomorrow," she said.

"We can pick him up at the airport and drive down toward Ingende," Kwame told her. "Unless we go down there tomorrow."

"He would not allow me more than twenty-four hours," Livie said. "But I insisted on forty-eight." She watched him. "So there's still time for us to get to know each other again." Kwame nodded. She added, "Mike and I can talk. He insisted on coming all this way out here with me. But you're the person I can really talk to."

Livie examined him closely because it was proving surprisingly difficult for them to talk. At last she asked, "You didn't fall in love with the Zairean woman married to the Belgian, did you? Your letter sounded as if maybe you had."

After a moment Kwame said, "Well, I certainly didn't expect to."

Livie looked away and took a swallow of beer. Then she examined him again. "Can we still be together?" she asked. "I mean: if she's married, does it matter what we do?" Kwame said nothing. Finally Livie asked, "Can I meet her?"

"She's gone to her village," Kwame said. He did not look at her. At last he said, "I'm going there myself in a few days. To marry her."

"Oh," Livie said.

For several moments they fussed with the plantains on their plates. Finally Kwame asked, "How do you like this African food?"

"Hate it!" she said. Then she laughed. "I hate African women too," she declared. She made a mock-pout and they laughed together.

"Are you doing bridewealth?" she asked. "The whole bit?"

"You know where to get healthy goats?"

"How many?"

"Twelve. A lot of cash too."

"You really love her, hunh?"

He nodded. "She's carrying my child." Livie looked a little surprised. But she managed to grin. "Thank you for not saying, 'You've been busy.'" Livie laughed. "She's very pleased to be pregnant. For an African woman—"

"I have done some reading," Livie said.

"I do love her," Kwame said.

"Are you bringing her back to the States?"

"Not for a while."

Livie looked carefully at him, but said nothing.

KWAME TOOK Livie to the Afrique. Tombolo put her into the room the Moulaerts had used. As soon as she was settled, Kwame took her out to Bomboko Congo, got her an Orangina, and found her a place to sit in the garden. Then he sought out the Badekas. They had already heard that he had been lunching at chez Kalima with a beautiful white woman with hair like gold. "Can you help me show her around this afternoon?" Kwame begged. "And have dinner with us? And can I spend the night here on your floor?"

"Are you afraid of her?" asked Badeka.

"I don't want Kalima ever to think that I slept with her."

"Kalima's not an American," laughed Badeka. "She's a Mongo. She doesn't care."

Kwame looked from Badeka to Théa and back. Was Badeka kidding him? "I don't believe that," he said. "Kalima threw Marike out of my room when she thought—"

"That was Marike, an ambitious Congolese schoolgirl," Théa said. "This woman has come all the way from America to see you."

"She would expect you to sleep with her," insisted Badeka.

"Don't you want to sleep with her?" asked Théa.

"Of course, he does," said Badeka. "He's a man, isn't he?"

"Then why are you afraid?" Théa asked.

"Because he's an American," Badeka said. "They make everything complicated." He grinned and turned to Kwame. "Go ahead and sleep with her," he advised. "If a woman comes from America to see you, you should be a good host."

"Impossible!" Kwame said. "I will not have Kalima thinking that I'm interested in her only until the first white woman appears."

"Is that what she will think?" Théa asked. Her gaze was amused.

Kwame did not know how to answer. So what would Kalima think?

"Do you suppose she wants to win from a failure of manhood?" Théa asked.

"She would prefer to know that you tasted them both," Badeka assured him, "and chose her."

Kwame felt confused. Appropriate middle-class American behavior lay in one direction; proper Mongo conduct lay in another. American attitudes would say that Mongo conduct promoted indulgence and AIDS. Mongo attitudes would contend that middle-class American behavior denied the reality of physical being.

KWAME AND the Badekas showed Livie the sights of Mbandaka. Théa made them a simple dinner and they all went together to listen to local rock 'n' roll at a nightclub. The Badekas left early, complaining of lessons to prepare. Kwame and Livie watched the combo and chatted until after midnight. When they returned to the hotel, Kwame waved to Tombolo in the bar and walked Livie to her room. She unlocked and opened the door and let it stand ajar. "Come in and talk to me," she invited. "I don't really feel that we've talked at all."

"So how is law school?" Kwame asked. He sat on the railing opposite her doorway.

"I'm supposed to tell you about law school while you're sitting there?" She scrutinized him. "We've never had trouble talking. Why is it so hard now?" He shrugged. "You've always been so articulate."

"Professorial and boring?" He laughed. "I guess my vocabulary's shrinking."

"Is it because you're getting married? Aren't we still friends?"

"I hope so." He added, "I think my vocabulary really is shrinking. I haven't articulated anything remotely complicated since I got here. Not even to myself. I haven't read a book in months."

"Come in," she said. "We'll talk complicated stuff. Can't you?" Livie gazed at him a long time. "This is really what you want?" she asked. "Marrying Africa?" He nodded. "You really want to turn your back on all you've worked for?" He nodded again. "You have such a great contribution to make back home."

"Do I? I feel more comfortable here."

"You have so many friends at home," she said. She put her hand on his chest. "So many people are counting on you." She kissed him—as a friend.

He swallowed. Her kiss had tasted sweet.

"I love you," she said. "I'll always count you among the most important people in my life. Maybe the most important of all." She kissed him again, very lightly, and gazed into his eyes. "But I'm afraid for you."

"Don't be. This is what I want."

"You're going to be a kind of Rip Van Winkle. You'll be in this place where nothing happens except for violent, tribal convulsions every ten or fifteen years. And then you'll come out—"

"Maybe not."

"You will!" She tapped on his chest as if she knew him better than he knew himself. "Your mind will get hungry for stimulation. You'll want to talk ideas with somebody! But you won't ever catch up with our world. It's moving too fast." She took his hands and looked deeply into his eyes. Her own eyes clouded with tears.

"Don't cry," he said. He knew she was right. He would want to return, maybe with Kalima, maybe not.

"I'll still want you then," Livie said. "I'll always want you. But the way we live is changing. When you come back, it'll be like we're spinning on different tops, mine much faster than yours, so much faster you can't jump onto it." She implored him. "I don't want to lose you."

She kissed him again, softly. The lightness and the nectar of her taste made him want her. And the smell of her, the feel of her thin, needful body pressed against him, the throbbing of the blood pounding in his head, the dim redness behind his closed eyes, the action of blood in his groin. He felt her moving and he followed her. They entered her room. He heard the door close. "Talk to me," she begged, but they kept kissing. He felt himself whirling, sliding, slipping away from Mbandaka, away from Kalima's world into Livie's, the world where he had grown up and he still belonged. The sweetness of her absorbed him and he who had traditionally been a person of the mind became a person of the moment. Impulse spun him, whirling, whirling, and when the spinning stopped, hours had passed and he was holding Livie as he always had and she was sleeping, smiling, holding tightly onto him.

As DAWN came up across the river, Kwame got coffee and rolls from the hotel kitchen and brought them to the room. He and Livie ate, then lay back in bed and at last words came to Kwame. They talked. Livie told him about the challenges and delights and the drudgery of law school, about prima donna professors and her classmates, some of whom had already washed out, and about living in Boston's South End. She discussed national politics and how legal training had affected her attitudes toward it and about issues that interested her: bolstering education, reducing poverty and racism.

He tried to explain what it was like living in the remotest part of the remotest part of the world: the allure of quietude and the great stillness, the glory of primordial rhythms, the rising and setting of the sun, the majesty of the clouds, the flow of life. He acknowledged the slackening of his intellectual vigor and its replacement with silence, watchfulness, his acceptance of man's smallness, and his need for harmony with the natural world.

"What's it like to love this African woman?" Livie asked.

"Simple," he said. "Not at all complicated." He was quiet, then sensed that she wanted to hear more. "Sex is easy here. It's a sex-conducive environment." Livie frowned. "As opposed to, say, Victorian England," he explained, "which was not conducive to it, with its emphasis on respectability and etiquette and Christian religiosity." Livie nodded, pleased to hear him talking again like a professor. "Here it's natural. No guilt attaches to it. Traditionally there's been little to do at night. And it's too hot to wear anything to sleep in. Flirtation and sex are primary modes of recreation. Extramarital contacts are widespread as they're bound to be in polygynous societies. Until AIDS came along there were no adverse consequences. Everyone wanted children and a girl's becoming pregnant out of wedlock occasioned no shame. In fact, it confirmed that she could produce offspring. That encouraged suitors." Livie smiled as if she could understand why Kwame found its simplicity attractive. "Out here," he went on, "men and women need each other to complete themselves. And to produce young. That's seen as the purpose of life."

After a moment of quiet Livie asked, "Will there be adverse consequences to your being here with me?"

"I hope not," Kwame said. "I feel badly about it."

"Do you?"

"Don't you? I'm engaged to be married."

"But there's so much for us to sort through. And this is part of it."

"My feeling badly: I know that means I'm reacting like an American. But I'm not marrying an American."

"I honestly didn't intend to seduce you," Livie said. "At least not last night. I really wanted us to talk."

"You didn't seduce me," Kwame assured her. "You pulled me back into American society. Our parts of it are very sex-conducive too. These things happen. And I needed to be pulled back before I took the leap. I needed to test what I really want to do."

"So it wasn't a bad thing?"

"Maybe not. Now that I've had the test." Kwame stared at the ceiling for a long time. "Maybe I'm crazy to think of taking the leap." Livie hoisted herself up onto her elbow and gazed at him.

"It's been sexual with Kalima," Kwame acknowledged, returning to his original line of thought. He smiled at Livie. "But it's always been sexual with us. My mother would be horrified at how easily I adapt to that. I've betrayed what she's always contended about us." He smiled; Livie smiled with him. "But here it's sexual in a way I'd never experienced before." He touched Livie's cheek to reassure her. "The American Way of Sex," he said. "It has that mix of prurience and Puritanism, predators and romantics, advertising, TV and entertainment media, permissiveness and repression. They're all wrestling around with you in the same bed. It's so complicated. So American."

Livie agreed. "We're all crazy."

"It's deeper now with Kalima," Kwame said. "She doesn't feel romantic love for me. But there's a respect."

"Lucky you two," Livie said.

KWAME LEFT her at the hotel and went to teach his classes. When he returned, she had dressed. They had the hotel kitchen pack them a lunch and Kwame took her out onto the river, out behind the islands that lay off the town to the sandbar where the night tracks of crocodiles formed patterns in the sand. After they ate, they talked about American policy in Africa. They argued about Mobutu. Livie contended that he was a monster and American policy makers were the Frankensteins who had created him. Kwame insisted that position was much too simplistic. She stuck her tongue out at him and did a monster walk around the sandbar. He tackled her and pulled her into the river.

Once they had stretched out on towels, she said, "I'm feeling that I've damaged things for Kalima. And I don't even know her."

"You haven't," Kwame assured her. "She has the baby. That's what she really wants."

Livie frowned. "What do you mean?"

"Well, everything is different now. I see that Kalima's people have been right all along. Why should a Mongo woman from the village of Bolobe marry me?"

"You're a catch, that's why."

"No. I'm a black American man at the end of the American century. A professor with a shrinking vocabulary who's lost the art of articulation."

"You are so full of shit," Livie said.

"Maybe," Kwame agreed. "But it's been fun to be with a woman again who makes a lot of the same assumptions about life that I do. Who's been trained to be curious and question authority. Who assumes the individual has responsibilities to himself that transcend the group. Who thinks I'm more important than the children I can provide."

"You are American, you know," Livie said. "There are always times when we do not want to be what we're stuck with being."

Kwame nodded. "I can't deny that it makes a lot more sense for me to marry an American woman, black or white, brown or yellow—and to make peace with being American—than it does to marry Kalima. And live a life that's totally foreign to who I am. You've made me see that."

Livie watched him. "But you're unhappy about it."

Kwame said, "I've sort of agreed not to take Kalima and the baby out of the Equateur for five years."

"But in that time you'll be transferred."

"I'll have to leave the service. Become an African. I've always wondered what that would be like."

"Can you do it?"

"Maybe not. Maybe—" He gazed at the African sky, the enormous clouds floating in that depth of blue. He thought how much he would miss them if he ever had to leave the Equateur. "Maybe you've rescued me," he said. "That's why you said you'd come. Mission accomplished."

"Do you hate me?"

"In a day or two I'll thank you." He pulled her to him and kissed her. "Without you I might have made the worst decision of my life. I really might have become Rip Van Winkle." She gazed at him and smiled. "The only real question I have to answer now is: When do I go home? Now or at the end of my tour?" He challenged her. "Whattaya think?"

"You won't like me saying this," she told him. "But if you know you belong in the States, why not go back now?"

He nodded and stood up and ran into the water. He swam so far out into the river that Livie worried the current would sweep him away.

WATCHING PASSENGERS leave the Air Zaire plane, Kwame felt the contentment that came from having spent the two previous nights with Livie. He felt admiration and even a bit of sympathy for the man they had come to fetch, a man who had the courage—and the resources—to come to Africa to protect a young woman he thought he loved. Especially when there was a possibility that she would reforge a relationship with her former lover. All Mike would be able to do then would be to congratulate them both and return to Kinshasa where he might be inclined to slit his wrists.

Kwame recognized Mike as soon as he stepped off the plane. His sympathies deepened. Livie's friend looked like an Armani poster boy: a smooth brow, hair cut long by a stylist, a strong chin lightly covered with manicured stubble, a pair of wire-rimmed, tinted glasses poised at the bridge of his nose. He had pale skin, the result of 100-hour workweeks at his computer and his phone. He looked like a rich American, determined to succeed at this business of vacation. His let's-get-on-with-it manner had been carefully honed at Harvard B School. He carried a laptop and a copy of *Vanity Fai*r and wore faded tailored jeans, a safari shirt, and hiking boots.

"He's nervous," Livie said. "Poor guy."

Mike walked toward them with exaggerated casualness, trying to relax a frame held rigid as if expecting to receive a blow. He smiled at Livie, scrutinizing her beneath a tight smile for some clue as to what she was feeling, and embraced her. Then he looked at Kwame who had dressed in the clothes Kalima chose for him to teach in. Mike seemed uncertain as to whether this man was his rival or a Zairean driver Livie had engaged to take her around the town. But he sensed Livie's affection for him.

"This is Kwame, Mike," Livie told him. "Kwame, Mike Ackerman." The men shook hands.

"Hi, Kwame," Mike said, still forcing his smile. He realized that this black liberal arts guy, this government official stationed in the middle of fucking nowhere, had won his girl. The smile stayed frozen on his face. Black guys always got the girls, his expression seemed to say, but he was still determined that he and Kwame would be friends.

"You survived Kinshasa," Kwame said. "What's it like down there?"

"No shooting yet. But the tension's so thick—"

"You could cut it with a tweezers," Livie finished flirtatiously. Mike looked miffed that she had swiped his cliché.

"We're glad you got out of there," Kwame said. "Welcome to the Equateur."

"Kwam wants to chase down some rumors about refugees entering the region," Livie explained. "So we're going for a little drive in the bush." Mike looked uncertain. Livie laughed and put an arm around his shoulder. "It'll be okay."

THEY DROVE four hours south of Mbandaka, sometimes creeping over rotting causeways across swamps, sometimes losing the road. At these times Kwame let Mike and Livie walk before the truck. Mike would talk to her quietly but with great intensity. Watching them through the windshield, Kwame sensed that Mike wanted to put everything into its proper box. He seemed to be demanding definitions when none could be offered. Had she and Kwame sorted out their relationship? If so, what was it? Where did he fit in? Livie was not thinking of staying in this godforsaken backwater, was she? Because he would not allow that.

As they drove on, Mike gazed at the landscape, then leaned forward, glancing at Kwame, and asked, "What exactly is it you're doing out here? I'm not sure I ever got that."

Kwame explained that he'd originally been sent to Mbandaka for a week. But the man operating the post had disappeared. "I later discovered he'd been killed."

"Whoa!" exclaimed Livie. "No shit?"

Kwame shrugged. He had remained in Mban. He said, "Needs of the service."

"Must've been pretty important to have somebody here," Mike remarked.

When he arrived, Kwame said, the embassy had concluded that the Mobutu era was ending. It seemed to want an officer in every part of the country.

"Just in case," Mike said.

"As things have turned out," Kwame noted, "all the action's been elsewhere. More than anything, this post resembles a Peace Corps operation. The embassy people are watching a civil war come their way and preparing for the worst. If they've forgotten about me, who can blame them? I head up a small library and a film and video service and teach classes at a secondary school. The classes are the most important thing I do."

Mike nodded, staring through the windshield.

"We're all three Americans," Kwame went on. "But I come from a different America than you guys do. It's been interesting, being here, to wonder if a black American has any deep background connection with Africa. Since the embassy's sort of forgotten me, I've wondered sometimes if I could just become an African."

Livie watched him. Mike said, "And you've concluded . . ."

"Sometimes I think yes. Sometimes no."

Under his breath Mike whispered, "Holy shit!"

They passed villages of mud-and-wattle huts, thatched with fronds. Sitting on stretches of bare, swept earth before the huts, villagers watched them pass. Naked children waved. Goats ran beside the truck, mesmerized by the vehicle's motion. Chickens squawked into the road. "I didn't know life could be so primitive," Mike said. "I mean we're in spitting distance of 2000."

"If, as an intellectual exercise," Kwame said, beginning at a place where he thought Mike and Livie could follow, "you

thought about becoming African—at least the Africans here—
you'd have to totally reorient your head."

"How do you stick it?" Mike asked. "These people are absolutely hopeless. Their bovine expressions. They live at the level
of instinct. If you want to develop Zaire," he wondered, "where
the hell do you start? What a management problem!"

"Kwame says there's a stillness here that renews the soul,"
Livie remarked.

Mike began to laugh, full of good humor. "I know you
mean it," he said. He leaned across Livie and slapped Kwame's
knee. "Because nothing's moved here in 300 years."

"Maybe if you get to know them," Livie suggested. Kwame
winked at her to thank her for coming to his aid.

"Bullshit," Mike replied. He laughed cannily. "You're shittin' us, aren't you, Kwame? You're doing intelligence work.
Right now we're trying to hook up with refugees, right?"

"I just told you what I'm doing here," Kwame said.

"You can admit you're CIA," Mike insisted. "Who would
we tell?"

They drove along for several minutes without speaking.

"If the worst comes with these Hutu refugees," Mike asked,
"what happens? Some of them killed Tutsis and they're being
chased by Tutsi soldiers. There could be killings."

Kwame nodded.

They passed a track heading west at a junction village called
Kalamba. The track led to Bikoro and beyond it to Bolobe.
Kwame gazed down the track, but did not say that Kalima
whom he loved and who was carrying his baby lived in that
direction. He did mention that he had shown videos in a village not far from here. He and Livie watched the track until it
was out of sight.

Five miles beyond the junction, they encountered a roadblock. Two soldiers had stretched the trunk of a sapling across

oil drums and now sat at one end of it on folding chairs they had commandeered from someplace. They brandished sub-machine guns and were drunk on local beer. When the film truck stopped at the roadblock, Kwame greeted the soldiers. They announced that the road was closed. It was impossible to get to Ingende. Kwame slid out of the truck. He shook hands and chatted with the soldiers. But they were adamant. No one could pass. Kwame wondered if the army commander at Wangata had set up roadblocks to prevent refugees from reaching Mbandaka.

Mike left the van. "Our friends here have been drinking," Kwame remarked. He spoke with surface casualness, but in warning. Mike was not deterred. Kwame wondered if he intended to show Livie that he could settle a matter that stymied his rival. From the way he strode to the sapling, it was clear that he regarded the roadblock as a management problem, one that Harvard B School gave him the skills to solve. He was, after all, one of those superior men who untangled dilemmas and created the world. "Careful," Kwame warned. Mike paid no attention. When he reached the sapling, Kwame said quietly, curtly, "Don't touch it." But he did.

The soldiers became immediately hostile. Possibly they were spooked by the paleness of Mike's skin, a pallor that Kwame knew some Africans associated with ghosts and death. Or they were irked by the assumptions of white superiority that Mike exuded but had no consciousness of communicating. Kwame said quietly, "Put it down. Move away."

"*Pas de problème*," Mike said in tourist French. He stepped back. The soldiers raised their rifles.

"Get back to the truck," Kwame suggested quietly.

"It's okay," Mike said. He asked, all geniality, what was happening down the road. The soldiers began to shout at him. He raised his hands to calm them. They shoved him. Kwame once more ordered him to be quiet.

When he kept on talking, a soldier raised his rifle and placed it against Mike's forehead. The other soldier pointed his submachine gun at the truck. Suddenly pung, pung, pung. Kwame felt the warmth of the air, the humidity on his skin, the churning in his stomach; he tasted the dryness in his mouth. Time so slowed for him that he heard each bullet as it hit the truck, puncturing metal. The two soldiers looked at one another; they seemed drunkenly baffled by what had happened. Kwame pulled Mike away. He hustled him into the truck. Livie was crouched on the floor. Kwame got in, backed the truck away from the roadblock, and sped off in the direction of Mbandaka.

"Jesus fucking Christ!" Mike said. "What was that?"

"You all right?" Kwame asked Livie. She said nothing, squirming onto the seat. As Kwame raced away, he watched the soldiers in the rearview mirror. Both men kept their weapons trained on the truck.

"What the hell's going on down the road?" Mike asked. "That'd be interesting to know."

Livie said, "Is the truck okay?"

"I think so," Kwame told her. "They hit a fender. Hopefully not a tire." And he thought to himself: These goddamn guys who create the world. What a pain in the ass!

THEY RETURNED to the hotel in time for a late dinner and ate it on the terrace overlooking the river. At length Mike said, "This place doesn't have 'tomorrow' written on it."

"It has 'now' written on it," Kwame replied lightly. "Has to because you and Livie are here." Mike smiled, pretty sure

Kwame was ridiculing him. "I've always told Livie that wherever she is, that's the center of 'now'."

"You're right about that," Mike said. Livie smiled at them both. "This place can't nurture creativity," he declared.

"Too much tradition," Kwame commented.

"A woman refuses to marry you unless you give her father goats," remarked Livie.

"No shit?" asked Mike. "That's really—"

"The divorce rate here," Kwame said, "is no higher than among 'people of our class.'" He and Livie exchanged a glance.

"Should be less," Mike interjected, "because tradition stifles ingenuity. It and creativity: they make for better lives. More comfort, convenience, efficiency. They flourish only where there's freedom, entrepreneurship, exchange of ideas. You better get back to the States, man."

"Otherwise," Livie said with a twinkle, "we'll think you're balmy, Kwame."

Kwame smiled at her. He understood that she was declaring to them both that she was siding with him. Mike reacted edgily, as if discovering that he had come all the way to Central Africa only to lose. But he said nothing.

"These people have wonderful social skills," Kwame said. "They really do have soul."

"I guess that's why there was so much bloodshed in Rwanda," Mike replied.

"I guess that must be why," Kwame said. He smiled at Livie.

While they finished their meal, Mike talked about how Africa might be transformed. Maybe he was showing off for Livie, Kwame thought. But, in fact, the guy really was bright. For three days in the country he had grasped a lot.

Finally Mike said, "I guess I better go. Let you two guys say your good-byes." He stood and shook Kwame's hand. He kissed Livie lightly on the cheek and said, "I'll sleep on the couch." He was making it clear that he knew he had lost and it was no big deal.

Livie watched him go. "He's really not a bad guy," she said. "It takes a lot of courage for him to leave me out here with you. He's afraid I'll stay here in Mbandaka if you ask me."

Kwame gazed off across the river, understanding that she expected him to announce his intentions. "You know what I don't understand about American life?" he said. "We are so trained to 'do,' to struggle, to compete, that we always feel a sense of failure about not doing better. At the end of our careers, when all the struggle-struggle-struggle is over, we feel that if only we had worked harder, if only our timing had been different, if only things had broken our way . . . Then we would be wealthier. Or more famous. Or have found true love. Or helped more people. At the end of American lives there is always a sense of not having done as well as we should have."

Livie shook her head. As usual, she did not agree with him.

"But it's true," he insisted. "Mike's in your room right now, thinking, 'If only things had broken my way . . .'"

"No, he'll be working on some project. He doesn't cry over spilt milk."

"You know what else I don't understand?"

Livie watched him a little impatiently. She wanted to talk about his coming back to the States with her, not this abstract stuff about a nonperfect world. Didn't Kwame understand that no place was perfect?

"America's creating a civilization where most of us will spend our lives in artificial, acclimatized environments. We'll work at computers, relax watching movies or TV. We'll exercise our bodies on the machines in the gyms we'll have in our homes. And we'll cut ourselves off completely from the natural rhythms of the physical world, from the flow of the seasons. That's a kind of folly. A kind of hubris."

"Kwame, most of us really are trying to live useful, productive lives."

"I sometimes wonder if the earth doesn't rebel against that hubris," Kwame said. Livie looked at him as if he were babbling nonsense. "With earthquakes, for instance. And fires, natural disasters, changing weather patterns. The earth is saying: 'I am still here. You cannot escape me.'"

Livie gazed at him. "Swami," she said, "you can't believe that. It's preliterate, prescientific babble." She grinned at him as if to say, "Gotcha!" But watching him, the grin faded. "You aren't coming back with me, are you?"

He shook his head.

"How can you stay? You're regressing to—" She did not finish the thought.

Kwame asked, "It isn't possible that I've found something?" Livie shook her head. He took her hand affectionately. "That's one thing you have to love about Americans," he said. "They're unshakably convinced that their way is best." She smiled and bit her lip. "I guess I'll stay out here in Africa."

"With the refugees and all we talked about today?"

He shrugged, knowing that he had made the right decision. He had loved her once, but he did not love her now. He watched her eyes fill with tears. "You mustn't cry," he said.

"Let me tell you something," Livie replied. She looked at him a long moment, trying to find words for her thoughts, and fiercely held his hand. "I understand the attraction of this place, I really do. But you're going to become ever more isolated. Is that what you want?" Kwame shrugged again. "Mobutu isn't the problem."

"Just a symptom."

Livie nodded. "Do you think this Kabila's really going to change anything?"

"Probably not."

"So what happens? It gets even worse than it is now?"

"Some places, yes. But not here. This really is the uttermost part of the earth. There's a kind of safety in that."

Livie shook her head, her expression contorted with horror and dismay.

"Embassy people," Kwame said, "the optimistic Americans, want to think the rebels will offer opportunities for 'new beginnings.' But how can that be? There's no foundation for that." He threw up his hands. "Kabila's moment is likely to be a prelude to—"

"Anarchy?"

"Possibly. There seem to be almost as many guns here as there are in the States. But it needn't be anarchy."

"Please don't stay," she implored. "I'm so afraid for you."

"Don't be. I'm in tune with things here. I don't want to live as fast as technology can push me. I don't want to think and live the way Mike has been trained to."

"It's so dangerous here."

"No more dangerous than New York or Los Angeles."

"Look what happened at the roadblock." Kwame smiled at her. "I'm afraid you'll get sick," she said. He shook his head. "Or that something dreadful will happen to you. These people can be so cruel."

"People get sick at home. The difference is they don't think they ever have to die. They think they can live five different lifetimes in fifty years. And never once know who they are. I want what is here, Livie."

She looked up at the stars. "Poor Mike," she said. "He knows I want to kiss you. He didn't want to see me do that."

Kwame leaned close to her chair and pressed his lips against hers. The taste of her made him think suddenly of all the things he would be abandoning when he married Kalima. He knew that now and then he would miss them.

Livie broke off the kiss and pulled her wallet from her jeans. She opened it and withdrew a photo from its plastic envelope. "This is for your wife," she said. "I've always loved it." She slid the photo across the table. It showed Kwame congratulating African voters in Cape Town.

They gazed at the photo, then at one another. "Thank you for coming," he said. "I hope you're happy wherever you are."

They kissed again. Livie said, "You too."

TOMBOLO WAS at the bar. Kwame took a stool beside him and ordered a beer. Tombolo mumbled a greeting. He had watched the three Americans at dinner. He knew that Kwame had spent the previous two nights with the golden-haired white woman. He knew that she had just left the terrace headed toward the room where the other white man waited. When Kwame's beer came, Tombolo scrutinized him curiously, carefully. But he said nothing; Americans were a species he would never understand.

"What's going on down at Ingende?" Kwame asked.

Tombolo shrugged. He would find out what Kwame knew first.

"Soldiers have closed the road," Kwame told him. "We almost got shot this afternoon."

Tombolo nodded. He said, "Stay away from there."

After a moment Mike appeared and slid onto the stool next to Kwame. "May I join you?" he asked. Kwame nodded his assent. Tombolo moved off. Mike ordered a beer. When the beer came, Mike said, "I need to thank you for saving my ass. That got pretty hairy out there."

Kwame agreed, "Those guys start drinking, watch out."

This was a good way for them to talk, Kwame thought. Sitting side by side they need not look at one another. But they could do that in the bar mirror.

For a moment they were silent. Then Mike said, "I had two days to kill in Kinshasa. So I talked to some people. Including the economics counselor at the embassy. I mentioned I was flying up here to see you."

Kwame smiled ruefully. "Did he know where Mban was?"

"He said, 'Mbandaka? We brought that guy out of there weeks ago.'" Kwame looked surprised. Mike watched him. "I said, 'I don't think so.' With that shitass State Department arrogance he said, 'I'm sure we did. We aren't leaving officers in places like that.'" Mike shook his head. "The embassy is in such panic about the Battle of Kinshasa that they can't keep track of their people."

Kwame did not know how to react. Was it really possible that the embassy had lost track of him?

Mike watched him in the mirror. "Mobutu returned to Kin last week. From Europe." Kwame nodded. "He'd had an operation for prostate cancer. He looked like a skeleton. He can hardly walk."

Kwame stared at the beer in his glass. Mike studied him in the mirror, then leaned close and said very quietly. "You saved my ass today. So let me save yours." Mike fixed his eyes on Kwame. "Don't get caught here. Let me repeat: Do not get caught here."

Kwame considered the advice.

"Mobutu's Zaire is not a country," Mike said. "It's a criminal conspiracy. Fed by money and violence. With the Cold War over, the money's gone. The US, Britain, France: they've all pulled the plug on aid. The IMF flushed Zaire. Violence is all that's left. Mobutu kills his own people, sometimes one by one; if they're ministers who've defied him, sometimes he sends the ANC on a killing spree.

"Across the country Kabilistes and Tutsi soldiers are chasing Hutus through the eastern jungles. They're massacring tens of thousands. Tens of thousands." Mike spoke slowly to let the words percolate inward. "Journalists can't find the bodies, but that doesn't mean those people aren't dead. Moreover those killers are coming here."

Kwame listened without speaking.

"So get out of here," Mike advised. "If there are people who are important to you"—Livie must have told him about Kalima—"take them with you. But get out. Because you're on your own here."

Kwame took a sip of beer, careful not to look at Mike.

"There's no government in Zaire," Mike said. "No law. Without government, people need families. You have no family here. Without family nobody gives a shit about you. When the chaos comes, nobody'll look out for you. Chaos is marching toward you right now."

Kwame said, "You must be glad to be getting out of here."

"Livie and I leave tomorrow night. That can't come quick enough. No offense."

Mike put his hand on Kwame's arm. The two men looked at one another. "You did good at the roadblock. I don't want you getting killed. So get out." They shook hands. Mike disappeared into the night.

Kwame drank his beer slowly and studied his image in the mirror. He and Kalima were about to create a family. But if trouble came, they would need more family than just the two of them. Would the Badekas be his family? Would Bonanga? Maybe it would not be possible for him and his family to stay the full five years in the Equateur.

NINETEEN

On the day before the Bikoro market convened, Kwame and Kalima fulfilled one obligation of the agreement Badeka had negotiated: that a marriage take place according to a custom that Kwame and his people would regard as binding. The couple exchanged vows in a Christian ceremony in the chapel of the convent where Kalima had studied in Bikoro. The Badekas served as witnesses.

The following morning, under the tutelage of Badeka, Kwame went to the market and bought a dozen goats in good health. They would be delivered in Bikoro. And so Bonanga came to Bikoro, accompanied by his wives and children, his brothers, their wives and children, and also by a number of Kalima's friends.

They arrived about midday and the ceremonies began. Kwame officially transferred his gifts of bridewealth, the goats and the first installment of cash, to Badeka. Badeka gave them to Kalima's oldest friend. This woman presented the gifts to Kalima. She and four other friends made a ceremonial inspection of the livestock. They counted the cash. Kalima then returned the gifts to her friend. The friend, in turn, offered them to Bonanga. Once he accepted the gifts, Kwame and Kalima became married in a ceremony that Kalima and her people regarded as binding.

The entire party walked back to Bolobe, the bride and groom strolling hand in hand, her mothers and the other women and the children singing, Bonanga and his friends driving the dozen goats.

Kwame and Kalima spent their wedding night in the abandoned house by the lake. It had been swept and cleaned. Pockmarked sheets of corrugated metal had been placed on the roof to protect the house from rain. As the newlyweds held one another, Kwame whispered to Kalima: "I missed you."

"Is this true?" she asked. "I heard you had a white woman come from America to take care of you."

"You think I sent for her?" he inquired. "I didn't even know she was coming. She was afraid she would lose me to Africa. She begged me to come home. I sent her away." Kalima did not reply. "If you don't believe me, ask Théa."

"Théa and I have already discussed these Americans," Kalima said. "That poor woman!" She smiled, pleased that he had chosen her.

"I love you," Kwame told her. It seemed a declaration that a man should make to his bride, especially since it was true. Kalima tenderly touched his cheek, assuming that these words had special importance in his culture. She placed his hand on her stomach where he could feel their baby growing.

At dawn Kwame bathed, using the gourd to rinse himself as he stood naked knee-deep in the lake. He had a strange feeling that it was different to rise in the morning a married man. What a curious thought! How could things possibly be different? When he returned chilled to his wife, he felt African and amorous. But that was not unusual. She smiled at him. Her love made her glow in the dim light of the house.

Kwame felt fulfilled. His love for Kalima seemed enormous enough to fill all space. With the baby on the way, his place in

Mbandaka and in Kalima's family secure, his wife full of love for him, Kwame felt as happy as he had ever been.

Now when Kwame awoke in the morning he knew without doubt that his existence had changed, but not in what ways. He had not changed; he assured himself of that. Even so, the world seemed a different place. He was now a family man; he had what his mother called "hostages to fortune." He had never understood what that meant. Perhaps that was the change. He was now a family man; he had hostages to fortune. He had now committed himself to a project from which there would be no escape, even if there was a divorce. That of protecting, nurturing, and providing for Kalima and their child.

It occurred to him that perhaps a family man should not walk around so often naked. Now when he and Kalima finished bathing together in the lake, he tied a cloth around his waist. "Why are you wearing a *pagne*?" Kalima asked him. "You are so beautiful without it."

He felt self-conscious. "A married man should not be displaying himself to the world."

"You can display yourself to your wife."

"Now that I am married, I will probably grow fat."

"I will see that you do."

"Don't you get fat."

"You will see me get very fat. In the next few months. And all your doing."

Later in the house he asked Kalima, "Do you feel different now? I do."

"Of course, I do! People I have known all my life in Bolobe look at me differently. I am now a married woman. The child I carry in my belly I will soon carry on my back." She gazed at him. "They look at you differently too. They think their eyes no longer deceive them."

"Meaning?"

"Maybe you are a black man after all."

ONE MORNING in Bikoro, moving through the market, Kalima stopped surveying goods and reached for Kwame's arm. Glancing at her, he saw her staring at strangers. A dozen of them straggled into town from Kalamba where the main road went north to Mbandaka. Dirt clung to their bodies and in the coils of their hair. Their clothes hung on them, ragged, filthy, smelling. Rather than walk, they lurched, staggered, pulled themselves along with canes. Fear contorted their faces.

In the days immediately after Kwame and Kalima were married, strangers like these infiltrated the town. Although few at first, they kept coming. They sat on the roadsides, wretched, exhausted. What was to be done with them? They needed food, clothes, toilets, places to sleep, to wash. They did not speak Lingala or Lonkundo and obviously they were starving. They begged for food; sometimes they snatched it from market vendors who failed to protect their goods. The vendors reported that the strangers were Hutus, hunted by Tutsi avengers. They had walked all the way from Rwanda. But, villagers asked, how was that possible? Wasn't that a walk of a thousand miles? In whispers, they wondered, was it not possible that some of them had also killed in the Rwanda genocide.

Kwame and Kalima realized that they must return quickly to Mbandaka. On the day they left, they rose at the first gray light of dawn. Half awake, Kwame stumbled outside, gooseflesh on his arms, and slogged into the lake. He gasped as the water rose to his waist, then ducked below its surface. Kalima joined him. "Invigorating!" he laughed.

"Enjoy. It will be hot on the road."

Dressed, their gear packed, they walked to Bolobe to bid farewell to Kalima's parents. Her mother said, "Maybe it is best for you to have your baby in Mbandaka."

"We know you'll want us there when you have it," remarked her father. "You have plenty of room and we are comfortable there."

Kwame picked up the basket of food Kalima's mother had prepared. Kalima fixed a steadying cloth on her head, took the basket, and set it into position. "We must go," she told them. "Or the sun will bake what you have given us to eat."

They left Bolobe, nodding and calling and waving to neighbors who rose early to watch them leave. Once they got onto the path toward Bikoro, Kalima told Kwame, "I don't want my parents living with us."

"Good," Kwame agreed with a laugh. "Neither do I."

"Perhaps it is best to keep my parents at a distance."

"You are beginning to sound like an *américaine*."

"You know how my father bosses everyone. While I was with them, he wanted me to wait on him as I had done as a child."

"Did you?"

"For my mother's sake. So she wouldn't have to."

Kwame was delighted that they had escaped Bolobe. Kalima seemed at last to see that she must resist her father's domination.

The day grew warm. Kwame felt the first rising of perspiration on his chest. As they walked on, Kalima said, "Even though my father took gifts from you, he tried to have me marry the man from Bikoro. Can you believe that?" She shook her head with irritation. "But because I was not willing, the man from Bikoro would not have me."

Kwame reached over to take her hand. They walked side by side. "When my parents come to Mbandaka," Kalima said finally, "they act as if my house—"

"Our house," Kwame emphasized.

She smiled. "You know I mean our house, the house you have so cleverly arranged for me. They act as if it was theirs. They don't realize they are guests."

Kwame stopped and pulled Kalima toward him. When he kissed her, she raised her hands to steady the basket on her head. Kwame declared, "No guests until— When?"

"Until the baby is born?"

"Too soon."

"Until it walks?"

"Too soon." They laughed. Kwame felt a sense of joy in this day. With every step his wife was sending Bolobe into the past. "Until it starts school."

"Too soon," said Kalima. She giggled. "Until it finishes university."

BECAUSE OF heavy traffic, the road north from Kalamba was in worse repair than when Kwame had crossed over it only a few days before, more dotted with potholes and pools of standing water. Ruts were deeper.

Strangers plodded along. Many seemed hardly able to keep moving. They were marshaling their last resources of energy to hobble forward. Others sat or lay at the roadsides. They begged for rides, for food.

Kwame and Kalima had been driving with the film truck's windows lowered. "Better put up the windows," Kwame advised. "Be sure your door is locked."

Raising her window, Kalima asked, "Is there nothing we can do for these people?"

"If there were only a couple," Kwame said, "I would gladly pick them up. But there are so many! They may try to take the truck." He told Kalima about Adriaan Moulaert. "It took him days to regain his strength. And he was young, strong. He had walked only from Kisangani. Some of these poor souls—"

With the windows raised, Kwame and Kalima began to sweat. Kalima continued to watch the ragged, exhausted strangers, wishing to be of help.

"If we stop for those we have room for," Kwame said, "they will all want to get aboard. We can't possibly take them. If we do, when we get to Mbandaka, what then? Where can we leave them? They'll want us to care for them."

Kwame had to drive carefully because of all the people on the road. Glancing at Kalima, he saw a sheen of sweat on her cheeks, a sad compassion in her eyes. Walking toward Bikoro, she had wanted to leave Bolobe behind. Kwame wondered now, as she watched the desperate strangers, if she wanted to return to Bolobe, to be once more the safe little girl who waited on her father.

At places where one of them should have checked the road, Kwame dared not stop. "If we stop, they'll overwhelm us," he told Kalima. He feared that refugees would climb on top of the vehicle or scramble inside it. Sometimes they hobbled toward the middle of the road in order to force the truck to stop. Kwame grimly persevered. He feared that he might hit these human roadblocks. But he drove slowly enough to permit them to pull themselves out of the way. Those with the energy tried to struggle aboard. They pounded at the windows. Kalima turned away, frightened by the fists and open hands slapping at her. Kwame feared they would somehow open the vehicle's doors, pull him and Kalima out, and attack them.

Kwame was sweating profusely. He was hungry and thirsty. But how could he ask Kalima to open the basket of food in the presence of starving people?

The film truck crossed a section of swamp. Kwame saw figures lying among manioc plants. He supposed exhaustion had overcome them, that they were sleeping. But slowing to peer at them, he realized they were dead. He said nothing about them to Kalima.

They neared the great river where the road split, leading both southwest toward Wendji and northeast toward Mbandaka. At the junction, Kwame came upon three bloated bodies lying across the road. They lay in pools of blood. Flies buzzed about them. Driving slowly Kwame stared in disbelief: a family, a man, a woman, and a child. Panga slashes scarred their heads and shoulders. A blow across the neck had all but severed the child's head. Kwame thought of their baby. "Don't look! Don't look!" he told Kalima. He reached out his hand to cover her eyes.

Hutu refugees, Kwame thought. The family had crossed the entire breadth of the country only to be caught by their enemies. He wondered at the hatred that motivated those enemies; they too had trudged across the country. Who were they? Rwandese Tutsis wreaking vengeance on both *génocidaires* and any persons suspected of being Hutu, even children? "Don't look! Don't!" Kwame kept advising. But Kalima saw the bodies. She began to cry.

Kwame wondered: Were local Zairean soldiers also killing strangers? Had they been sent to prevent refugees from entering Mbandaka? Hadn't the officer at the military camp assured him, "We will handle this matter in our own way"? Would Mbandaka set its military garrison on the refugees?

Kalima kept asking, "Isn't there anything we can do?" She placed her hands against the windshield so as not to see the road. She looked beseechingly at him.

"Let's hope it's safe at the house," Kwame said.

He turned the truck northeast toward Mbandaka. Refugees fleeing toward Wendji must have hoped to cross the river there, he thought. If they got across, maybe their Tutsi enemies would give up the chase. The trampled condition of the road, however, showed that most refugees had headed toward Mbandaka. Ever more bodies sprawled in pools of blood across the road.

Closer to town Kwame came upon soldiers digging a deep, wide trench. Others shoved bodies into it. Still others stood guard, AK-47s at the ready. They gestured Kwame to stop. Instead he floored the accelerator. "Hold on!" he instructed Kalima. "Hold on!" He raced the truck down the middle of the road, horn blaring. Kalima screamed, clutching the dashboard. Her scream frightened Kwame. He yelled at the top of his voice. Pedestrians scattered. Soldiers scrambled out of the way.

Nearing the Berton house, Kwame slowed the truck to a crawl and turned. As he approached the house, worn and ragged men emerged from roadside vegetation. They wielded pangas, machetes. They hobbled beside the film truck, pounding on it with the broad sides of their pangas. Kwame saw dozens of exhausted refugees at the house. He gritted his teeth, turned the truck, and raced off. Kalima stared in horror at her home, overtaken by strangers. "What's happened to everyone?" she cried. Her people working at *le snack* had been living there. Kwame sped toward town. Kalima watched her home until it disappeared from view.

Some of Kalima's people had rented a house in the *cités*. Kalima directed Kwame to it. When he parked outside, Kalima burst from the vehicle, whooping and calling her people. They came racing from the house. Kalima embraced them. Kwame remained in the truck, bent over the steering wheel, trying to control his emotion, endeavoring not to cry. Kalima's people came to shake his hand. Soon some of them were weeping, recounting what they had witnessed.

Kwame pulled himself out of the truck. He found Buta and drew him aside. "What happened at the house?" he asked.

"While we were at *le snack*," Buta said, "the strangers moved in."

Kwame leaned against the truck fender, too tired to stand. "Are all of our people safe?" he asked.

Buta nodded. "We didn't dare to go inside. The strangers implored us to help them. But how could we? We had already shared the food at *le snack*. We took what they allowed us to take and came here."

Kwame said, "They threatened us with pangas they could hardly lift."

"They cannot fight," Buta said. "But they are so many. Like locusts, like army ants."

In the house Kwame stripped off his tee shirt, washed his face and torso. Kalima opened the basket of food from Bolobe. They ate, sharing the food with the others.

"How have things been in town?" Kwame asked.

"Come outside," Buta said. Kwame pulled a clean tee shirt from his backpack and followed Buta to the truck. They stood behind it, hidden from the house.

"It was bad at the dock," Buta said. He spoke quietly. Most refugees had gathered at the port, he said, trying to get passage across the river. But soldiers found them there.

Kwame asked: "Zairean soldiers? Tutsis? Kabilistes?"

Buta did not know. There was no attack, he claimed, no fighting between soldiers. The Kabilistes and Tutsis came into town, he had heard, as brothers, in order to hunt refugees. They found Hutus at the docks. Hundreds of them. Anti-Mobutu Kabilistes instructed pro-Mobutu soldiers to give commands in Lingala. They shouted: "Zaireans, fall to the ground!" The Hutu refugees spoke no Lingala. They remained standing. The soldiers opened fire on them.

Kwame sat on the ground. He had no energy to hear the report while standing.

Buta reported that soldiers massacred not only strangers, but local people as well. When the firing started, panic swept the crowd. People jumped into the river. Many drowned. Others were shot in the water. When the soldiers ran out of bullets, they used pangas, rocks, clubs, any weapon that came to hand. "Go to the dock," Buta said. "You will see clothing and belongings that refugees dropped as they ran into the river."

"And the bodies?" Kwame asked.

"For the crocs," Buta said.

"And *le snack*?"

"We haven't been back. No one goes into town."

"And the library?"

Buta shook his head.

"Lofale? Anatole?"

"Gone to their villages."

Kwame thought he must check on the library. He found a bed in the house and napped for an hour. He told Kalima where he was going. He would not take the truck; it might be commandeered. He walked through the late afternoon neighborhoods of small homes to the main road. Probably it was foolish to do this, he told himself. He felt drained from the driving. Even so, he started toward town. No one was on the streets.

When he reached the post office, he saw out in front of the library the palm frond canopies of *le snack*. Soldiers idled in their shade, drinking beer, yakking, their AK-47s lying on the ground. Kwame moved forward. The soldiers fell silent. They watched him. When he stepped into the cultural center's yard, they reached for their weapons.

Kwame's senses revived, grew sharp. "Tata?" he asked. "Tata Anatole? Is he— In the house at the back?" He chattered nervously.

The soldiers glanced at one another. They did not rise. They stared at him.

He wondered if they understood French. "*Mbote!*" he called. He started slowly toward the back of the building. "Ça va?" he kept asking. "Okay? Ça va?"

None of the soldiers spoke. They watched him. Several were smoking hemp. Its odor filled the air. One of the soldiers waved a hand to let Kwame pass.

"Anat?" he called. "Anatole?" The entry doors were open. Books littered the floor. He was certain Anatole would not be there, but he moved toward the house, calling his name. A soldier slept in the entryway of the *boyerie*.

Kwame glanced behind him, then moved through the back entry into the library. Every few steps he called out, "Anat? Anat?"

His heart beat fast. He saw men asleep in Mason's bedroom. It was now a barracks, without furniture except for mattresses brought in from somewhere. The Zaire map had been ripped from the wall. Still visible were Mason's scratchings: "The horror! The horror!" Kwame moved forward on tiptoe.

In the library, books lay open on the floor. Some were ripped open as kindling for fires set to keep down mosquitoes. Kwame left by the front door. He went down the steps. He waved to the soldiers, showing that his hands were empty. He walked away quickly, feeling the soldiers' eyes on his back.

Outside the office of Air Zaire, he stared at the route map. He could hardly think. "What now?" he asked himself. Did it make any sense to remain in Zaire? No. To fly to Kinshasa? No. The battle to overthrow Mobutu would take place there. It might be taking place there now.

He caught his breath and thought of his arrival in Mban-daka so many months before. What hopes he'd had! To accomplish something constructive for the underdeveloped world. And something for himself. What a way to leave Zaire! In flight from a dysfunction that like army ants ate everything in its path.

He entered the airline office. "I am closed," said the *chef de service.*

"Are flights still leaving?"

The man measured Kwame. "Sometimes."

"I need two tickets for Bangui. Are planes going there?"

"Tomorrow noon," said the *chef.* "Then not for another week. If the airport remains open. But I am closed."

"I'll give you a credit card." Kwame reached for his wallet.

"I am closed," the *chef* insisted. He shook his head; he would not accept credit. "Everything is turmoil in Mban," the man said.

Kwame removed his credit card and driver's license from his wallet and handed them to the *chef.*

The *chef* shook his head. "Who are you?" he asked. "How do I know it's your card? Pulling things from a wallet doesn't mean they're yours."

Kwame said, "I am the American living here." Through his fog of fatigue he remembered Odejimi's hundred-dollar bills. He had carried them in his wallet ever since the night he had found them in the doctor's room. "Here's something for your kindness." Kwame handed the *chef de service* two hundred-dollar bills. "Here's my credit card and some American money. Hard currency." The two men examined one another. "It's always useful to carry hard currency."

The *chef* scooped up the two bills. He felt their consistency and stuffed them into his trousers. He processed the tickets, issued boarding passes. He placed the documents into an

Air Zaire envelope and handed them to Kwame. "Tomorrow morning at eleven."

"We'll see you then," Kwame said. "I trust you can help us board the flight. My wife has never flown."

"Glad to help, *M'sieur*."

"I'll count on it," Kwame said.

He did not know if Kalima had a passport, even if she had visited Belgium. It would be the job of the *chef* of Air Zaire to get Kalima onto the plane. Once in the Central African Republic, Kwame would throw himself on the mercy of the American Embassy. He would leave it to them to sort out Kalima's travel status and find a way to get them both to America.

Kwame stuck the ticket envelope into his shirt. Disregarding his fatigue, he hurried back to the *cités*. The red globe of the sun was now moving behind the horizon. He strode along so as not to get lost in the confusion of small streets. He must reach Kalima before night fell.

Kwame took Kalima to the Badekas. They had returned to Mbandaka several days earlier. They all embraced, relieved to see each other. In the comfort of these friends, Kwame felt his energy revive.

"Have you come through this business safely?" Kwame asked.

"Safely, yes," Badeka assured him.

"But devastated by sadness," added Théa. "It will be years before Mbandaka recovers from this."

Kwame asked if he and Kalima could spend that night at the school. Their house was now sheltering refugees. Tutsi soldiers were using the library as a barracks. The Badekas insisted that they stay with them. Kwame suggested that the couple give

Kalima some tea. There were a couple of errands he needed to run.

Before he left, Théa took him aside. "You must get Kalima out of Mbandaka," she said. "Otherwise she will internalize what she sees. It will affect the baby."

"Explain to her that she must leave," Kwame pleaded.

He took a crate of plantains, a gift from the convent in Bikoro, to the priests at the Catholic mission. When he asked about the Onatra docks, the priests glanced about to check who might overhear. Two priests had been at the docks. They had witnessed the massacre. Hundreds slaughtered, they confirmed. Women and children. Bodies thrown into the river. There were mass graves now in every cemetery in the town. Kwame asked about the number of dead. One priest estimated 500, the other 2,000.

At the Afrique, Kwame saw an unusual number of patrons on the terrace. Many were tall and thin: Tutsis. Kwame bought a drink for Tombolo. "Don't think this means good business for me," the hotelier complained. "These men do not buy their drinks. They're turning my reputable place into a bordel." Tombolo insisted that he had seen no one killed, but he had heard gunfire and screaming and seen bodies floating on the river.

"I went down the Ingende road about ten days ago," Kwame said. "There were army roadblocks. Why were they set up?"

Tombolo did not know. Perhaps soldiers hoped to stop the refugees from entering Mban, he suggested. Tombolo insisted, "It's best to know nothing about this business." Kwame asked if soldiers from the army camp had participated in the massacres. The hotelier merely shrugged.

Kwame related what he had heard from the priests.

"If those priests had sense," Tombolo whispered, "they would mind their own business." Many refugees had survived, he assured Kwame. Local people were sheltering them and giving food to those hiding out. Some had already crossed the river; others would follow. "It is best to know nothing. And to say nothing."

Kwame could hardly believe that local Zairean troops had allowed Tutsi soldiers, tribal thugs, to enter Mbandaka and murder hundreds of exhausted, frightened, starving refugees.

"A terrible business," Tombolo said. "But you white men!" He inspected Kwame with scorn. "So sentimental! Those strangers were not our people." He raised his glass to patrons newly arrived in the bar. "They were not our people," he repeated. "Some of them were killers. They did even worse things to Tutsis. Are we to let them take over our town? Without money? Or food? Camping in our yards? Shitting in the streets? Spreading SIDA? These Tutsis solved a problem for us that we might have had to solve in the same way ourselves."

When Kwame left the Afrique, he shook Tombolo's hand and thanked him for being a friend.

"I won't be seeing you again?" Tombolo asked.

"Probably not."

AT THE Badekas', Kwame found that Kalima was taking a nap. He went quietly into the bedroom and positioned a chair so that he could watch her sleep. He prepared the little speech that he expected he must give to win her agreement to leave. In his mind he rehearsed all the occasions when she had demonstrated courage by adjusting to new situations: entering the relationship with Bonanga's friend; leaving her family for the convent; leaving the convent for a life with Vandenbroucke; defying her parents to return to him. He would extol the entrepreneurship that led her to develop *le snack*. He would praise her beauty and education and speak of his confidence that she could master any challenge set before her. He would explain that he could not become an African, although he had tried. However she could become an American. Even if there were things about his country that distressed him, he had come to understand that he could not run away from what he was. He needed to embrace it and that embracing would be easier if she were with him.

When he finished this recitation in his mind, he found Kalima watching him. He leaned over and kissed her. "You're here. You were gone so long! I was afraid something had happened to you."

"I'm right here. And I'm going to stay beside you."

"Did you hear what happened at the port?" she asked.

"How did you hear?"

"Buta's people told me." She reached out to take his hand. "We cannot stay here," she said. "We have a baby on the way."

He nodded in agreement.

"My head keeps calling up pictures of that family we saw on the road. I think of that child—" Tears shone in her eyes. "We cannot stay here."

Kwame told her what he had arranged. "You knew that sometime we would go to America," he told her. She nodded. "But not so soon."

"We must go there," Kalima said. "My parents would not want their grandchild born in this place of death."

Kwame assured her that they would figure things out in Bangui. Perhaps he would extricate himself from his present job and return to university teaching. They might live in a university community where her being Congolese would be a matter of interest, even fascination, to many of the people they met. "As for Bolobe—"

Kalima sighed, "There is no going back to Bolobe. After what I have seen today, I will go wherever you take me." She smiled at him. "Even on an airplane!"

KWAME WOKE in the night, his back warmed by Kalima's body. He sat on the side of the bed, the air cool on his back. He had been married less than a week. But in that time everything in his world had changed. While he was transferring bride-wealth to Bonanga, Tutsi soldiers from Rwanda, and possibly Zairean soldiers from Mbandaka, were slaughtering refugees at the Mbandaka port. Impossible to believe! He could not conceive that it had happened and nothing would be done. He had listened to shortwave news. There were no reports of the massacres. Could a thousand people be slaughtered in Mbandaka and no one even know? No one ever care?

Across the room Kwame saw his mother. She was standing in her kitchen, leaning against the counter, her arms folded across her body. They had not spoken in a very long time. Appraising him, she began to talk. She asked, as she always did, "What are you taking from this experience, son? What are you learning from it?" He did not know how to answer.

"At the university," she reminded him, "you used to claim that America and white education had captured your head. You remember that? But your heart, soul, and body, they were black, you said, were African." Although he did not remember ever saying such things, he did not deny that he might have spouted off that way. "Was studying African literature a way to make your head African?" He smiled at that; perhaps she understood him better than he understood himself. "Going to the uttermost parts of the earth, was that your attempt to become African?"

Had he ever really played with such an idea? Becoming African? No! He didn't think so.

"The uttermost parts of the earth." Kwame smiled. His mother saw them as a trial of fire that he had chosen to walk through. He entered those uttermost parts as a young man she loved and admired and respected. But how would he come out? Would he come out at all? What would his experience there be?

Mason had gotten lost in the uttermost parts. That's what his mother would conclude. Mason could send extravagant fulminations to Dad and yet write tender letters to Stephanie, letters he never sent. He yearned for his wife, but chased teen tail and got lured into Mme Berton's trap.

Had Odejimi lost himself as well? In sex and drugs, whiskey and tobacco? Kwame thought of the occasion when he and Odejimi and Madame Van, as she had been then, had played sex all day, the two men competing, sating their bodies in hers, fueling their excess with whiskey and the breakfast of champions.

"You almost lost yourself there," his mother told him.

"I truly came to love her," he replied. "I hope you'll meet her soon."

"You almost got lost," his mother repeated. "Your father and I were so worried. But now you have married her and have a child on the way. You came as close to becoming African as it is possible to come. Getting lost entirely was a very close thing."

"Don't badger the boy," his father said. Kwame smiled. He had not seen his father in the kitchen shadows.

"You've got hostages to fortune," his mother reminded him. "Get them safely out of Zaire."

EARLY THE next morning Kwame drove to the post office. He engaged a soldier sitting out front to guard the vehicle, promising him zaires. Inside he tried to place a call to the American Embassy in Kinshasa. The operator shook his head. No calls were getting through to Kinshasa. A battle was in progress there.

Kwame made a call to the American Embassy in Bangui. That took an hour, but he got through. He explained to the duty officer who he was and mentioned the massacres that had occurred in Mbandaka. The officer had heard rumors of them. Kwame explained that he and his wife would be arriving by plane in the early afternoon. He requested that an American officer meet them. His wife who was pregnant would be traveling without a passport. The duty officer assured him that someone would greet them in Bangui.

THE BADEKAS took Kwame and Kalima to the airport. Kwame gave Badeka the film truck.

Before going to the plane, he walked alone to the fence that edged the tarmac. He stared off across the runway at the walls of trees he had watched when he first arrived in Mbandaka. He thought of that day, of the four men who had walked out of the jungle, carrying pangas; they stood before him, staring. He thought of the teenage girl, naked to the waist, carrying the log on her head. He thought of Odejimi, driving out of the jungle after a rendezvous with Mme Berton. "Mister Johnson," he had grumbled. "That execrable tract. Had to read it in school." Kwame smiled, remembering that. He had been scheduled to remain in Mbandaka only a week. He thought of first beholding Madame Van, so full of mystery, of her becoming Kalima, of his falling in love with her so genuinely that he sent Olivia Carlyle back to America and committed himself to Kalima and their child.

The plane was called. Kwame and Kalima embraced the Badekas. What friends they had been! Teaching their students had been Kwame's best experience in Mbandaka. He and Kalima stood in line to move out onto the tarmac. Good to his word, the *chef de service* supervised Kalima's boarding the plane. Kwame started across the tarmac. Ascending the stairway to the plane, he gazed at the tall clouds floating over the dense vegetation of the jungle. He had a deep affection for Africa. As things turned out, he was taking it with him in a young African wife who would soon present him a child.